Praise for *Looking for Enza*

"Richly atmospheric and blistering with tension…a perfect holiday read."   **Zoe Strachan**

"Smooth prose and a dramatic story…The interweaving of narratives provides richness to this world of personal and political struggle."   **Elizabeth Reeder**

"You can see, taste and feel the dusty red roads of the South African bush in this rich, evocative exploration of love, jealousy and betrayal in post-colonial Zambia in the 1970s."
Jackie Copleton

"A wonderful, mesmerising story, full of love and longing."
Carmen Reid

"A compelling tale of a young woman returning to her childhood home to confront her past."

Sarah Maine

"I was seduced by the sultry, dreamlike colours of Africa; hooked by the insistent drumbeat of menace that pulses through the novel."

Sandra Ireland

Praise for *Paris Kiss*

"Flows from the page like a piece of art."   *Sunday Mirror*

"This makes a touching tale of friendship, love and betrayal set against a colourful backdrop of the Paris art world."
France magazine

"An intense and satisfying story – an insight into the constraints on passionate and talented women in the Parisian art world at the turn of the century. It will haunt you."
Sara Sheridan

Also by Maggie Ritchie

Paris Kiss

LOOKING FOR

EVELYN

MAGGIE RITCHIE

Saraband

Published by Saraband,
Digital World Centre, 1 Lowry Plaza
The Quays, Salford, M50 3UB
www.saraband.net

10 9 8 7 6 5 4 3 2 1

ISBN: 9781910192849
ISBNe: 9781910192856

Edited by Laura Waddell
Cover image: from a 20th-century African print (copyright unknown)

Typeset by Iolaire Typography Ltd.
Printed and bound in Great Britain by Clays Ltd, St Ives plc

MIX
Paper from
responsible sources
FSC® C018072

For Michael and Adam

ALL GROWN UP

Lusaka, Zambia – May 1993

Chrissie Docherty rolled her shoulders to ease the stiffness and heard a crunch. The barman placed a gin and tonic clinking with ice in front of her and she drank half of it down, relishing the cold ache in her throat. She sighed, trying to relax, and settled herself on the bar stool at the Ridgeway Hotel. It had been a bone-jarring drive along potholed roads down from Lake Tanganyika, where she'd been camped out with the rest of the press pack. A Scottish millionaire who was the scion of an engineering dynasty, his wife and young son had been missing for more than a month from their adventure holiday in Zambia. They had last been seen setting sail alone in a small fishing boat on the treacherous lake that was as wide as a sea.

In the Glasgow headquarters of *The Journal*, Chrissie had begged the news editor for the assignment, told him about being brought up in Zambia, and how it would give her an edge over the other journalists. She'd held her breath while he considered, seeing him think it was a risk to use her, a relatively untried reporter. She hoped he couldn't tell she was spinning him a line: it had been twenty years since she'd last set foot on southern Africa's red soil and her childhood memories were hazy at best. But the ruse worked and she was out of the office, on the way to the airport before he could change his mind. Before she left, the Chief Reporter, one of the old hands who had always treated her with a mixture of lust and contempt, sauntered over to her desk where she was frantically packing her

1

briefcase with passport, notebooks, contacts book and a tape recorder. Chrissie braced herself for a sarcastic remark laced with sexual innuendo. To her surprise, Scotland's most hardnosed and unreconstructed journalist gave her a grudging smile. Bob Macintyre handed her a folded-up piece of paper. She opened it warily to see a phone number and a name.

'This is the Beeb's man in that part of Africa,' he said. 'Duncan Cairns is old school, a gentleman of the press – not like me, eh?' He winked and for a moment Chrissie thought he was going to make a move: the Chief's hands could move as quickly as a striking snake. But he only straightened his tie and grinned at her. 'Cairns and I go back a long way. If you mention my name, he'll help you out.'

Chrissie had been grateful and met Cairns when she arrived in Zambia, hoping for an insider's view. But he knew as little about the missing family as the rest of the press pack, who mooched about on the edge of the lake day after day, ignored by Zambian police inscrutable behind mirrored shades. When the rescue came, the two surviving members of the family were whisked away to an unknown destination. But luck was with Chrissie. In the end, she had been the one to track down missing James Cameron and his son and get an exclusive, thanks to the friendship she'd struck up with her driver. Gabriel was a Chewa, and Chrissie's childhood friend had been from the same tribe. She dredged her memory and was surprised how readily her tongue spilled out the driver's native language, Chichewa. Gabriel, it turned out, knew the night porter at the hotel where the family was holed up. *He is my mother's sister's son*, he told her in the language that had always made her think of shallow water running over stones.

Once Chrissie was in, she used her charm to secure the interview. Cameron bristled when he saw her, but his expression softened when he heard her accent. Tommo, the photographer, helped to break the ice with banter about football matches he'd covered. After a while, Cameron began haltingly to tell them about the sudden squall that had blown in and taken them by surprise.

'I lost control of the wheel and the boom swung round and next thing I knew Fiona was in the water. I tried to reach her but she went under another wave.' His voice broke and he stared at his hands as if accusing them of treachery. 'I couldn't jump in after her – I had to stay and look after Stephen.' Cameron gave Chrissie an anguished look. 'He's only nine. I couldn't leave him.' He wept and Chrissie sat quietly and let the stranger's pain seep into her bones. It was the price she'd paid time and again. Later she'd write a sensitive piece, turn the sorrow into a story that would help the family come to terms with this senseless accident, but for now her job was to listen. Cameron wiped his face and told them how he'd kept his young son alive by catching river fish, which they had devoured raw, how they'd been delirious with sunstroke and near death when a helicopter had spotted their uncovered boat, a mere speck on the vast emptiness of Lake Tanganyika. Chrissie scribbled her way through half a notebook and the photographer took candid shots of the family. She only relaxed when they were back outside, squinting at the afternoon sun, her head buzzing with Cameron's words.

Nobody else had a sniff of the story and the news editor had boomed his appreciation down the crackling telephone line, telling her to take a few days off, she'd earned it. Now Chrissie was exhausted and empty, but relieved to have filed the last of her copy. She wanted nothing more than to down a few drinks in the hotel bar and rehash the story with Tommo, but he was still upstairs in his room, doing inexplicable things to strips of film with a hairdryer to wire pictures back to *The Journal*.

Chrissie plucked at the back of her white shirt; it was already sticking to her despite the cold shower she'd taken. The ceiling fan only stirred the warm air that came in from the hotel garden. She caught the nose-nipping turpentine scent of green mangoes on the breeze. Ever since she'd stepped off the plane at Lusaka airport, she'd been knocked off balance by the confusing jumble of smells, sights and sounds that took her back to her African childhood: the cloying sweetness of coconut oil, the overwhelming pungency of dried river fish, the purple froth of jacaranda blooms down Cairo Road, the soft harmonies of African voices. As she'd walked through the crowded streets, every corner seemed to be haunted by ghosts from her childhood. A thought kept niggling at the back of her mind, as if she'd forgotten to do something. Chrissie frowned into her drink. What was it? Usually when she was out of town for the paper she

3

was clear-headed and focused on the job in hand, but on this trip her mind was wrapped in fog, as warm and oppressive as the African heat she had once tolerated effortlessly as a child. She squeezed her eyes shut and tried to pinpoint what was making her so uneasy.

Memories from her childhood drifted through her mind like mist from the lake: a boy sitting in a tree eating a green mango; the same boy lying in a dim hut with flies at the corner of his eyes, drinking his tears; the steel flash of a machete as it caught the sun; a woman in a yellow dress splashed with crimson. *There was something she had to tell her dad, what was it?* She opened her eyes and the memories scuttled back to their corners. A dread began to grow and take shape in her mind: she was sure now that something terrible had happened when she was a child, something so awful that she had erased it from her memory. And she had been involved somehow. But the more she concentrated on recalling the past, the more elusive it became. Perhaps if she stayed on for a few days like the news editor had suggested, her memories of that time would come back fully. Chrissie flexed her fingers, stiff from scribbling longhand. From experience she knew the best way to remember would be to stop thinking about it and relax – the same technique she used when she couldn't think of a way to write the first lines of a news story. If she let her mind wander, the memories, like the words of a story, would tumble out of the dark corners unbidden.

Chrissie looked at her watch and sighed: Tommo would be ages yet. She jiggled her foot and looked around the bar, being careful to scan for weirdoes. Sitting on her own in a bar didn't bother her but her friendly, open face made her a magnet for nutters. Running her fingers through her short hair, still damp from the shower, she surreptitiously checked out a group of Chinese businessmen who were being schmoozed by some government suits. Zambia had changed dramatically since the 1970s, when it was just emerging from nearly a century of British rule, full of copper wealth and hopes for the future. The Zambian Copper Belt had once been the world's largest source of copper ore. But prices had collapsed after the oil crises in 1974 and 1979, plunging the country into debt. From being second to South Africa in prosperity, Zambia was now one of Africa's poorest countries.

At the airport, Chrissie had noticed that all the signs were in Chinese as well as English. The Chinese were everywhere, dressed in hard hats and suits, taking smiling photographs of each other. They were the new *bwanas* who had taken over the faltering copper mines and set them to work again. As long as the mines were profitable, the new bosses didn't seem to care if a handful of miners were killed, and they brutally shut down strikes. In the bar, Chrissie strained to listen in to the conversation at the nearby table and watched the Zambians in suits laughing and pressing drinks on the Chinese. She couldn't hear what they were saying from her perch at the counter, but no doubt they were trying to persuade their guests to take over another failing copper mine or build a railway line. The suits looked prosperous and Chrissie wondered if civil servants in Zambia were still known as *wabenzies*, because the official car was always a Mercedes Benz.

She crunched an ice cube and switched her attention to the far corner of the bar, where a couple of backpackers had their tongues down each other's throats. None too clean, decked out in bandanas, leather bracelets and bead necklaces, they would never have been allowed over the doorstep of the Ridgeway she'd known as a child. Back then, it was the smart place for whites to have cocktails and a nice meal served in the old-fashioned way on linen tablecloths with silverware and polished crystal. It had been an oasis where they could still pretend that independence had never happened, that Zambia was still Northern Rhodesia and the capital Broken Hill. When Chrissie used to come here with her family, her mother had always worn her best dress and pearls, her beehive lacquered stiffly into place. There would be chicken in a basket and Fanta for the kids; deluxe export whisky and steaks for the grown ups. Back then, the hotel had seemed exotic, a palace of luxury after the colonial station where the Dochertys lived in a bungalow alongside a handful of other whites, mostly teachers at the training college where her father worked.

Twenty years later, Chrissie had followed her homing instinct and booked in here rather than into the more modern Intercontinental, which was where most journalists and visiting politicians stayed, and where you were bound to see ANC guys in exile from

South Africa, huddled together in the swish lobby as they talked about their dream of ending apartheid. But Chrissie wasn't here on a political story, and she'd never liked hanging out with the press pack. She loved the Ridgeway's shabby colonial style: the ceiling fans, potted palm trees, and waiters in white jackets. The bar looked out over a garden filled with the flowering bushes and trees she remembered from her childhood, their names enough to conjure a time when the world was fresh and clean and clear: *jacaranda, mimosa, magnolia, frangipani, bougainvillea, hibiscus.* The whoop-whoop of a hoopoe came through the open glass doors and she imagined its crested head bobbing as it called to its mate. She'd already spotted that the pond was still there and wondered if it was still inhabited by the small crocodile that had fascinated her as a child. With her brothers and sister, she'd crouch at the edge of the water as they dared each other to poke it with sticks.

Chrissie blew her hair out of her eyes and was about to order another drink, when she stopped, struck by a ghost from her past. But the man sitting at the other end of the bar was too solid to be a ghost. Chrissie studied her old enemy. He was hunched over his drink in sweat-stained khakis, his fair skin broiled by years in the sun to a reddish tan. His coppery hair had faded and he had aged badly, but it was Gerry Mann all right.

He must have felt her staring at him because he turned his head and raised his glass. 'Buy you a drink, love?'

Chrissie suppressed the urge to tell him not to call her love, or flower, or pet. She had had enough of those names on her long climb to *The Journal* by way of newsrooms in rural backwaters where the male reporters still thought it was 1953, not 1993, and that a woman journalist should stick to writing about knitting patterns and scone recipes. Chrissie swallowed her irritation and slid off the bar stool. Gerry Mann had known her as a child growing up in Africa; he might have some answers to why so many of her troubled memories were beginning to resurface.

He grinned and patted the seat beside him, obviously thinking he had made a bar room conquest. 'What'll you have, love?'

'Gin and tonic, please.'

He turned to the elderly barman. 'You heard the lady, Innocent.'

'Yes, sir.'

Mann held out his hand; it was large and moist with the afternoon heat. She took it and quickly rubbed it on the back of her khaki trousers. He didn't seem to notice and smiled at her again. The corners of his eyes crinkled and she realised he must have been handsome once before alcohol and the sun took its toll.

'Gerry Mann,' he said, the 'a' flat, northern English.

Chrissie sat down and didn't return his smile. 'I know who you are.'

Mann gave an uneasy laugh. 'That's funny, I've never met you before, but you know me, or so you say.' He narrowed his pale blue eyes, now empty of their early friendliness. 'Why don't you tell me your name, love?'

'Well, it's not love, that's for sure,' she said with a light laugh that held some steel. 'I'm Chrissie Docherty. You knew my dad in the Seventies. Jim Docherty.'

Mann frowned. 'British Council Jim Docherty? Chalimbana Jim Docherty?' She nodded. He put down his drink, all smiles once more. 'Well I'll be buggered! I remember you now: you were a right skinny little rat.' Chrissie winced. As a child she'd been all knees and feet, her gangly limbs not suited to the short dresses and white socks of her childhood. She had filled out and now she was glad of her long legs and the natural slimness that meant she could eat what she wanted. Mann seemed to share her appreciation; Chrissie didn't like the way he was looking her up and down, as if he were choosing a prime cut of meat. He peered down her shirt and whistled under his breath. 'Look at you now, though – all grown up.' Chrissie's hand went to her top button and she felt her cheeks burn when she realised it had come undone. She did it up and twisted away to take a slug of her drink, determined not to let him get the upper hand. He seemed to read her discomfort and laughed softly. 'Well, well, well, little Chrissie Docherty.' Chrissie wanted to get up and leave but she couldn't move, like a rat transfixed by a snake. Gerry Mann wiped his mouth and shuffled his stool closer. 'How is your old man, anyway?'

She answered curtly. 'He's retired now and living back in Edinburgh.'

'He won't like that, not Jim Docherty of the British Council. Won't like not being the big panjandrum, any more, I'll bet.' Chrissie turned back to study Mann. She had underestimated him as a drunken buffoon, but he was perceptive in a squirrelly, unkind way.

'I wouldn't quite put it like that,' she said. 'But, you're right, he hates being home – the weather gets him down and he misses his driver. Mum likes it, though, being around us, and her grandchildren.' Mann pretended to yawn. He really was maddening.

'Same old story I've heard a million times,' he said. 'The expats who can't get used to life with the ordinary mutts back home.' He leaned even closer and tapped her knee so she had to cross her legs to get some distance. 'But what brings you back to Zed, little Chrissie? I thought your lot never came back.'

She took a gulp of her drink and the ice chinked against her teeth. Chrissie knew a slur masked as a joke after years of having to defend her unusual upbringing. She'd lost count of the number of times she'd been asked belligerently: 'But where are you actually *from?*'

She eyed Mann coolly. 'My lot? What do you mean by that?'

He laughed, his eyes wide with disingenuousness. 'Yeah, you know, diplomatic brats, moving from one country to the next, no roots, no loyalties, nowhere to call home.'

Chrissie looked down at her drink to hide her expression; the bastard could still get to her after all these years. She wanted to kick him in the shins but instead painted on her best reporter's smile.

'Roots are over-rated, don't you think? They tie you down. Me, I like being free; I can go anywhere I want. Lets me do my job, no one to answer to.'

'What is your job?'

'Journalist.'

That usually elicited a frown of contempt from people, but Mann looked at her thoughtfully. 'That so? What are you covering?'

'The boat that went AWOL on the lake.'

'Oh, yeah, the tourist who got himself lost. Poor sod, I hear the wife went overboard and they haven't found the body. The crocs will have got her by now.' He narrowed his eyes. 'So, you've been sniffing around with the rest of the vultures.' Mann bared yellow teeth at her as if to show he was only joking. He waited for her to

8

give him a tight smile and took another slug of his drink. Chrissie watched his neck flush with the alcohol. He spoke more loudly now, inhibitions dissolving in the whisky. 'Silly bugger – only had himself to blame, trying that sort of caper during the rainy season. I don't understand this new breed of tourist. They used to come to gawp at the lions and elephants, now it's all climbing Kili over in Tan and bungee jumping into Vict Falls.'

Despite herself, Chrissie enjoyed the way Mann spoke to her as one local to another, using the familiar shorthand. He waved his empty glass at the bartender to call him over, but Chrissie put her hand over her glass. She'd already had a couple on an empty stomach and didn't want to make a fool of herself. Mann drank neat whisky as if it were water. The guys back at the newspaper could knock it back but they wouldn't be able to keep up with an old Africa hand. Her parents' house – wherever they happened to be in the world – had always been stocked with boxes of whisky and gin, cases of wine stacked on top of crates of beer, all to keep the social wheels lubricated during countless parties full of diplomats, government ministers, and their cohort of wives. Gerry Mann was from that same generation, who drank as if they were immortal. Or maybe they didn't expect to live long enough to pay the piper. Chrissie watched Mann wrap both hands around the refilled tumbler to control his shakes. The years of hard drinking had started to take their toll. She knew the signs: the yellowed whites of the eyes as the damaged liver struggled to filter out the poison, the flushed face with its oily sheen, the slack, waxy skin and distended stomach. But when Mann spoke there was no slurring; just by listening to him you wouldn't know his veins held more Johnnie Walker than blood.

He shifted on his stool and studied her in turn. 'So you're a hack, eh? I might have guessed – you were always sneaking about the place earwigging private conversations.' He grinned again and this time there was no mistaking the malice. 'Who do you write for then, *The Times*?'

Chrissie suppressed a smile. She remembered the rolled-up copy of *The Times*, the expat Bible that used to be airmailed to every British bungalow in Zambia, two weeks out of date. 'No, I work for *The Journal*.'

He looked blank. 'What's that? Some local rag?'

Chrissie bridled. 'We sell more than *The Times* and the rest of the broadsheets put together.'

Mann smiled unpleasantly. 'Chippy aren't we? So what you're saying is you work for a mass-market trashy title.' He tilted his head and eyed her beadily. 'That means your bosses will have plenty of cash for stories.'

Chrissie shrugged and tried for indifference; annoyed she'd let him get to her again. She took a deep breath to control her temper. The Chrissie she used to be last time she was in Africa, the nine-year-old tomboy, would have thrown her drink in Gerry Mann's sneering face and run out of the bar as fast as her skinny legs could carry her. She tried to remember she was a professional woman now, a year off thirty. She'd held her own with worse creeps than a washed-out old schoolteacher. Chrissie sipped her drink before replying.

'We do sometimes pay for stories, if they're good enough.'

'Interesting.' He leaned towards her so their noses were almost touching. Before she pulled back, Chrissie smelled the whisky on his breath and underneath it something else, something rotten. 'Normally I wouldn't have time for the blood-sucking capitalist press,' Mann said. 'But seeing as your old man was a friend, I'll make an exception.' Chrissie bit back a reply. Her dad had never had much time for Mann. 'How is the old bastard, anyway?' he said.

Chrissie sighed. Short-term memory loss was one of the least endearing qualities of drunks: he'd already asked her about her dad. 'Glad to be out of Zambia. He said the only way he'd come back was at the head of a tank column advancing down Cairo Road.'

Mann laughed. 'It's a bugger of a place, right enough, but it's ruined me for anywhere else.'

Had it ruined her too? Chrissie had always found it hard to settle in one place. She'd worked hard to convince herself that Scotland was home, but since coming back to southern Africa, she realised she felt more at home here. She thought she'd had enough of being a foreigner in someone else's country, weary of seeing the surprise in people's faces in Lisbon, Madrid, Caracas, when they heard a fair-skinned Celt speaking like a native. All her life, she had carefully learned customs, jokes and languages and worn them like camouflage to fit in, and when she'd moved to her own country as a teenager, that had been the hardest shift of all. The truth was, she was from everywhere and nowhere. Maybe Mann was right: she was just another expat brat with no roots.

He pushed his empty glass at her. 'How about you buy me a drink or three on expenses? It'll be worth your while. I know all the dirt around here – all the secrets.'

Chrissie doubted her paper would be interested in gossip from the expat circle, but she was curious. There were things about her childhood she could only half remember but Gerry Mann might be able to help her. Besides, she'd always wanted to find out more about that turbulent time, just after Zambia had gained its independence. Her parents didn't like to talk about those days, and whenever she broached the subject, they'd start to reminisce about their other postings: India, Spain, Venezuela, Portugal – anywhere but Africa.

Chrissie followed Mann across the room to a quiet table overlooking the garden. A passing waiter in a pristine white jacket and gloves smiled at her as if nothing had changed since the 1970s; as if the city outside the high walls of the Ridgeway wasn't a broken-down war zone between the handful of rich people living behind security gates with their home cinemas and armed guards, and the desperately poor. In Lusaka, the threat of violence was ever-present: burglaries, carjackings and rape. She'd read it in the eyes of the aid workers as she rode with them in gleaming white off-roaders, in the way the foreign correspondents huddled together in the bar of the International. But here, in the Ridgeway, it was as if time stood still. Chrissie watched weaverbirds flit over the pond, chasing flying ants through the violet dusk. A hornbill called out its harsh warning and another memory clawed its way out of the darkness. The hornbill was a harbinger of death: that's what the villagers used to say in Chalimbana, where she'd grown up in the bush. She'd always been superstitious, and at home she skirted ladders and saluted single magpies. The hornbill gave another rasping cry and she suddenly felt hot and dizzy. There was a buzzing in her ears, like a cloud of blowflies. Chrissie squeezed her eyes to shut out the racket. In the red darkness behind her eyelids she heard the whoosh of a machete, the sickening chop as it hit bone; she saw a stray dog lapping at the edge of a red puddle, the flies swarming to the feast. When she opened her eyes, Gerry Mann was staring at her.

'You're awfully white, love, even for a Jock.'

Chrissie stood up slowly. She heard again the telltale buzz in her ears, and knew that if she moved too quickly she'd pass out. The fainting spells had started in Zambia when she was a child, ever since she'd been so ill that year. She shook her head to clear the fog. Chrissie closed her eyes and saw a man digging in a graveyard under the bright penny of a moon; a fever-dream face at her window; the rustle of snake scales on a tiled floor. A whisper curled around her brain: *You're next, little white rat.* She dabbed her upper lip with the napkin the waiter had wrapped around her drink to protect her fingers from the ice-cold glass.

Chrissie held onto the back of the chair. 'Excuse me, I'm just going to nip to the loo.'

'Shouldn't have had ice in your drink. S'why I take mine neat.'

When Chrissie returned, her face still wet from the cold water she'd splashed on it, she felt better. Mann started talking before she'd even sat down, his tongue loosened by the whisky.

'I must still have been headmaster of the secondary school in Chalimbana when you were last here. Have you paid a visit back to the old place?' She shook her head and regretted it when she had to press down on a fresh wave of nausea. Mann waved his drink expansively, spilling a little on his khaki shorts. 'You should, but it's not the same.' He sighed. 'S'gone to the dogs, like the rest of Zed. We had such dreams, such high hopes after independence. It was going to be a new Eden.' He wiped his hands over his eyes and seemed to refocus. 'Anyway, I've done all right for myself. I'm an academic now, political science lecturer at the university – proper *nabob*, as your dad would have put it.' Mann motioned to the waiter. 'Jim Docherty was an India hand through and through, but he never understood the Africans.'

Chrissie's parents had spent their first tour in India. People in the colonial service used to say you were either an Africa or an India hand and that once you'd been on one continent you couldn't stick the other. Mann was right: her parents' house was full of books about the Raj and brass and ivory ornaments of Hindu gods. Even after all this time, they still yearned for the Punjab.

'No, your old man never understood the Africans, not the way I do.' Mann impatiently waved his empty glass in the air. 'He had good intentions, but these Council johnnies never stay anywhere long enough. Not like me.' He jabbed a finger at his chest. 'Me, I stayed on and tried to do my best for the country, wanted to do some proper good, you know, not skip out after a few years like some I could mention. Jim had his heart in the right place, but what could he do in the four years he was here? Teach a few primary school teachers better English?' He banged his glass on the table, bringing the waiter scurrying to refill it. 'Nah, it's us, the ones who stuck it out, who made a real difference.'

Chrissie watched him drain off half the glass of whisky, his face turning darker shade of red, and wondered why as a child she'd been so frightened of this pathetic drunk. She realised he'd always been jealous of her father; it explained why he'd singled her out and been so unkind to her. As a child, she'd been an easy target. Well, she was all grown up now. Chrissie wished she hadn't agreed to have a drink with him, and looked around to see if the photographer had come down yet, but there was no sign of him. Her skin felt hot and she wiped her upper lip again. She wondered what she'd been ill with when she was little and whether she was getting it again. Chalimbana had no doctor then, and she'd been too ill to travel to Lusaka. If it had been malaria, it could be coming back for a second bite of her. Sweat pricked her hairline. She pushed her glass to one side. Mann was right: it was stupid to have asked for ice in her drink, a tourist's mistake. Chrissie gripped the arms of her chair and half rose, about to leave Mann to his maundering, when she caught a familiar name.

'What did you say?'

'Do you remember Evelyn Fielding?' he said.

Chrissie sat down again, electrified. That name! It echoed around the chamber of her memories. She saw pale hair, pale skin powdered with freckles, an English rose in Africa. Something terrible had happened back then, and with a sudden certainty she knew Evelyn was at the centre of it. Chrissie frowned as she tried to pull back

13

the curtain to her past. All she remembered was that it had been *a bad business*, that's what they'd said, the adults as they whispered in corners, glancing her way to make sure she couldn't hear. She shook her head to clear it. What she did know was that Evelyn Fielding had left Africa in a toxic cloud of scandal twenty years ago, and that the mention of her name intensified the dread that had been growing in her since she'd come back to Africa.

'I remember her, but only vaguely,' Chrissie said, trying for nonchalance but failing. 'I think she was our next-door neighbour in Chalimbana for a while.'

''S'right, lived right next to old Jim Docherty and his brood.' He smacked his lips. 'She was a damn fine looking woman, Evelyn, still is. Bumped into her in town the other day, getting supplies. Hadn't seen her for years.'

Chrissie started. 'I heard she went back to England.'

Mann didn't seem to hear her. The lines around his eyes softened with longing and for a moment Chrissie saw again the handsome man he must have been. Then he surprised her.

'I've never loved anyone like I loved her,' he said. And, to Chrissie's alarm, she saw his eyes redden and fill with tears. He cleared his throat and visibly pulled himself together. 'No, Evelyn never left Africa; she just let everyone think that she had. She runs a safari lodge up country, south-east of Kabwe at Luangwa.'

Chrissie stared at Gerry Mann as more whispered conversations drifted back to her: *she killed that man as sure as if she'd pulled the trigger... a white woman... the shame of it... poor Robert.* She struggled to remember what had happened. There was a terrible fuss but the details had been kept from her as a child. It was around the time she was sick and Chrissie's memories were jumbled up by fever and the passage of time.

She sat up straighter. The news desk had given her some time off and she had never been to the Luangwa Rift Valley: she would use this free time to track down Evelyn and perhaps she would be able to shine a light into the dark corners of her mind, where the nightmares lurked. Maybe she could still the unease that had dogged her for years and made her leave the light on at night. *There was something she needed to tell her dad.* Chrissie was gripped with an overwhelming urge to find Evelyn Fielding, to leave right this minute and find out exactly what had happened all those years ago. She went over the reasons again, as if to convince herself she was acting rationally: she would lay her ghosts to rest, she had a few days to herself and she had never been up country. There was nothing to stop her.

Chrissie fumbled in her bag for her notebook and pen. 'Out past Kabwe, did you say? Can you remember any more details?' she said, writing. 'I'd like to find her.'

He shrugged but his eyes were sly as he looked at her over the rim of his upturned glass. 'I can't remember just now, had a drop too much, bit pissed.'

Chrissie clutched his arm. 'I'll make it worth your while. You're right, my paper has deep pockets.' Her news editor would kill her if he found out but she could fudge any payment to Mann on expenses. Chrissie was sure now that there were secrets from her past to unlock and that Evelyn held the key. Mann's eyes were closing and she shook him awake. 'Gerry, will you tell me how to find Evelyn?'

'Okay,' he said, and muttered directions. Chrissie was writing fast when a hand landed on her shoulder. Damn, she'd forgotten about Tommo. He wouldn't want to go off grid with her; she'd have to persuade him. She was brave but not stupid. Zambia was not always a safe place for a white woman travelling on her own.

Chrissie turned to smile at the photographer, but he was looking past her at Gerry Mann, his lean face suspicious. 'You all right, Doc? Who's this?'

'Tommo, this is Gerry Mann, a friend of my father's from the old days. How do you fancy a trip out into the bush, to a safari lodge, to visit an old friend of my family? The news desk has given us a few days' grace and you could take some snaps for that portfolio you're always threatening to put in for an award.'

''F'sake, Chrissie, if we've got some free time I'd rather book a microlight over Victoria Falls, more dramatic, like.'

'We can do that too, on the way back.' She touched his arm. 'Please, Tommo, I really want to go. I'll owe you one.' She waited, willing him to say yes. He was happily married with a couple of kids now but they had a history, going back to their early days in regional newspapers when they were both marooned in the north of Scotland. She smiled and tucked her hair behind her ear. 'What do you say, are you up for an adventure?'

Tommo grinned and pushed his hand through his dark hair. 'Aye, go on then. But I'm driving.'

'That's the spirit, Jock.' Tommo narrowed his eyes at the hated moniker, but Mann didn't seem to notice. He banged his empty glass on the table. 'Now, how about another drink?'

Chrissie put her notebook away while Tommo ordered another round. Gerry Mann would have a bear of a headache in the morning but that was his lookout. She'd got what she wanted out of him, now it was up to her to do some digging. All her life, she had been haunted by the half-remembered events that had taken place in her African childhood. She would go to Kabwe and find out the whole story.

THE UPSIDE DOWN TREE

Tommo was sulking in the Land Rover's passenger seat, oblivious to the red sun hanging low and heavy above the eastern rim of Africa.

'I can't believe you talked me into a wild goose chase just so you can catch up with some woman from your past,' he said. 'I should be flying over Victoria Falls now, hanging out of a plane with my camera.' Chrissie swerved to avoid a pothole and grinned when Tommo clutched his stomach.

'Quit moaning,' she said. 'It's just for a few days. We can try to fit in the Falls when we get back. Besides, the way you were sinking the pints and whisky chasers last night, you're in no fit state to loop the loop in a microlight. Have a kip and you'll wake up in a better mood. Here.' Chrissie took one hand off the wheel, rummaged in her shirt pocket and threw him a packet of painkillers. 'There are a couple of bottles of Fanta in the cooler behind you.'

'This stuff's mingin',' he said, reaching for a bottle. 'Why don't they sell normal ginger in Africa?'

'I don't think Zambia's ready for Scotland's other national drink.' Chrissie saw a clear stretch of road ahead and put her foot down. Tommo popped three pills and chugged down a Fanta.

He pulled his skip cap over his eyes and settled in for a sleep. 'Wake me up when we get to wherever the fuck it is we're going.'

Chrissie concentrated on the road. They'd come off tarmac a few miles east of Lusaka and were now driving over red dirt, packed hard and filled with gaping cracks wide enough to trap even a Land

17

Rover's tyres. Unlike Tommo, she didn't have a hangover. She'd woken early that morning and smelled the air, fresh from one of the last showers of the rainy season. Raindrops clung to the open mouths of the trumpet-shaped flowers of the morning glory that climbed around her hotel balcony. She had picked one to tuck behind her ear before remembering their milky sap was poisonous. Now she scanned the horizon through a bug-smeared windshield, her eyes thirsty for the primary colours of Africa. Her senses were more alert than they had been in years, as if she'd broken free from a long grey dream. Here, everything was in the uncomplicated colours of a child's painting: the sky a true blue, the earth a rich red, and the trees blooming with splashes of crimson, purple and yellow. It was the beginning of the dry season so there was still a carpet of vivid green left over from the rains. Chrissie drove past sugar cane fields worked by women bent over their hoes with babies tied to their backs, and she remembered chewing on the split cane as a child, sucking at the sweetness and spitting out the fibre. There had been a friend with her, a little African boy. She frowned. What was his name?

The Land Rover jolted over a bump in the road and Tommo groaned in his sleep. In the rear view mirror, she saw a huge snake stretched fatly out behind them. She thought she must have killed it, but after a moment its coils jerked and it slithered into the bush. Chrissie shuddered; she hated snakes and couldn't bring herself to look at them, even the harmless milk snakes she'd seen in tanks. It was the way they moved and the primeval stare of their obelisk eyes, the flicker of tongues, and their careful, curved smiles. She glanced down at her notebook, tried to read the directions she'd scrawled, and took the next turning. The dirt road was more overgrown now, disappearing in some places beneath the tendrils of thick-leafed vine that crawled along the ground. For the next couple of hours, Chrissie drove without seeing a village or anyone else on the road, the scrubby landscape broken only by the occasional stunted tree. She drove up a hill, the wheels churning and whining against the shifting dirt, and saw a grove of giant baobab trees ahead with bulbous trunks and naked branches thrust desperately up into the sky like fat old men pleading for mercy. She slowed the Land Rover to look at them. They were so odd these trees, the way they seemed to grow upside down with their roots waving in the air, scrabbling for purchase where there was none. The road disappeared into a shallow river and as the Land Rover splashed through it, Tommo woke up.

'Where are we, Doc?'

Chrissie cut the engine and squinted at the directions but couldn't make any sense of them. They both stared out of the muddy windscreen at the strange trees. Tommo pointed at the grassland stretching ahead to the horizon.

'Where's the road gone?'

Chrissie pulled a road map out of the glove compartment and started unfolding it. 'I think I took a wrong turning.'

'For Christ's sake, give me the map. This is what happens when you let a reporter do the driving.'

They got out and laid the map flat on the bonnet and peered at it together, but only the main roads were marked. In the southeast, where they were heading, there was a whole lot of nothing. Tommo swore with guttural force and began to walk away towards the trees.

Chrissie called after him. 'Where are you going? Tommo? Don't play silly buggers.'

He waved without turning round. 'I've got to take a leak.'

Chrissie picked up her notebook and read the directions again, but she didn't recognise any of the milestones Mann had slurred at her. They were supposed to have driven past a water tank but she couldn't remember seeing one. A shield bug crawled across the map and she brushed it off, careful not to crush it. They were called stinkbugs for a reason and gave off a rank stench a bit like fresh coriander. The sun was high now and burning the back of her neck. What the hell was she doing here? She stretched. Her back and legs were stiff from working the Land Rover's heavy pedals and a walk would loosen her up. She followed the direction Tommo had taken, towards the baobab grove. It was cool under their shade. She leaned against one of the massive trunks and looked up into the twisted branches.

'What are you looking for, Chris?' She had spoken quietly, but her voice rang out in the quiet and a bird took flight in a clatter of feathers. The trees stood silently around her while she tried to gather her thoughts, sent into turmoil by a visit from Duncan Cairns earlier that morning. She had been finishing her breakfast on the terrace, her mind on the journey that lay ahead, when the BBC journalist had sauntered into her sightline.

'Thought I'd try and catch you before you head off to the UK,' he said with an affable smile. 'You're a hard person to track down.' He sat across from her and looked around at the garden with its flowers and birds. 'Great place – old style, colonial. I thought everyone stayed at the Intercontinental.'

'I've always liked the Ridgeway.'

'Well, I wanted to congratulate you on bagging that interview with Cameron.' He had a pleasant voice, Scottish with the rough edges rubbed off to suit the Home Counties listeners. Despite his years living in the sun, his face was smooth; he smiled with his eyes and had a quiet confidence and an easy, comfortable manner. Chrissie realised his charm was practised but she also knew she could trust him.

She poured him some coffee. 'Thank you, that means a lot coming from you.'

He laughed. 'London weren't too pleased with me this morning when they saw the spread in *The Journal*. How did you manage to get to Cameron?'

'A friendly face, good contacts and a dollop of local knowledge.'

Cairns raised his eyebrows over his coffee cup.

'You're not the only old Africa hand at this table,' Chrissie said. 'I grew up here, in the bush.'

'Really? That's interesting. You're altogether an interesting young woman, if you don't mind me saying, not at all what I expected from a *Journal* reporter.' He saw Chrissie's frown and hastened to smooth over his gaffe. 'I'm a Glasgow man myself; read it growing up, man and boy. Shame to see such a fine campaigning paper taking a nosedive downmarket. Bloody bean counters, eh?'

His expression was affable, but Chrissie knew when she was being patronised, no matter how beguilingly, and rose to the defence of her colleagues.

'I'm proud to work alongside some of the best journalists in the country,' she said, glaring at him. 'I'm sure our two million readers agree.'

Cairns laughed and loosened his tie. He was handsome in a sharp-faced way in his crumpled linen suit and a white shirt that showed off his working tan. 'Touché. That'll teach me to be sniffy about the red-tops.'

Chrissie grinned, relenting. 'Especially when we beat you to the story.'

The older man spent the next twenty minutes regaling her with anecdotes. Chrissie thought she was immune to reporters' war stories, but Cairns had interviewed Amin and he knew all the ANC guys – he'd had dinner with Joe Slovo and Nelson Mandela. Later that day, he was going to slip over the border to Zimbabwe to interview Mugabe.

Chrissie pushed her plate away with a sigh, her triumph with Cameron forgotten. 'You've got a great job, Duncan. You get to cover stories that matter.'

'I don't know, you're doing not doing so badly for a young reporter – I'd have done anything to have covered a story like this when I was your age. A family adrift on a dangerous crocodile-infested lake, the mother dies and the father and his son cling to life for weeks before a dramatic rescue. It's got everything, like a Hollywood film script, only better because it's real life.'

He asked her about growing up in Zambia and she told him about her strange early life, living on four different continents before she'd finished school. He widened his eyes.

'Radio 4 listeners would love you. They can't get enough of all that daughters of the empire stuff. And you have a good voice. ' He considered her for a moment and Chrissie knew he was about to tell her why he'd sought her out. 'Will you take some advice from an old lag?' She nodded and he went on. 'If I were you I'd get out of *The Journal* while I could – they're notorious for burning out reporters.'

Chrissie opened her mouth to defend her paper again but he held up her hand. 'I know, I know, you're loyal and you're grateful because they've given you a staff job. But if you're not careful you'll wake up one day and you'll be fifty and wonder what happened to your life.'

Chrissie chewed her lip and thought. Since joining the paper she'd been part of a team, so intent on covering the next news story she hadn't stopped to think if it was the right place for her. She'd turned a deaf ear to one of the older reporters, a staunch union man who'd been made redundant, when he'd warned her to get out. Chrissie had been on nightshift and helped him carry a couple of black bin bags out to his car.

'Things are about to change – and not for the better,' he'd said. 'You may be the blue-eyed girl right now but you'll find out soon enough that we're all dispensable, just cogs in a machine for making money.'

Now Chrissie looked straight at Cairns. 'What else would I do?'

He met her eyes. 'You could come to Kenya, as a freelance stringer for all the national papers, and file the odd item for the Beeb. I'd show you the ropes, teach you how to slice tape on the go and handle a Uher.' He tapped the recorder the size of a briefcase that now sat at his feet. She'd seen him lugging it everywhere. 'I cover a huge patch – thirteen countries – and I could do with another pair of hands, someone who knows how things work out here. They want me back in London in a couple of years. You'd be in with a good shout for my job, and I'd put in a word for you, of course.'

Chrissie caught her breath, held it, and let it out slowly. 'Are you serious?'

He spread his hands. 'Never been more so. Nairobi's a good place to live, a lot more civilised than Lusaka. The downside is you live out of a suitcase. I don't get to see much of my family, but it's a hell of an exciting time to be a reporter. The South African elections are coming up next year and Mandela has a huge support base. Could be a whole new era for Africa. You're a single girl, aren't you? No ties, it would be perfect for you.' He leaned towards her. 'What do you say?'

Chrissie chewed a fingernail and thought. She'd be recording history as it was made, living and breathing Africa every day. But she'd made Scotland her home. Finally, after years of travelling and saying goodbye to friends, she'd settled. Besides, she had a coveted staff job and freelance life was risky. Did she really want to uproot and start all over yet again? Throughout her adult life, Chrissie's transient, restless nature had pushed her on, never staying too long in one city or with one boyfriend. She'd always chosen men whom she knew she could discard without a wrench when she moved on. At *The Journal* she'd found some kind of stability.

'I'll think about it,' she told Cairns, remembering what one of her earlier mentors had told her: a good reporter never closes doors.

He handed her his card. 'Here's my number in Nairobi. I'll be on the road for the next few days, to Zim first to see what that old fox Mugabe's been up to, then to Jo'burg to catch up with the township riots, and on to Pretoria to interview Mandela.' He smiled at her. 'If you take my advice, you'll do more than think about it. You're young enough to take risks, and I can tell that Africa is in your blood. Once you've lived here, it never leaves you. I spent my childhood in Nairobi, so I know what it's like. You'll miss it.' He sat back and folded his arms, lecture over. 'When do you go back home?'

'Not right away. I'm going up country first. There's a woman I used to know who runs some sort of safari beyond Kabwe, thought I'd look her up.'

'You don't mean Evelyn Fielding?' Chrissie nodded, startled. 'I tried to interview her a few years back when I was doing a From Our Own Correspondent on whites who had stayed on after independence. She wouldn't open up and it was a wasted trip, but she's a striking woman and I'm glad I met her. I was quite taken with her, I must admit.' He rubbed the side of his sharp nose. 'It's an odd set-up where she lives, like an old English country estate that's been transplanted to the middle of the nowhere. She's been living there for years – a white woman running her own place, smack bang in the bush for all that time, right through the troubles and the land seizures. She must be a remarkable person.' Chrissie stood up to shake Cairns's hand, desperate not to waste anymore time. She had to get to Kabwe. The urge to find Evelyn was like a tug on a string that led to her gut.

Now, in the baobab grove, Chrissie placed a hand on the tree trunk and the other on a low hanging branch. 'I used to climb trees but never one like you,' she whispered. She hauled herself up until she straddled a branch near the top. From there, she could see out over the great grassy plains and towards the blue hills in the north.

A breeze lifted her hair and she closed her eyes and felt the sun in her face. When she opened them she saw a snake in the red dirt below, its emerald body coiling in an 'S' as it skimmed towards a hole in the ground. Chrissie cried out and wobbled on the branch, nearly losing her balance. The snake must have seen the flash of movement because it stopped and turned its head towards the tree and looked up at her. It was green and long and she wondered if it was a black mamba – one of the deadliest snakes in Africa – but its mouth was closed and she couldn't tell. Her thighs grew slippery with sweat as she gripped the branch. If the snake came up the tree and it was a black mamba she wouldn't stand a chance; she'd be dead. *In ten seconds flat.* Her brother Hamish's words came back to her. She could see the snake's tongue flickering as it watched her. They stared at each other as the afternoon sun freckled her arms. Chrissie could hear the blood pounding in her ears. Then, as quickly as it had appeared, the snake turned its head away and slipped into the hole. She let out a breath and leaned against the baobab's trunk. Somewhere nearby a hoopoe began to chug away, as if sounding an all clear. Coming back to Africa had shaken her to the core but somehow her encounter with the snake had released the tension that had been building inside her and given her a moment's respite from the gnawing anxiety. The tree trunk was warm against her back. Chrissie wanted to kick off her boots and stay in this tree and not have to think about her future. A bell rang and she looked down. An elderly African man on a bicycle bumped over the grass towards her. She climbed down the tree and waved.

'Please, can you help us?' she called to him. 'We're lost.'

The old man shook his head and spoke a tribal language she didn't recognise but that could have been Nyanja. Her few words of Chichewa or the hotchpotch slang they spoke in Lusaka wouldn't help her now. Damn it, why hadn't she picked up a phrase book in the city? She remembered what Gerry had told her about Evelyn's estate and asked the question that every Zambian knew in English. She pulled out the map from her pocket and showed him the blue shape.

'Where is the lake?'

The old man smiled and spoke in his language full of murmurs

24

and clicks. He pointed and Chrissie shaded her eyes and followed his finger to an undulating sea of grass and stunted acacia trees. She heard Tommo rustling through the scrub and beckoned him over.

'He doesn't speak English but he knows the lake nearest Evelyn's place. Only thing is, I can't understand his directions.'

Tommo reached into his pocket. 'Leave this to me.' He handed a note to the man and began to pantomime riding a bicycle and driving, then pointed at the Land Rover and at the man. Understanding dawned in the old man's face. He nodded and got on his bike and began to shakily cycle away. Tommo wrenched open the jeep door and ushered Chrissie into the passenger seat.

'Come on, Doc, we're going to follow the bike.'

'Or, why don't we put his bike in the back and give him a lift there?'

He struck his forehead. 'Aye, good point. Ho! Old yin!' The cyclist stopped and looked back. Tommo grinned at Chrissie as he got out of the Land Rover. 'We're a good team, eh Doc?'

'Yeah, look at us,' she said. 'Two numpties lost in the African bush. Just don't ever tell anyone about this.'

EVELYN

They let the old man off when they'd reached the main road. He had traced his finger along their map to show them where to go. It was nearly nightfall when they arrived at a brick and stucco arch on a hill. Below them, the lake shimmered like a sapphire in the bat-filled half-light. In front of them, a drive flanked by lush green gardens swept towards an English-style country house. With its turrets and porticoes, they could have been standing in Sussex, if it weren't for the red soil beneath their feet and the bowl of cobalt blue sky streaked with pink, gold and purple by the death throes of the giant copper sun. There was no sign of life and Chrissie was reminded of abandoned castles in fairy tales, wild thorn bushes protecting the sleeping princess within. But this place was well kept with the edges of the pristine lawn cut sharply, the beds full of cheerful orange marigolds and tree trunks painted white half way up their trunks to fend off marauding insects. A peacock shrieked, splitting the quiet, and Chrissie jumped, her heart racing.

Tommo laughed. 'What's got into you, Doc? You're not usually this nervy.' He shrugged when she told him to shut up and got out of the car to start taking pictures. Chrissie joined him, shivering in the cool air. Tommo lowered his camera and whistled. 'Some place, this.' Chrissie looked out over the valley spread below and felt a great sense of peace settling into her bones.

'It's the most beautiful place I've ever seen,' she said. She pulled on her jacket and they walked towards the house. In the dusk,

Chrissie saw the glimmer of pale hair: Evelyn was sitting at a table under a jacaranda tree, drinking tea with a blonde man. Both their faces were cast in shadow. Chrissie's breathing quickened and shallowed with nerves as she drew near. She stopped a few yards off and studied Evelyn, who was absorbed in work and hadn't noticed their approach. The table in front of her and her companion was littered with ledgers and brochures and scattered with the jacaranda's blue flowers. Chrissie noted how Evelyn had changed and how she'd stayed the same. She must be in her mid-forties by now and her pale hair had a few streaks of silver. Her once creamy skin had taken on the deep tan that comes of years of living in the African sun, and there were lines around her eyes, but despite having lost the fresh bloom of youth, she seemed more poised and sure of herself. Evelyn was, if anything, even more beautiful than Chrissie remembered, and beside her Tommo whistled softly under his breath and reached for his camera.

Evelyn looked up from the papers she was working on and started. 'Oh, I wasn't expecting anyone.'

Chrissie smiled. 'I'm sorry, we should have phoned ahead. A friend told me about this place – we've come all the way from Lusaka. I hope it's not inconvenient.'

'That's all right, the phones are never reliable anyway,' Evelyn said. 'Have you come for a safari?' She pointed her pen at Tommo's camera. 'Or are you writing a travel piece? Either way, you've come at a lovely time of year, and you're welcome at Pembroke.' She stood and shook hands with them. 'I'm Evelyn Fielding, and this is Johann Frank, who manages the farm and our safari business. I don't know what I'd do without him,' she pressed his arm and he stepped out of the shadow of the tree. Chrissie had never seen Johann before, but felt as if she recognised him. He smiled as if he too had been waiting a long time to meet her. Tall and loose-limbed, he had the light eyes and dark-blonde hair of a Northern European. By rights he should be steering a ship through a cold sea under a pewter sky, but he looked utterly at home in Africa.

'Afrikaaner?' she said and put out her hand. His grip was warm and callused.

He smiled. 'No, but I am Dutch,' he said in unaccented school-taught English. 'I can understand Afrikaans quite well, but I have a different outlook from my Boer cousins.' Chrissie noticed he hadn't released her hand and she reluctantly pulled it away. She could sense Tommo waiting beside her and she stepped aside so the two men could greet each other. The photographer introduced himself to Evelyn and Chrissie wrenched her attention back to the older woman.

'I don't know if you remember me, it was so long ago.' She took a breath and hurried on. 'It must be twenty years and I was a child then. I'm Chrissie Docherty. I used to live next door to you in Chalimbana.'

She was shocked to see Evelyn cry out as if in pain. Johann leaned over her, concerned.

'Are you all right?' he said. He was so tender and careful with her that Chrissie wondered if there was something between them. A woman like Evelyn would always have a man in tow. Chrissie was surprised at the sour tone of her thoughts. She recognised them as an echo from the past: Evelyn had often been judged by other women and found wanting.

Evelyn waved Johann away. 'I'm fine, don't worry.' She patted his arm as if he were an over-solicitous son, and at once Chrissie was ashamed of her petty jealousy – she barely knew this man and she was practically laying claim to him. She made an effort to be professional. Evelyn had collected herself too, and turned to Chrissie, calm once more but guarded. 'I do remember you, of course. You were such a funny, skinny, little thing. Look at you now, so tall and elegant. Are you a writer?'

'A journalist.'

Evelyn frowned. 'And what brings you here? Are you working on a story?'

Chrissie took a deep breath and decided the direct approach was best. 'No, it's nothing to do with my job. I'm here to find out about my past, and I was hoping you would help me do that.'

Evelyn tucked a strand of hair behind her ear with a shaky hand. 'Johan, would you take Chrissie's colleague – Tommo isn't it? – into the house and show him around?' He nodded and she managed a smile. When the two men had walked away, Evelyn turned back to Chrissie. 'I don't know what you mean. What about your past, and what do I have to do with it?' Her voice was steady but she avoided meeting Chrissie's eyes.

Chrissie wasn't going to be thrown off track so easily, not after having come so far. Evelyn was ready to talk, but she would have to use all her powers of persuasion.

She sat and touched the other woman's arm. 'Please, don't pretend. I know you can help me: I can't remember much but I am certain of that. I witnessed something terrible when I was a girl and it damaged me.' Her eyes pricked and she swallowed and started again. 'This hideous, shapeless fear is always with me, has been with me since then. When I'm in its grip, I can barely breathe or move. And I have these strange, terrifying flashbacks that don't make any sense: there's always blood, flies, and a nameless, sickening violence.' Her voice had risen and she looked around and dropped it. 'Coming back here has made it worse, but at least I'm beginning to remember and I'm sure it all goes back to you. I keep seeing this image of you in a yellow dress, covered in blood. I'm trying to sort the nightmares from reality but I can't make sense of it. '

Evelyn glanced at Chrissie and twisted her head towards the lake below, as if looking for a way out. After a while she sighed and turned to face her. 'I thought I'd erased my past when I began a new life out here, but I should have known it would catch up with me. After all, what I did was unforgivable.' She took a sip of cold tea and grimaced. 'When you walked across the lawn towards me earlier, I tried not to look at you for as long as possible. Ridiculous, really, like a child trying to make its fears disappear by hiding behind its hands. This day of reckoning was always going to arrive. I knew I couldn't hide forever.'

Chrissie felt a pang of compassion, but her need to find out the truth was even greater now that she was so close to it and she pressed on.

'I don't want to hurt you by opening up old wounds but perhaps it would help to talk. I've interviewed many people who have suffered alone and in silence, and they always feel better afterwards. Sometimes I'm the only person they ever open up to – their friends and family can't handle their pain.'

Evelyn turned up the corners of her mouth. 'Confession is good for the soul, isn't that what Father O'Brian used to say?' Naming the priest, who had been a friend and protector to both of them all those years ago seemed to give her strength and she sat up straighter. 'How did you know where to find me?'

'I bumped into Gerry Mann.'

Evelyn's mouth tightened. 'Of course, it would be him. Gerry wouldn't think twice about giving me away.' She looked out again over the valley and the emerald lake and the blue hills fading into the distance seemed to calm her. 'I suppose you're right: it's time I stopped running away and face up to what I did. But not tonight.' Evelyn stood up and gestured towards the house. 'I'll tell you everything, but not now. You'll be tired after your long drive and it's a long story.'

She linked her arm into Evelyn's and led her into the house where they met Johann and Tommo in the hall. 'Johann, will you see to our guests? Make sure they are comfortable, and have something to eat. The Impala and Kudu rooms are empty.' She turned to Chrissie. 'We have a party of Americans staying with us, but they are out on safari, so we'll have the place to ourselves for the next few days.' Evelyn lowered her voice. 'Perhaps you're right: it will be a relief to talk.'

Chrissie watched her walk away and felt another pang of remorse. Tomorrow she would make the other woman stare into the deep well of her past, and God only knew what demons would crawl out of the dark. Perhaps she should have left Evelyn alone here, in this sanctuary she had created in the hills, but the compulsion to know more was overwhelming.

'Thank you,' Chrissie called after her.

THE PAST

Chrissie woke at dawn. Outside her window, the sky was lightening, the morning alive with the sound of roosters crowing and the clatter of pots and pans from the kitchen. She'd forgotten that the day in the bush started so early, before it grew too hot to work. Evelyn had said they would talk after breakfast, so Chrissie had time to spare. She pulled on her clothes and headed out to explore the estate.

Chrissie ducked behind the house, staying out of sight of the kitchen staff, who were sitting in a group at the open back door. She would usually have stopped to say hello, but she wanted to be alone. Besides, they were having a break, chatting and smoking together; they might not welcome having to be polite to a guest. She compromised and waved at them as she strode past, noticing that the men were in khaki trousers and T-shirts, and the women wore blouses and skirts, but their hair was covered with turbans. Chrissie was glad to see this remnant of the traditional African printed cloth she remembered from her childhood. She'd found the sight of everyone in cast-off Western clothes dispiriting since being back, especially after she'd found out that the charity shop clothes – donated so well-meaningly – were sold in great piles in the market by traders who bought in bulk and were putting the Zambian textile factories out of business.

Chrissie's thoughts were interrupted by a lion's roar. Intrigued, she reached a wire enclosure and walked down its length until she came upon an alarming sight: Johann pinned to the ground by a lion, its open jaws working at his head. She sprinted towards the gate and pulled open the bolt before realising the danger she was putting herself in. The lion stopped what it was doing and regarded her with mild curiosity. Its eyes were yellow suns and she was close enough to see the scars on its broad snout. Chrissie's insides turned to water, and she looked about to see if there was a rock or a stick she could use as a weapon.

She heard a muffled laugh and Johann emerged from underneath the lion. It rolled over onto its back, its paws folded on its chest like a domestic cat.

'Oh, hey, Chrissie,' he said and ruffled the creature's mane. 'Meet George. The great lump has got spit all over me.' He scratched behind its ears and the lion head-butted Johann, knocking him over. Chrissie sank to the ground, her legs finally giving way, and started to laugh. 'What's so funny?' Johann said, sitting up.

'I thought that lion was eating you for breakfast,' Chrissie managed.

Johann face folded into a wide smile. 'George wouldn't hurt a fly, would you, *bokkie*.'

Chrissie remembered the Afrikaans term of endearment, which translates as little buck. The Boer couple on the neighbouring farm had called her that when she was a child. That and *popje*: dolly. She shuffled over to Johann and watched him play with the lion. His hands were broad and square – tanned, practical hands. She made herself look away. She'd be on a plane back home in a few days. He was an attractive man but there was no point in getting close to him. Chrissie had learned that lesson early on: don't get too attached, it only causes pain when you move on. And Chrissie was always moving on.

'He's so tame, why doesn't he bite?' she said.

'I brought him up as a cub. He was an orphan – poachers may have taken his mum, or the pride left him behind, I don't know. I found him a day's drive from here, practically dead from dehydration, his fur matted, skin clinging to his ribs. I thought he'd had it, but a couple of bottles of milk and a little boiled chicken later and he was as good as new. I hand fed him, so he thinks I'm his mum, don't you?' Johann fell onto the lion and they wrestled. The animal's huge paws were pinned around his chest and Chrissie was alarmed until she saw its claws were sheathed. She put out a hand and stroked its massive, tawny pelt, surprised at how soft it was.

As Johann walked her back to the house, Chrissie stole surreptitious looks. He was tall, more than six feet, spare but strong under his shirt, as far as she could tell. She was so busy studying him that she tripped over a hole in the ground and had to clutch at his side. She reddened, feeling like an idiot, but forgot her embarrassment when he crouched down next to the hole.

'Snake hole,' he said, peering inside.

Chrissie pulled at his arm. 'Let's go. I don't want to be bitten.'

He laughed. 'Don't tell me you're afraid of snakes. I thought you were brought up in Africa? It's me, who grew up in snake-free Amsterdam, who should be frightened.'

'It's silly and I know they avoid us, but I've always been terrified of them. I have this recurring nightmare about a black mamba, its mouth open so you can see the black inside. It's coming towards me, and I can't move or scream.' Chrissie realised Johann was looking at her and began to walk away from the snake hole so he had to follow. When they were walking abreast, she said: 'What brought you to Africa?' As they wandered back to the house, stopping every now and then to prolong their conversation, he told her he had studied zoology at university.

'I'd always loved animals as a child but I was never allowed to keep a pet – my family lived in this grand old canal-side apartment and my mother thought animals were dirty creatures.

'Our home was beautiful, but I felt hemmed in by all those houses standing shoulder to shoulder, the shops and bridges and the maze of alleyways. I was trapped by the canals and the grey sea, by everything being so man-made and so damn cleverly *engineered*,' he said. 'I wanted wide open spaces, to be in the wilderness.' He stopped outside the lodge house and opened his arms to the valley below. 'Now, I am a tiny speck of humanity in the middle of all this and I love it. I'm free here. I could never go back now. Do you understand what I mean?'

Chrissie shaded her eyes as she looked up at him. The sun had climbed higher, whitening the sky. 'Yes, I understand. When I left Africa, I lived in cities for the first time in my life. I had to get used to roads choked with traffic, to schools corralled by iron railings, crowds and high buildings and hard pavements, being stuck indoors for hours and hours at a time, wearing shoes and layers of itchy, heavy clothes to keep out the cold.' She stopped and plucked a purple bougainvillea blossom from the wall of the lodge, twirling it until its white heart was a blur. 'But I also felt safe, the way I never had in Africa. It's one of the reasons I've come here, to find out why I was so scared all the time. Something terrible happened when I was a child, there are things I can't remember, or only half-remember in dreams.'

'Are you sure you want to remember?'

'I'm afraid of what I'll find out, but yes, I think I have to.'

Later, back at the house, Evelyn poured Chrissie a cup of tea. They were alone, the remains of breakfast scattered around them. Johann, knowing they wanted to talk privately, had offered to take Tommo around the estate.

'You may be interested in how we run the safari,' he told the photographer. 'It provides jobs and we're self-sufficient here, with our own farm, a school, a shop, and a well-stocked clinic, all run by the workers and their families.'

Chrissie had shot Johann a grateful look as Tommo shouldered his camera and climbed up into a safari truck with him. She sipped her tea and waited. Evelyn turned her cup round and round in its saucer as if she didn't know where to begin. When she looked up, Chrissie saw dark shadows under her eyes, showing she had slept badly.

'So, you want to know everything.' Evelyn paused and Chrissie nodded. 'And you promise you are not going to write about this?'

'I promise.' Chrissie chewed at a fingernail, eager to question Evelyn but wary of frightening her off. 'When I try to remember my childhood here it's like looking in a shattered mirror. I can only see fragments and distorted pictures. I need to make sense of it to be at peace.' Chrissie was horrified to find herself tearing up.

Evelyn stared at her in anguish. 'You poor girl, of course I'll help you.' She put a comforting hand on Chrissie's arm. 'I'm afraid you saw too much, when you were a child and too young to grasp what was going on. But you're old enough now to understand, and perhaps, to forgive me.'

Chrissie wiped her eyes and smiled at her. 'I'm sure you don't need my forgiveness.'

'Oh, I do, I most certainly do.'

Evelyn began to talk, haltingly at first, her voice gaining strength as she stepped further back into their shared past until the words tumbled over each other. Chrissie bent to hear every one of them, like a thirsty person straining to catch every drop of water. As Evelyn's story unfolded, Chrissie saw how its threads were woven into the threads of her own story, until the intricate pattern of the whole was revealed. Over the next few days the two women met and during walks around the grounds and cups of tea in the shade, Evelyn gradually revealed what had happened to her, to them all, twenty years ago. And the more Evelyn talked, the more Chrissie remembered, until it was as if she were nine years old once more and still living in Chalimbana.

At first, Chrissie tried to question Evelyn about the snatches of memory that troubled her: the blood, the flies, the stained dress. But Evelyn stopped her.

'There's always a reason why people like me, like your parents, came out to Africa and left everything behind.'

'My parents had no choice – my father was posted here. They never wanted to move to Africa, they've made that clear enough over the years.'

Evelyn's laugh was dry. 'That may be true in part, but I'm sure your father relished the chance for an adventure in Africa, for new horizons. I know I did.' She narrowed her eyes at Chrissie, as if calculating. 'You're about the same age I was when I came out, so perhaps you'll understand what it was like for me.'

Rain

London – June 1973

Evelyn was working at an art gallery in Soho when she met Robert
Fielding one rainy summer evening. It was coming down in grey
sheets when he pushed open the doors and ran in, shaking the water
from his hair like a dog. She noticed him because he looked so out of
place in his dark suit in a sea of polo necks and corduroy jackets. He
was also extraordinarily good-looking: spare but broad-shouldered,
pushing back his dark hair, wet from the rain. There were shadows
like bruises under his eyes and he had a distracted, restless air, as if
he'd rather be somewhere else. Evelyn didn't blame him. He'd obviously only come in to get out of the rain, but he picked up a glass
of wine and peered at a painting. She giggled when he sipped the
warm German hock and made a face, looking around for a place to
put down his glass. He appeared so in need of rescuing that Evelyn
pushed her way towards him through the tight groups of gallery
hangers-on, all screeching like seagulls with their backs firmly to the
art. She was deeply bored with her dead-end job at the gallery, with
London and with her life, and this stranger intrigued her: he was so
different from her usual crowd of aspiring artists, out-of-work actors
and penniless writers, all vying with each other to be more cynical
and jaded than the next. When she arrived at the stranger's side,
he was staring at a bulbous sculpture with such frank disgust that
she laughed out loud. Startled, he turned towards her and nearly
knocked over the exhibit.

'Damn it! I'm terribly sorry.' His accent belonged to another generation: at once clipped and drawling. Her arty friends affected to sound like London cabbies or adopted a transatlantic twang, but this man was unashamedly English and upper class.

'Oh don't be sorry,' she said, righting the sculpture. 'It's a perfectly hideous piece.' She had to tip her head to look up at him. The lines around his eyes were like white spokes against his tan. When he smiled, the white disappeared. He looked back at her without self-consciousness. The rain that had been throwing itself at the plate glass window stopped and the last of the evening sunlight came out, lighting up the drops of water in his hair like crystals. She laughed again and put out her hand.

'Hello. I'm Evelyn.'

'Robert Fielding,' he said, not letting her hand go. 'You seem to find me awfully funny.'

'There you are, Evie. I've been looking for you everywhere,' Patrick, her ex-boyfriend spoke into her ear and made her jump. She hadn't heard his approach over the hubbub. Now he gripped the back of Evelyn's arm just hard enough to make her wince, forcing her to let go of Robert's hand. The two men eyed each other. She edged away from Patrick, who smirked at the other man.

'Robert, Patrick Fitzgerald, the artist who made the piece you were just admiring,' she said.

Patrick took a drag of his cigarette. 'It's called '*Love*'. What do you think?' The question was a challenge and he narrowed his eyes at the other man through a thick cloud of smoke.

Robert frowned at the sculpture, a concrete donut stabbed with a rusted iron spike. Evelyn understood his bewilderment: she'd spent three years at Art College trying to get to grips with pieces like this and had learned early on not to talk about whether she liked a work of art or, God forbid, that she found it beautiful. *But does it work?* Her tutors would demand. When she started going out with Patrick, Evelyn had soon learned to keep her mouth shut and wait for him to talk about his work. After graduating, she'd drifted into a summer job at the gallery and four years later she was still here. Now she was twenty-five and felt stuck. The gallery job was meant to be a stopgap while she put together enough material for an exhibition, but she'd quietly given up on making it as an artist and had stopped drawing

37

altogether. Boredom and self-loathing had driven her into the arms of Patrick, who was as bafflingly cruel as his work. Even now, after his appalling behaviour had forced her to break up with him, he wouldn't let her alone, assuming she'd come to her senses and go back to him.

Patrick rolled a cigarette and began to talk about his favourite subject: himself. 'Let me help you out. You see, what I'm trying to do here is push the boundaries, you know what I mean, mate?' Robert looked slightly appalled at being addressed like a plumber's assistant but Patrick didn't seem to notice his expression darken. He waved his cigarette stub loftily, sending sparks and ash over Evelyn. 'It was Rodin who said that sculpture is the art of the hole and the lump. In that respect, and that only, I happen to agree with the old bastard.'

He rolled and lit another cigarette and carried on talking about space and textures. After a while, Evelyn stopped listening, and so apparently did Robert. Over Patrick's head, he sought her eyes and once again she found herself unable to look away. Sensing he didn't have his audience's full attention, Patrick fell silent and looked from one to the other. When he spoke, Evelyn recognised the note of menace lying just underneath his Irish lilt. He stabbed a finger at Robert. 'I haven't seen you around before, have I?'

Robert was still looking at Evelyn and answered distractedly. 'No, I don't expect you have. I'm not usually in London, you see. I live in Africa.'

Patrick put his arm around Evelyn's shoulders. 'Africa, is it now?' He whistled. 'Isn't that something? I suppose you don't get to see much in the way of art or culture out in the wilds, eh? Too busy hanging on to the British Empire and keeping the natives in their place, what, what?'

His smile was affable but the parody of Robert's cut-glass accent was unmistakable. Evelyn would have sniggered along with him only a few months ago, but she was sick of this kind of cheap dig at the expense of people who weren't artists – *civilians* Patrick called them. She furrowed her brow at Robert trying to signal her disgust to him, but all his attention was on Patrick now. He had gone completely still, his eyes burning into Patrick's. Evelyn felt a stab of sympathy for her ex.

When he eventually spoke, Robert's drawl had turned icy. 'Is that what you call this – art?' He flicked his eyes over the sculpture and back to Patrick. 'I don't know how you fellows can stand to be creeping about indoors all day messing about with paints. I prefer to be outdoors, living life rather than looking at it. This sort of thing is all very well, I suppose,' he glanced at the sculpture with distaste, 'but it's not what you'd call man's work.'

Patrick, who liked to think of himself as a working class hero – even though his father was a mild-mannered schoolteacher – and liked to challenge other artists to fights in Soho's drinking clubs, was silenced. He would probably have stalked away to preserve what was left of his dignity, but Evelyn made the mistake of snorting into her glass of wine. Patrick glared at her and she remembered how fragile his ego was and felt a pang of pity. But perhaps she'd become too used to protecting his feelings. It was about time someone put him in his place. She smoothed a strand of her pale hair behind her ear and allowed herself to openly admire Robert, running her eyes over his beautifully tailored dark suit and his lean and hungry look. Patrick in his threadbare velvet jacket looked like what he was next to him: a dilettante and a phony. Evelyn's frank interest in Robert and the comparison between the two men wasn't lost on Patrick. He clamped his arm more tightly around her shoulders.

'Come to the pub, Evie, darlin', the whole gang's going.'

She tried to shake him off. 'No, Patrick, I don't want to.' He ignored her and pulled her towards him so she staggered slightly on her heels.

Robert put his hand on Patrick's arm. 'She told you she didn't want to. Let her go, there's a good chap.'

The two men stared at each other and Evelyn held her breath. No one had ever stood up for her the way Robert was doing now. His hands hung at his side now, curled into slight fists and there was a tension in his shoulders, as if the muscles were bunched, ready for action.

Patrick dropped his eyes first. He brought out his tobacco tin and began to roll another cigarette. It was like watching a cat back away from a fight, grooming itself to save face. He took his time lighting his cigarette before he smiled at Robert.

'You can have her if you want. I've finished with her.' He turned on his heel and walked away. Trembling with rage, Evelyn watched him approach a critic and start insulting him loudly enough for the whole gallery to hear. 'Concocting more of your uninformed tripe for your so-called newspaper, Morton? You're pathetic. Typical critic – you can't create anything yourself, so you sneer from the sidelines at those of us who can and do.'

Evelyn watched Patrick jab his finger in the journalist's face; she wanted to stride over and bend it until it snapped.

Robert leaned towards her and spoke gently. 'Are you all right? I'm sorry. I shouldn't have been so rude to him but he was unspeakable to you. I'm afraid he's taking it out on that poor chap over there instead.'

'It's not your fault. Patrick can be vile. But I spent days persuading *The Times* to send someone to this opening and now he'll trash the exhibition and Chester will be in a filthy mood with me.'

'Chester?'

'He's the gallery owner. My boss. I'm supposed to be in charge of publicity, as well as the hanging, and being polite to potential customers.'

'Is that what you were doing with me? Being polite?'

'Oh no, I…' She saw he was smiling and she laughed. 'I could never be polite to you.'

'I'm delighted to hear it. Why don't you continue not to be polite to me over dinner and a decent drink? This stuff is filthy.' He put down his glass next to the ugly sculpture and some wine splashed the concrete. 'Oh dear,' Robert said. 'Actually, I rather think that's an improvement. Dissolves the boundaries, so to speak.'

Evelyn pretended to frown. 'Yes, the indivisible line between the self and the other is now soaked in plonk.' She laughed and took his outstretched arm. 'All right, let's go.'

It was raining hard and they ran across the street to shelter under a shop awning. A gust of wind threw a bucketload of rainwater at them and Robert unbuttoned his coat. Evelyn hesitated for a moment only before stepping into the warmth. He wrapped his arms around her and it was like coming home. It shouldn't happen this fast, but she didn't care. She'd once seen a woman drop her keys in the street and a stranger stop to pick them up for her. When they straightened up, he put his arms around her and kissed her. Evelyn understood that impulse now: she had nothing to lose. When Robert kissed her, their faces were wet with rain but she didn't care and clung to him as the sky emptied itself over them.

WHITE ROSES

For the rest of the summer, Robert courted her in the old-fashioned
way, as if he really had just stepped out of the 1940s. He would
arrive promptly at her digs with pale, creamy roses, and over dinners
at Claridges or the Ritz, he told her about his life in Africa.

'It's Zambia now, of course, since independence in '64, but I still
think of it as Northern Rhodesia. We've done a pretty good job of
handing the country back without any guerrilla wars or bloodshed.
Kaunda – that's the president – is doing his best, but nationalising
the copper industry has been a disaster. Foreign investors are…'

Evelyn's attention wandered when Robert talked about politics
or economics, but when he told her about hunting for big game,
and what it was like to sleep under canvas while lions roared in the
night, she sat up and listened, breathless with excitement. She loved
to hear about his childhood, growing up practically wild in the bush.
He'd desperately missed Africa when he was sent away to boarding
school in England and counted the days until he could go back at
the end of every term. He dreamed of being finished with school
so he could go back to Africa for good. But his family left Africa to
come back to England when he was in his teens. As soon as he could,
he took a job with the Colonial Office, who had sent him to work all
over the Federation of Rhodesia and Nyasaland, as the neighbouring Zambia, Rhodesia and Malawi were then called. His days were
spent trekking through the vast empty veldt to settle disputes with
the paramount chief – the 'headman' Robert called him – of each

of the tribes. Evelyn liked the exotic names of the different peoples and tried to memorise them: Lozi, Ngoni, Tonga, Lunda, Bemba, Kaonde, Luvale, Chewa, Nyanja...

'When independence came, I stayed on as an advisor to the new Government,' Robert said. 'They wanted me to live in Lusaka, but I've never liked city life and found somewhere in the bush where I could stretch my legs, a former colonial station called Chalimbana. It's about an hour's drive outside Lusaka but I don't go into the city much – try to stay away from the office as much as possible. The Zambian civil service is a shambles. None of the locals have much more than primary education let alone any experience of government, and nepotism is rife. When you get a government job as a *wabenzie* you're expected to employ your extended family.' He shrugged. 'It's deeply entrenched in traditional African culture, but it does make my job rather tricky. I'm afraid there's a lot of work to be done if they are to make it alone now the British have upped sticks. We have to help train them: we owe them that at least.' He took her hand across the table. 'Listen to me banging on about my job. I'm sorry, darling. I'm on my own so much out there, I think I've forgotten how to talk to women. You must be bored out of your mind.'

But Evelyn shook her head and asked him to tell her what Africa was like, what it was really like. So he told her about the bush babies that wail at night like human infants, how he slept out on the veldt, the stars scattered across the inky sky, about the rich red earth streaked through with malachite, mica and copper, and the blue hills that stretched hazily into the distance. Evelyn listened spell-bound. It all sounded so much more exciting than her dreary life in London. She couldn't know that Robert was never usually this talkative, that homesickness had made him so. Already she knew she wanted to marry him and live in Africa, so she forced herself listen when he talked about the Copper Belt that had made it the most prosperous country after South Africa; how before independence only a handful of British colonial officers had administered the huge, nearly empty country where scattered nomadic tribes scraped a basic existence from the earth.

'When I went out to the Federation in the 1950s only three per cent of the population was white, and that scared some people who thought they could be murdered in their beds at any time. It meant some of my colleagues in the Colonial Service took a heavy-handed approach when they were dealing with the headmen, but I didn't find it necessary. I'd grown up with these people.'

Robert grew passionate when he told Evelyn about his hopes for Zambia to become even more prosperous than it already was.

'It's underdeveloped but the red earth is rich and fertile, ripe for farming. A few Boers have ventured north from SA to set up farms but we need more like them to set up good working farms and really make the land work, bring jobs, food and prosperity, train up the locals, make the country self-sufficient.'

Evelyn knew agriculture and economics were important, but her imagination really caught fire when Robert showed her a dog-eared postcard he kept in his pocket. It was of Victoria Falls, an aerial photograph of the winding Zambezi River plunging into a vast opening in the earth. Tons of water cascaded into the abyss sending up clouds of spray.

'It's one of the wonders of the world,' Robert said, and her breath caught in her throat. He told her about David Livingstone trekking north into the unknown territories and how he stumbled on the Falls, how the locals were terrified of legends about water demons and refused to go near it. Evelyn wriggled in her seat and listened avidly. This was more like it! Her ideas of Africa had been gleaned from Rider Haggard and Edgar Rice Burroughs novels. Growing up in a sleepy market town in Surrey, she'd gobbled up the adventures to fill the acres of time between tennis matches and horse riding. The only daughter of a stockbroker, she had dismayed her parents when she'd moved to London instead of settling down with one of the nice young men with a steady job in the City. By the time their fears were realised, it was too late: her heart had been broken by Patrick, a man so thrillingly bad she had been sure she'd never get over him. But now here was Robert, with his tales of thunderous waterfalls, big empty skies and hunting in the bush. With him, she could put the failures of the past behind her and do something meaningful at last. Evelyn wasn't quite sure what that would be, but she was convinced she would find it in Africa.

Robert proposed one night over champagne and oysters in the Ritz and, giddy on Dom Perignon and the chance of a new life, Evelyn accepted without hesitation. She took him to meet her parents and he charmed them with his correct manners and the way he treated Evelyn like a fragile treasure. Her father, who had always tried to impress on her the importance of marrying a man with enough capital to yield a decent income, realised the marriage would take his daughter several notches up the social scale, and assumed Robert had the means to match his cut-glass accent. He clapped Robert on the back and declared himself delighted. Evelyn's mother wasn't so sure.

'He's so much older than you, darling. Forty-five – that's nearly my age. And you're so young, still a child really,' she said as she helped Evelyn pack to go back to the city.

But Evelyn was twenty-five and didn't feel young any more. She was sick of London: the rainy streets crammed with miserable office workers, the leaden skies, and the poky attic flat with other girls' tights dripping over the bath. She'd grown to loathe the tedium of sitting in an empty gallery all day listening to Chester bitch about clients. Africa would be an adventure, and it would take her far away from Patrick, who still wouldn't leave her alone, even though she was with Robert. Especially now she was with Robert. He'd taken to turning up at the gallery when she was working, circling her, like a cat that hadn't finished tormenting its prey.

Now she threw the last of her clothes in her bag, her jaw set. 'What does age matter? I love him.'

Her mother tucked a strand of Evelyn's hair behind her ear. 'Of course you do, darling. But try to think of the future. The age difference may not matter now, but when you're forty he'll be sixty.'

Forty seemed years away to Evelyn. She shrugged and laughed. 'Oh Mother, try to be happy. I am.'

And she was: surprisingly, delightedly. Evelyn found that a handsome, mature man who quite clearly adored her, who took her out to dinner and lavished compliments on her, was a wonderful distraction from the despair she'd dragged around with her since finding out Patrick had been sleeping with her friend. Another artist, Miranda performed 'happenings', rolling her naked body smeared with luminous paint on rolls of canvas taped to the floor. At first Evelyn had been pleased when her sophisticated friend and her boyfriend hit it off, until the day she walked in on them at Patrick's studio and found them entwined on the stained mattress he kept for his models. Miranda had smiled lazily up at Evelyn. *Why don't you join us, darling? No? Oh, don't be so bourgeois.*

Evelyn had fled, appalled and in tears, their laughter trailing after her as she clattered down the stairs. When she'd told the gallery owner, a bitchy old Soho queen, that Patrick had betrayed her with Miranda, the daughter of a baronet, he had sniggered. 'He's traded up, sweetie.' She'd been stung.

But now she was the prize. Evelyn liked the way the maître d' pulled out her chair and deferred to Robert in his handmade suits, scenting both class and money, how women in Parisian dresses and serious jewellery turned their heads when he walked into a restaurant or theatre foyer. They looked at him hungrily before catching sight of Evelyn. It gave her a flicker of triumph to see them drop their eyes, outmatched.

The only sour note in their courtship was struck when they visited his family in the Cotswolds in the run-up to the wedding. His sister picked them up at the station in a vintage open-top sports car she called Swifty, as if it were a pet. Evelyn froze in the cramped back seat, a nasty wind whipping her hair into her eyes, while Pamela shouted news at her brother above the racket from the engine.

The family home was straight out of the pages of *Country Life*. The autumn sun bathed the stone façade in golden light, but inside it was as dark and cold as a mausoleum. Robert's father stomped into the hall, which was empty apart from a dilapidated hat stand and a tarnished suit of armour, shook Robert's hand and nodded at Evelyn before disappearing, never to reappear during that endless, uncomfortable weekend. Evelyn, accustomed to the middle class comforts of central heating, plentiful hot water and thick, fitted carpets, suffered terribly. At night, she shivered under icy sheets, her toes bashing against a 'stone pig', a tepid stoneware bottle that was supposed to take the chill off the bed but only made it feel clammy. When Robert snuck into her room and put his arms around her she was glad of his warmth. As his mouth found hers in the chilled darkness, it seemed to Evelyn that he still burned with the heat of Africa.

On their last day, Robert's stepmother, a scrawny woman with cold eyes the colour of sea-washed glass, studied Evelyn as she perched on the sofa with the silky head of a Pekingese resting in her lap.

'Don't stroke Pongo so, hard, his eyeballs will pop out – it's a fault in the breed,' Clarissa snapped.

Evelyn laughed but realised with a stab of panic that she was serious. 'Oh, I'm sorry.' She snatched her hand away and looked desperately for Robert, but he was standing with his back to her at the other side of the cavernous drawing room. He'd been shut up with his father in the study all morning and had made straight for the whisky when he came out, looking murderous. Evelyn turned back to Clarissa and tried to think of something to say to break the frigid silence. She began to ask about the garden, but the older woman interrupted her rudely.

'Who are your people?'

Startled, Evelyn started pulling at the dog's ears again but stopped when she saw Clarissa frown. 'Um, my father is a stockbroker. Is that what you mean?'

'Not really, no.'

There followed a brutal interrogation about Evelyn's family background that soon revealed she was woefully lacking in breeding, unlike the Pekingese with its inadequate eye sockets. She bent her head and answered the barrage politely, but finally lost patience when Clarissa asked her if she dyed her hair. *Only it's so brassy, you see.*

Evelyn stood up and brushed the dog hairs off her lap. 'I love Robert very much, and he loves me, and that is all you need to know about me.'

Pamela, who had been sitting quietly on one of the many sofas anchored like icebergs around the drawing room, rose and came to meet her. She pulled Evelyn towards her with fingers reddened and roughened by years of living in this draughty pile.

'My dear,' she whispered to Evelyn. 'Don't mind Clarissa, she can be horrid but she's not a bad old stick once you get to know her;

she has a kind heart.' Pamela's smile softened her homely features: a strong nose, a high, bony forehead and the same square jaw as Robert. She was what the English call handsome when they mean to be kind to a plain woman.

Evelyn glanced at Clarissa, who had taken the sulky Pekingese into her own lap and was feeding it treats. 'I've met cobras with kinder hearts,' she said.

Pamela laughed and drew her into a love seat in a corner, out of Clarissa's earshot. 'She's a pussycat compared to my mother. You would never have got near Robert if she were still alive. Florence wouldn't have stood for the competition. She was a great beauty in her time – the whole county was in love with her.' Pamela looked up at a portrait of a dark-haired woman with pale skin, huge dark eyes and a crimson mouth. Her shingled hair was glossy as a blackbird's wing and her satin eau-de-nil evening gown draped the curve of her hips. Her creamy breasts looked as if they should be eaten with a teaspoon, one quivering bite at a time.

Pamela sighed and turned away from the portrait as if it tired her. 'Mother was terribly *glamorous*. We were worried when Robert said he was bringing you here that he'd bring someone like her, as he has in the past. This family has had quite enough glamour – and the scandal that inevitably follows.'

Evelyn was intrigued; Robert had never mentioned a scandal. More pressingly, she wanted to know about Robert's other girl-friends.

'What do you mean about a scandal?'

Pamela lit an unfiltered cigarette, a Senior Service, the sort of thing a labourer would smoke. She puffed at it for a bit and blew the smoke out of her impressive nose. 'Well, there was Charlie. She broke Robert's heart before he went out to Africa. He'd spent years chasing after her. Charlie was quite something – straight out of the society pages. Presented at court, inherited diamonds, as highly strung as a greyhound, you know the sort of the thing.' Evelyn didn't but nodded so Pamela would carry on. 'Anyway, she turned out to be a heartless little fortune hunter. Her father had squandered the family money on the gaming tables and she was penniless, look-ing for a meal ticket. But when Charlie found out the old man had disinherited Robert – that's probably what they've been fighting about today – she ran off with a chinless duke who happens to own half of Scotland. Robert was never quite the same and took himself back off to Africa, heartbroken.'

Evelyn glanced up at portrait and looked away from Florence's hard eyes. 'And your mother, what was she like?'

Pamela stubbed out her cigarette in a plant pot. 'Robert adored her and she him, but she had no time for me – too much of a plain Jane for her.' Her bark of laughter turned into a cough. 'You'll find out soon enough that none of us can live up to Florence's memory. There's nothing quite like a tragic dead mother – or mother-in-law – to make life difficult.' Pamela looked over to Robert, who was staring out of the window into the darkness. 'She left so much damage in her wake, you see.'

'How old was he when she died?'

'Five. Only five. Poor little sod.'

Evelyn's heart contracted. She wanted to run over to Robert and put her arms around him, to smooth away the deep groove between his eyes and take away the pain. At that moment he turned towards her and saw her looking at him. When he smiled at her, it was like the sun coming out after a storm.

On the train back to London, Evelyn wanted to ask Robert about his mother, but he looked drained, the blue smudges back under his eyes.

'Thank God that's over,' he said and looked out onto the sodden fields as they sped past them through another summer shower. He loosened his tie and grimaced. 'I can't breathe in England. I've got to get away from here.' He reached for her hand, desperate now. 'You will come back to Africa with me, won't you? I couldn't live without you, not now.'

'Yes, I'll come with you.' He pulled her towards him, so close she could feel his heartbeat. Evelyn had never held someone else's life in her hands before. She closed her eyes and lost herself in the kiss.

As the train raced towards London, Evelyn watched the pale sun keep pace through the smeared glass. Soon she would be in Zambia with Robert. She closed her eyes and tried to imagine the hot African sun on her face.

AFRICA

September 1973

Evelyn stepped off the Dakota plane into a new world. The warm air clung to her and smelled of wood smoke, oil and dust. She shaded her eyes and looked up into the upturned blue bowl of the African sky. Before her, a landscape the colour of yellow ochre stretched to the horizon.

She was taken aback by the smallness of Lusaka, the capital of Zambia. She had expected a busy city, but it was more like a sleepy frontier town in the Wild West, with low buildings that flanked the main street. The covered pavements gave little respite from the afternoon heat, but down the middle of Cairo Road there was a line of trees, heavy with purple blooms. *Jacaranda.* She whispered the name, feeling its softness in her mouth. Under the trees, sellers sat cross-legged in the shade in front of blankets strewn with incidental treasures from the copper mines in the north: green whorled malachite polished into gems for rings and bracelets, amethysts cleft open like fruit to show their purple and white hearts, copper bangles said to have healing powers. The hawkers showed her slim antelopes carved out of ebony and primitive masks made from bark, urging her to buy in their strange language. Evelyn flitted from blanket to blanket, trying on beaded bracelets and holding malachite eggs in her hand. Robert leaned against a tree and watched her.

In their room at the Ridgeway Hotel, she sat at the dressing table and tried on an amethyst necklace she'd bought, admiring the way it deepened the blue in her eyes. Robert frowned when she turned round to show him.

'A trinket from the bazaar,' he said. 'I can't have my wife wearing that.' He brought out a leather jewellery case from his pocket. 'I was going to give you these when we got to Chalimbana, but you'd better have them now.' The pearls had a pink lustre and were so cold when he dropped them around her neck that she gasped. 'They'll warm up against your skin, take on a sheen from its oils,' he said.

Evelyn laughed. 'You funny man, who told you that?'

He stood behind her, his fingertips on her shoulders. 'My mother. They were hers. When I met you, I had them sent out and restrung in Bond Street.'

'They're beautiful.'

And they were, but the pearls were heavy and seemed to drag Evelyn down by the throat. Since that peculiar conversation with Pamela, she had burned to find out more about Robert's mother. But every time she started to ask about her, he shut down and grew morose. She fingered the cold pearls and thought better of it: he'd been so happy since they'd arrived in Africa; as soon as he'd stepped off the liner at Cape Town it was as if he'd shrugged off his melancholy along with his heavy coat. He'd strolled through the shouting crowds of porters and hawkers on the dock, quite at home in the hubbub, whilst she'd shrunk from the outstretched hands of the children who ran alongside them in bare feet, tugging at her clothes.

Evelyn studied her husband in the mirror; the shadows under his eyes were less marked and he seemed at peace. She didn't want to darken his mood by asking him about his mother's death. Instead, her reflection smiled up at his and she touched the pearls at her neck.

'Thank you darling.'

He pulled down the strap of her slip and kissed her shoulder. Evelyn turned round and caught the warm cup of his mouth in her own. Outside the open window a bird was calling *hoop-hoop-hoop* over and over again while the songs of grasshoppers rose and fell in waves.

Later, Evelyn lay naked on the bed and watched Robert change into a khaki shirt, shorts and knee-high socks. The ceiling fan stirred the languid afternoon heat.

She yawned and stretched, warm as a cat. 'Darling, all you need is one of those old-fashioned Rider Haggard hats to complete the look.'

He grinned at her and pushed an electric shaver round his chin. 'You mean a sola topee? The old man used to wear one of those. Still got it somewhere.' He turned and tickled her foot. 'Come on, lazy bones, get dressed and we'll have a couple of sundowners in the courtyard.'

Evelyn sat on the terrace looking over the hotel garden and watched the sky turn rosy. A pair of yellow and black weaverbirds flitted back and forwards over the pond, hanging upside down on their complicated pouch of a nest to feed their chicks. In the green water below a crocodile floated, waiting for one of them to fly too low. *Don't worry, Madam, it is quite tame* the waiter had said, noticing her alarm as he placed their drinks on the table. A hoopoe – the bird she'd heard earlier – jumped from branch to branch in the tree, dipping its crested head up to the setting sun and back to the ground like a mini oil drill as it chugged out a warning. All around her, periwinkle blue morning glories and red hibiscus opened their trumpet mouths and the whitewashed walls bloomed with the heady sweetness of honeysuckle. Africa was like a brightly coloured dream, a dream that seemed more intense and real than anywhere Evelyn had been before. In Africa she could be someone new.

She changed into an apple green sundress for the drive to their new home. Ten miles into the bush, the dress was dark with sweat under her arms. Africa, hot and dusty, roared in through the Land Rover's open windows. Evelyn lifted her hair so the breeze could cool the nape of her neck.

She peered through the mess of crushed insects on the windscreen, hoping to see exotic wild animals roaming the yellow plains: the elephants, leopards, giraffes and zebras she'd imagined. But, all she could see was an expanse of dry scrub and trees that looked as if they had been pressed down by a giant hand. Her teeth jarred as the Land Rover jumped over a pothole. On the horizon, water mirages were thrown up by the play of heat and dust. They had arrived in Zambia in the dry season, when the land is parched and waiting for the rains. Evelyn had lived all her life in England, where even the summers could be cool, and found the dust suffocating, the air unbearably hot. A headache nudged at her temples as the sun bore down on her through the windshield. The roar of the engine failed to drown out the cicadas' never-ending screech and she winced. In the past few days she'd already learned to dread the escalating whine of their call, which signalled the hottest part of the day when it was best to find shade and a cool drink. Evelyn moved her back away from the plastic seat cover and plucked at the front of her dress. It had seemed so pretty and stylish when she'd bought it in London but she now realised it was too tight for the heat.

She shouted over the racket from the Land Rover: 'How much farther, darling?'

'Not far now, another ten miles or so.'

Evelyn put her arm around Robert's neck and pulled him towards her for a kiss. The jeep swerved and bounced over a rock. He shook her off and turned his attention back to the ruts in the dirt road. Evelyn chewed her lip and stared straight ahead, stung. It was true that Robert had relaxed since their arrival in Africa, but she'd begun to notice an ever so slight distance opening up between them, as if he'd begun to slip away from her and back into his job. He'd been distracted all morning since coming back from an early meeting with some government ministers. Now his air of irritation made Evelyn think of her father who disappeared behind a newspaper after work while her mother hovered, anxious to please, ignored and growing more invisible with every passing year. Well, that was not about to happen to Evelyn; she would not fade obligingly into the background. She twisted in her seat and pulled up her dress and opened her thighs so the white triangle of her pants showed. Turning to Robert with a small smile, she put her left hand on his thigh and slipped it under the cuff of his shorts and let her fingers rest there. He glanced down at her lap and groaned slightly. She felt a stab of triumph as the Land Rover swerved off the road and he stopped the engine.

Later, Robert still had his hand on her thigh when they drove towards a sign marked 'Chalimbana'. They turned off the main road and bumped over a cattle grid. Half a mile along a red dirt track, they stopped in front of a cluster of white bungalows. Evelyn studied her new home, excitement draining out of her like champagne emptied into a sink. Their bungalow was small and suburban with a crazy paving path leading up through a neat apron of grass to the veranda. She could hear children playing somewhere and see a badminton net strung across the neighbouring garden. Her heart sank; were it not for the bougainvillea climbing up the walls, she could be back in Surrey.

Robert seemed oblivious to her mood. 'We should get you in out of the sun.'

He jumped out of the Land Rover and walked up the veranda steps, whistling a tune that Evelyn recognised. It was a sentimental Irish tune that Patrick used to sing to her. Evelyn wondered what he was doing; what he'd make of his Evie in the African bush. He had turned up at her leaving party at the gallery, maudlin drunk, and begged her not to marry Robert. *Do you love him? You can't possibly love him. Have you slept with him yet?* He'd grabbed her arms hard and tried to pull her in for a whisky-scented kiss. But she's had enough of those. She'd pulled away from him and run out of the gallery and all the way to Robert's hotel.

Now Evelyn shook her head free of the memory of the desolation she'd seen in Patrick's eyes. She stepped out of the Land Rover and smiled up at her husband, who had turned to wait for her. He held out his hand to her and she ran lightly up the steps. All that hurt and confusion with Patrick was at an end. Robert had saved her and brought her to Africa, to start a new life. She slipped into his arms. He kissed her gently and swung her off her feet so she had to cling to his neck. Evelyn tucked her face into his neck and breathed in the faint sandalwood of his shaving soap. She wouldn't think of Patrick anymore. She was Mrs Fielding now: a married woman.

Robert pushed open the screen door, careful not to bump her feet in their heels – so impractical for the bush, but she was vain about her ankles. For a moment Evelyn couldn't see anything in the darkness after the glare outside. He set her down and she held on to his arm, off balance.

Robert laughed and caught her. 'Steady, don't want you keeling over in front of Sixpence.'

A man stepped out of the shadows and stood there, waiting. Evelyn laughed nervously. Robert had told her they'd have a houseboy working for them and she'd pictured a young village boy whom she would treat with kindness and perhaps even teach to read. But this was a middle-aged man with white frosting his wiry hair, and a sour expression. She put out her hand uncertainly. He ignored it. Embarrassed, Evelyn let her hand drop.

Robert nodded at him. 'Sixpence, it's good to be home.'

'Yes, Boss.'

'Bring us some sundowners, there's a good fellow – whisky and soda for me, gin and tonic for Madam. Then you can shoot off to the compound.' Sixpence disappeared through the swing door into the kitchen and Robert put his arm around Evelyn and gave her a reassuring squeeze. 'Servants don't like change, but don't worry, he'll soon get used to you. Sixpence is a good sort; he's been with me for twenty years. Came into my employ in Malawi and followed me from one posting to the next, from there to Southern Rhodesia and finally to Zambia. I wouldn't be without him. I'm sure you'll get on like a house on fire after a while.'

Evelyn wasn't so sure. Sixpence refused to look at her while he put the drinks down on the cane table on the veranda and walked away without a word when she stumbled out her thanks. Her shoulders didn't drop until she heard the back door slam and saw the top of his head above the reed hedge that ran along the garden as he walked away from the house.

She kicked off her sandals and tucked her feet under her on the sofa. 'Sixpence is a funny name. Is it a nickname?'

'No, it's his real name. In southern Africa parents often call their children after an event around the time of the birth, or a name they think is lucky, or that might bring the child wealth or schooling. You can tell the ones who have been to mission schools – they favour the Old Testament.'

Evelyn laid her head on Robert's shoulder. 'I like it. It's so different here, from everything I've ever known.' They sipped their drinks as the sun became a ball of molten copper and slipped beneath the watchful blue hills, turning the sky flamingo pink.

Robert sighed and waved his glass at the hills. 'It's good to be home. I couldn't stand London – noisy and grey and full of whey-faced men in suits. I only stuck it out to bag you, you know.'

Evelyn stretched out and put her feet on Robert's lap. She'd already come to love this time of day, when the shadows turned purple and the heat abated. She wanted to keep him talking.

'If you hate London so much, why ever did you go back?'

'Head Office called me in for a debrief, some sort of policy review, but it was a waste of time; Whitehall wasn't interested in hearing about Zambia's problems. Too busy clapping each other on the back because the handover in '64 was so peaceful. They don't want to hear about problems, or that the new Government is floundering in the dark.'

Evelyn reached for his hand and squeezed. No wonder Robert had been irritable; he had a lot of responsibility. She should have been more understanding. They sat quietly. In the distance an animal called out –something between a bark and a howl.

Robert turned to face her in the half-dark. 'But there was another reason I went out.' He paused and sipped his whisky. 'I wanted to build bridges with my father, get him to cut me back in to the will, and persuade him to release my inheritance.'

'What for?' Evelyn swung her feet to the ground. 'Are we in trouble?'

'No, nothing like that, it's for Pembroke, our lodge in the south-east of Zambia. It's where I grew up. When Father went back to England he abandoned it. I've always wanted to restore it to the way I remember it. The old man just let it go to ruin, damn him.'

Evelyn remembered what Robert's father had been like at their wedding: he'd barely spoken to his son and ignored her completely. The acidic Clarissa hadn't been much better. She had slid her eyes over Evelyn's short white dress and the white jasmine in her hair, smiled thinly and gone off to speak to someone more important.

Now Evelyn was curious; Robert rarely spoke about his child-hood, but perhaps here, close together in the darkness of the bush, he would open up about his past. She prompted him: 'You never told me about Pembroke before.'

'I suppose there hasn't been time. I'll take you there some day. But it's a sad place – roof's gone and the termites have done for most of the furniture.' Robert took a deep swallow of his whisky. 'My mother loved it there, called it paradise on earth.' Evelyn went still. Robert had never talked about his mother before. She said nothing and willed him to go on. He was quiet for a moment and the sound of the crickets grew louder in the silence between them. After a while, he began to talk in a low voice, as if he were telling her about a dream. 'I used to sit at her dressing table, watching her paint on her lipstick. It was dark red, like a slash of blood. And her skin was white, like porcelain, against her dark hair, like the Snow Queen in the fairy tale. I used to wonder if her skin would be icy to the touch. I remember her scent, Lily of the Valley. I thought she was the most beautiful woman in the world.' He traced his fingers down Evelyn's wrist. 'Until I met you, of course.'

She pictured a small boy, standing just out of reach of this cold woman, desperate to touch her but not daring. A helpless fury gripped her on his behalf. Evelyn put her arms around him now, the way his mother should have and pressed her face into his neck. She waited for him to go on talking but he only stroked her back.

She moved away but kept her hand in his. 'You've hardly talked about your mother, only that she died when you were a child. What happened to her?'

He studied their clasped hands. 'It might have been malaria or dengue. It's hard to tell, there are so many fevers out here.'

'How old were you?' Evelyn knew the answer – she'd remembered Pamela telling her – but she wanted to keep him talking.

'Five or six, I don't quite remember. All I know is I was sent back early from my first term as a boarder. They'd already buried her in the English cemetery in Broken Hill, but Father took me out to her grave. Someone had planted orange marigolds in the red dirt that covered her. Mother could never bear their scent. I remember thinking it should have been lilies so she could smell their perfume while she slept.'

Evelyn stroked back a lock of hair that had fallen over his forehead. 'I'm afraid I don't wear Lily of the Valley,' she said.

'No, you smell of England, of apple blossom and freshly cut grass.' He turned his face up to hers. They were so close she could see the hazel flecks in his grey eyes.

'You saved me, Robert Fielding.'

'No, my darling,' he said. 'It was you who saved me.'

There was a movement behind them and Evelyn started. Green buds were bursting open like stars to reveal long thin petals, luminous white against the darkness. They looked like sea anemones waving in the current.

She knelt on the sofa to get a better look. 'How extraordinary. What are they?'

'Spider lilies. Some people call them moon flowers because they only come out at night.' Evelyn looked up at the huge moon that hung in the sky. The flowers looked as if they were drinking the moonlight. Robert pulled her back to sit next to him and traced the line of her cheek down to her neck. She closed her eyes with pleasure. He spoke softly. 'It was the first thing I noticed about you in that bloody awful gallery – your skin, milk-white, like a moon flower.'

Evelyn opened her eyes and smiled at him. 'How poetic, darling.'

He smiled back but wouldn't be joked out of his mood. 'You were so different from the women out here – those harridans propping up the bar at The Ridgeway. I tried taking one of them out once – Shirley? Shelly? Some bottle blonde.' He shuddered. 'She had a laugh like a rutting baboon and the kind of leathery skin that's been out in the African sun too long.'

Evelyn laughed. 'That's not very chivalrous, Robert Fielding.'

'Unkind, I know, but so true.' He stroked her face again. 'I couldn't take my eyes off you all the while that Irish bastard was clutching at your arm. I wanted to punch him in the face.'

'Poor Patrick, he didn't stand a chance. As soon as I saw you, I longed to go to bed with you.'

'Well, that can easily be arranged, my darling.' He pulled Evelyn to her feet and led her inside.

Later, in the inky darkness, she lay under the mosquito net. It was too hot even for the cotton sheet that Robert had pushed down to his hips. Evelyn listened to the crickets, soothed now by their chirrups, and was nearly asleep when she heard a scuffling sound outside. She sat up and turned on her bedside lamp. A shadow sprang away from the bedroom window. Evelyn's heart thundered in her chest. She was aware again of how isolated they were in the vast emptiness of the bush, and began to understand why the colonials lived in English bungalows: to remind them of the safety of the Home Counties and to fend off the wild African night. After a while of listening for more noises, her breathing slowed. It must have been a trick of the light. Evelyn lay down next to the reassuring breadth of Robert's back. She was safe with him; he wouldn't let anything happen to her. The fan moved the warm air across her face and she closed her eyes.

ROASTING LEMONS

Evelyn took her cup of tea out to the veranda of her new home. The red tiles were cool beneath her bare feet. The blue mountains were shrouded in mist; soon the sun would burn it off and the heat would rise up from the red earth, but for now Evelyn relished the fresh morning. There was a movement behind her and she turned to see Sixpence standing in the shadows, watching her from behind the screen door. She tried to call out a greeting to him but it died in her throat. He turned his back on her and padded back to the kitchen. Evelyn looked down at her cotton housecoat and naked feet and wondered if she'd embarrassed him. She didn't know what to make of this servant, who glided silently from room to room. Evelyn didn't relish being left on her own with his surly presence all day. When Robert left the house, dressed for work, she followed him to the car and held on to his arm through the Land Rover window.

'Do you have to go? It's only six o'clock.'

He kissed her distractedly goodbye, his mind already on the day ahead. 'That's when the working day starts in Africa. I've some catching up to do with the headman.' He put the jeep into gear and waved as he drove off.

Evelyn walked slowly back into the house. It was the first time they'd been apart since their wedding. The day stretched before her. She could straighten up her new home but Sixpence was already mopping the floor, a yellow dust cloth tucked into his trouser belt.

Besides, it would get hot soon and she wouldn't have the energy. Robert had told her that the rains would bring relief from the searing heat when they came. Evelyn didn't know how she would bear the heat until then; it drained her, forcing her to take naps in the hottest part of the day. But it was cool now, and she would explore her surroundings before the sun climbed higher. She dressed quickly and went back out into the garden. The swing door opened behind her and she froze.

'Madam, would you like some tea?' It was the first time Sixpence had spoken to her.

Evelyn turned to face him, shading her eyes. Damn, it was already getting hot. 'Oh, that's kind, but no thank you, Sixpence. I think I'll go for a walk, it's such a lovely day.'

He frowned. 'It's not safe for Madam to walk alone.'

She laughed. 'Nonsense. I grew up in the country. I can look after myself.'

Sixpence turned on his heel without another word. The door banged shut behind him. Evelyn bit back the urge to call him back and tell him off for his bad manners. She didn't know how to handle this mute resentment and suspected it was because she was white. It seemed naïve now, but she hadn't given the colour bar – as everyone here seemed to call it – a moment's thought before she arrived, assuming that independence had swept away the divisions between the races. In London, she'd been 'briefed' by a camp older Foreign Office mandarin whose only advice had been to make sure she had a silk umbrella. *Only thing to keep you dry during the rainy season*, he'd drawled before going back to his files. There had been no helpful tips about how to deal with a truculent servant who clearly detested his new mistress.

Nor had there been a warning about the rampant insect life that flew, crawled and hopped everywhere. Evelyn stepped gingerly over a hissing column of soldier ants and walked further into the garden. The air was growing warmer and she felt the sun on her bare arms. She was determined to make the most of what was left of the coolness before the cicadas began.

As she walked around the garden, along the borders with their pungent marigolds, and brushed her fingers against the sweet honeysuckle that grew everywhere, she began to feel better. In Africa she was free; she could do anything. Nobody knew her here, not even Robert, really. Here nobody knew she was a failed artist, one of Patrick's cast-offs to be pitied and sniggered about. Evelyn stretched out her arms and spun around slowly with her eyes shut. This was her chance of a new beginning; she would never be lonely or humiliated again. She leaned against a tree with red flowers and imagined its strength soaking into her. In Africa, she would take risks and have adventures. In Africa, she would do exactly as she pleased. Emboldened, Evelyn decided to stop worrying about Sixpence. He was in her employ after all. She was Robert's wife; this was her home and she would run it as she damn well pleased.

For a start, she would brighten up the poky little bungalow with flowers from her own garden. Evelyn was reaching up to break off a frangipani bloom – its creamy flesh so different from the papery dog roses in England – when she heard children's voices coming from next door. She walked over to the reed hedge that separated the two gardens and peeked through a gap to see a skinny white girl squatting next to a black boy in torn khaki shorts. A bleach-haired toddler in nothing but a pair of socks played in the dirt nearby. The older girl and the boy, who looked about nine or ten, were huddled over a fire. They were poking at a round, charred object and didn't notice Evelyn until she moved to get a better look, making a noise. The girl nudged the boy until he stopped what he was doing. They both stared.

Evelyn smiled and waved. 'Hello.' The smaller girl stood up and waved back. She took a step towards Evelyn, and walked straight into the the the fire. 'No!' Evelyn cried out and dropped the flowers. Tearing at the gap in the hedge to make it larger, she squeezed through and ran towards the little girl, but it was too late. The child's screams ripped the air as a burning ember stuck to her sock. The older girl picked up the toddler under the arms to try and shake it free, but she staggered and they both nearly fell. Evelyn reached them and yanked off the sock. The toddler's chubby foot was red and beginning to blister.

'That's a nasty burn,' she said, picking up the child. 'Let's go and find your mummy.' Evelyn patted the little girl awkwardly on the back and made a shushing noise she thought might comfort her, but she only opened her mouth and howled more loudly. Evelyn shifted the sobbing child onto her hip and ran towards her neighbours' veranda, the older girl and boy trotting by her side like a pair of gun dogs. Evelyn reached the stairs and called out: 'Hello? Is anyone home?'

A woman in an apron, her hands floury, burst through the screen door and ran down the steps. She pulled the little girl off Evelyn and held her tight.

'There, there, my little chick, my little hen,' she crooned. She looked at Evelyn over the child's head and spoke sharply. 'What happened?' Evelyn wrung her hands. This was a terrible start. What if the woman blamed her for the accident?

'I'm so sorry,' Evelyn said. 'I couldn't stop her in time. She stood in the fire, but I don't think the skin is broken.'

The woman turned her child's foot in her hand. After a while, to Evelyn's relief she put the toddler down. 'Hush now, it's only a wee burn, you'll be all right.' She smiled warmly at Evelyn and held out her hand. 'I'm Grace Docherty. You'll be Robert's wife, Evelyn isn't it?' Evelyn nodded and smiled back. 'Come away into the house. I'd better put some Germolene on Catriona's foot. Thank goodness you were there to help her. Come in, come in. I'll make us a cup of tea.' Grace was halfway up the stairs before she noticed her older daughter, who had been skulking in the background. She turned on her. 'Christine Docherty! You should have been looking after your wee sister. What have I told you before? No more fires!' The girl hopped from foot to foot with frustration while Evelyn looked on, trying not to smile at the furious scowl.

'But, Mum! How are we supposed to roast lemons without a fire? I was being careful, I promise. It was Cat's fault. I told her to stay away, but she followed Elijah and me.' She balled her fists. 'And now we're not allowed to make fires anymore. It's not fair!'

'That's enough, Chrissie,' Grace said. 'I don't want to hear another word out of you. Off you go.'

Chrissie took the boy by the hand. 'Come on, Elijah, let's look for mangoes.'

Grace called after her: 'And I don't want you eating mangoes at this time of year. They're not ripe and you'll end up with a sore stomach, like last time.'

Chrissie glared at her mother over her shoulder as she marched off. She looked so murderous that Evelyn had to swallow a bubble of laughter as she followed Grace into the bungalow.

GREEN MANGOES

As Evelyn recalled that day, it came back to Chrissie in vivid detail. Up in the tree on the other side of the dirt road, she had bitten into the hard, white flesh of a green mango. She remembered how it had tasted bitter but held the promise of the succulent fruit. The dried sap from the stalk had been sticky on her teeth and the fruit's flesh hard and white. Now her memories of the rest of the day returned.

Back then, Chrissie swung her legs against the crackled bark of the branch she was sitting astride and looked out over the valley, at the brown river winding its way through the red dirt to the lake, and the tall, yellow elephant grass that grew higher than a man. The acacia trees held their gnarled bare hands up to the sky, but she knew that just before the rains came they would sprout green leaves to catch every last drop of water.

Chalimbana, with its handful of white bungalows, its two thatched churches and the teacher training college where her father worked, stretched before her along the flat bed of the valley. She twisted her body to see where the river dipped down towards the lake and the village with its round thatched huts clustered around a big tree where meetings and parties were held. Apart from rare trips into Lusaka, the village was at the edge of Chrissie's world. She had been told she'd been born in India, but her family had moved to Zambia when she was a toddler like her sister Cat, and she couldn't remember anything other than eating rice in the cool darkness of the kitchen in Hyderabad, and the softness of her ayah's skin when she hid her face in Mary's neck. Africa was all she knew, except for the single winter she'd spent in Scotland three years ago when her dad had gone back to university in Edinburgh before returning to Zambia. She had tried her best to forget that time. It had been like a film – a cold film shot in black and white. She'd been happy at her little school in Chalimbana but miserable at the Scottish school, chilled by the Victorian building and baffled by the iron railings that imprisoned the children. The hard tarmac that covered the playground had bloodily gouged her knees every time she'd fallen. Unhappiness had wrapped itself around Chrissie like a damp fog all the time she'd been there. When the family had returned to Africa a year later, Chrissie had plunged back into what she considered her real life and Edinburgh had been reduced to nothing more than a monochrome dream. The possibility of leaving Africa again never entered her mind. This was her home, her *kraal*.

And now a new person had come into her narrow world: Mrs Fielding. With her blonde hair and big blue eyes, pouty pink lips and slim legs, she looked like one of the Sindy dolls that Chrissie's grandmother mailed out every Christmas and birthday for her and Cat. The sisters had quite a collection now, all permanently naked as they had a mania for washing the dolls' clothes in basins in the gardens. The teddy bears also got a good daily scrubbing and were now balding as if they had alopecia, even the ones owned by her older brothers, Hamish and Angus.

Chrissie wanted to talk about the fascinating Mrs Fielding and called out to her friend, Elijah, who sat a little apart on the same thick branch, his legs dangling. One of the houseboy Samson's ten children, he was about Chrissie's age.

'Elijah?' Chrissie shuffled up to be near him but he was tinkering with a car he'd made from old bits of chicken wire and didn't look up. She peered over his shoulder and watched his deft fingers twisting the wire into shape. All the African boys made these intricate models fitted with long steering columns so they could run along, pushing them in front of them. They were much more fun than her brothers' collection of Dinky cars and she knew that Angus and Hamish coveted the home-made toys. Elijah was concentrating hard and Chrissie had to yank his khaki shirt.

He frowned and bent the mudguard into shape. 'What is it?'

Chrissie wanted to impress him and thought hard. 'Isn't Mrs Fielding pretty?'

He shrugged. 'She is a Madam.'

Chrissie sighed; she would never get his attention this way. Then she remembered that boys like dangerous things. She thought for a moment and said in a hushed voice: 'Guess what.' A pause for effect, but Elijah still didn't look up. 'There's a black mamba in our garden.'

That made him look up, and his eyes widened with excitement. He spoke quickly. 'You should be careful. This is a very dangerous snake. It can kill you.' He put the flat of his hand on his chest. 'I know this. My mother's sister was bitten.'

Chrissie wriggled even closer to Elijah on the branch. Her breath came in quick, uneven bursts. 'Did she die?'

Elijah shook his head slowly. 'No.' Chrissie sighed. She'd been hoping for a gruesome story – some frothing at the mouth at the very least, like when a rabid dog bit you. Elijah looked around and lowered his voice so she had to lean in to hear him. 'The witchdoctor came and gave her medicine.'

Chrissie gasped and looked around too. She knew who the witchdoctor was – Nyirongo, the messenger who ran errands for the college. She'd heard her father talking about the problems he caused. Nyirongo came to the house every day to deliver newspapers and magazines from back home. Chrissie didn't like the way he stared at her, and how he was amiable to her in front of her parents but tried his best to scare her when she opened the door on her own. Hamish called him Bug Eyes behind his back and imitated the way he stared when he was trying to frighten them. The village children were terrified of him and Chrissie had spent so much time at the servants' compound with Elijah that she'd soaked up some of their fear. She tried to be brave now and remember how her brother laughed at 'old bug eyes'.

'Hamish says Nyirongo isn't a real witchdoctor, that he can't cure anyone from a black mamba bite. My dad says he's a faker too.'

Elijah looked around, his eyes wide. 'Ssssh! He'll hear you, he's got spies everywhere.' He pointed at a weaverbird nest hanging above their heads. 'Even the birds tell him things. If he finds out what you said, he'll put a curse on you, blow blue powder through your door. You'll be dead quick-quick.'

Chrissie shivered, as if a tick had buried itself into the back of her neck. But she prided herself on being as brave as a boy and was about to tell Elijah her brother's nickname for the witchdoctor, when she saw a man walking down the road towards them. It was Nyirongo. Fear began to gnaw a hole in her stomach. Hamish was wrong after all, and Elijah was right: one of the witchdoctor's familiars had heard her say she didn't believe in his magic, and he'd come to punish her.

She grabbed Elijah's arm and whispered, 'Look!' They held their breath as they watched him come closer. When he was directly under the tree, so close Chrissie's feet nearly grazed the top of his head, Elijah let out a whimper. Nyirongo stopped and looked up through the leaves. He put down his bag without taking his eyes off the boy and began to mutter in Chichewa and wave his hands about, as if he were casting a spell. Chrissie noticed a wet patch spread across the front of her friend's shorts, and a bud of anger opened inside her chest. All her life, she would find it easier to stand up and fight for others than for herself. Now she shook her fist at the witchdoctor and shouted: 'You leave Elijah alone, or I'll tell my dad.'

Nyirongo turned to stare at Chrissie. He bared his teeth in a grin, took hold of the lowest branch and swung his legs up and started to crawl slowly towards them. Chrissie screamed and Elijah dropped his wire car in the dust under the tree and tried to scramble higher, sobbing openly. Nyirongo lunged for the boy and grabbed the back of his shirt. Elijah started to keen like a terrified animal. The sound enraged Chrissie further and she kicked at Nyirongo's face as hard as she could.

The man whipped his head round and grinned at her. She'd split his lip and his teeth were bloody, as if he'd been eating flesh. It was Chrissie's turn to whimper in fear.

'What is this?' Nyirongo hissed in English. 'A tasty little white rat! This is just what I need for my cooking pot.' He licked his split lip and began to inch along the branch towards Chrissie, long yellow fingernails reaching for her leg. She tried to move away from him but her back hit the tree trunk: there was nowhere left to go. Chrissie watched, frozen, as Nyirongo got nearer and nearer until his hand closed around her ankle. She started crying and shook her leg but his grip tightened. When she tried to scream no sound came out. Chrissie turned her head away and squeezed her eyes shut so she wouldn't have to look at him as he pulled her slowly towards him. She thought she could hear flies buzzing close to her ears; the buzzing grew louder until it became the roar of an engine. Nyirongo let go of her ankle and used some of the Chichewa swear words Elijah had been teaching Chrissie. She opened her eyes and saw a truck rumbling along the road in a cloud of dust. Brakes squealed and a man in an African print shirt and black trousers got out and waved off the driver. He walked over to the tree, put his hands on his hips and stared up at them.

'What the devil is going on here? Get down from there, man, and leave those children alone.'

Nyirongo dropped to the ground, all sheepish smiles and rounded shoulders. He wrung his hands and bobbed his head. 'Hello, Father, we were just playing a game.'

Chrissie wiped her eyes with the heel of her hand and was glad to see the friendly, lined face that belonged to Father O'Brian looking up at her. He said Mass at the tiny Chalimbana church the Dochertys attended every Sunday and had become close friends with her parents over the years. He must have only been in his early fifties then but looked older, worn out by repeated bouts of malaria and the harsh life of a missionary priest. He had a white shock of thick, wavy hair – what her granny called Irish hair – and his Celtic skin was lined from exposure to the African sun. Tom O'Brian adored all the Docherty children and paid particular attention to Chrissie. She in turn doted on him and now she waved at him from her perch among the mango leaves.

The priest shaded his eyes and called up to her. 'Is that you, Chrissie? And young Elijah too? Are you all right?'

'Yeah, we're okay,' she said. But it came out wobbly and high-pitched, giving away her earlier tears.

Father O'Brian turned on Nyirongo, his hands on his hips, and let out a torrent of Chichewa. Chrissie didn't understand more than a couple of words but she could tell he was angry. The witchdoctor hung his head and muttered back.

'What are they saying?' Chrissie whispered to Elijah.

He covered his mouth to hide his laughter. 'He is telling Nyirongo to get back to work and stop his nonsense,' he said, his eyes bright. 'He is saying, leave the children alone or he will kick his bottom all over the village so he cannot sit down for many days.'

Chrissie snorted behind her hand, and the two children nudged each other in the ribs and giggled as they peered down to watch Nyirongo walk away, his feet kicking up little clouds of red dust. Reckless with relief, Chrissie stood up on the branch and called out a singsong after him: *see you later, alligator*. Nyirongo turned and shot her a look so malevolent that she sank down on her haunches and hid her face behind a clump of green mangoes.

Below them, Father O'Brian picked up the wire car that Elijah had dropped and whistled in appreciation. 'This is very good, Elijah. Is it Mr Docherty's Bentley?'

'Yes, Father.' The children climbed and slid their way down the tree and Elijah was soon showing him how he'd copied the vintage car's sweeping curves. Father O'Brian squatted down next to him and listened intently, his long face serious under his white hair.

'And all made out of chicken wire, you say?' He shook his head. 'You boys are so clever.' He pretended to think, tapping his finger on his lips. 'But do you know? The strangest thing has happened: all my chicken wire has disappeared and my chickens are wandering about the mission garden, eating the seeds I planted. Now, isn't that a great mystery? I wonder where it could have gone?' Elijah giggled. The priest stood up and rubbed the boy's head. 'Go on with you, you wee rascal, your mother will be looking for you.' He turned to Chrissie, who had been hanging back, shyly tracing circles in the dust with her feet. 'And here's my favourite little maid. I'm on my way to see your parents. Will you walk with me?'

Chrissie gave the priest her broadest smile and waved goodbye to Elijah. She skipped all the way along the road and up the drive to the bungalow, hand in hand with Father O'Brian, all thoughts of curses, witchdoctors and black mambas banished under his warm benevolence as she chattered to him. When they reached the bungalow, her mother came out with Mrs Fielding. Chrissie had forgotten all about her new neighbour but now she gazed with admiration at her creamy skin and pale hair, the slimness of her waist in her buttercup yellow dress. Chrissie changed her mind; she didn't look like a Sindy but more like one of the beautiful creatures pictured in her mother's magazine, showing off the latest fashions from back home. Chrissie sped up to get a closer look, dragging the priest behind her.

The priest was laughing when they reached the veranda steps. 'She's talked my ears off, Grace, and now she's running my legs off.' Chrissie's mother smiled at the priest. She always looked younger and happier around Father O'Brian. It never occurred to Chrissie until years later what it must be like for her mother stuck out in the bush, unable to drive, looking after four children miles away from doctors and shops. Evelyn's arrival must have seemed at first like a boon to her mother: a fresh face from home to talk with and share the long, hot, empty hours. Or perhaps it was the arrival of Father O'Brian that made Grace Docherty smile so. He was one of the few people who could wipe away the frown lines carved between her eyes. Either way, Chrissie remembered that afternoon as if it were illuminated: the adults shining with goodwill, the elation from seeing the hated Nyirongo sent packing, the warmth of the priest's hand around hers.

Her mother held out her arms to Chrissie, her earlier wrath forgotten and kissed the top of her head. 'Poor Father O'Brian, let him have some peace. Go on inside and help set the tea tray.'

'Sure, I'm only teasing, I don't mind a bit that Chrissie is a wee chatterbox,' Father O'Brian said. 'Don't I always have time for my favourite little maid?' He lifted Chrissie up and swung her through the air. She squealed and he let her down. Chrissie gave his waist a quick hug and ran into the house to find Hamish and tell him about her encounter with Nyirongo. Now he would have to believe her that the witchdoctor had magic powers. And that only Father O'Brian's magic was stronger.

71

TIFFIN

Evelyn, Grace and the priest watched Chrissie disappear into the house.

Father O'Brian laughed under his breath. 'Look at her go. I don't know where the child gets her energy in this heat. Does she ever stop moving, Grace?'

'Only when she sleeps, like all my children.' She put her arm through his and drew him towards Evelyn. 'Tom, this is Evelyn Fielding.'

He took Evelyn's hand in both of his. 'Ah, Robert's young bride. You're the talk of the district.'

Evelyn wasn't sure how to respond. She was slightly irked that everyone she met seemed to know who she was already. Another reminder of the village mentality she thought she'd left behind. She swallowed her irritation and studied this man who didn't look like any priest she'd ever met before, with his African print shirt and black trousers.

Evelyn was horrified to hear herself saying: 'Where's your dog collar?' She clapped her hand over her mouth. 'I'm terribly sorry.'

His weathered face broke into a smile. 'Did you think I'd be in a cassock with rosary beads hanging off my belt? I'll leave that to my Jesuit brothers. I'm what you call a White Father. We dress like the people we live among, so it's clothes from the local tailor for me.' He looked down at the colourful shirt and frowned. 'It could be worse – the first White Fathers got their name from wearing Arab robes in North Africa.' He took out a handkerchief and wiped his forehead. 'Mind you, at least that get-up would be cooler. I'd wear shorts and jungle boots if I could, but the people might mistake me for a colonial, and we can't have that.'

Evelyn frowned. 'My husband wears shorts. And he works for the Colonial Office.'

Father O'Brian spread his hands. 'Ah, but Robert is an exception to that poisonous breed, a prince among men. He is what Jim Docherty would call a pukka sahib – one of the old school. Robert was born here and loves this place and its people almost as much as I do. And he stayed on after the other government men packed up and left. It's a pity some others didn't leave, the ones who only come here to exploit the copper – jumped-up carpenters and joiners living like kings off the sweat of our black brothers as they toil in the mines.'

Grace shook her head at the priest. 'Now, Tom, Evelyn's only just arrived and doesn't want to hear one of your political rants.' She ushered them into the bungalow. 'Come away in out of the heat. I've made shortbread, and there's fruit scones and a Dundee cake.'

Tom O'Brian sighed happily. 'Grace Docherty, you bake cakes my mammy back in Waterford would have been proud to put her name to.' Grace walked ahead of them and he whispered to Evelyn: 'She's a darling woman, and to cap it all, her husband likes a drop of the hard stuff – a bit like myself.' He called to Grace. 'Jim wouldn't happen to be at home now, would he? I've a few things to go over with him.'

Grace laughed and showed them into the sitting room, which had the same functional G-plan furniture as Evelyn's new home. The only difference was that it was cluttered with brass and ivory Indian gods rather than ebony and mahogany African animals and masks.

'Don't worry, Tom,' Grace said. 'Jim's home and the whisky tray is all set up. Mind you don't drink too much. We don't want you setting a bad example to your flock.'

The priest rubbed his hands together and eyed the drinks. 'My flock could drink me under the table any day. I'll have to put in a bit of practice so I can last the pace next time I'm sitting around the calabash with the elders, trying to find out what's going on in the village. Those crafty buggers always manage to get me too drunk on *chibuko* to remember their secrets.'

Grace handed Evelyn a plate of scones covered with a domed net to keep off the flying ants that seemed to be everywhere, their silvery wings fluttering desperately as they danced their last waltz. An embroidered cloth trimmed with African beads protected the sugar bowl from the invaders.

'*Chibuko* is the home brew the Africans make from millet,' Grace explained to Evelyn. 'It looks and tastes like vomit. I don't know how Tom can drink the stuff.'

He looked mournfully at the cup of tea he'd been handed. 'Sure, it's not too bad after you've had a few. Anyway, it's a sacrifice I'm willing to make for my vocation.'

Grace raised her eyebrows at Evelyn. 'You're a noble man, Tom. Your place in heaven is assured.'

Evelyn laughed. She was warming to Grace, who had seemed so capable and stern when she'd first met her, but clearly had a wasp-ish sense of humour. She didn't seem to be in the slightest awe of Father O'Brian and called him by his first name as if he were an ordinary man. Back home, Evelyn's mother treated the vicar with the timidity and reverence his title demanded. She remembered how sharply her mother had spoken to her father for having alco-hol on his breath when Reverend Soames graced their home. The Docherty family, it would appear, had an altogether more relaxed attitude to the clergy and Evelyn rather liked it. She liked the priest too. He teased Grace, but with a kindness and affection that Evelyn suspected brought out her neighbour's softer side.

A compact, bearded man barrelled into the room followed by Chrissie, who walked slowly, like a flower girl behind a bride, as she concentrated on not dropping a large fruitcake.

'Hello, Tom,' he said. 'What are you doing drinking tea? I've managed to get hold of a bottle of Glenfiddich.'

The priest put his hands together as if in prayer. 'God Bless you, my son.'

Evelyn stood up to be introduced but Jim Docherty only nodded tersely at her before bustling off to sort out the drinks. She sat down again, feeling discomfited. Evelyn was used to men who wielded charm like a stealth weapon. She didn't know what to make of this Scotsman whose brusque manner verged on rudeness.

Evelyn grew quiet during the afternoon tea as she listened distractedly to Grace, who talked endlessly about the shortages at the Chalimbana store, as if this tiny settlement were the only known universe. She didn't seem at all interested in Evelyn's attempts to entertain her with tales of London life and the famous artists she knew. As darkness enveloped the small bungalow and the gas lamps were turned on – they were in the middle of yet another blackout – Evelyn settled back against the sofa and tuned out of the conversation. The window darkened and she imagined the wild bush stretching for miles on every side of the bungalow with their little group corralled inside, the house beaming out its comforting yellow light into the night, a tiny oasis of Britishness in the vastness of the African night. Grace was right, she realised: it was absurd to talk of art galleries and Piccadilly restaurants. England was another world, one they'd all left behind. Their old lives didn't matter here; they had all been reborn under the African sun.

Evelyn sipped her tea and smiled at Grace. She was a generous-hearted woman, who had clearly decided to take Evelyn under her wing. They fell into a comfortable silence and, as if in accord, turned to hear what the men were saying. Evelyn gathered that Jim Docherty was in charge of the teacher training college in Chalimbana. He spoke with such fervour that she could tell he was one of those men who was driven by their work. She learned that the British Council had posted him to Zambia to oversee a modern language laboratory at Chalimbana College to improve the teachers' English. The men's voices had grown louder as they worked their way down the whisky bottle.

The priest held his glass out as Jim stood up to top him up. 'I caught that devil Nyirongo today trying to scare the living daylights out of Chrissie and Elijah.'

'It'll take a stronger character than that to scare my Chrissie,' Jim said, smiling down at his daughter who was drawing on the floor in front of the priest. The girl was quiet but Evelyn sensed she was listening to the men talk just as avidly as she was.

Jim sat down again heavily and rubbed his eyes under his glasses. 'That bugger Nyirongo is a bloody nuisance, though. I've just lost another batch of graduates from Lusaka thanks to his mumbo-jumbo. He told them they didn't have the right tribal scars on their faces to protect them from witches and, of course, they believed him. They left because they were convinced there was a ghost in the compound, saying they could hear it moving about outside in the dark. I offered to spend the night with them but they said it wouldn't come if I were there. Apparently, witchcraft doesn't work on white people.'

Father O'Brian shook his head. 'Ghosts! It'll just be the cattle roaming about.'

'More than likely, but they insisted on leaving all the same. I had to put them on the back of a lorry in the middle of the night.'

Evelyn leaned forward to join the conversation. 'Did you say witches? Surely there are no such things in the modern world?'

Jim laughed wryly. 'Aye, but you're not in the modern world now, Mrs Fielding. Welcome to Africa.'

'Evelyn, please, you make me sound like an old married woman.' She dimpled at him but it had no effect.

The priest, on the other hand, seemed to relish the chance to be gallant. 'Sure, you're a young slip of a thing!'

Jim ignored them both and thoughtfully polished his glasses. 'I've made a study of the traditional belief system of the tribes around here. It's fascinating – the ancestor worship, the witch hunts, the way they force a person they believe to be possessed to dance themselves to death. But it's one of the biggest impediments to progress.' He sighed. 'I'm afraid it makes no difference whether we believe in magic or not: it's as real for the people who live here as electricity is for us.'

'Jim's right,' Tom O'Brian said. 'They nearly all believe in magic, even the ones who attend Mass every Sunday and call their children after all twelve of the apostles. The traditional religion was here thousands of years before we arrived and it's not going to go away because we think it's a lot of nonsense.'

Evelyn laughed to cover her discomfort: she didn't like the idea of witches and witchdoctors, spells and curses. You could see how people would believe in these things out here, where the bush seemed to be crouched outside the settlement, waiting for the yellow porch lights to go out.

The priest brushed shortbread crumbs from his shirt. 'This fella Nyirongo, I'd like to wring his neck with one of his magic spells.' He snorted. 'It's nothing but a scam to rob people who are so poor they only just manage to scrabble a living from the earth. Old Nyirongo charges through the nose to protect the villagers from imaginary curses. If something bad happens to them – a crop fails or one of their family becomes ill – it must be the result of an evil spell cast by a witch. Or if your neighbour has a spot of good luck and you're jealous, why then, he must be a witch! The man's a parasite, feeding off the worst of human nature.'

Evelyn shivered despite the heat. She'd heard drums beating last night when they'd arrived and they seemed to fill the air with soft menace. Perhaps it was this sense of danger that sharpened the colours in Africa and made her feel more alive.

The priest was shaking his head and still talking about the scourge of witchcraft. 'It's just as bad up in the hills, even though we work so hard at spreading the Word of God.' They all looked out of the window and stared at the hills, black now against the navy sky. 'I suppose I should be getting back.' Father O'Brian sighed but made no sign of moving from his armchair. He patted Chrissie's head, which was tinged with copper in the light of the gas lamps, and Evelyn wondered about the loneliness of a priest's life, deprived of a wife and family.

'Is that where you live, Tom, in the Chalimbana Hills?' she said, trying out his Christian name.

'Yes, I run a mission up there. It's not too bad,' he said, as if he'd read her thoughts. 'I have some lay helpers and a couple of hard-working nuns who won't touch whisky. But they're good souls, for all that, bless them. They help me run the clinic and teach the hill village children their ABC, if we can catch them long enough, that is.' The lamplight softened his craggy features. 'You should come up and see us once you've settled in a bit. We could do with an extra pair of hands at the clinic.'

Grace stood up and briskly collected the cups and glasses. 'Don't be daft, Tom; Evelyn doesn't want to go up to the hills. I don't know how anyone can live up there,' she said with a shudder. 'It's even more remote and primitive than Chalimbana, and that's saying something. Aren't you afraid you'll get hacked to pieces in your bed one night?'

'The angels protect lunatics and drunks,' the priest said with a chuckle, 'and I suppose I'm both. Besides, the Africans like us White Fathers. We help them plant gardens so they have food all year round. I learned quickly when I came out here in the 1950s that you can't preach to people who are starving, you have to help them in more practical ways first.'

Jim Docherty stretched his legs. 'You'll need more than divine protection living in the hills. Jacobs would tell you to get a gun.'

Evelyn looked at Grace for an explanation.

'Piet Jacobs has the biggest farm around here,' she said. 'He's your best bet for fresh meat and fruit and vegetables.'

The priest frowned. 'I hear Jacobs can be hard on his farm boys, a typical Afrikaner.'

'He's a farmer,' Jim said. 'A good man but a pragmatist.' He grinned through his beard. 'Just like you, Tom.'

Father O'Brian huffed and made a show of looking at his watch. 'I really should be going. Now, before I go, and speaking of Jacobs, do you think you could ask him if could spare us another ox, Jim?'

'What happened to the one you spent months training to take the plough?'

'There was a wedding feast.'

'Don't tell me it ended up in the pot?' Jim started laughing and fetched the whisky bottle. 'Here, you'd better have one for the road.'

Father O'Brian sighed happily and held out his glass again. 'It's no wonder I drink.'

Back in her bungalow, Evelyn stepped out of the bath and padded across the floor, leaving a trail of wet footprints on the polished concrete. She stood naked in front of the mirror and enjoyed the sensation of her skin drying in the warm air. The cotton dressing gown was cool as she slid her arms into it. She was still tying it when she came out of the bathroom and saw Sixpence hand Robert a pile of ironed shirts. The servant kept his head bent, but his eyes slid towards Evelyn and she pulled her dressing gown closed at the neck.

She waited until she was alone with her husband before she spoke. 'I can't get used to having someone in the house all the time. It doesn't feel right to have a servant.'

Robert threw the shirts onto the bed where they landed in a heap. 'Your mother had help with that big house in Surrey, didn't she?'

Evelyn picked up the shirts and began to refold them. 'We had a daily, of course, but Mrs Jenkins was like one of the family.'

'Well, Sixpence has been with me for years. You'll get used to him. Besides, I can hardly turf him out – he's too old to work on Jacobs's farm or in the mines up north. He'd have to move to the city, away from his family, and no good comes from that.' Robert began to undress. 'A house job is considered a good job.' Robert slid under the sheets and watched her cross to the dressing table. 'The Masters, the couple who live up the road, tried to do without a servant when they first came here from Malawi and it caused a lot of bad feeling in the village. I had a hell of a job keeping the peace. In the end, they saw sense.'

Evelyn let the subject of Sixpence drop. She didn't want a quarrel, and she didn't want to admit that it wasn't having a servant that bothered her: there was something about the way Sixpence watched her that made her uneasy. She laid down her silver hairbrush and picked up a split amethyst she'd bought at the street market in Lusaka. The light from the lamps shone through the purple. Evelyn had made the bedroom her own with her necklaces draped over the mirror and her make-up and perfume scattered about in pretty boxes and bottles. She loved the way the mosquito netting over the big mahogany bed made it into a secret place, where she could have Robert all to herself. It was here he relaxed enough to take off the stiff mask of authority he wore for his job, and where he treated her with the tenderness that had first drawn her to him.

She climbed into bed beside him. 'I met the neighbours today.'

'The Dochertys? He's a decent sort, even if he is a raving Scot Nat. Does a good job at the college.'

'I found him a bit gruff, but Grace is kind. They've invited us to a party.'

'Oh God! I can imagine nothing worse. I hope you said no.'

Evelyn put her hand on his chest. 'Please, Robert, I'd like to go. I don't know anyone here. It's lonely all day while you're out at work. I feel at a bit of a loose end hanging around this house with no-one to talk to.'

He pulled her closer. 'All right,' he murmured into her hair. 'We'll go if you really want to. They'll all be dying to get a look at Robert Fielding's child bride: they'll have been talking of nothing else for weeks.'

She laughed kissed him on the mouth. 'Thank you, darling.'

Robert sighed. 'At least Jim Docherty will have some decent whisky. You can always rely on a Scot to have a full drinks cabinet.'

Evelyn was about to turn off the lamp when she realised she must have dropped her silk scarf on the way back from the Dochertys. It had been a present from her mother.

'I'll be back in a minute.'

Evelyn pulled on her robe and went out to the veranda to look for her scarf. What she saw made her stop in her tracks. Sixpence was holding the scrap of silk to his nose, his eyes closed as he inhaled her scent. She stepped back into the shadows and watched him stuff the scarf into his pocket and begin clearing away the glasses. A flush of blood warmed Evelyn's neck. She waited in the shadows for her heart to quieten and crept back to the bedroom door before Sixpence could see her.

MELTING POT

The party was going strong and Blue Mink's 'Melting Pot' was playing on the music centre when Evelyn and Robert arrived at the Dochertys'. A couple of young VSOs in mini-dresses were swaying their hips, drinks held high, while they sang along to the chorus. One of the girls, who had long, straight hair like Joan Baez, bent over to choose a cigarette from a silver box on the coffee table and her knickers flashed under the short hemline. Evelyn raised her eyebrows at Robert but he was busy shaking their host by the hand.

'You'll take a dram, Robert?' Jim Docherty shouted through the noise. 'I'm afraid it's only a blend. I had a twelve-year-old malt that came in the diplomatic bag, but Tom O'Brian had the last drop.' He bared his teeth at Evelyn and thrust a drink into her hand. 'You'll find Grace over there with the rest of the wives,' Jim told her with a dismissive nod before he gripped Robert's elbow and turned his back on her.

Evelyn peered through the cigarette smoke. Grace sat on the sofa with a large woman in a print frock and a couple of stringy women with skin like cured tobacco, one in an electric blue trouser suit and the other in a psychedelic maxi dress in acid yellow and bright pink – colours that shouldn't be in the same room never mind the same garment. Evelyn was glad she'd chosen a simple but expensively cut black cocktail dress that came demurely to her knees but artfully showed off her calves, narrow shoulders and arms she knew were as slim and graceful as a ballerina's. The pearls Robert had given her gleamed, opaque and heavy against her pale skin and she resisted the temptation to play with them to calm her nerves. The line of seated women appraised her like a panel of judges and she turned away from them in panic to talk to Robert. But he was following Jim into the crowd and only mouthed 'good luck' over his shoulder in response to her desperate look. Evelyn glared at his back and pretended not to see Grace waving her over. She hated being lumped in with 'the wives'; it reminded her too much of her parents' bridge parties back home. Evelyn looked around the room in despair. She could have been back in Surrey: all that was lacking was a group of men in golf jumpers. Her heart sank: she had travelled half way across the world only to end up in the sort of suburban backwater from which she'd fled to London. Her cheeks burned in the heat of the press of bodies and she took a sip from her glass. Fruit bumped against her teeth and she tasted mint and cucumber.

She looked at her drink incredulously. 'Pimm's No 1 Cup. In Africa!'

'I know, ridiculous, isn't it? It's Jim's idea of a woman's drink,' said a voice behind her ear. Evelyn hadn't realised she'd spoken aloud and started. A man with sandy hair and freckles held out his hand. He was only a little taller than her with fleshy features that just stopped him being handsome. But his eyes were lively and his expression warm and open. He held out his hand. 'Gerry Mann, headmaster of the secondary school. You must be Evelyn Fielding, the mystery woman we've all been talking about and *dying* to meet.'

Evelyn rested her hand lightly in his. In faded jeans with his hair curled around the collar of his open-necked cheesecloth shirt, he stood out among the other men in safari suits and their wives in luridly patterned party frocks. He was eying her with interest and a buzz of excitement coursed through her. A little flirtation wouldn't do any harm, and it would pay Robert back for abandoning her in a room full of strangers. She pulled at a curl of hair that had escaped her chignon to frame her face, and put the end of it in her mouth.

'Everyone I meet seems to know who I am before I open my mouth,' she said, the corners of her lips tugging upwards to hint at the mischief in her eyes. 'I'm hardly a woman of mystery.'

Gerry leaned in conspiratorially. 'Chalimbana is a small place.

82

If you have any secrets you might as well confess them now and I'll send out a memo. It'll save the gossips a lot of time.' He nodded over to the wives, who were openly staring at them now. When he raised his drink to them, the row of women slid their eyes away and went into a huddle. Evelyn didn't want to upset Grace and gave an embarrassed wave to signal she'd come over in a minute. But she had no intention of leaving Gerry's side, not yet anyway. He was so easy to talk to and this was the sort of silly, arch conversation she'd enjoyed with her Soho friends. It was so easy and pleasurable, like slipping into a bubble bath. Gerry's eyes never left her face and Evelyn gave him one of her warmest smiles. She ignored the warning heat that crept up her neck. After all, why shouldn't she enjoy the company of this charming man? It was delicious to gossip with an ally and for the first time since she'd come to Africa she didn't feel like an outsider. Evelyn took another sip of her drink and made a face. Gerry laughed.

'I can see you're going to liven up our little suburban outpost.' He waved at the smoky room. 'Shall I give you a guided tour of the residents of your new home?'

'If you like, although I demand to know all their secrets, which is only fair, after all, if they are soon to know mine,' she said.

Gerry clinked his glass with hers. 'Done.'

She pointed at a burly man in a bush shirt and shorts talking to her husband and Jim Docherty. The blonde giant laughed loudly at something Docherty said and white teeth flashed in his tanned face.

'Who's that chap, the one built like a prop forward?' Evelyn said. 'He looks as if he's been fed on steak and milk all his life. Is he American?'

Gerry's tone was sour. 'Piet Jacobs is a Boer.'

Evelyn frowned over the background chatter. 'A bore?'

He raised his voice. 'No, a Boer, an Afrikaner, although he's a bit of a bore too.' Gerry grimaced. 'Don't bother with him – Jacobs is a Neanderthal, a complete racist. Exploits the men who work on his farm for a pittance. You should hear the way he talks about them, as if they were slaves and he the plantation owner.' He pointed with his drink at a white haired man in a cream suit with a much younger woman hanging onto his arm. 'Now he's interesting – John Masters, a writer who collects African stories. The woman clutching at his arm is his second wife. They had a bad time in Malawi – a botched burglary that ended with her being attacked. They never talk about it but she hardly leaves the house.'

'That's awful!' Evelyn said. 'Why don't they go back to England?'

'Some of these old Africa hands are stuck here; they've been here so long they don't have anything or anyone to go back to, and they get used to the life.' Evelyn noticed that the woman kept darting her head like a bird on the lookout for a predator.

'Poor thing. Do you think she's homesick?'

Gerry studied her and dropped his cynical tone. 'Why, do you miss home?' Evelyn's eyes smarted as sudden tears threatened and she looked into her drink. When she spoke, Gerry had to lean his head towards hers to hear her.

'Not exactly, it's just so different here, from what I'd imagined. I thought it would be a big adventure and that I'd feel freer, somehow, living in the bush. But I don't feel free, I feel trapped. It sounds silly, but I don't quite know what to do with myself here.' She looked into his eyes and saw the concern there. She didn't want to flirt any more but longed more than anything to confide in another person. 'Do you think I'm pathetic?'

'Don't be daft,' he said. His flat vowels revealed his northern roots and for some reason made her trust him. 'Look,' he said, all business. 'Can you drive?'

Startled, Evelyn said: 'No, I've never learned. Why?'

He shook his head. 'No wonder you feel trapped. There's a whole country out there waiting for you. But to discover the real Africa, you need to be able to drive otherwise you'll be stuck in the house and end up like that lot.' He nodded towards the wives.

She thought he was being unfair but let it go. 'That's all very well, but how am I supposed to learn out here? Robert's away all day and far too busy to teach me.'

Gerry grinned at her and they were conspirators again. 'I'd be glad to. No, really, it's no trouble. And I know you'll pick it up in no time, a clever woman like you. What do you say?'

She knew Robert wouldn't like it, but Evelyn ignored the thought and clinked glasses with her new friend. 'I say yes, please.'

'That's my girl.' He took the empty tumbler out of her hand. 'Now, how about I fetch you a proper drink?'

As Evelyn watched him walk over to a table loaded with bottles she felt so lit up with elation that she was sure Robert would notice. She looked around the room for him but couldn't see him. She searched for Gerry and when the crowd parted she saw him at the drinks table. There was a movement and she saw Chrissie's face peek out from underneath the tablecloth. The girl held her finger to her lips and Evelyn smiled: Chrissie Docherty seemed to have a talent for getting into mischief. Evelyn raised her arm in a wave but found herself gripped from behind and spun round to find Robert glaring at her. She'd never seen him so furious and shrunk away from him.

He spoke through clenched teeth. 'We're going home. Now.'

She is Footing the Ball

Chrissie sat with Hamish under the drinks table and spied on the party. It was quiet under there and they could escape the noise and smoke while evading adult detection. They had a bowl of groundnuts between them. She'd helped her mum shell them and roast them earlier, a chore that had seemed to last forever but which made the nuts taste even better. Chrissie licked the salt and flecks of papery red skins from her fingers and scanned the guests. She had been watching Mrs Fielding talking to Gerry Mann. He'd had one of his arms around her back and was smiling too much, looking like her cat when he'd caught a bird. Gerry Mann was always jolly and laughing, but he made Chrissie uncomfortable. His jokes were draped in a hidden skein of meaning; she hated the way he smirked at the other grown-ups over her head. And he talked to her in a familiar, knowing way, as if she were another adult. Chrissie tried to avoid him where possible. She much preferred being ignored, or the kind of grave affection that Mr Jacobs and Father O'Brian showed her.

Gerry Mann was coming towards the table where she was hiding and she shifted further back under the table out of sight. But after a while, she couldn't resist peeking out again. He'd stopped to talk to someone and was laughing loudly, his face turning a deep pink. Elijah had told her that his pupils at the secondary school called him *Monkey's Bottom* in Chichewa because he went red when he shouted at them.

When Chrissie sneaked another look at Mrs Fielding, she had obviously spotted her and waved. Chrissie tried to signal to her not to give away her hiding place when Mr Fielding appeared at his wife's side. The villagers had a nickname for him, too: they called him *Maganga*, The Rock, because he worked for the British Government that had built all the stone buildings. The name suited him at the moment: his face looked like it was carved from stone. He could be stern and aloof, but you knew where you were with Mr Fielding. He would never laugh at you and he was someone you could go to if there was trouble. Her father had told all the children that if the balloon went up, they were to fetch Mr Fielding. Chrissie had seen *Around the World in Eighty Days* at the open-air cinema and couldn't wait to see a hot-air balloon come flying over Chalimbana. She looked for her father, who the villagers called *Mandala*, Spectacles, after his glasses had saved him from a spitting cobra one day. Chrissie shivered as she remembered the jet of venom that had come shooting out of the snake's reared head. Samson had run out of the house and bashed in its head in with a *panga*, but when Hamish had dared Chrissie to pick up the tail, its body had twitched and she'd screamed and dropped it. Hamish had nearly wet his pants laughing and the memory made her turn and glare at him. He had his mouth full of peanuts and opened it to show her the mess inside. Chrissie rolled her eyes at him and went back to watching Mr and Mrs Fielding. They looked as if they were having one of those whispered adult fights no one was supposed to notice. She wondered if The Rock had seen Mrs Fielding laughing behind her hand with Monkey's Bottom, the way the older village girls did when the boys teased them. Chrissie was watching Mr Fielding almost drag his wife towards the door when Hamish dug his elbow into her ribs.

'Hey, Chris!'

She thumped him back. 'Ow! What is it?'

'Watch out, incoming at twelve o'clock.'

Their mother's legs arrived in front of them, followed by her head as she bent down and peered under the tablecloth. She looked cross, even upside down.

'Chrissie! What are you doing down there? You're supposed to be helping. Come out and pass some plates of food around.'

'Do I have to?'

'Yes you do, young lady. I won't ask you twice.' She clapped her hands. '*Jaldi jaldi!*' Chrissie crawled out. When their mother rapped out Hindustani commands, the Docherty children knew she meant business. Chrissie shifted from one foot to the other while her mum beat the dust off her dress and fussed with her hair. 'Look at the state of you. What happened to all your lovely curls? I don't know why I waste my time putting your hair into rags.'

Chrissie scowled at her feet in their horrible shiny leather shoes and white socks and flexed her toes. She hated wearing shoes. She stuffed her hair behind her ears and hoped her mother wouldn't find out that she'd put her head under the garden tap that morning to get rid of the hated curls. Her mother pushed a platter of crackers covered in tinned paté and slices of olive at Chrissie.

'What about Hamish? Why doesn't he have to help?'

'He's a boy. Now, go on with you.'

Once their mother was out of earshot, Chrissie bent down and hissed at Hamish: 'It's not fair!' Her brother scrambled out from under the table and swept a handful of crackers off the plate, stuffing them into his mouth.

'I'm off to play football with Storah,' he grinned, and sauntered past her, hands in his pockets. 'Have fun at the party, squirt.' Chrissie lunged for him, but he was already dodging through the crowd of grown-ups – a trick he said he'd learned playing rugby. Angus, their older brother, had taught Hamish about rugby in the Christmas holidays when he'd come back from Scotland. When Chrissie had asked him what boarding school was like, Angus had scowled at her and gone off to find Storah, his friend from the village. Now Hamish played with Storah while Angus was away. Hamish went to a boys' school in Lusaka, but he'd have to go away next year too. Chrissie didn't question why the boys were sent to boarding school and why she went to the local school; it was just the way things were.

She pushed through the crowd and offered the plate to Mr Jacobs, who was now talking to her father. He crammed a cracker into his mouth and patted her head absentmindedly.

Mr Jacobs waved the bottle of Castle beer in his big paw at Chrissie's father. '*Ja*, it was another *panga* murder, you know with a machete. A bad business – they chopped him up into little pieces and the police had to use a dustpan and brush to sweep what was left of him into a basket.' Chrissie stood rooted to the spot, staring up at Mr Jacobs, who took another cracker from her plate and ate it calmly, as if he were talking about the new crop of strawberries on his farm rather than murder. 'This fellow was from a different tribe – Ngoni, I think – and he was getting a bit too friendly with the village women, if you know what I mean.'

Chrissies tried to imagine someone chopped up with a *panga*. She looked up at Mr Jacobs hoping he'd say more, but he only ruffled her hair again.

Her dad shook his head. 'Christ, what a country!'

'I keep telling you, Jim, keep a shotgun under your bed. That nightstick of yours is no use.' Mr Jacobs gulped from the upturned beer bottle and sighed and wiped his mouth. 'I tell you, the country has gone to the dogs since independence. Some of my farm boys have been getting cheeky, the younger ones, you know? The older ones know what side their bread is buttered.' He sighed again. 'You've got to remember we're outnumbered and now they're in charge. These people are like children, they need a firm hand or they'll run riot. Thank God Fielding is back: they listen to him. My word is law on the farm, but he's got the ears of the village headman. There may be a new regime in Lusaka, but out here old habits die hard and he's still the British *boma*.'

Chrissie's father crossed his arms and looked up at the big farmer. 'I don't agree with you Piet. People here need education and training, and that's what we're giving them at the college. Do you realise less than one per cent of the population has completed primary school? And that there are only about a hundred African university graduates in the whole country?'

Mr Jacobs snorted. 'Again with this, Jim! When will you learn that what they really need are jobs to put *nshima* on the table – and it's men like me who give them work.'

Their voices grew more heated and Chrissie realised there would be no more talk of the *panga* murder. She took the plate of snacks over to her mother, who sat on the sofa next to Mrs Jacobs. With her ample chest and cotton print frock, the farmer's wife looked frumpy next to Chrissie's mum, in her tailored linen dress embroidered with gold lilies, her white fingers covered in ruby and sapphire Indian rings in rose gold.

Mrs Jacobs pulled Chrissie onto her lap and kissed her. 'Look at you *popje*, you get bigger every time I see you. Grace, you're so lucky to have two girls. God only gave me boys, all grown up now and living in Rhodesia, their poor mamma forgotten.'

Chrissie leaned against Mrs Jacobs' warmth and listened to the women talking.

'Lotte, did you see Robert Fielding arguing with his wife?' her mother said to Mrs Jacobs. 'He should never have married that young girl. She told me they've only known each other for a few months.'

Mrs Jacobs shifted in her seat to get more comfortable. 'Isn't he a bit old for that sort of thing? Piet and I love Robert, but he's always been such a loner, and moody too. I can't imagine him as anything other than a bachelor. The Jones girl's mother will be furious. He took Shirley out a few times and the mother was already planning the wedding. Where did he find this one?'

'He met her in London, apparently, in some gallery. She's an artist.'

'An artist! My God! Poor girl! What was Robert thinking? She'll never survive out here.'

Chrissie wondered what was wrong with artists, and why anyone would have trouble surviving in Chalimbana.

'Evelyn's a sweet little thing,' her mother said. 'But she hasn't a clue about life in Africa. Robert had no business bringing her to Zambia, let alone out here to the bush, miles away from Lusaka, the shops and the club and other young people. I remember when we were first posted out here. It was difficult, but I had the children to keep me busy. It's the women without children who really struggle. They've nothing to do – not even the housework.'

Mrs Jacobs nodded. '*Ja*. The men like it here, they have their work, but it can be lonely for the wives. It's different for me, I grew up in the bush and I've got the farm, and that big fool over there to cook for.' She nodded affectionately towards Mr Jacobs. '*Ach*, don't worry about it Grace, this new girl will learn how to cope, give her time. Like you say, once the babies come, she'll just have to get on with the house and the kiddies and whatever and what have you.'

One of the other women leaned forward. 'Well, Gerry Mann seems taken with her. She'd better watch out – people can be terrible gossips in a small place like this.'

The women's voices grew lower and more hurried. With her mother distracted, Chrissie knew it was a perfect time to escape the party, but first she had to get rid of the platter. She wriggled off Mrs Jacobs's lap and picked her way through the throng, her eye on the swing door to the veranda and freedom. The adults she squeezed past ignored her but she knew there would be trouble when she walked into Gerry Mann back at the drinks table.

'Watch out!' He held two glasses up. 'You nearly spilled Mrs Fielding's drink.'

Chrissie was going to tell him that Mrs Fielding had already left with her husband when she spotted Mr Masters and became distracted. He wrote books of African stories filled with magical animals: foolish frog kings and crocodiles who tricked them, and Chrissie was reading them slowly to make them last. She felt Gerry Mann poking her in the back.

'Hey, I'm talking to you.' Chrissie turned round and steeled herself to speak to him. Her voice sounded high and prissy with nerves.

'Hello, Mr Mann. Are you enjoying the party?'

'*Are you enjoying the party?*' he mimicked, sending the blood to her face. 'You expat brats are all the same, making small talk, handing out drinks and canapés. Precocious, I call it. Not an attractive trait in a child.'

Fury bloomed in Chrissie's chest and she fought the urge to kick him in the shins. Instead, she picked up another plate of crackers.

'Excuse me, I have to hand these around.'

'Why, of course, it's been a pleasure talking to you. We must do lunch,' he said in a falsetto and sniggered.

Chrissie walked away, her back rigid, and kept walking until she was out on the veranda. The sky was pink behind the trees at the edge of the garden and Hamish and Storah cast long shadows on the lawn as they played football. It would be dark soon. She put the plate down on the veranda's tiled floor, sniffed and wiped her nose on her arm. Chomsky, her tabby cat, emerged from under the raffia sofa, flapping his ears as if he was trying to get rid of an itch inside them, and began to lick at the paté. Chrissie sat down next to him and took off her tight shoes and white socks. She watched him eat for a while and began to feel better. By the time he had finished and was cleaning his paws, she'd forgotten all about Gerry Mann. Hamish called out to her and she jumped up and ran over the patchy lawn to where he and Storah were kicking a ball made from rags and chicken wire stuffed with newspapers.

'*Bwanji!* Storah,' she called.

'*Ee. Bwanji!* Chrissie.'

Hamish passed her the ball. 'Hey, Chrissie, want to play? She plays nearly as well as a boy, Storah.'

Storah nodded gravely. 'She is good at footing the ball.'

Chrissie sent the ball spinning across the grass and smack into the trunk of the frangipani tree. Hamish threw his arms in the air and ran around the lawn shouting, 'Goooooaaaaal for Scotland!'

'Very good, Chrissie. You should be playing for Zambia,' a deep voice said.

Chrissie turned round to see Henry Cizinga, the new college principal, with his wife. Chrissie thought Mercy Cizinga looked splendid in her traditional costume, her turban and long dress printed with the national colours of Zambia: green for the rich farmlands, black for the people, orange for copper from the mines and red for blood. Mr Cizinga, in contrast, was smart and sombre in a black suit and a white shirt, but a wide smile split his face.

Chrissie's father came out into the yellow light of the veranda where the moths had begun to gather and ushered the Cizingas into the bungalow. It was darker now and the sky was turning purple. Chrissie went back to playing football with Hamish and Storah. They hadn't been playing long when Mr and Mrs Jacobs came out of the house and climbed into their pick-up truck. They slammed the doors shut without stopping to say goodbye. Chrissie caught sight of Mr Jacobs's face in the half-light as they drove past. He looked angry and didn't wave back at her.

She dribbled the ball over to Hamish. 'What's up with Mr Jacobs?'

He shrugged. 'Dunno. Come on, Chris, your turn to be in goal.'

After everyone had left the party, Chrissie and Hamish went to join her parents on the veranda, drawn like the moths by the halo of light and by the low murmur of their parents' voices. Cat had woken up and come out of bed to look for their mother and was now curled up in her lap asleep, thumb in mouth, her cheek as creamy and soft as a frangipani petal. The Jacobs had left a gift of biltong for the children and Chrissie sat across from her parents and gnawed on the salty beef strips. Hamish had stationed himself behind their mother and had a strand of her hair between his teeth. He had the strangest habit of eating her hair.

The ice clinked in their mother's drink and she sighed and shifted Cat's weight, bending to kiss her untamable, white-blonde hair. 'The Jacobs weren't too pleased to see the Cizingas.'

Chrissie's father rubbed his eyes under his glasses – a sure sign he was upset. 'I couldn't not invite the college principal. Piet and Lotte have to realise that times have changed.'

Her mother stared out into the darkness of the garden where fireflies spiralled like sparks from a bonfire. 'I saw a snake today, a green loop hanging off the veranda roof. It swung its head down to look at me and hissed. The strange thing is, its mouth was all black inside.'

'Sounds like a black mamba,' Chrissie's father said. 'You should have called Samson, he would have dealt with it. They're extremely poisonous. They say their bite will kill you in an instant.'

'I thought it was rather pretty, but then I don't mind snakes,' her mother said mildly.

Chrissie shivered. She hated snakes. In the distance she could hear faint drumming.

Her father cocked his head in the direction of the village and stood up. 'I'm going to patrol the perimeter fence. Jacobs told me there's been another *panga* murder. In this heat, before the rains, everyone's on a short fuse.'

Chrissie watched the beam from her father's torch flash around the darkening garden; it bounced high up into the miombo tree and caught a bush baby's eyes, turning them into shiny green pennies. Every night, their mother would let them look for the bush baby but Chrissie had never seen it before.

'Look, Mum there it is!' she cried. Her mother turned her head and caught Hamish unawares still with her hair between his teeth. She put her hands up to her head and winced.

'Hamish Docherty, will you stop eating my hair! Both of you get to bed, it's late. Here, take Catriona with you.' She handed the little girl to Chrissie, who staggered slightly under her warm heaviness.

Hamish pulled open the swing door. 'Come on, Chris. Race you. Last one in bed is a green hairy egg. With purple spots on!'

'No fair, I've got Cat.'

They ran off, Chrissie's skinny legs flailing as they giggled and slid down the corridor, the red-wax concrete floor slippery as an ice rink from Samson's daily polishing.

In bed, Hamish and Chrissie crept in either side of their little sister. She slept with her arms flung back on the pillow, eyelashes casting shadows on her cheeks in the moonlight that was streaming in from the mesh window. Hamish was supposed to sleep in his own room but ever since Angus had left for boarding school he'd been scared of the dark. Chrissie pretended to believe him when he claimed he only came into the girls' room to protect them.

'Hamish.'

'What?' They were whispering, even though Cat slept soundly.

'Do you think the snake will come back? The one Mum saw.'

'The black mamba? Samson says it lives in the crooked tree at the bottom of the garden. He tried to smash its head with a *panga*, but it was too fast. He says we're not to climb that tree anymore. It's the deadliest snake in the whole of Africa. You heard Dad – one bite and you're dead in ten seconds flat. There's no cure.'

Chrissie pulled the covers up to her chin. 'I bet the witchdoctor can cure you. Elijah said he has a cure for everything, even sleepy sickness.'

'Sleeping sickness, you baby. I told you, the witchdoctor is just the silly old messenger, and he doesn't have any magic cures. You shouldn't believe everything Elijah tells you. He's only a little one, like you.'

'Am not little.'

'Are.'

'Am not.' They went on like this for a while. Chrissie was drifting off to sleep when there was a scratching at the window and a hideous face snarled at them, lit up eerily with blood-red light. She sat up in bed and screamed and Hamish jumped out of bed and made for the door. There was a hoot of laughter from outside and they heard her dad crashing away into the darkness.

'I wish he wouldn't do that,' Chrissie said.

Hamish came back to bed and punched her arm. 'Don't be such a girl. The brother and sister snuggled into Cat, who hadn't stirred through their dad's trick. Her breath smelled sweet and her shock of fine, blonde hair stood up like a halo.

'Hamish, did you see Mr and Mrs Fielding fighting? I wonder what it was about,' Chrissie said.

He yawned. 'Dunno, who cares?'

'Do you like her? I think she's nice.'

'She's just another boring grown-up.'

But Chrissie knew from the way the adults had talked about her that there was something different about Evelyn Fielding. The party had left her uneasy: Mr Fielding had looked so furious, and then Mr and Mrs Jacobs had seemed angry too. The air was heavy and seemed to press down on her. She wished the rains would come. Cat's little body was like a hot water bottle and Chrissie rolled over to a cool spot, falling into a troubled sleep. That night she dreamt of a black mamba, its mouth open wide to show the darkness inside.

CRACKS

Evelyn lay on the bed with a wet cloth over her eyes, which were reddened and sore from crying for hours. Her head throbbed and her limbs were heavy with fatigue. She could hear Robert in the shower. Their fight had been like a storm ripping through the bungalow, his anger and jealousy a towering force that had taken all her strength to stand up to. The names he'd called her! No one had ever talked to her like that – not even Patrick when he was drunk. A sigh shuddered through her chest but her tears were spent. He'd rampaged from room to room, throwing things at the walls, his face contorted with fury, while she stood in the path of the hurricane, her arms crossed tightly, her protests shouted down. She waited until he had walked out on to the veranda, where he sat with his head in his hands, his back curved in despair. Evelyn sat down next to him and laid a hand flat on his back. He flinched but she kept it there.

'I'm only going to say this once,' she said quietly, feeling his heat through his shirt. 'You have no reason to be threatened by Gerry Mann or anyone else. I love you.'

His shoulders shook and she realised he was crying. He turned suddenly and took her in his arms. 'Forgive me,' he said, choked, and tried to kiss her. She kept her face away from his.

'You frightened me. And you hurt me. Don't ever speak to me like that again.' He had nodded and taken her to bed, where he had been at his most tender with her. But it was as if a cold shard of glass had been inserted into Evelyn's heart.

Now she removed the cloth from her swollen eyes and went to sit in front of her dressing table. She took off her pearls and as she put them in their box she noticed the purple bruises on the inside of her arm where Robert had wrenched her away from the party.

'I have to be my own person,' she told her reflection. 'I can't be frightened of my husband. I won't be my mother.' Her father had never shouted and made a scene like Robert, but he could be cold and whenever he was in one of his moods she and her mother had tiptoed around him. It was an icy, controlling kind of bullying and she'd watched how her mother, desperate to please him, had faded over the years.

She hardly saw Robert over the next week; he was away early in the morning and back sometimes after she'd gone to bed. He was setting up a new district court system, he'd explained, and would be away even more over the next few weeks.

'If I don't come home, don't worry, it just means a meeting's run late and I've stayed on at the Ridgeway.'

She nodded and tried to care, but something had shifted in her heart, as if the fight had left jagged cracks in the walls of their marriage. One day, when Robert had been away overnight, Evelyn watched a car drive up to the house. Gerry Mann got out and walked towards the house.

'The lovely Mrs Fielding! Are you ready for your first driving lesson?' he called.

Evelyn was delighted to see a friendly face. She'd seen Grace a couple of times but she was always so busy with the children. She'd found the days interminable; the oppressive heat made her too languid to do anything other than sit in the shade of the veranda and stare out at the blue hills. She'd taken out her sketchbook and started to draw them but the soft pastels, made for European skies, were wrong for the colours that shimmered under the African sun.

Gerry grinned at her. 'Well? Are you coming?'

She hesitated. Her husband wouldn't like it, even though she'd reassured him after the fight that she had no interest in Gerry. But Robert need never know: he wouldn't be back until well after sundown. Besides, she would go mad on her own in this house, trapped indoors by the heat and the miles of bush on every side, with Sixpence lurking in the background watching her every move. Learning to drive would give her freedom. If she waited until she asked Robert, it would cause another row, and she couldn't face that. Anyway, he'd only say no, and Evelyn hated to be thwarted.

She smiled at Gerry. 'I'll just get my bag.'

He opened the driver's door for her. 'Come on, you won't need your handbag in the bush.'

Evelyn ran down the steps and got in behind the wheel. The engine was running and she pressed the accelerator so it revved loudly and chased a flock of parakeets out of a tree into the cobalt sky. Gerry got in beside her and showed her how to work the pedals and gears. The car lurched forward a couple of times and then they were off, slowly at first, then faster as Evelyn gained confidence, the car eating up mile after mile of red road as they drove out of Chalimbana and into the bush.

THE BRAAI

The week after the party, Chrissie was helping Elijah make a guitar out of an old paraffin oil tin, stringing wire through holes he'd punched in the metal, when she saw Mr Jacobs's bakkie turn into the drive. She watched her father came out to meet him; they stood beside the pick-up truck, hands in their pockets.

'You left sharpish the other night, Piet.'

Mr Jacobs studied his jungle boots for a while. He cleared his throat. 'Jim, if you're going to have those people at your house again, will you let us know? We can't be at the same parties. I'm sorry, but that's the way it is for us.'

Elijah pulled at Chrissie's arm and she passed him another piece of string without taking her eyes off the two men. Her father didn't say anything but took off his glasses and rubbed his eyes. The silence stretched between them until Chrissie could bear it no longer. She ran over to Mr Jacobs and threw her arms around him. He laughed and squeezed her so hard she thought her ribs were going to crack

'*Haai*, Chrissie. *Hoe gaan dit?* One of the farm dogs has had puppies. Would you like to come and see them? *Ja? Goed.* Go and find your mum. We'll cook up a braai.' Chrissie started up the steps just as her mother came out on the veranda.

'Mum! Mr Jacobs says there are puppies on the farm, and he's invited us to a barbecue. Can we go?'

'*Ja, kom.* Lotte and I have a side of beef we want you to take off our hands. Since the kids went away to Rhodesia, we've got too much of everything. You'd be doing us a favour.'

Chrissie knew her mum had been worried about food shortages. There was nothing in the Chalimbana store except bottles of bleach and a few sacks of mielie-meal.

'We can't go on like this,' her mum had said to a neighbour only a few days ago. 'I'm running out of tins. At this rate I'll be feeding the kids *nsima* and *kapenta*.' Chrissie hoped not; she found the corn porridge slimy and tasteless, and the pungent smell of the dried river fish turned her stomach. Now Mr Jacobs was offering to help them out.

Her mother looked pleadingly at her father. 'Jim?'

There was a small silence while the adults looked at each other and then Chrissie's father held out his hand to the farmer. 'Of course, we'd be delighted. Thank you, Piet, you're a good man.'

Mr Jacobs slapped him on the back. 'Ach, it's nothing, *my bru*. I'll go and start the braai.' He got into the bakkie and leaned out of the window and waved. '*Sien jou later*.'

Chrissie's mother called down from the veranda to Mr Jacobs. 'Wait, Piet, can I bring Evelyn Fielding? Her husband's away on business and I don't like to think of her alone.'

'*Ja*, of course. But I just passed her coming out of the farm – she was all over the road, nearly drove me into the ditch. I don't know why women are allowed behind a wheel. She was with that *khaki* schoolteacher, you know? The one who thinks he's Joe Slovo and talks to me like I'm a complete *domkop*.'

Chrissie caught a look pass between her parents that she couldn't interpret.

'That sounds like Gerry Mann,' her father said.

As the truck disappeared in a cloud of red dust, her mother shooed Chrissie into the garden. 'Go and fetch Hamish, he'll be up in the tree house. Jim, away and change your shirt.'

Later that day, when her dad finally stopped the Bentley outside the Jacobs's farmhouse, Chrissie got out on shaky legs, still feeling carsick. They'd had to stop a couple of times on the way to let her out. While she bent double over the side of the road, her father

100

lugged two buckets of water out of the boot and washed the dust off the car with chamois leather.

'Honestly!' her mum said more to herself than the kids when Chrissie got back in the car. 'What's your father like fussing over his precious car? Only he would think to bring a vintage car out to the bush.' Chrissie closed her eyes and tried not to breathe in the smell of old leather. Her dad started the engine and the Bentley went on its sickeningly smooth way. She wished they'd gone in the Landie; it clattered along through the potholes but didn't make her sick. Every time the Bentley dipped like a liner riding the waves, her stomach slid up her throat.

At the farmhouse, Chrissie took deep breaths while the grown-ups asked the usual questions – hello and how are you and how was the drive? Mrs Jacobs must have noticed Chrissie's pallor and broke away to hug her. She smelled of starch and carbolic soap.

'Want to see the puppies, *bokkie*?'

Chrissie straightened up and grinned. 'Hamish, you coming?'

'Nah, Mr Jacobs is going to let me drive a tractor.'

Chrissie took Mrs Jacobs's hand and they walked across the big dirt yard towards the barn. The air smelled of burning wood and she began to feel better. The bitch was one of the Jacobs family's fierce guard dogs, a brindle Rhodesian Ridgeback. When Chrissie lifted one of the pups and held it to her face, the mother didn't growl but only lifted her head and watched. The puppy was warm and smelled of sour milk and its eyelids were gummed shut with a sticky infection. Chrissie began to feel sick again and was glad when Mrs Jacobs asked her to put it back.

'Come on, *bokkie*, Piet will have the meat nearly ready by now. Now, I want you to pile up your plate – you look like you need a good feed.'

Back at the house, the steaks were charring on the braai and the long *boerewors* sausage was coiled like a fat snake on the grill. Mr Jacobs and her father were standing in front of the cut-off petrol drums, laughing and drinking beer. Chrissie had just sunk her teeth into a corncob, blackened in places from the grill, when she heard the roar of an engine. She turned to see one of Mr Jacobs's farm-hands at the wheel of the bakkie.

The brakes squealed and he called through the window: 'Bwana! Come quick! Rebel soldiers in the sugar cane fields by the river.'

Mr Jacobs put down his plate and wiped his mouth. 'Christ, they must have snuck in over the border from Rhodesia. I need to take care of this, Jim. *Damn dit*, the country is going to the dogs.' He turned to the farmhand. 'Moses, go and fetch the rest of the boys. Meet me round the back of the house and I'll get the guns.' He walked off towards the house and gave two sharp whistles. Two enormous Ridgebacks scrambled out from underneath the veranda, where they had been panting in the shade, and trotted beside their master, their ears and tails up, ready for a fight.

'Do you want some help?' Chrissie's dad called after him.

The farmer looked grim. 'No, stay here and look after the women and kiddies. This is my land and I'm still the bwana here. I'll send the bastards packing.'

THE SUGAR CANE FIELD

Evelyn pressed her foot to the accelerator as they reached a blind summit and for a glorious moment they were airborne before the car thumped back to earth.

'Woah! Take it easy,' Gerry said. 'I think I'd better drive for a while before you kill us both. Pull over here.' Evelyn slammed on the brakes and they lurched forward in their seats.

She grinned at Gerry. 'Sorry. Got a bit carried away there.'

He ran a hand through his sweat-soaked hair. 'Well, at least you don't lack confidence behind the wheel.'

Outside the car, a field of sugar cane stretched as far as she could see, the long pointed leaves rippling together in the wind like the waves of a dark green sea. The sky was cloudless and blue and the sun blazed down on them unhampered. On the horizon, though, she could just make out steel-grey clouds banked on top of each other. A rivulet of sweat ran down her spine and she closed her eyes, wishing the clouds would race over the fields towards them, bringing their cooling rain. When she opened her eyes she thought she saw a man standing in the middle of the field, but he must have ducked down out of sight. Gerry got out of the car and stretched and she followed.

Evelyn shielded her eyes and pointed into the fields. 'Did you see that?'

He frowned. 'What am I looking for?'

'I thought I saw someone in the fields.'

'Could be baboons, I hear they're a pest. A troop of them can strip a field in a few hours.'

'No, it was definitely a man.'

He shrugged. 'A farm worker then.'

She took a breath. 'Gerry, I think he had a gun. And he was in uniform, like a soldier.' They stood very still and watched the field for a while. Then they both saw it: a dark furrow opened up and men were running towards them, guns pointed.

'Get back in the car, quick!' Gerry shouted. But by the time they'd run around to the doors, slipping and sliding with terror, they were surrounded. Evelyn froze, her breathing heavy. She counted five men dressed in a ragbag of military fatigues and toting guns. Their eyes were reddened with drink and one of them was chewing on a strip of sugar cane, sucking out the juice and spitting out the fibre. These men weren't in any kind of regular army.

One of them, who had an air of authority, stepped forward and pointed his gun at Gerry. 'You, give me money.' Gerry reached into the back pocket of his jeans and held out his wallet. The leader tucked the gun under his arm and pulled out some notes. 'Twenty kwacha!' He threw the empty wallet at Gerry's feet and turned his gun towards Evelyn. 'What about you?'

She didn't like the predatory way he was looking at her and took a step backwards. 'I don't have my purse – it's in my handbag, back home.' Evelyn remembered what Robert had told her about his authority in the region. 'My husband is Robert Fielding. He's with the Government. You should let us go.'

The leader frowned at her and swung the gun back to Gerry. 'This one is *Boma*?'

'No,' she said. 'He's not my husband.' The man laughed knowingly, and the others did the same. Evelyn realised her mistake at once. She opened her mouth to try again when Gerry butted in.

'Hey, my brother, cool it. I know all about your struggle. You're from Southern Rhodesia, right? You're the Patriotic Front, with Mugabe and Nkomo, fighting for your freedom.' The other man tilted his head but didn't answer. Gerry began to gabble desperately. 'But, don't you see, I'm on your side. Black power!' He made a fist in the air and looked hopefully around the men. The one with the sugar cane hadn't stopped chewing and spat lazily at Gerry's feet.

The leader studied Evelyn. 'We are brothers, huh? That's good, because brothers must share everything.' He reached out a hand to stroke her hair and she shrank back. 'Yellow and soft, like a doll's,' he murmured. He turned back to Gerry, his fingers tightening in her hair. 'Hey, brother, can we all play with your dolly?' And the other men laughed. Before she could move away, he pushed her roughly to the ground.

Gerry leapt forward and shouted: 'Leave her alone!' Two of the men grabbed him by the arms and held him still, while the leader placed his gun on the car bonnet and unbuckled his belt. Evelyn tried to squirm backwards, kicking her feet against the dirt to get away and ended up with her back against the fifth man's boots. He squatted down and held her by the shoulders. 'Go on, Captain, you first.'

The leader knelt between her legs and pushed them apart, fumbling with his trousers. Evelyn could smell the acrid sweat off him, and something else, the sweet smell of cannabis and the sour stench of beer on his breath. When she tried to push him off with her body, she felt a sharp blow to her head and a warm trickle from her temple. Evelyn turned her head away and tears squeezed from her eyes. She heard a voice pleading, *no, no, no, no* and realised it was her own. The leader clamped a hand over her mouth and shifted on top of her. Evelyn tried to make her mind go blank and pretend she was somewhere else, but the testosterone-laden heat from the man's body was too real. He yanked at her pants and she cringed and shut her eyes when shots rang out. *Oh God, they've killed Gerry*, she thought. The leader jumped off her and began to run, the other men following. Evelyn scurried over to the side of the car and watched a pick-up truck drive into the sugar can field after her attackers. The back of the truck was filled with men, shooting their rifles into the air. Evelyn felt an arm around her shoulders and screamed and tried to shake it off.

'It's okay, it's okay, it's only me,' Gerry said, and she turned and hid her face in his shirt and began to sob. That was how Piet Jacobs found them when he burst out of the sugar cane field.

'Those bastards!' he said, breathing heavily as he towered over their crouched figures. 'If I'd caught them I'd have shot them in the head.' He took off his shirt and bundled it into a pad that he pressed against Evelyn's head. 'Are you all right?' She nodded and started crying again. 'Bastards,' he said again. 'It's come to this – they dare to attack a white woman. This would never have happened before.' Jacobs and Gerry each took an arm and helped Evelyn to her feet. 'I'll take her back to the farm, you'd better make yourself scarce.'

'Don't you think I should see a doctor?' Evelyn managed to say.

'What doctor? The nearest one is in Lusaka. Lotte can patch you up – she's had plenty of practice, better than any doctor.'

'What about the police, surely we should report this?' she said.

'No police,' Jacobs said firmly. 'We deal with things ourselves out here.' He spoke to Gerry. 'If you know what's good for you, you'll lie low. You shouldn't be out here with another man's wife.'

'But we were only…there's nothing…' Gerry stuttered.

Jacobs put up his hand. 'I don't want to know and I don't care. But I know Robert Fielding. You'd better get out of here.'

Evelyn's legs had begun to shake and she let Jacobs lift her into the passenger seat of his pick-up truck. There were shots and faint cries in the distance. The noise of the engine drowned them out and she leaned her head against the window, exhausted. On the horizon, the clouds rumbled and she wondered if it was raining in London. It was her last thought before she fell asleep.

Evelyn woke to a murmur of voices. It was dark outside and she was laid out on a sofa under an open window. She wondered where she was and looked around the room. A pair of eyes stared down at her from the gloomy rafters. A scream died in her throat when she realised the eyes belonged to the head of some kind of wild boar. After a while she made out that it was a warthog, a hunter's trophy. Next to it an impala gazed at her helplessly. The wall was covered in animal heads, most of them antelopes of one kind or other, their horns spiralled like sugar barley. Evelyn tried to sit up to get a better look and clutched her head in pain. It was a moment before the attack came back to her, and she whimpered.

Lotte Jacobs bustled through from the next room, wiping her

hands on her apron. The sofa creaked when she sat down next to Evelyn and began to rub her back in soothing circles. 'Hush now, *bokkie*, you're safe here. You've had a big fright but you're going to be okay. I've washed the cut on your head but it doesn't need a bandage. Lie down again for a bit while I make you some tea. Then Jim will take you home.'

She left and Evelyn stared at the sorrowful impala. The voices drifted in from the veranda and she recognised them now as those of Jim Docherty and Piet Jacobs.

'Can you believe President Kaunda is backing this Patriotic Front mob – you should have seen them, Jim, what a raggedy bunch of up-to-no-good thugs. They're lucky they were fast runners and got away from my boys. Didn't realise they had a jeep tucked away behind some trees on the other side of the fields. They must have set up camp a few days ago; there were empty tin cans and rubbish everywhere.'

Evelyn moved along the sofa so she could hear more clearly. Jim Docherty spoke next.

'You think they were guerrilla fighters from over the Rhodesian border?'

'*Ja*, sure of it. I don't know what President Kaunda's playing at, giving them house room. He's asking for trouble. Doesn't he know what they are capable of? They call themselves freedom fighters but they're nothing but a bunch of murderous gangsters. Look at what they nearly did to that poor girl.'

There was a silence then Jim Docherty spoke. 'What they did – what they nearly did – was terrible, but that doesn't change my views. Ian Smith shouldn't have broken away from British rule and declared unilateral independence before there was a chance for proper elections. Putting the whites in charge without a vote – that's just asking for trouble. Now he's stuck with this awful civil war with no end in sight. Smith is the one I'd call a thug.'

'Ach, Smithy isn't so bad,' Piet said. 'He's protecting his people, the people who made Rhodesia what it is, who built it out of nothing, like my father did with this farm. People like us, we have as much right to be here as the blacks.'

'But it's their land, your father came up from South Africa and took it off the natives, probably bought it for a pittance, just like the mining companies when they snapped up the copper mines from the Barotse paramount chief.'

Piet snorted. 'And how the hell do you think the Barotse got their hands on that rich copper land in the first place? I'll tell you – by invading some other tribe and taking it off them. That's the way things are done in Africa. It's survival of the fittest. You think democracy is the answer? Look at what happened here last year with Kaunda, when he declared Zambia a one-party state with his precious UNIP in charge. So much for all the promises made at independence. The power has gone to his head, and now he's giving sanctuary to Mugabe's Patriotic Front so they can make raids into Rhodesia and scuttle back here to safety – and cause the kind of trouble we saw today.'

Piet's voice was rising as he got into his stride. 'And because KK has offered his so-called brothers sanctuary, Smithy has closed the borders and we Zambians can't get anything in or out of the country. Rhodesia was our main trade route to South Africa and the rest of the world. One Zambia, One Nation – that's Kaunda's rallying cry. Well I say, One Zambia, One Hell of a Mess!'

Jim Docherty spoke more loudly to be heard over the Boer's growl. 'It's early days, Piet, there are bound to be teething problems with a new government. And while they try to find backers to build a railway line to Tanzania, there are other trade routes opening up – the TanZam Road to the port of Dar es Salaam.'

'Tssh! That's the worst road in the whole of Zambia, and that's saying something. I tell you, we were better off under you *blerrie* Brits.'

'I agree, it's not a perfect state of affairs,' Jim Docherty said, and Jacobs snorted again. 'But you've got to look at the positives – the schools that have been built in every district, secondary as well as primary. There used to be only schooling for whites with rural blacks getting a few years at primary if they were lucky. Do you know that before independence there were only two secondary schools for blacks in the whole country, both mission schools? Soon there will be universal education, and that's got to be progress. Education is the great leveller – we've always known in Scotland that it's the only way up and out. My own father had to leave school at thirteen to go into the steelworks to support his brothers and mother. He was stuck in a manual job, but he encouraged me to go to university, and there will be families all over Zambia with the same idea. It'll take time, but I'm optimistic about the future. This is still one of the wealthiest countries in Africa.'

'Ja, but for how long? The Indians have all been sent packing, just like in Uganda when Amin took over. That means the shops aren't being run properly – the natives don't have a clue about stocktaking and whatever and what have you. How long before they think they can farm, too? Before they come looking for my land? And it could happen – we're vastly outnumbered. That's why I have to show them who's the boss. Can you imagine my boys trying to run this place without me? It would turn back to bush in a couple of weeks, I tell you.'

Evelyn heard a deep sigh. 'Piet, you're impossible.'

'I'm a realist, Jim. I know this country and I know these people. They weren't ready for independence; they aren't capable of running their own affairs.'

'I've heard that argument before, in Scotland. But Piet, don't you see that if you let someone else run your country, you'll never be ready for independence?'

Lotte came back into the room with a tray. She put it down in front of Evelyn and, hearing the raised voices, shut the window.

'Ach, those two, they are always arguing about politics. Then they get drunk together and they are best of friends again.' Evelyn took the cup of tea that was handed to her and winced at the sugar that had been piled into it. Lotte noticed. 'Drink it, it's good for the shock.' She poured herself a cup and sipped it while she watched Evelyn. 'You look better, your colour has come back.' She sat back in her armchair and was quiet for a while. A cuckoo popped out of its clock and counted to eight.

Evelyn pushed back the blanket off her. 'I should be getting back.'

'Ja, soon. Jim will give you a lift. He took Grace and the kids home earlier and came back to check on you.'

'That was kind of him. I thought he disapproved of me.'

'Ach, Jim can be a bit dour, as he would say himself, but he has a good heart. Like your husband.'

There was a pause. Evelyn put her teacup down. Why was Robert always the hero? She felt her cheeks grow warm and something burst inside her.

'What do you know about my husband? You all think he's this noble, fair man, the *Boma*, one of the old school, isn't that how Tom O'Brian described him? But behind closed doors, he can be cold as ice one minute then erupt into this jealous rage the next.'

Lotte put her own cup down and sat forward in her chair. 'Now, you listen to me, Evelyn Fielding. I do know your husband, very well as it happens. And I know he'd be furious if he found out you were driving about in the bush with Gerry Mann.' Evelyn started to protest but Lotte put up a hand to stop her. 'I know there's probably nothing in it, but there's already been talk about the two of you – the way you were carrying on at the party, touching his arm and whatever and what have you. And Robert is a jealous man, as you know. Which is why Piet won't mention to him what happened today. He'd hunt those men down and kill them, and then he'd go looking for that schoolteacher for exposing you to danger.'

Evelyn put her head in her hands. 'I know, he was so angry just to see me talking to Gerry.' She looked up, her eyes full of tears. 'He frightens me when he gets like that. I don't understand why he's so jealous.' Lotte came and sat next to Evelyn, rubbing her back once more like a mother would to her child.

'I've known Robert all my life,' she said after a while. 'We grew up together, he was like a younger brother to me.'

'What?'

'Robert was just a little boy when his mother died, and it broke him, like a clay pot. But you're his wife – you hold great power. You can mend him by stopping up the cracks with love.' Lotte shook her head. 'Robert's a complicated man, not like my Piet. He is a good man, but he can be a little boring if I'm honest.' She looked wistful. 'Life with Robert would never be boring.' She sighed. 'Such a sad childhood he had.'

'You mean his mother dying?' Evelyn said.

'*Ja*. We were both kids at the time, me a few years older. When his mother died, his father brought Robert back from school in England and then forgot all about him. He used to come over to our farm all the time; ate as if he were starving. Mamma did what she could for him but there were twelve of us. Once he asked her if he could come and live with us and she had to tell him he couldn't. He put his head in her lap and she held him until he stopped crying.' Mrs Jacobs wiped her eyes.

Evelyn touched her fingers to her forehead. 'But surely Robert's father would look after his own son? He was only five.'

'The old man was broken-hearted, nearly went out of his mind with grief. They say he had been madly in love with his wife, that she was a real beauty. When she died, he wouldn't have anything to do with Robert. The child must have reminded him too much of his wife. Robert was all alone – his sister Pamela was only a baby and was sent back to England to be raised by an aunt. In the end, the house girl took pity on him and brought him back to the village with her. We used to see him sitting with the other children under the big village tree, this little white boy among all the blacks, listening to the old women and their stories. After about a year, Tom O'Brian had a word with Robert's father and he was sent back to school in England. I don't know what was worse.'

They sat in silence for a while and Evelyn tried to imagine Robert as a child, running wild, afraid and alone, taking comfort where he could find it, like the street urchins she'd seen running along side the cars, begging for coins. Evelyn wanted to scoop the young Robert up in her arms and give him all the love that had been taken away from him. But she realised she couldn't make him happy by pretending to be what she wasn't. She would be a good wife to him, but she had to find her place in this strange, empty country.

'That reminds me, Father O'Brian has asked me to work in his clinic and I think I'll give it a go.'

'Are you sure? It's no picnic up there in the hills.'

'I need something to do, to feel useful.' Evelyn didn't know why she was telling Lotte, perhaps because it felt good to be able to confide in another woman. 'This is a beautiful, wild country and I know I'll grow to love it. But my days are so empty. Don't you ever get bored?'

Lotte laughed. 'Bored? I don't have time to be bored. A farmer's wife is always busy.' She picked up a seed catalogue that was lying on the table next to her and used it as a fan. 'It takes a while for you British girls to settle in. You should have heard Grace when she first came out. She got used to it, but she has the kiddies to look after.' She gave Evelyn a long look. 'What you need is a baby.'

It was stuffy with the window closed and Evelyn lifted her hair to dry the sweat on her neck. 'I don't want to be just another colonial wife, sitting at home while my husband is out doing whatever it is he does. I can't live like that; I want to make a difference, do something worthwhile. Robert's gone so much and I don't know what to do with all the hours.' Evelyn let her hair drop and looked down into her hands. There was dried blood on them and she thought she might cry again. She saw again the leader's face close to hers, the beads of sweat on his brow, his breath in her mouth. *No! No! No! NO!* Evelyn pushed the images out of her head. The attack would not break her; she would not be a victim. Evelyn shook her head to rid it of the images. 'Father O'Brian has asked for my help, so I'm going to volunteer for the mission clinic.'

Lotte sighed. 'Tom is an interfering old woman, but you do what you need to do to make you happy.'

'I feel it's my duty.'

Lotte's face hardened. 'Your only duty is to your husband, and soon enough it will be to your children. If you go up to that mission, you won't get any thanks for it. This country has changed.' She looked away and her expression softened into one of sorrow. 'The truth is, they don't want us here. Sometimes I think the sooner we've all left, the better.'

THE CLINIC

Evelyn wiped the sweat out of her eyes with the crook of her arm. It had been a bad labour and the room smelled rusty with blood. The young mother lay asleep on a blanket on the floor, a groove of pain still carved between her eyes. Her baby reached out its plump arms to Evelyn, fists waving in fury as it opened its mouth in a cat's cry of hunger. She picked it up from the cot and put her finger in its mouth and the baby, a little girl, tried to suck before arching her back again. Terrified she'd drop the baby, Evelyn rocked her and tried to remember a nursery rhyme to sing to the child. When she couldn't think of any, she hummed her old school hymn instead.

'Ye gates lift up your heads on high...' The baby opened its mouth again and screamed. Evelyn swung her arms faster but that only made things worse. 'Please don't cry, please don't cry, hush, hush.' Evelyn held the hot little body to her neck and winced as the cry became a nagging keen in her ear. She held the baby away from her and regarded its bawling face. 'Oh, bugger and damn and blast, why won't you stop, you fiend?'

'Dear God, that's no way to talk to a little one.' Father O'Brian strode into the room and Evelyn nearly wept with relief. 'Here give the wee soul to me.' He took the wriggling bundle off her, deftly tucked it under his arm, and reached for a bottle. In a few seconds, the baby was making contented little grunting noises. As she suckled, the little girl stared at the priest as if he held the answer to the mystery of life.

113

Father O'Brian nodded at the baby's mother lying on the floor. 'Sister Bernadette has done all she can for Chikondi, but these girls come in anaemic. They're not fit for childbirth. She needs a blood transfusion if she's to see tomorrow.'

Evelyn crouched down beside the girl and pulled the sheet up to cover her breasts, which were high and small. She's still a child, Evelyn thought. She ought to feel for a pulse, but didn't know how, and realised how useless she was. It was hot in the room and she went to the window and opened it wider. Outside, a group of small boys were admiring Robert's Land Rover, which she'd taken to driving up to the mission in the hills. She'd asked Robert to teach her to drive and he'd been surprised at how quickly she'd picked it up. Evelyn was careful not to mention the lesson she'd had with Gerry, or what had happened out in the sugar cane field. Now she leaned on the windowsill and watched the boys. One of them pushed a toy car made of wire in front of him and the others chased after, begging for a turn.

Evelyn turned to the priest, who was still feeding the baby. 'I'm not much good as a nurse,' she said. 'But I can drive. I'll take Chikondi to the hospital if you help me put her in the Land Rover.'

The baby had fallen asleep and Father O'Brian laid her gently in the cot. 'I suppose it's worth a try.'

Outside the clinic, a woman with a baby strapped to her back bashed maize into mush for porridge with a wooden mortar and pestle that was nearly as tall as her. She stopped her rhythmic work and watched them carry the girl to the Land Rover. Evelyn didn't meet her eyes and instead concentrated on her task. She knew the hill village women were suspicious of her from the way they smirked behind their hands and wouldn't meet her eyes when she talked to them. The men were worse; they stared at her openly from their stools in the shade of the village tree. They'd spend all day there, drinking beer and gossiping while the women pounded the maize, hoed the scrappy gardens and washed enamel plates under the stand pipe, usually with a baby on their backs and a runny-nosed toddler clinging to their legs.

Father O'Brian eased the young mother into the back of the Land Rover and Evelyn took the wheel. He climbed in beside her and she over-revved the engine, desperate to get away from the stares. In the rear view mirror, Evelyn saw the woman raise the pestle high above her head and release it with a thump into the mortar.

The hospital was filthy. The missionary clinic was basic but at least it was clean. The air in the Lusaka hospital was a miasma of stale sweat and vomit overlaid with the pungent, throat-clogging stench of human excrement. Soiled bandages stained red with blood and yellow with iodine lay discarded in corners, and the floor was occupied by families crouched next to the sick person they'd brought in. They tended to pots of dried fish and wild spinach while the patients lay in silent misery on mats.

A harried doctor swept through the ward. He took one look at the young girl slumped between Evelyn and the priest and shouted at a porter to put her on a gurney. Evelyn tried to tell him about the labour, how she'd lost a lot of blood and that her name was Chikondi, but the doctor interrupted her.

'Yes, yes, I see this every day, she's anaemic,' he said, his accent and blonde looks identifying him as a Swede. 'They don't eat enough protein, it's all that maize and cassava. I'll try a transfusion, if we have enough blood that is.' He walked away before Evelyn could thank him. She'd never felt more helpless.

Tom O'Brian covered her hand with his. 'You go home to your husband, my child. I'll stay with Chikondi.'

Robert wasn't at home. He was at yet another series of crisis meetings with the *wabenzies* and wouldn't be home for a few days. Evelyn bathed and changed into a clean dress. She sat on the veranda and tried to settle her thoughts by looking at the sun painting the blue hills gold and pink. She pictured Robert with his shirtsleeves rolled, his hair sticking up because he'd run his hand through it in exasperation. The civil servants had little experience of government, he'd told her, and meetings could go on for hours, days even, in the traditional African way. It was no use trying to hurry things along, as everyone would smile and nod and agree but nothing would be decided.

The sky was darkening to violet and Evelyn wondered if she should help herself to a whisky and soda. Through the mesh swing door she could see Sixpence in the sitting room, waxing the floor with rags tied to his feet. She didn't want him to think she was the kind of woman who drank on her own while her husband was away at work – just another bored white woman with not enough to do. She sighed and tucked her feet under her bottom. Robert was away so much these days, and she'd taken to spending longer and longer at the clinic, but it wasn't the satisfying, worthwhile work she'd thought it would be. Her lack of even the most basic medical or nursing experience made her more of a handicap than a help, and she had the impression the nuns worked around her, too kind to ask her to get out of their way and go home.

Evelyn saw headlamps in the distance along the road into Chalimbana and wondered who was approaching. Not Robert, that was for sure. He was hardly at home, and when he was he was morose and preoccupied. She shifted off her seat and decided she would have that drink after all. As she poured the whisky, she let herself think about why Robert's mood was so black. Ever since the attack, she'd flinched away from him in bed at night. The last time he had tentatively put his hand on her shoulder, she had tried, she really had, but when she opened her legs to him, she could only see the leader's eyes staring into hers; Robert's hand on her thigh became his and her muscles went into a spasm of alarm so it was impossible for Robert to enter her without her feeling excruciating pain. She'd gritted her teeth for a while but pushed him off and wept uncontrollably, her back to Robert, who, appalled, had tried to comfort her. He'd soon given up and they slept with their backs to each other, curled into their own shells of resentment and loneliness. Evelyn knew she should tell Robert about the sugar cane field, but she was too ashamed; deeply, sickeningly ashamed.

Now she watched the headlamps grow nearer and turn into her drive. A car door slammed and Gerry Mann appeared out of the gloom. Exhausted from her day at the clinic and desperate for someone to talk to, Evelyn ran lightly down the steps towards him. She was so relieved to see his familiar face that she was too friendly, smiled too widely, and took his arm in hers. Gerry's eyes stretched and a flush of pleasure darkened his face as she drew him close for a kiss on the cheek.

'Gerry, darling!' Evelyn was aware of speaking in a trilling falsetto but couldn't seem to stop this fevered outburst. 'How lovely to see you! Come and have a drink.' She felt her hand pawing at his arm. 'I insist you tell me all your news, immediately!' When she led him up the steps to the cool of the veranda she noticed with a jolt of irritation that Sixpence was standing behind the screen door, twisting a cloth in his hands.

'Madam?'

She waved him off back into the house. 'No need to get us drinks, Sixpence, I'll be mother.' Her voice was harsh in her own ears but Gerry didn't seem to mind. He kept looking at her out of the side of his eyes, as if he were aware of new possibilities.

They sipped at their whiskies with a dash of soda. The alcohol hit her empty stomach and made her reckless. Evelyn knew she was talking and laughing too much while Gerry watched her. After a while, she stopped in mid-sentence and found she couldn't go on. She stared at her hands, rubbing them together over and over, as if trying to wash them clean. Gerry put down his glass and put his hand over hers.

'Are you all right, Evelyn?' She shook her head, not trusting herself to speak. 'I'm sorry I haven't been to see you since, you know, since that day, I thought it best to give you some time to yourself. But perhaps I was wrong to do that.' Her eyes began to prickle and she blinked away tears. Now her nose was running. Oh God! She picked up a paper napkin and wiped it. Gerry pretended not to notice and poured them both another drink, without soda this time. He settled back into the chair. 'Tell me what's wrong,' he said. And he listened while she told him about the nightmares that woke her, and how every time she closed her eyes she saw the rebel leader bending over her, his hand on his buckle. And, worst of all, how she was terrified they would come back for her.

'I've tried to make myself busy, to forget about it, but it hasn't worked,' she said. Between ragged sobs, she told him about the mission: about the flies, and the dirt, about the barefoot children in rags with swollen bellies, their ashy skin covered in ringworm; about the hostile, worn-out women and the men who sat under the trees drinking and looking at her. 'I've never seen such poverty before, I just feel so useless,' Evelyn said, blowing her nose hard, not caring that her eyes would be puffy and red. 'Lotte Jacobs was right – they don't want me there. The hill women disapprove of my short skirts. Apparently it's okay to have bare breasts but God forbid you show your legs! And they think there must be something wrong with me because I don't have children. *They* pity *me*, can you believe it?' She drained her glass and Gerry topped it up. 'I've never really done any work like this before. Every single person up there – even the young children who work in the fields and look after the babies – is more competent than me.'

Evelyn told him about the clinic staffed by nuns who weren't medically qualified but who seemed to know what to do. They were patient when they had to show her again and again how to paint the children's heads with purple medicine when they came in with ringworm or how to dress the men's wounds – horrific *panga* slashes from drunken fights that left them with arms hanging by a string or severed fingers, the wounds bright red against their skin. 'A man came in last week with an axe embedded in his head,' she said. 'He was still conscious and talking. He died later, of course. The worst of it was no-one seemed shocked apart from me.'

Gerry was silent for a while. 'Evelyn, may I give you some advice? I know it's not what you want to hear, but believe me when I say in the kindest way possible that you're wasting your time up there.' She opened her mouth to protest but he carried on. 'It's not that they don't need help, but you're just not cut out for it. You're an intelligent, woman, an artist. They need someone practical and hard-headed, who isn't reduced to tears by the plight of a sick child or a dying man – the sort of women I grew up around in the North who roll up their sleeves and get on with it, and have a full night's sleep after. But you're different, Evelyn, you're sensitive.'

She bent her head. 'Weak, you mean.'

'No, not at all. You're wasted up there. If you want to make a difference, really make a difference, I have a job for you, one that's more suited to your talents.' He stood up and held out his hand to her. 'Dry your eyes and come with me. There's someone I want you to meet.'

Evelyn followed him obediently to his car. As Gerry shut the car

118

door behind her she saw Sixpence on the veranda. He was rubbing the glass tabletop hard, as if to eradicate all signs of her. He straightened up, holding their glasses in his fingers, and stared at her like one of the hill village men. Evelyn wondered briefly how much he hated her, and found she didn't care any more. The setting sun was in her eyes and she put on her sunglasses, turning her head so she couldn't see Sixpence. She shouldn't have to put up with this in her own home. There was nothing else for it: Robert would have to get rid of him. As he drove, his hands steady on the wheel despite the whisky, Gerry told her Jim Docherty had introduced him to a young man who wanted to become a teacher.

'Jim can't see it of course, but I think he's got far more potential than that. While the other student teachers are trying to get to grips with basic English, it turns out he's read the complete works of Shakespeare and Dickens, as well as Flaubert and Goethe. And he can quote Milton by the verse-load. But the damnedest thing is, he's a gifted artist. Apparently, he had a scholarship to study fine art at university in Uganda, but had to interrupt his degree when Amin took power last year. I'll let you judge for yourself, but with the right support I think he could be a great artist. And that's where you come in,' he took his eyes off the road and touched her lightly on the arm. 'Didn't you say you had a fine art degree, and that you worked at a London gallery?'

Evelyn watched the giant copper sun as it sank behind the hills and seemed to set fire to the veldt. Soho seemed a million miles away and a hundred years ago.

'I was at St Martin's but I was only really a Girl Friday at the gallery.'

'But you know talent when you see it?'

'I suppose so.' She could feel her spirits lifting: a promising young artist! She could help an artist, and feel useful.

Gerry thumped the steering wheel. 'I knew you'd be just the person! You'll see, Joseph Makelele is the genuine article, a diamond in the rough. With help from us, he could go all the way to become Zambia's first great artist.'

WHERE IS THE LAKE?

September 1973

Chrissie remembered the first time she met Joseph. It was a strange, foreboding day. The rains had still not broken but the black-edged thunderclouds were getting nearer, pressing the air down so she thought her ears were going to pop. Her mother had gone to lie down in the dark with a cold cloth over her face.

'Go and play, and take Cat with you,' she had told Chrissie and Hamish after they had barged into her bedroom for the fourth time.

Chrissie and Hamish, with Cat between them, stood at the edge of the shaded veranda as if they were at the side of a pool about to jump in. Chrissie shaded her eyes against the glare from the garden and pointed at the trees on the other side of the patchy lawn.

'Let's play high-up tig.' It was their favourite game and could go on all day, even into the next day. If you had your feet off the ground you were in the den, but the minute they touched the ground you were for it. Hamish cocked his head to one side. 'OK. I'll give you a ten-second start. Cat, you can have a longer one.'

They watched Cat in her dirty white muslin dress run over to the flame tree with its sprays of red flowers and start to climb it. She sat down on a low branch and squinted at them under her too long fringe.

'My tree!' she called. Chrissie and her brother rolled their eyes at each other, the game forgotten. They walked over to the flame tree and looked up at their little sister. Her mop of hair shone against the green. She stuck out her tongue. 'My tree! My tree!'

Cat had assigned them all trees, even though she was the littlest. Chrissie's was the frangipani, which was too easy to climb, and she hated how the creamy petals were thick and smooth like skin, and how they bled a milky sap. Hamish had the miombo, the highest tree in the garden where he had built his tree house. You had to be careful as it spat out its winged seedpods with a crack that sounded like a rifle shot.

Hamish shook his fist at Cat. 'You can't own a tree, you little twit. I'm coming up.' Cat folded her arms and opened her mouth and screamed. Within seconds Hamish had scaled the tree and clamped a hand over Cat's mouth. 'Shh! Ow!' He shook his hand. 'She bit me!' He jumped down and scowled at Cat, who grinned back.

Chrissie stretched up her arms and swung from the lowest branch, her toes scuffing the dirt. 'Just leave her up there, Hamish. Let's play football instead.'

'Nah, I'm going to wait here until she comes down. And then I'm going to climb this tree.' Hamish slid his back against the trunk of the flame tree until his bottom touched his heels. Chrissie sighed; he would stay like that for ages, and Cat was just as stubborn.

Chrissie gave up and went round to the back of the house, where the kitchen door opened out onto the vegetable garden. Her dad had worked hard but the carrots only grew to the size of a thumb and the potatoes were full of holes when pulled from the ground. The only things that grew well were runner beans. She picked one of the furry leaves and stuck it to her chest like a badge. Samson came out of the darkness of the kitchen and stood in the doorway.

'There's peanut butter today,' he said. 'You want some?' Chrissie couldn't believe her luck. She followed him into the kitchen and thickly spread a slice of her mother's homemade milk bread with peanut butter.

'Thank you,' she said through a sticky mouthful. Samson nodded and went back to his cooking. Chrissie made the unexpected treat last all the way to the servants' compound on the other side of the garden gate, where Samson lived with his family. She lifted the catch and walked over the hot, hard-baked ground, glad of her flip-flops. Samson's wife was washing the youngest boy under the outside tap, rubbing his head with a cake of pink carbolic soap and pouring the water over him with her cupped hand. Two of Elijah's sisters were sitting in the shade of a tree, the older one twisting and tying the other's hair into hoops and whorls using black thread. Chrissie sat on the lid of the corn store and watched for a while. There was some spilled corn next to her and she amused herself by throwing it to the chickens, which were scrabbling and pecking in the dust. At last, Elijah came out of the house with its corrugated iron roof and she jumped down to meet him.

'Where are we going?' she said as they ran out the other side of the compound through Samson's pumpkin patch.

'We are going to the store. There is peanut butter.'

Chrissie waited on the steps outside next to a sack of toffees and a crate of dusty Fanta bottles while Elijah shopped for his mother. It was too hot inside and the soupy air smelled of dried fish and soap powder. The peanut butter had made her thirsty and she longed for a Fanta, but she hadn't brought any *ngwe*. She shaded her eyes and watched a young man stride up the path carrying a suitcase with a belt round it. He was tall, and wore a long leather coat with wide lapels over an open-necked patterned shirt and flared trousers. Chrissie thought he must be hot and bothered in all those clothes but there was a swing to his walk. And when he saw her sitting in the shade his face broke into the kind of wide and friendly smile that made you want to smile back.

Chrissie shaded her eyes and squinted up at him. '*Bwanji.*'

The stranger put down his cardboard suitcase and clapped his hands in greeting. He sat down next to her and reached for a Fanta, twisted it off and handed it to her before doing the same for himself. The drink was warm but it was sweet and fizzy. He flashed his toe-tickling smile again and she giggled.

'My name is Joseph Makelele,' he said and held out his hand.

She shook his hand. 'Hi, I'm Chrissie.'

'Hello, Chrissie. I am very glad to make your acquaintance.' He smiled again. 'When I came round the corner, you looked like a little lizard hiding from the sun.' Chrissie wrinkled her nose, delighted with the compliment. Lizards were her absolute favourites and she'd been trying without success to catch and tame one for weeks.

Joseph put down his Fanta bottle and turned to face her. 'Now, can you help me, I wonder, little lizard? Where is the lake?'

Chrissie wiped her hands, dusty from the Fanta bottle, down the front of her dress. 'There is no lake.'

He clicked his tongue. 'There is always a lake wherever there are people living.'

Chrissie stood up. 'No, this place was built by *MuZungus*, by Europeans. But there is a lake out there, beyond the village.' She pointed towards the collection of round huts with their thatched roofs.

He put his head on one side. 'No lake! What kind of barbarous place is this? *All torment, trouble, wonder and amazement inhabits here: some heavenly power guide us out of this fearful country.*' Joseph winked at Chrissie whose mouth had fallen open. 'That's from *The Tempest*. Have you read it? No? You should. So, little lizard, if there is no lake in this Brave New World, how should I wash after my journey?'

Chrissie hopped down the steps, pulling at his arm. 'There's a tap around the side of the store. Come on, I'll show you.' She hunkered down and watched Joseph put his head under the tap to wash off the dust. It looked so good that Chrissie copied him. Afterwards, they sat back down on the steps and finished their Fantas.

'Have you come to learn to be a teacher at the college?' she said.

Joseph pretended to look alarmed and bent his head to hers and whispered. 'Do you have magic powers? How do you know this?'

She nudged him with her elbow. 'It's obvious – everyone new here comes to study at the college. My dad works there. He's called Mr Docherty. Do you want me to take you to see him?'

'That would be very helpful. I'm glad I bumped into you today, Chrissie Docherty.'

'Okay, I'll just let Elijah know.'

Joseph had such long legs that Chrissie had to run and skip to keep up with him.

'You don't look like a Chewa or a Bemba,' she said. 'What's your tribe?'

He laughed slowly and it was like honey pouring out of a jug. 'I am Lozi, from Barotseland. Do you know where that is?'

Chrissie shook her head and he pointed to where the sun sank over the hills every night. 'Far away, over to the west. But my family live in Lusaka now.'

Her father stood behind his desk at Chalimbana College and shook Joseph's hand. Pinned to the wall behind him, next to Chrissie's drawing of a house with a blue strip of sky and a red flower, was a map of Zambia covered in red pins. Her dad pushed another one in.

'Barotseland, you say?' Her father opened a book and looked up the index. 'Ah here we are.' He read aloud and Chrissie came round the desk to listen more carefully. 'The Barotse are cattlemen from the Barotse floodplains of the Upper Zambezi. They originally came out of Zaire in the eighteenth century. Now a minority, they were once the ascendant aristocracy in their region.' He studied Joseph over his glasses. 'Interesting.'

An aristocrat! Chrissie stood behind her father and looked admiringly up at Joseph.

He winked at her. 'Yes, sir.'

'And what is your language, Joseph Makelele?'

Chrissie hung over her dad's shoulder as he wrote 'Lozi' down in his notebook. He'd studied linguistics at Edinburgh University, which was why their cat was called Chomsky. That was the year they'd had to leave Africa and she'd had to go to school in Scotland. The playground didn't have any trees to climb and the Scottish sun had seemed tiny and so pale she could hardly see it in the grey sky. Chrissie had not understood the teacher when she said 'Get out your jotters', and she had to wear lace-up shoes and socks every day. Now she wriggled her toes in her flip-flops and watched her father trace his finger on the map of Zambia while Joseph told him how he had come to Chalimbana from his homeland.

'First I took the line of rail.'

'From Barotseland?'

'No sir, from Ndola to Lusaka. I worked in the mines. My father and mother and my brothers and sisters live in Lusaka now, and I visited them before I came here. My father works in the city as a clerk with the *Boma*.'

Chrissie's dad hummed happily into his beard. 'So, if you lived in the Copper Belt, you'll speak some Town Bemba too.' He put his hands in his pockets and studied the young man. 'The mines, eh? That can't have been easy.' Joseph nodded and looked unhappy. 'How old are you?'

'Twenty-four.'

He made a note in his book. 'Go on – you took the line of rail from Ndola. How did you get here from Lusaka?' Chrissie knew there was no railway station in Chalimbana, only the red roads.

'I took a bus some of the way. And I walked until a man in a pick-up truck gave me a lift, a Boer. He left me a few kilometres from here.'

'Ah, that'll be Piet Jacobs. Try to hire you for his farm, did he?' Joseph ducked his head.

'Thought so. Bet he told you it was a waste of time training to be a teacher, eh? Don't listen to him, Joseph. You chaps know the value of a good education, just like I did. It's the only way up and out.'

'Yes sir, it's what my father always told me. He had a scholarship to study at university in South Africa but his mother died and he decided to stay at home and look after the younger ones.'

Chrissie's dad made a noise in his throat. 'My own father had to leave school to work in the steelworks.'

'Yes, sir. It was hard for our fathers.'

'You went to a mission school?'

Joseph ducked his head again. 'Yes, with the Presbyterians. Reverend Milne was a good teacher. He saw that I could draw well and encouraged me. He also taught me to stay away from alcohol, so I am teetotal, sir.'

'The Presbyterians do a lot of good work in Africa; you'll have a decent grounding. What level of education did you reach?'

'I have my secondary leaving certificate, and I completed two years of a BA in fine art from Makerere University in Kampala.'

Dad raised his eyebrows and looked at Joseph over his glasses. 'That's impressive.'

'My father went to school with President Kaunda and lobbied him personally for a , scholarship.'

'And now you want to be a teacher?' Dad put down his notebook and pen. 'Wouldn't you be better off finishing your degree?'

'There is no more money, sir, I would have to get another

scholarship and I don't know if that is possible. Besides, my father is getting older and I need to provide for my brothers and sisters, just like he did, and your father too.'

Chrissie's father picked up the letter Joseph had given him. 'The mission school is paying for your training and they want you to go back and teach there. Is that what you want?'

'Yes, sir.'

'I'm more than happy for you to become a student here, but we've had some trouble recently. The latest batch of students was Nyanja. There was some foolish talk of spirits and they wanted to leave. They said they didn't have the right initiation scars for protection. I see you don't have tribal scars. Am I going to have the same problem with you, Joseph?'

'No sir, I am a good Christian. I don't believe in traditional magic. Mr Milne taught me it was nothing but superstition.'

The men shook hands and as Joseph bent forward, Chrissie noticed a coin on a string around his neck, like the charm that Elijah wore to ward off spells. Just then, she sensed someone watching her and turned round to see a shadow flit past the open door, like a snake slithering into the bushes. She ran to the door and saw Nyirongo walking down the hall, his messenger bag swinging empty by his side, his bare feet whispering on the cement floor.

BEST LAID SCHEMES

When Gerry took Evelyn to meet Joseph, the first thing she noticed was how beautiful he was. His face was all angles: a high, intelligent forehead, pronounced cheekbones and a square jaw. But his lips were wide and soft, his brown eyes deep-set and fringed with thick lashes. Tall and willowy, he moved easily and seemed perfectly relaxed to be around her. When she praised his drawings, he smiled with unabashed joy and looked at her with an openness that was welcome after the hostility and barely veiled resentment she'd met from the hill villagers and in her own home from Sixpence. And Joseph's work! It was so fresh and vigorous. Evelyn had never seen anything like it, and grew more excited as she looked through his sketchbook. It was like no student's work she had ever seen and far surpassed anything they'd had at the Soho gallery. Gerry was right: Joseph had the potential to be a great artist.

'These are amazing, just breathtaking,' Evelyn said, her hands full of drawings of men toiling in the copper mines, faces shining in the heat, features thrown into stark relief by the dim light from the underground lamps. Others showed children playing five stones, hens pecking in the dirt around them, and women bent over cooking pots, shucking corn and selling vegetables spread out on a blanket. They were simple but knowing: the work of a gifted artist. The sluggishness and despair brought on by the drudgery at the clinic were gone; instead Evelyn felt as if every nerve in her body were on high alert. 'You say you weren't able to finish your degree?'

she said. 'But you must continue your studies, you must! You have so much talent.'

Joseph shook his head. His voice was a gentle hum that vibrated through Evelyn's bones like a tuning fork.

'You are very kind, Mrs Fielding, but what I must do now is become a teacher, go back to my village in Barotseland. Without a teacher the children will not learn to read and write. And my family, they need my salary. My brothers also need to finish university, and there are many mouths to feed.'

Gerry Mann put his hand on Joseph's shoulder. 'Perhaps you should think about applying for another bursary.'

'No, my father has already asked and I cannot get any more money from the Government.'

Gerry thought for a moment. 'Have you thought about studying in Europe? There are international grants I can help you with through my contacts at the University of Zambia. Joseph, you're a bright young man with lots of potential – think how travel would broaden your horizons as an artist.' He turned and appealed to Evelyn. 'What do you think?'

'I think it would be a crime to let such talent go to waste,' she said firmly. 'Joseph, why don't you let me help you prepare a portfolio while you get your teacher training certificate? We can work at my house, I've got bags of time and the dining room is a big, light room that we never use. It would be perfect for a studio. You could come after class. What do you say?' Her heart hammered in her chest while she waited for his reply.

Joseph gathered the papers together and looked from Evelyn to Gerry and back again. He ducked his head. 'I would like that very much. Thank you.'

Gerry clapped him on the back and Evelyn laughed with relief.

'It's a plan!' she said, 'Our plan.'

Joseph smiled and the room seemed to grow brighter. 'I will go to university in Europe, yes,' he said. 'And then I will be a teacher, like you, sir.'

When her husband came home that night, Evelyn told him about her plans to help Joseph Makelele. Robert was sitting on the bed and she couldn't make out his expression from behind the mosquito net.

'Why would you do that?' he said after a while. 'Presumably he's here to be trained as a teacher.'

'Yes, but he has this wonderful talent, and besides, I want to do it.' She pulled aside the netting and sat down next to him, her hand seeking his.

'First the clinic, now this – are you bored?'

'I am, I'm afraid, but only when you go away. I'm not bored of us.'

He was silent for a while. They had grown used to silences in their marriage but Evelyn desperately wanted to do this; it seemed like her last chance to salvage her dreams of a new life in Africa. She squeezed Robert's hand. 'Please, darling. I need this.'

He turned to speak to her, his face in shadow. 'I know we haven't been... *close* over the last few weeks, but I want this marriage to work. I don't want you to be unhappy. I know you're lonely, that you haven't adjusted to Africa yet, all that takes time. But I'm not sure this project is the answer. Wouldn't it be better if we tried for a family?' He kissed her hand. 'I've always wanted children. If you had a baby, perhaps you'd feel different, settle more into life here.'

Evelyn thought of her mother, sitting in the big empty house in Farnham surrounded by photographs of her and her brothers, long gone to jobs and their own wives. Being a mother had kept her busy, but in the long run it hadn't made her happy. Now that her mother was alone in the house, she filled her days polishing surfaces already gleaming and plumping cushions, waiting for her husband to come home.

'I want more than that, Robert. I want to do something with my life.'

'What could be more important than bringing up a child?' He withdrew his hand. 'Does Jim Docherty know about this plan? I'm not sure he'd appreciate you and Gerry Mann distracting one of his students with something as impractical as art classes.'

'No, he doesn't. And I'm not going to tell him either. I get the impression he doesn't approve of me. He'll put a stop to it, say it's not relevant to Joseph's studies, that I'm not qualified to teach.'

'And he would be right on both counts.'

Evelyn felt the blood rise in her face. 'Thank you.'

'Docherty is no fool, you know. He'll soon find out what you're up to when he sees you at the college.'

Evelyn looked down at their hands, now nearly as brown as Robert's. She spoke casually. 'I could teach him here.'

Robert stood up. 'That's out of the question, I forbid it.'

Evelyn stood up and faced him, outraged. 'What do you mean, you forbid it?' They glared at each other for moment before she laughed lightly and put her hand on his chest.

'Let's not quarrel, darling.' But Robert shook her off, his expression rigid. This wasn't the affable man with the dry laugh she'd met in London, the man who adored her and everything she did. Here, in Africa, he had reverted to type: a white man in charge. Evelyn realised how little she had known about him back in London. She let her hand drop and spoke coldly. 'Why do you object to me mentoring a young artist? Is it because he's black?' He ran his hands through his hair and she could see where it had begun to go grey at the temples.

'Of course it's because he's bloody black, and because you're a white woman. It wouldn't look good.'

Evelyn folded her arms across her chest. 'You sound like that Neanderthal Jacobs.' Robert closed his eyes and pinched the bridge of his nose. He put his arm around her and made her sit down. Evelyn kept her back stiff.

'I keep forgetting you don't know what it's like here,' he said. 'That there are unspoken rules we all follow in order to live side by side without killing each other. It's only a few years since there was a colour bar, with everyone strictly segregated: whites, blacks, coloureds and Asians,' he said. 'There's not supposed to be a colour bar anymore but we still follow the same rules and everyone knows how it works. This is a small place and people will talk. If you take him up, it won't do this boy any good, either. His own people will shun him.'

Evelyn fought to control her temper. 'For God's sake! Joseph isn't a boy: he's a young man, old enough to make his own decisions without worrying about idle gossip. As am I.' Robert took her hand again. She desperately wanted to push him away; instead she felt the calluses on his palm, traced the white scar where his knuckles had

130

once split open. A hunting accident he'd said. The knife had slipped when he'd been gutting a gazelle.

Evelyn kept her eyes on the scar while she spoke carefully and quietly. 'I need to do this. I don't want to be another useless white madam with too much time on my hands. I can't be that person. I won't be that person. I want to love Africa the way you do, but to do that I need to get involved, not just be an onlooker, an outsider.' She raised her eyes to his and let the tears spill unchecked down her cheeks. 'I'm so unhappy.' He was listening to her now, looking at her intently, the way he had the first time they'd met. She kissed his mouth, felt his lips soften. 'Let them talk,' she said. 'The world is changing. I know Joseph has real talent but he needs encouragement. Your work is important, advising the new Government so they can run their own affairs. Well, this is work I can do.' Evelyn kissed him again and felt the heat build between them. For the first time since the attack, she wanted her husband, desperately. She climbed into his lap and pushed him back onto the bed. 'If I can do this one thing, I know I'll be happy again. And then I'll be ready to have a baby, I promise.'

131

SPIES

Chrissie was playing spies with Elijah when she saw Joseph arrive at Mrs Fielding's bungalow. She and Elijah had snuck through a hole in the fence between the two houses and hidden in the mulberry bush. The bush must have rustled because the leaves parted and Joseph peered down at them.

'Hello, little lizard' he said.

She put her finger to her lips. 'Shh! Don't tell anyone we're here.'

He smiled at Elijah. 'What is the game, little brother? Tell me and I will keep your secret.'

'We are spies. I am James Bond, my number is oh-oh seven and I am licensed to kill,' Elijah said.

Joseph put his head to one side as if he were thinking hard. 'Who is this James Bond?'

Elijah spread his palms to explain. 'The Queen's spy, On Her Majesty's Secret Service.' He grinned. 'I saw him in a film.' Chrissie's father had started open-air screenings at the college, projected on to the outside wall. The audience sat on benches while moths and white flying ants danced in the glow from the film.

Joseph hunkered down and whispered, 'You are very noisy spies.' He laughed in his throat, softly, and Elijah and Chrissie began to giggle. He shushed them and looked around, as if checking for enemy agents. 'You must be quiet, like the leopard, then you will be first-class spies.'

They watched him go up on the veranda and knock on the screen door. The Fieldings' new maid opened it and stood for a moment, her hands behind her back, swinging her hips a little. Chrissie remembered her mum talking to her dad. *Have you heard the latest? Evelyn Fielding tried to fire poor old Sixpence, but Robert wouldn't have it – Sixpence has been with him for years. She came over here looking for sympathy but I told her it wasn't worth falling out with her husband, that she'd just have to learn to get on with Sixpence but that she should take on her own maid as well, a Jehovah's Witness, otherwise she'd be robbed blind. I asked Samson to send round one of his relatives.*

'Look, it is Precious,' Elijah said. 'She is my sister. She came to back to live with us when her husband didn't want her any more. He was angry because she could not have a baby.'

Chrissie didn't know what Elijah was talking about. She had never really thought about babies and where they came from, and didn't want to think about it now. Chrissie made pretend binoculars with her fingers and studied Precious. She wrote 'new maid' in her spy book and beckoned to Elijah. They crept out of the mulberry bush and up to the veranda wall, stealthy as leopards, just as Joseph had said. Chrissie could hear a murmur of voices that grew clearer as they drew nearer.

'I'm sorry, I do not speak Chichewa, please speak English,' Joseph was saying. Chrissie and Elijah peered through a gap in the concrete walls and saw Joseph's big, bright smile that was as warm as the African sun. Precious giggled and put her hand over her mouth. She smoothed her white apron over her pink gingham uniform and looked at him shyly.

'Do you have a girlfriend?' she said in English.

Joseph shook his head and laughed. 'No, until today I had not met anyone as pretty as you.'

Precious beamed at him. 'To ask me out, you should have gone to the kitchen door, not the front door.'

Joseph looked up at her, his eyes wide, and stammered: 'Oh, I'm sorry, Miss, I didn't come to see you, I...' Chrissie heard Mrs Fielding's voice, high and piercing after the lilt of Precious and Joseph's conversation. Elijah had once told her that Europeans sounded like dogs barking when they talked.

'Joseph, is that you?' Mrs Fielding called from inside. 'Come in and we'll find a quiet corner. I've managed to find my drawing materials.'

Joseph smiled sheepishly at Precious, who stood in his way, glaring, and squeezed past her. After the screen door slammed shut behind him, Precious stayed on the veranda and slapped her own face with a sharp crack. Chrissie winced and sat back on her heels, unsettled. When she looked again, Precious had taken up a brush and was sweeping the veranda as if she were punishing it. Sixpence came out and began setting the table for lunch. Elijah shuffled closer to her to get a better look, standing on a twig and breaking it. Sixpence looked in their direction, like a cat that has heard a mouse in the bushes. Chrissie and Elijah ducked down and after a moment he turned his attention to Precious as she started to speak in English.

'That Barotse, he thinks that white lady is better than me? I'm not good enough for this cheeky mission boy? Plenty village boys like me, yes they do, but the Barotse always think they are better than the rest of us – tch.' She sucked her teeth and banged the broom against the steps releasing a cloud of dust and dead insects. Precious stopped sweeping and hid her face in her apron, her shoulders heaving as if she were crying. After a while, she wiped her eyes and began talking to Sixpence in Chichewa. He stood still as a boulder and listened. When he answered her, Chrissie could hear the urgency in his voice and he gestured wildly, as if telling Precious what to do. The maid took a step backwards and said *iyayi*. No! They walked back into the house, arguing. What were they talking about? Chrissie wished she could speak better Chichewa; their words had been like a fast-flowing river and she couldn't follow what they had said. She turned to Elijah and saw that he looked frightened. She pointed towards the disused chicken hut that was their den and they raced towards it, bent double.

When they got to the hut's black mouth, Elijah poked a stick in first to make sure there were no snakes and Chrissie followed him in. They were proud of their den: it had taken days to shovel out the layers of chicken manure and build up the walls with some spare bricks they'd found. They used a sheet of corrugated iron for a roof, and it had become Chrissie's job to keep the floor clean with her toy dustpan and brush. She pulled on the evening glove she'd stolen from her mother so her knuckles wouldn't get scraped raw on the beaten earth floor and began sweeping.

'What did Sixpence say?'

Elijah leant his chin on his knees and watched her. 'He said Precious should speak to the witchdoctor.'

Chrissie stopped brushing and sat down opposite him, their knees touching. 'To Nyirongo? Why?'

'He said the Barotse is a *nfiti* and has put a spell on their madam to make her love him.'

Chrissie frowned. 'Sixpence said Joseph is a witch?' She remembered the charm hanging around his neck, the silver coin threaded with string. A witch wouldn't have a charm against other witches – it didn't make sense. 'What will they do to Joseph, if they think he is a witch?'

Elijah shook his head. 'Bad things, to make him sick, maybe to make him die.'

Chrissie pulled off the glove and threw it into the corner. 'We have to help him. Joseph is on our side, he's a goodie. We should go back to Mrs Fielding's house and warn him when he comes out.'

Chrissie and Elijah made their way back through the garden and crept around the Fieldings' bungalow. When they heard music coming from a side window, they crouched down underneath it to listen. Chrissie put her finger to her lips and Elijah nodded. She poked her head above the windowsill, and what she saw made her forget to duck back down. Joseph held Mrs Fielding in his arms and they were spinning round and round the room, like the two dancers on her music box. Mrs Fielding's cheeks were pink and she was laughing. Chrissie held her breath: she'd never seen anyone look so beautiful. Elijah pulled at the hem of her dress but she batted him away, so he came up for a look too. After a while, Elijah giggled and grabbed Chrissie's hand and pulled her to her feet, and they began to dance too. The two children went round in circles, copying the adults, their bare feet kicking up little clouds of dust as they swayed and dipped to the rise and fall of the music. It came to an end and the record crackled on the turntable. Chrissie and Elijah went back to the windowsill and watched Evelyn put on another record. Chrissie was so intent on the scene that she didn't notice someone had come up behind her until her ear was pinched hard and she and Elijah were jerked away from the window. Chrissie kicked out and was dropped on the ground. She stared up at Sixpence who scowled down at them, his arms crossed.

'Don't you hear your mother calling for you?' he said to Chrissie. He pointed at Elijah and spoke to him in Chichewa. When he bared his teeth and growled at them, they ran as fast as they could, scattering in different directions. When Chrissie got to the fence, she stopped and looked back. Sixpence stood at the open window, as still as a leopard, watching Mrs Fielding and Joseph dance.

WHITE GLOVES
AND PETTICOATS

Joseph held Evelyn lightly, his hand barely touching the base of her spine, but they swooped and spun around the room as if they were one person. As they waltzed, she threw back her head and closed her eyes, and felt the back of her neck prickle, as if she were being watched. She opened her eyes to see a shape at the window: the silhouette of a man with the setting sun behind him. Joseph whipped her around again and when she next faced the window it was empty. A trick of the light, she thought. She smiled up at Joseph and he grinned back at her.

Joseph had been reluctant to dance at first. He'd held his pale palms out to her as if for inspection and frowned. 'I have no white gloves. We always wore white gloves at the missionary school dances. And the boys wore suits and the girls coloured dresses with many petticoats. They looked so pretty, like butterflies.'

Evelyn had laughed. 'Well, we may not have white gloves and I certainly don't have layers of tulle and netting, but I want to dance, so, shall we?' She'd put her head to one side. 'We'll call it a Ladies' Excuse Me. Don't tell me you're going to turn me down? That would be bad manners.' She'd taken a record out of its sleeve – it must have dated back to the 1950s from the artwork – and put it on the turntable. The room had instantly filled with big band, dancehall favourites and they'd both laughed when she'd stepped into his arms.

As they'd turned around the room, their feet working together, her shoulders had begun to relax for the first time in weeks. Robert had been spending longer and longer away from the house, meeting the chiefs in the district to set up the new district court system. He'd been exhausted and travel-stained after these trips, but instead of leaving him alone to rest, she couldn't stop herself babbling at him, desperate to talk to another person after yet another lonely day. As the weather grew hotter and the grasslands turned dry and brown, Evelyn felt as if she was fading too, and that one day there would be nothing left of her but dust. When Joseph had arrived at the bungalow earlier that afternoon with his drawings, cheerful enthusiasm, and quick, enquiring eyes, it was as if the rains had come at last.

They had spent the best part of two hours looking at his work and as he'd talked about it, he'd become more animated, Soon they were laughing, heads together like colleagues, Evelyn making suggestions as he listened gravely or explained what he was trying to achieve. At first, she'd assumed she would be able to help him put his work in context by teaching him about modern art movements, but she'd had to revise her opinion when she picked up a drawing that was all angles and planes.

'My Cubist period.' His laugh was self-deprecating. 'It was too derivative of Picasso and his friend Braque. These are better, I think.' He'd pulled out a sheaf of drawings in coloured pastels: vivid market scenes of women hawking fruit, men leaning against oil drums drinking beer, children chasing chickens through the legs of adults. They'd taken a break then, and he'd spied the dance record, taken it out of its wire rack and looked at it so wistfully she decided they should have some fun together.

As they spun round and round the room smiling at each other in delight, Evelyn imagined Joseph walking through Bloomsbury to university lectures, a portfolio under his arm, a muffler around his neck and wearing a velvet jacket, every bit the artist. She would introduce him to gallery directors and arrange exhibitions. *Yes, I did discover him* she would admit with a modest smile, *but his talent, so powerful, so vibrant, speaks for itself, don't you think?* And with the lightest of laughs she'd say, *Like Picasso, only the real thing!*

'Excuse me, Madam.'

Precious was standing in the sitting-room doorway holding a soup tureen. Joseph dropped his arms and stepped back, but the waltz music kept playing. Evelyn crossed the room and picked up the record player's arm; it skipped across a track, scoring a deep scratch into the black vinyl.

She spun on her heel to face the maid and raised her voice. 'For God's sake, can't you see I'm busy?' Evelyn bit her lip. She hadn't meant to snap at the girl, but it was too late to take it back now. She pressed her hand to her hairline, damp with sweat from the dancing, and made an effort to moderate her tone. 'Yes, what is it?'

Precious wouldn't look at her. Damn it, the girl was going to sulk. As if it wasn't bad enough dealing with Sixpence. When she'd hired her at Grace Docherty's suggestion, Evelyn had wanted to befriend the maid so she'd have an ally against Sixpence, but her chummy overtures had been met with alarm and, more recently, a barely detectable smirk of derision.

Precious lowered her eyes and covered her mouth. 'Madam, dinner is ready.' She lifted the lid off the tureen and Evelyn could smell the curried chicken. Her stomach turned over: mulligatawny again. Couldn't Sixpence cook anything else?

'All right, I'll be along in a moment. Joseph, will you join me for dinner?' His eyes widened and she heard Precious gasp. What was wrong with these people? You'd think she'd just asked him to come and watch her undress. Joseph shook his head and mumbled. 'No?' Evelyn said, unable to quell her irritation at the absurdity of the situation. They had just been talking like equals, dancing together, for Heaven's sake. 'Well, we can resume our lesson at the same time next week.'

He gathered up his drawings and left the room without looking at her. The ease and friendliness they'd shared had disappeared as soon as Precious had come into the room. Evelyn watched Joseph as he walked back out into the dry wall of heat: his shoulders were hunched as he trudged through the dust. The sooner she got him out of this place, the better.

My Father's House

A few weeks after the art lesson, Gerry Mann was driving away from the house when Robert arrived back from his latest trip. It was dark and Evelyn waited for him at the top of the steps in the yellow pool cast by the veranda light.

'You're back early,' she said.

He turned to watch the plume of dust disappear over the hill. 'Evidently. What was he doing here?'

'Just paying a friendly visit, you know.'

Robert's face darkened. 'No, I don't know.'

A bubble of anger rose in Evelyn's chest. 'Gerry's a good friend. What's wrong with that? I have no one else to talk to – you're away so much. And when you do come back, you shut yourself away with your papers. I don't know why you bothered to marry me, you don't seem to care for my company at all.' Evelyn stopped herself; her mother used the same plaintive voice with her father when he came home, rumpled and weary from the office.

Robert walked up the steps and put his arms around her. 'I'm sorry. I've been having a rough time of it lately. Work is… well, I won't bore you.' He let her go and they sat down together on the veranda. 'I know I've been neglecting you, and that I've been a bear.' He ran his hand through his hair. 'I've another meeting with the bastarding *wabenzies* tomorrow, God help me. I'm just not cut out for this job – can't get a thing done. The civil service is a complete shambles. I didn't think I'd still be doing this; it's not what I planned for us. My bloody, bloody father.'

Evelyn kicked her sandals off and tucked her feet under her. Robert looked worn out, but at least he was talking to her again. 'You thought you'd be running Pembroke by now?' He nodded and she laid her head on his shoulder. 'Tell me what it's like.'

Robert stared down at his hands, loosely clasped between his legs. 'It's like nowhere else on earth.' He looked up and she saw that his eyes were ringed with fatigue. 'Would you like to see it?'

'I'd love to.'

His doleful expression lifted and he looked ten years younger. 'Come on then,' he said and pulled her to her feet. 'We'll need an early night if we're to leave at first light.'

She straightened her skirt and laughed. 'What about the bastarding *wabenzies*?'

He grinned. 'Bugger them. Go and pack, we're going on safari.'

She was heading indoors when he put his hand on her shoulder and asked: 'What did Mann want?'

Evelyn kept her expression neutral and matched his tone; she didn't want to spoil his mood with another ridiculous fight. Robert was bound to disapprove of the real reason for Gerry's visit. 'Oh nothing much. I told you, just a social call.' She didn't tell him that Gerry had proposed taking her to Lusaka to meet some of his political activist friends, or that she had readily agreed. Helping Joseph had woken Evelyn from a dream and she was buzzing with energy, restless to take action. Why shouldn't she broaden her political horizons, as Gerry put it? The world was changing, that's what everyone kept saying. And Evelyn wanted to change with it.

She slipped through the door into the house but Robert called after her: 'Well, don't get too chummy with Mann; he has some dangerous ideas and he keeps some odd company. Since Kaunda declared a one-party state there has been a clampdown, a ban on political meetings with agitators thrown out of the country, or worse. There's already a file on Mann – he's trouble.'

It was uncanny, almost as if Robert knew what they'd been talking about. How did he know so much about Gerry's political leanings? She remembered what Jim Docherty had said: Robert was the *Boma* and the Africans respected him as the law around here. Perhaps they feared him, too, and brought him offerings of secret nuggets of information. She tried to make out his expression through the screen door, but he had turned away and stood with his back to her, looking out at the shadows the moon cast over the hills.

Robert was already dressed and had packed the Land Rover when he woke her before dawn.

'The roof in the old place was threatening to fall in the last time I was there so we'll probably have to camp out,' he said. Evelyn ran to change into a pair of canvas trousers and her tennis shoes when he frowned at her summer dress and high-heeled sandals and asked: 'Is that what you're wearing?'

He drove for hours without stopping and Evelyn watched the sky lighten into a rose gold before settling into a deep blue untroubled by clouds. It was the height of the dry season and Robert told her they would see plenty of game as the herds roamed the bush looking for water, but all she could see for miles was brown scrubland. At first they passed women on their way to market with bundles on their heads, barefooted children on their way to school, and men on bicycles. But as they travelled further east, they were alone in the African wilderness. It was impossible to talk for long over the din of the Land Rover's engine, and soon Evelyn leaned her head against the window, her eyes growing heavy. She was about to succumb to sleep when she saw a family of giraffes loping along beside them, keeping pace. She leaned forward and begged Robert to stop, but when he cut the engine they veered away and galloped off into the bush. Robert started the engine again and they rode off with a lurch and crunch of wheels.

'Don't worry, plenty more of them where we're going,' he shouted.

And he was right. They passed wildebeest with their long, mournful faces, and a herd of pot-bellied zebras swung in an arc, kicking their hooves behind them. The sun was high in the sky when they started to climb a hill track, the engine revving and tyres spinning as the Land Rover strained against the gradient. Evelyn was stiff and sore by the time they drove under an arch with 'Pembroke'

142

picked out in contrasting bricks. Robert stopped the Land Rover and they got out. Below them a lake shimmered like a sapphire. Evelyn watched a flock of pink flamingos take to the sky, circle, and settle again on the water. Robert took off his bush hat and wiped his forehead with the back of his arm. He came to stand beside her.

'I used to dream about this place when I was at school in England.' He put his face up to the sun and Evelyn watched the strain leave him.

'You should be here,' she said. 'It's where you belong.' She looked out over the lake and felt at peace, her restlessness stilled by the sight of the ruffled surface of the water. 'It's strange, but I feel as if I've been here before,' she said.

Robert put his arm around her waist and pressed her to his side. 'There's a local legend that this is where God used to live. He was lonely and created the first man and woman out of clay from the lake and put them in charge of the animals. But the African Adam and Eve and their children soon made a mess of things, and God was so disgusted he climbed up into the sky and never came back.'

'There are worse places to be abandoned,' Evelyn said. 'So this is the Garden of Eden?'

'Yes, with crocodiles. The lake looks tempting but I wouldn't advise taking a dip.'

'Even with crocodiles, it's the most beautiful place on Earth. No wonder you dreamt about it. Why ever did your family leave?'

Robert shook his head. 'Let's not spoil the day. Come on, I'll show you around.'

They drove up a broken driveway past an overgrown rose garden where the bushes had returned to their wild state so the thorny branches lashed the side of the Land Rover. On the other side of the thicket lay what had once been a lawn and was now a tangled meadow of dry grasses where butterflies danced. And beyond was Pembroke. The brickwork was crumbling and the roof had fallen in, but Evelyn could see the bones of its beauty through the decay.

She got out of the Land Rover and gazed at the house in delighted astonishment. 'It's an English stately home. In the middle of Africa.'

'My mother loved England. It was the only way my father could persuade her to come out here,' Robert said. He pushed open the heavy door, which had been chewed by termites, and they walked into the cathedral-like space. Cracked flagstones stretched out across the vast hall and half a staircase spiralled upwards before disappearing into nowhere, like a surrealist's dream. Shafts of light flooded in through the arched windows and fell in golden pools. Evelyn stepped into one of them and looked up into the light.

'It's like swimming in sunlight,' she said, holding out her hands.

'You look like you're made of gold,' said Robert in a hushed voice.

Evelyn spun round slowly. 'Can we sleep here tonight?'

Robert laughed. 'If the roof doesn't fall in on us. I'll get the camping things. And then let's eat, I'm starving.' He cooked steaks and eggs over a primus stove, refusing to let her help, and afterwards they drank strong coffee laced with brandy from a flask.

'This is the best meal I've ever had,' she said.

He wiped steak juice off her chin with his thumb. 'Food always tastes better on safari.'

Evelyn began to unbutton her shirt. 'What else is better on safari?'

He pushed her gently on top of the sleeping bag and pulled at her waistband. 'Let's find out.'

Robert lit an oil lamp and hung it from the branch of a small tree that had pushed its way through the flagstones. He opened a canvas tube and unrolled the paper it held, smoothing it flat on the floor. Evelyn watched him in the flickering light cast by the fire he'd made in the hearth. Here, in this primitive shelter, she felt closer than she'd ever been to him. Now, perhaps she could tell him about the attack in the sugar cane fields, explain to him why she'd pushed him away for weeks, that it wasn't through disgust but fear. She drank some more brandy to give herself courage and went to crouch beside him. The night air was chilly this high up and she'd pulled on one of Robert's sweaters.

She peered down at what looked like plans. 'What are they for?'

Robert pointed to one section. 'It's Pembroke, or what I'd like it to become. This is where I want to build the farm, so the estate could be self-sufficient.' He pointed again. 'And this is the village, with a clinic and a school and a subsidised store. The goods can be brought in by truck from Lusaka once a month.'

Evelyn smoothed a corner of the blueprint. 'What about running safaris?' She looked around at the cavernous hall. 'This place would make a wonderful lodge. Plenty of people would pay a fortune to stay here.'

Robert looked at Evelyn as if seeing her for the first time. 'It could work' he said slowly. 'But it's all a pipe dream. I don't have the money to do any of this – my father made sure of that.' He rolled up the blueprint and put it away, distracted once again, and Evelyn realised the moment had passed and she'd missed her chance to tell him about the attack in the sugar cane field.

While Robert set up their camp beds, Evelyn explored the old house. Most of the rooms were empty, the windows curtained with overgrown creepers that turned the light green. In one room, scattered with torn picture books, she found the iron skeleton of a child's cot, it's bedding eaten away by termites. In another, the ruined carcass of a four-poster bed listed to one side, its silk canopy tattered like so many flags after a battle. Evelyn's foot knocked against something solid that rolled away and she bent to pick it up. It was a scent bottle, its contents dried to a yellow smear. The faded label read *Lily of the Valley*.

'That was my mother's.' Evelyn gasped. She hadn't heard Robert come up behind her until he spoke. He put his hands on her shoulders. 'Are you all right?'

Her heart was racing. 'You gave me a start, that's all.' She stepped into the room and her tennis shoes left prints in the fine dust. 'Was this her bedroom?'

'Yes.' He walked over to what was left of the bed and stared down into its dark recess. 'This is where I saw her last. In bed with my father's best friend.' Robert's face was corpse-pale in the underwater-tinted light. Evelyn wanted to touch him, comfort him; but she also wanted to know more.

'Go on.'

He stared into a speckled mirror that still clung to a crumbling plaster wall, as if he could see into his past. His laugh was a bark – shocking and violent, like a curse. 'Good old Uncle Bill. He was the great white hunter, taught me to shoot, how to survive in the bush, even knew how to fly a plane. He was every English boy's idea of a hero, but he turned out to be an utter shit.'

Evelyn put her hand in his and felt along the familiar lines on his palm. She had often looked at the framed photograph Robert kept of his mother, and now she imagined that perfect face with its arched eyebrows and glossy, shingled hair lying on a pillow next to her lover, her perfect lipstick smudged and eyes sleepy with sex while her child looked on in white-faced shock.

Evelyn pressed his hand to her mouth. 'My darling, how awful for you. What did your mother do?'

Robert's voice was dry. 'She didn't see me.' He jerked his head as if he were shaking water out of his hair. 'I ran out of the house all the way to my nanny's room in the servants' compound and stayed there until I heard him drive away. I had to go back to boarding school the next day and when my mother tried to kiss me goodbye I turned my head away. I walked out of the door without saying goodbye to her. I wanted to hurt her. A week later the headmaster called me into his office and told me to be brave, that my mother was dead. I don't remember what happened next, but I'm told I went along the corridor that overlooked the quad, smashing all the windows.'

Evelyn heard him breathe deeply and imagined a crack opening up in a wall. She had never seen him so vulnerable. Like most men of his class, an austere boarding school regime had taught Robert to keep his emotions under house arrest. But now it was as if he had stepped out of his protective carapace to stand before her, naked. She wanted to weep for him; for his cauterised feelings, for the self-contained, rigid man he had been forced to become.

He took her into his arms and spoke into her hair. 'That's why, the thought of you, with someone – I couldn't bear it, don't you see? I thought you'd been seeing that bastard Gerry Mann.'

Evelyn pulled away and smoothed the hair away from his darkened eyes. She decided then she could never tell him about that terrible day in the sugar cane field. It would kill him.

CHICKEN IN A BASKET

Chrissie and Hamish sat with their mother under the big mimosa tree in the courtyard of the Ridgeway Hotel. The drooping yellow blossoms brushed the tops of their heads and made a gold-green arbour for them. Cat was asleep on their mother's knee, thumb in her mouth and cheeks pink. It was hot even in the shade and Grace was fanning them both with the menu. Chrissie kicked the bench as she waited for lunch to arrive and looked around the courtyard at all the families with kids, wondering what it would be like to live in the city all the time. Mum didn't like it, said it was dirty and dusty, a nothing town in the middle of nowhere, but to Chrissie, used to the emptiness of the bush, Lusaka was a bustling metropolis full of fascinating sights. She liked to pick up the malachite eggs with their polished green swirls and the copper bracelets, laid out on the vendors' blankets under the frangipani trees that divided Cairo Road. The city's main thoroughfare was now named Independence Avenue, but it was still better known by its old name. When it was first built, Cairo Road was supposed to go all the way up to Egypt. Chrissie was wondering what it would be like to go to school on a camel and live in the desert when she spotted Mrs Fielding in the corner of the restaurant. She was laughing and tossed her head so her pale hair swished over a bare shoulder. Chrissie raised her hand to say hello but couldn't catch her attention.

'Who are you waving at, Chrissie?' her mum said.

'Mrs Fielding over there.' She pointed and her mum twisted

round with difficulty, Cat still on her lap, but turned back quickly. A waiter put their food on the table; the chicken in the basket smelled good in the sun. Chrissie crammed some chips into her mouth. 'Did you see her? She's over there with Creepy Gerry Mann.'

'Eat your lunch and don't talk with your mouth full.' Her mother spoke sharply and frowned behind her sunglasses. Chrissie wondered what was wrong, and why she didn't get up and say hello to Mrs Fielding, and why she hadn't gotten on to Chrissie for calling Gerry Mann creepy. She wanted to ask her mother why the atmosphere was so tense, but didn't know how to ask the question, just that the afternoon had soured. Hamish put out his hand to steal her chips and they started to squabble and kicked each other under the table for the rest of the meal. Chrissie forgot all about Mrs Fielding and Gerry Mann until much later, during the car journey home to Chalimbana.

Their parents were talking in the front while Hamish and Chrissie showed Cat how to play Snap on the back seat. Cat was cheating but they didn't mind because they liked to hear her crow with laughter every time she won.

'The audio equipment's arrived,' their father said. 'It's stored in the office – you should see it, huge crates, must have cost a packet. They're going to bring them to Chalimbana on lorries as soon as the language lab's ready. Shouldn't be long now, just the thatched roof to go on. Did I tell you it'll be the largest thatched building in the whole of Zambia? What do you think of that, Grace?' He grinned and slapped the steering wheel.

'Big deal,' their mother sniffed.

Chrissie went still to listen more closely and saw Hamish do the same. Mum was in a filthy mood, and had been snapping at them all afternoon while they trailed around the empty department stores and waited for their lift home. But their father failed to pick up on her mood and carried on talking to her rigid profile.

'Come on, Grace, you must admit, it's some achievement bringing the latest technology over to the middle of the African bush. The audio equipment will help the students learn English intonation. Just now, I get them to repeat a simple declarative sentence and they sing it back to me, in harmony. Very musical it is too, but not quite the Queen's English.' He laughed lightly, ignoring his wife's stony expression.

'I don't know why you bother.' Another sniff, louder this time. Hamish and Chrissie looked at each other over Cat's head. Hamish drew his finger across his throat and pointed at the back of their father's head with his thumb. Dad spoke through his teeth and slowed down his words as if he was talking to an idiot and Chrissie lowered her head, knowing a storm was about to break.

'I bother, Grace, because it's my job, and it's an important job. They desperately need teachers here, and better schools. It's the only way for them to make it on their own. We can't just abandon them, not after years of depriving generations of even the most basic education.' He stuck out his chin. 'We Scots helped to build the Empire and it's only right that we see it through, do our duty.'

'Empire! Duty! Would you listen to yourself? What pompous rubbish! They don't want us here. You should be thinking of your own family, stuck in this godforsaken place in the middle of nowhere, filth and disease everywhere, no decent shops, that awful school, and the children running wild.'

'The kids are perfectly happy – I'd have given my eye teeth to have the kind of freedom they have growing up. Living in Africa! I could only dream about countries like these when I was their age. Thank God for Andrew Carnegie and his libraries. I learned about the wide world from books, just think Grace, our children live in it.'

Chrissie agreed with her dad: she couldn't imagine living in the grey town where her father had grown up and where her grandmother still lived, with its row upon row of council houses. The year she had spent in Edinburgh had convinced her that she never wanted to go back. Just then, Chrissie had a moment where she felt completely present and alive, filled with a bright, clear joy, for the big copper sun, the dusty air, the red dirt roads and the brown grasslands that rolled away into the blue blur of the hills. The sensation was fleeting and vanished when the car bumped over the cattle grid, which meant they were nearly home. Her mother's beehive hit the roof of the car. She clutched it and started taking pins out, stabbing them back into place with a ferocity that told Chrissie her mood had worsened if anything.

'May I remind you, Jim Docherty, that one of your sons is in boarding school, thousands of miles away, and that your other son, who is only eleven, is about to join him there. I didn't have children to send them away.' A tear rolled out from under her cat's eyes sunglasses, and Chrissie winced. She saw that Hamish was looking studiously out of the window, oblivious to Cat's attempts to fold each playing card in half.

Her father rubbed his eyes under his glasses. 'Grace, we've been over this a hundred times. The chaps at the Foreign Office say it's for the best, that a public school will give the boys connections, a good start – better than I had.'

'There was nothing wrong with where we came from. You should never have brought us here. I miss home.' She started to sob and Chrissie wondered whether to risk patting her mother on the shoulder, but decided it was too dangerous.

'Grace, you forget what it was like at home: the small-mindedness, people sitting over their wee half-pints asking what religion you are or what bloody school you went to.' He rolled his shoulders as if shaking something troubling off them. 'I couldn't go back to that. And what about everyone knowing your business? Sneering if you wanted a different life?' He banged the steering wheel. 'I'll not go back to it. I won't.'

'For God's sake, Jim, can you no ...' They were both shouting now and Chrissie tried to stop listening. She looked desperately at Hamish but he wouldn't turn round. Cat had her thumb in her mouth and was trying to shove her head into Chrissie's armpit. Her mum's voice was shrill. 'And this is better? Stuck out here in the middle of bloody nowhere, away from our families? We should be at home, where people at least know how to behave.' Chrissie's father was taken aback, and the tension in the car eased. It was like the wind dropping after a squall.

'What do you mean?'

'I saw that Evelyn Fielding at the Ridgeway with Gerry Mann. It's disgraceful the way she's carrying on.' Chrissie's father was silent for a while, watching the road as he negotiated the Bentley around a pothole the size of a small swimming pool. He wound down the window to help him steer and let in a hot blast of dusty air.

'I'm sure it was all perfectly innocent,' he said once the window was closed again.

'There's been talk that she's spending an awful lot of time with him while her husband's been up country on government business.'

Dad clucked his tongue, his anger forgotten. 'Talk! There's always *talk* amongst the wives. Don't you have anything better to do?'

'It's not right – she's a married woman. Would you like it if I went out for lunch with another man?' The car turned into their drive and stopped outside the house. Chrissie's father leaned over and stroked the side of her mother's face.

'No, no I would not,' he said softly.

Her mother smiled. 'Och, Jim.'

And Chrissie, who had been holding her breath, sighed.

THE BOTTLE SHOP

Evelyn sighed and put down her napkin. 'That was delicious, thank you.'

Gerry grinned at her. 'I knew a trip into town would cheer you up, and the Ridgeway always does a good lunch. Consider this a holiday from bungalow-land.' He pushed aside his plate and clicked his fingers for more drinks.

Evelyn looked out over the garden for the weaverbirds she liked to watch. She stretched her legs out underneath the table; it felt good to be out of the house and away from Chalimbana. Robert was away again and she'd just started to climb the walls with boredom when Gerry had shown up and reminded her of their plan to meet some of his activist friends. She'd hesitated for a moment, knowing Robert wouldn't like it if he found out, but just then the wind had pushed open the kitchen swing door and she'd spotted Sixpence and Precious huddled together in whispered conversation. She'd picked up her handbag and hurried out the door with Gerry: anything to avoid another day of being watched and silently judged by their resentful faces.

The waiter approached their table and Evelyn put her hand over her glass. 'Not for me.'

'Nonsense,' Gerry said. 'You need the quinine for the malaria.' She removed her hand and the waiter poured a jigger of gin into her tumbler and a splash of Indian tonic. His white gloves made her think of Joseph.

'Thank you for sending Joseph to me.'

'How's he doing?'

Evelyn picked up her glass and took a sip. It was too strong but it was deliciously cold and she drank some more. 'I don't know how much I'm helping him, if I'm honest. His work is so original and I don't want to spoil it by teaching him lots of dreary tricks. And, technically, he's already pretty proficient. Joseph is a one-off but I'm not sure he realises it. I wish you would tell him.'

Gerry Mann drained his whisky. 'Drink up and you can tell him yourself.'

'He's not here, is he?' Evelyn looked around but saw only white faces seated at the tables. Wasn't that the Dochertys? She tried to catch Grace's attention but she was busy gathering up the children and they were gone before she could wave hello. 'I think I've just seen Grace Docherty.' She said. 'I wonder why she didn't stop? She's usually so friendly.'

Gerry pulled out her chair. 'If it was Grace, she'll be gossiping like mad about us, mark my words.' He waved his hand dismissively. 'Don't mind her, the nosy mare. Tell you what, let's give her something to gossip about and leave arm in arm.'

She hesitated then took his arm. Outside the hotel, she saw Grace and her children standing in the shade of a jacaranda tree. When she looked over at them, Evelyn suddenly felt ashamed of her childishness and dropped Gerry's arm. Her neighbour had been kind to her and here she was behaving like a naughty schoolgirl. Gerry rested his hand on the small of her back to guide her across the road and Evelyn regretted how familiar she'd allowed him to become through a mixture of loneliness and vanity. She fell back to walk behind him a pace and he turned and smiled at her.

'Come on, slow coach. We're going to meet up with Joseph, and some friends of mine. I think you'll find them interesting.' He lowered his voice and took her arm again. 'They're trying to set up a new pro-democracy party, in opposition to Kaunda. But you're not to tell your *Boma* husband about this or my friends will get into hot water. It'll be our little secret.'

They went up a series of side streets, which took them away from the centre of the city and into a maze of houses that were little more than shacks with zinc roofs. Old women sat on low stools at their doorways and watched them as they scurried through the dirt-packed streets. Skirting a ditch full of empty bottles and cans, they came to a door in a wall. Gerry knocked and they waited. Evelyn could hear music, loud and pulsing, with electric guitars whining. The door opened a crack and Gerry muttered something. He slipped inside and she followed close on his heels. They plunged into a hot throng of young people in Afros and bell-bottoms, the men in loud shirts and the women with blouses tied under their breasts to show off flat stomachs. They swayed and clicked their fingers to the music coming from a makeshift stage at the end of the walled compound where five men slouched over their instruments. The air smelled of pot and sweat, mixed with the sour smell of home-brewed beer. Gerry grabbed a couple of bottles from a petrol drum filled with ice and water and handed money to a man with reddened eyes. Evelyn took a sip and made a face.

'You don't like our *shake-shake*, eh?' Red eyes put his head back and gave the slow laugh that she now recognised served to cover annoyance.

She smiled uncertainly and took another drink, forcing the sour beer down her throat. 'Not at all, it's lovely, thank you.'

Gerry, unaware of her discomfort, grabbed her by the arm and led her further into the crowd towards the wall of music. He shouted in her ear, his face flushed and eyes bright. She could only catch some of what he was saying: ... *grooviest Zam Rock band in... psychedelic rock and funk... mixture of Jimi Hendrix and James Brown...* She nodded and pretended to share his enthusiasm but was dismayed when he started jerking his body to the music. She was aware they were causing some amusement and when someone jostled her so she was pressed against his chest, Evelyn shouted over the noise: 'Can we sit down?'

Gerry pointed to a cluster of white plastic chairs and some electric cable spools that served as tables. A group of young men stood up and made space for them, greeting Gerry like an old friend. He introduced Evelyn to them as students at the University of Zambia. It was quieter in their corner and soon the men started talking politics, as if taking up a conversation they'd had before many times.

'The problem with Jim Docherty and the other British Council johnnies,' Gerry was saying, 'is they can't see that we need to radicalise young Zambians, not just teach them English and impose our education system on them. Really, it's just another form of colonialism. When they sent out Docherty, I assumed he'd be a kindred spirit; a comrade. I thought working class Scots were all supposed to be socialists, but he's as reactionary as they come – just another lapdog of British imperialism.'

Evelyn liked the way Gerry's eyes shone when he spoke and the way the young men seemed to hang on his words, but she wasn't sure she agreed with him. From what she'd seen of Jim Docherty, he was nobody's lapdog. Still, Gerry was so passionate. She wished she could muster the same enthusiasm for... well for anything. Since returning from Pembroke, now that Robert had taken himself off on yet another trip, she had found herself slipping into a sort of languor, made worse by the heat that banked up more every day as the rains threatened but never arrived. When Gerry had proposed this trip to Lusaka to see 'the real Africa' she'd hoped it would shake her out of her torpor.

She studied his profile as he gestured and banged the table, and a thought stole into her mind: perhaps she ought to be with a man like Gerry: a man of conviction, who lived in the present, not the past. He was younger than Robert and didn't seem so weighed down by convention and responsibility. She listened to his flat vowels, the way he swore without thinking and she found herself wincing. There was no getting away from it: his background was different from hers. It meant he was uninhibited and irreverent, and perhaps that's why she enjoyed his company so much, but today she found herself embarrassed by the loudness of his voice and his wild gestures. She was aware of people watching them and wished he would quiet down. Evelyn took another sip of the disgusting beer and tried hard to pay attention to the conversation. She was clearly not expected to contribute as all eyes were on Gerry, but she was content to listen. He was talking about revolution and empowering the youth now, thumping the table with his fist for emphasis and making the bottles jump.

'KK is as bad as the colonials were. We've got to get rid of him. It's

time for a new generation of young Zambians to grab their destiny!'
he said.

The afternoon wore on and the more Gerry talked and drank, the
less attention he paid to Evelyn. She looked at his mouth opening
and shutting without taking in a word of what he was saying and
was reminded of her father talking about the Government's failings
to his golf cronies. It seemed men were boring when they talked
politics, wherever you were in the world. A girl in jeans stretched
tight over an ample bottom, with her Afro tied back with a scarf and
large hoops in her ears, brought them a tray of beers. Gerry paused
and said something in her ear as she bent over him and she laughed
and bumped his shoulder with her hip as though indulging a pesky
uncle. Gerry's put his arm around the girl's bare waist and stroked
it with his thumb. The girl's eyes took on a professional blankness.
The exchange made Evelyn uncomfortable and she looked away and
watched the dancers moving lithely to the music, like sea anemones
in an ocean current. Her thoughts, too, began to drift, but when she
heard another familiar name she tuned in again.

'Take Tom O'Brian. He means well, but the missionaries are
misguided fools,' Gerry was saying as he waved his beer bottle
about. 'They think they're helping, but really they're only putting a
plaster on a wound when the whole bloody leg needs amputating.'

One of the university students spoke in such a gentle singsong
you had to listen carefully to hear the rebuke in his voice. 'Father
O'Brian is a good man. He does a lot of work in Lusaka with the men
who come from the villages to find work. It is not easy to be away
from your people and there are too many tribes in Lusaka all mixed
up. It is difficult to know who you are. The church is our family here.'

Evelyn was glad someone else had spoken up for the priest.
If she'd been sitting on the Dochertys' veranda or at the Jacobs's
farm she might have spoken out in Tom O'Brian's defence, but
she instinctively knew these men would not welcome a woman's
opinion. She'd been aware that one of them had been watching
her from across the table for a while. When she caught his eye, she
looked away but it was too late. He stood up and she saw he was
wearing his shirt unbuttoned all the way to his low-slung waistband.
He rested his hand on the hard muscle of his stomach and stared at

her. Gerry was arguing about 'colonials in cassocks' and didn't look up. The man came over and put out his hand, indicating he wanted to dance. When she shook her head and smiled nervously he bent down and spoke into her ear.

'What's the matter, white lady, don't you dance with black men?' A wave of heat crawled up Evelyn's back and sweat prickled between her breasts. Appalled at being taken for a racist, she put her hand in his and sprang to her feet, following him into the crowd. Pushed tightly together by the other dancers, the man gripped her around the waist with both hands and swung his hips to the beat. She felt his erection grow against her thigh and tried to wriggle free but this only seemed to excite him more. He crooned in her ear along to the music and Evelyn could smell his sweat and the oil he used in his hair. His arms locked behind her and he began to rub against her body rhythmically. Evelyn tried to get her hands in between them to push him away but she found with a jolt of horror that she had only managed to trap them against the bare flesh of his stomach, down near his waistband. He closed his eyes and groaned. Evelyn looked over at the table for help, but Gerry was still talking, waving his damned beer bottle. It was no use: he'd abandoned her. She tried to shove the man away again but he just laughed softly. Evelyn didn't know what to do. Her throat tightened and she fought for breath in the suffocating crush. When she closed her eyes the face of the gang leader from the sugar cane field swam before her and she began to panic. There were bodies pressing into her on every side; she couldn't get free. Robert, where was Robert? She needed her husband. Why had she come out on her own again? Robert could be cold and controlling, but he would never have left her alone in a place like this, at the mercy of strangers. The man pushed his face close to hers and she twisted her head away, desperately searching for a friendly face, but all she could see was the sea of people dancing as if one to the thudding rhythm. She was the only white woman at an African shebeen. She was a fool. Just then, another man pushed his way through the crowd towards her and she cringed when he tapped her on the shoulder.

'Hello, Mrs Fielding, may I have this dance?'

'Joseph!' She didn't try to hide her relief.

His smile was as wide and friendly as ever, but she noticed for the first time that here he carried himself with an air of easy authority. Perhaps it was his height, and the long leather coat he wore that swung open over a colourful shirt and white, flared trousers, but she was aware that her dancing partner had moved away from her slightly. Joseph turned his smile on the other man, who scowled back.

'You are one of Mr Mann's friends, aren't you?' Joseph said. 'You are Mwewa Ozumba.' The man nodded and Joseph laughed in a friendly way. 'I saw you sitting with Mr Mann when I came in.' He glanced around and lowered his voice conspiratorially. 'Let me tell you, my friend, that I heard some Yellow Shirts asking if anyone had seen you.' Ozumba looked around in fear and let go of Evelyn. She watched him fight his way through the crowd and out of the door into the street, and once he had gone took a deep, ragged breath. A drunken couple lurched past, knocking her off balance, but Joseph caught her by the arm.

'Thank you,' she said and straightened up. He kept his hand on her arm and it made her feel safe. 'How did you get rid of him? And who or what are Yellow Shirts?'

He grinned. 'Government agents who do not like people breaking the law by gathering together in a public place and talking against the President.'

She felt her heartbeat slow and smiled up at her saviour. 'And of course, there aren't any of these Yellow Shirts here at all; you made it up to get rid of him.'

'Oh, no.' He pointed to the table next to Gerry Mann. 'There are two over there. You can tell they are undercover police because they are speaking ZP, which is Zambian police slang. They are too stupid to remember to talk like normal people.'

Evelyn looked closely and saw two men in white shirts, black slacks and lace-up leather shoes. Their hair was cut close to their heads and they wore aviator sunglasses. They weren't chatting or moving to the music like everyone else; they were sitting still as if listening hard behind their dark glasses.

'Oh dear, this is terrible. I should warn Gerry.'

'Do not worry; they will not arrest a white man, especially in front of all these people. But he is putting the others in danger, and he should not have left you alone.' He frowned. 'It is not safe for you here, Mrs Fielding. You are too beautiful – it makes you vulnerable. *She walks in beauty, like the night / Of cloudless climes and starry skies; / And all that's best of dark and bright / Meet in her aspect and her eyes.*'

'Byron. I love that poem.' Evelyn coloured and ducked her head, suddenly shy. She was used to compliments but it was the first one Joseph had given her. Perhaps she oughtn't to have danced with him alone in her home; he probably had a crush on her now and no doubt he expected to dance with her. But when she looked up at him, he was watching the undercover officers. And when he put his arm around her without touching her to shield her from the press of bodies and began to lead her back to her table, she felt the tiniest bit disappointed. After all, he had saved her. He deserved a dance. Where was the harm? It was beginning to get dark and strings of coloured lights had come on. The air was warm and the crowd had thinned a bit, seeming joyful to her now rather than threatening. The band began to play what sounded like a rumba only more sensuous, and the rhythm was irresistible. Evelyn put her hand on Joseph's arm and he turned round.

'I don't know how to dance to this music. Will you show me?'

He smiled and took her in his arms. This was different from the dance in her dining room. Joseph moved as if his limbs were filled with mercury, and she found herself relaxing into his rhythm, swaying her hips and allowing herself to lean into him until the lines of their bodies touched at every point. Evelyn rested her cheek on his chest where his shirt opened and felt the warm smoothness of his skin against her cheek. The music coursed through her until she was no longer aware of her surroundings, only the touch of his hands on her back and the pulse at the base of his neck where her cheek was pressed.

'Hey, little brother, how's it going? And who is this beautiful girl?' Evelyn woke as if from a delicious dream to see friendly eyes peering down at her from a wide, round face. Joseph released her and threw his arms around the newcomer.

'Jeremiah!' There followed a great clapping of backs, arm punching and wrestling. Joseph pulled himself out of a headlock, laughing, and turned to Evelyn. 'This certified lunatic is my big brother, Jeremiah.'

'Pleased to make your acquaintance, Madam,' Jeremiah bent over her hand in mock chivalry. 'I'm sorry to hear of your affliction. It must be terrible to lose one's sight, but I suppose that explains why you have allowed my brother to dance with you.' Joseph pretended to cuff him around the head and he ducked. 'Hey! Watch the 'fro!' Jeremiah took a comb out of his pocket and fluffed his hair. 'Hey Joseph, are you brave enough to introduce your friend to the rest of the brood?' He talked behind his hand to Evelyn. 'I warn you, they are a desperate bunch, but as long as you don't make any sudden movements you'll be safe.'

Evelyn laughed and followed the brothers to another makeshift table where four men whose infectious grins and similar features showed them to be Joseph and Jeremiah's brothers. They were like a pack of friendly dogs, who joked and traded insults while constantly touching each other: rubbing heads and pushing each other off their chairs, helpless with laughter. They beckoned Evelyn to sit among them and fired questions at her.

'How did you meet this reprobate? His art, you say? Don't give him a big head, we've been hearing about Joseph the Genius since he was still wetting his pants,' said one, who might have been called Samuel. Their Old Testament names had been shouted at Evelyn so quickly she couldn't possibly remember who was who.

Another – Zebediah? – pointed at Joseph. 'While he was getting all artistic we were out slaving so one day we can actually earn a crust, eh Joseph? We are all studying sensible degrees; me I'm going to be an engineer, mechanical, and so is Jonah. Jeremiah will be an engineer, electrical, Zach an accountant and Samuel is studying to be a vet.'

'Hey! I've done some honest toil, too,' Joseph said, laughing. 'What about the mines?'

Jeremiah's chubby face turned into a scowl. 'That was very stupid of you, little brother. There was no need to do that when Father lost his job. We would have pulled through, we always do.' He turned to Evelyn with a beatific smile. 'We Zambians are very resourceful, you know. It is our best quality.' He flung his arm around Joseph's

160

shoulders and kissed him loudly on the side of his head. 'This is our brother, a free spirit, who we love so much, our mother's favourite son – she used to chase the rest of us around the *kraal* with a broom if we didn't help with the chores while head-in-the-clouds drew in the corner.' He laughed the same honey-over-stones laugh as Joseph's. 'But I don't mind as I am the most handsome. Look at him,' he rubbed Joseph's head affectionately. 'My little brother! His only fault is he doesn't drink, not even a drop of *shake-shake*.' He picked up an empty Fanta bottle in front of Joseph and shook his head in disgust.

The brothers, funny and warm, seemed to accept Evelyn and her friendship with Joseph with ease and for the first time since she'd arrived in Zambia, she relaxed in the company of a group of Africans. And when Gerry and his activists joined their table, she was relieved the brothers' cheerful banter overwhelmed any attempts at political talk. From being ignored and irrelevant, Evelyn became the centre of attention. The Makelele brothers sought her opinion on every subject as their conversation danced from books and art to popular music. Her head was still singing as Gerry drove them back through the darkness to Chalimbana and as she jumped out of the car at her bungalow, waving him off. She made her way up the path, humming and swinging her hips to a calypso that had stayed in her head.

Robert stepped out of the shadows on the veranda. 'Where the hell have you been? Do you know what time it is?'

Evelyn giggled. 'You sound like my father.'

'Are you drunk?'

'Bit squiffy, that's all. Been dancing in Lusaka.' She reached him and tried to take his arms. 'Why don't we dance now? Come on, you used to take me dancing in London.'

'Stop it!' Robert gripped her by her shoulders and Evelyn sobered up as if she had been sluiced with cold water. 'I can't have my wife out to all hours dancing in the Lusaka Club – don't you know how people talk?' He shook her, and Evelyn nodded mutely, scared. She knew that she couldn't tell him she'd really been at a bottle shop. Robert's eyes were hooded, his face threateningly close to hers and she turned her head away. The closeness they'd had at Pembroke was gone; she had been a fool to think she had broken through his

161

defences. It was like stepping back into a recurring nightmare and she steeled herself to face his anger. But suddenly Evelyn was tired of being on the defensive. She hadn't done anything wrong, just been out with some people her own age, dancing, drinking, and having fun.

'You're hurting me. Again.' She spoke coldly and took a step away from him.

He blinked as if waking from a dream and released her. 'Evelyn, I'm...'

She didn't wait to hear the rest and walked into the bungalow, leaving him standing on the veranda, his outline silvered by the full moon.

WITCHES

'When the moon is full, the witches fly through the air in baskets or ride on hyenas. They go at night to the graveyard to eat the flesh of a person who has just died,' Elijah told Chrissie as she collected lucky beans from where they had fallen from the tree. Later she would string the shiny red and black beans together to make a necklace.

Chrissie sat back on her heels and glared at Elijah. 'That's a lie.'

'It is true. If you don't believe me, come to the graveyard tonight with me, after the watchers go home. They are burying my mother's sister's husband today. In the village they say there must be a witch around here, and this *nfiti* will call other witches to make a feast of the dead body.'

Chrissie narrowed her eyes, not wanting to believe him, but at the same time longing for it to be true. 'Why do they say there must be a witch?'

'Many people are sick and now some are dying. They say a *nfiti* has been putting poison into their food, a poison made from dirt.'

'From this?' Chrissie grabbed a clod of dried mud and crumbled it into red dust.

Elijah shook his head impatiently. 'No, this dirt is for spells, it is made from hair or fingernails. The witch steals it from you and also collects the dirt from your footprints, or picks up your *bibi* when you go to the toilet.'

Chrissie made a face. 'That's horrible.' But she crept closer. 'What else do witches do?' Elijah scooted over on his bottom and looked around as if to make sure no one was listening. He was so close his springy hair rubbed against her forehead. Her mum was going to be furious when she got ringworm again, but it was worth it to hear the village secrets.

Elijah whispered: 'After the *nfiti* kills you with the poisoned dirt he tells all his *nfiti* friends and they come to the grave at night. Their eyes are red and they each have a *nbobo* with them.'

Chrissie started to whisper too. 'What's a *nbobo*?'

'It is the animal servant of the *nfiti*. It can be a hyena or an owl or a leopard, sometimes a black mamba, but not an ordinary one. This one has a hood, like a cobra.' Elijah spread his hands behind his ears and Chrissie shivered. It reminded her of the tree at the bottom of her garden that she and Hamish called the black mamba tree. Samson had chased one of the snakes and it had slipped into a hole underneath. Whenever she thought about it, she imagined the snake looped around a branch, waiting for her. Now she could see it in her mind's eye: it raised its head and listened to the call from a witch, slipping out of its coils and silently moving down the trunk as it headed to the burial ground next to the abandoned Jeremiah village.

Elijah put his chin in his hands and they stared at each other, neither wanting to blink first.

'Do you know what the *nfiti* do when they dig up the body?' he said. Chrissie shook her head. 'They use magic to bring the person back to life, and then they torture him and drink his blood and eat his flesh. If you don't believe me, we could go and see, like spies. But perhaps you are afraid.'

Chrissie stood up and the lucky beans spilled out of her lap and scattered in the dirt, the necklace forgotten. 'I'm not afraid. We'll need a torch. I can get my dad's.'

Elijah touched the leather pouch that always hung around his neck. 'Also, you need a charm, like this *cibalilo*. When I was born it was over my head and my mother kept it for me. It has powerful magic.'

Chrissie's Irish grandmother had also been born with a lucky caul and kept it in a leather pouch in her special drawer. She had told Chrissie that sailors would pay a lot of money for the birth sac that went around a baby; it was supposed to keep them from drowning at sea. Gran had let her touch the caul so she would have good luck and be protected from bad things. It had felt dry and papery. Chrissie wished she had it now to wear around her neck.

That night, Chrissie and Elijah stole through the old village that had been abandoned years ago, the ruined huts casting shadows in the silvery moonlight. The drums had been going all evening and grew louder the closer they got to the graveyard. The moon went behind a cloud and they drew together, following the circle of yellow light cast by the torch. A skinny village dog kept them company for a while, growling only at Chrissie as if he could scent that she was not from the village. Elijah threw a stone at it and the dog slunk off into the bush. The sound must have disturbed something because there was a clatter of wings above them. Elijah grabbed Chrissie's arm; she dropped the torch and it went out.

'Get off! What did you do that for?' she said.

'Look, *nbobo!*' Elijah pointed up to a tree where an owl, backlit by moonlight, watched them from its perch.

Chrissie picked up the torch and clicked it on and off and on and off: nothing. 'It's broken! Dad will be furious.'

Elijah sidled around a hut with a roof that had rotted away. When he stopped, Chrissie bumped into him. She started to tell him to move but he hushed her and pointed into the blackness of the bush where lights flickered in the distance, as if someone were carrying a burning branch through the trees.

'Look they are playing. The *nfiti* send out their souls at night to fly through the air,' he whispered. 'They go into people when they are asleep. Sometimes they cut off a person's head and play football with it. And then when they wake up, they have a headache.'

Chrissie straightened up and put her hands on her hips. 'I thought you said the witches rode about on hyenas, with their eyes all red. I knew you were a big fat liar.' They heard a low rumble of voices and Elijah pulled her back down and into the door of the hut. Chrissie held her breath as several pairs of feet trudged past. She wondered if Elijah was telling the truth and there really were witches, but the feet were going in the other direction, away from the graveyard. She heard someone laugh and call out goodnight in Chichewa. When it was quiet again, they came out from the hut.

'It was only the graveyard watchers,' Elijah said. 'They have left and now the *nfiti* will come.' He sounded so certain that Chrissie began to think it might all be true: that witches roamed the bush at night, desecrating graves. In the darkness it was all too easy to believe in witchcraft. The owl spread its wings and swooped over them so low that Chrissie ducked. Her heart hammered so loudly in her chest she was sure it could be heard. She desperately wanted to go home, to be tucked up in her bed next to Cat with Hamish in the next room, but Elijah beckoned and she tucked the broken torch into her back pocket and followed him.

The moon was so bright now it showed them a path that wound through the tall grass. They followed it until they reached the fence around the graveyard. Chrissie peered into the square of dirt dotted with lopsided crosses. She just had time to see a newly dug mound of dirt before the moon went behind a cloud and plunged them into darkness. The two children sat down by the fence and waited. After a while, Chrissie heard Elijah's stomach rumble. She had sneaked a peanut butter sandwich out of the house and now she tore it in two and handed half to him. She didn't know how much time passed but her bottom was going numb when they heard a scraping noise and Elijah clutched her arm. It was someone digging. Chrissie tried to swallow but the clot of bread and peanut butter in her throat wouldn't go down. She spat it out, got to her knees and peered through the fence. The someone was singing quietly and digging: a man by the sounds of it. His voice rose every time the spade hit the dirt. The moon came out from behind its cloud and the graveyard was bathed in moonlight, the rusty metal crosses throwing long shadows on the ground. The man had his back to them and Chrissie slowly, slowly stood up to get a better view, holding her breath as if that would make her invisible. She could see that the man had stopped digging and was now kicking the grave dirt around with his bare feet. He had a bag slung around his body and reached into it, pulling out thin white bones that he scattered over the disturbed grave. In the bushes, a scuffle and an animal shriek split the graveyard quiet, and the man turned around and saw them. For a few frozen seconds Nyirongo and Chrissie stared at each other before Elijah grabbed her and she started running, her feet scrabbling over tree roots and potholes as she hurtled after him through the darkness. *I'm going to fall and break my neck. Mum and Dad will be sad and Hamish will wish he'd been nicer to me. I wonder if Cat will remember me when she's bigger?* They ran and ran all the way home, the breath tearing at Chrissie's throat until she thought she would be sick. When they reached the mango tree near her house, they were too scared to stop and say goodbye. Chrissie didn't stop running until she reached the back door, slammed it shut and threw the bolt. She stood there, trembling and panting, pressed up against the door until she was sure no-one was coming after her.

That night, as Chrissie slept curled around Cat, the rains broke. While the drops hammered on the corrugated iron roof and turned the dust into rivers of red mud, she dreamed about a black mamba. It reared up in front of her, opening its mouth to show the blackness inside.

THE CURSE

Chrissie didn't see Elijah for a few days even though she waited for him every morning by the mango tree. He wasn't at school and she thought his mother must have kept him off school again to help gather in the crops in their garden before the rain ruined them. At school, Chrissie was restless, moving between the European girls who played elastics and hopscotch, the African girls who played five stones, and the Indian girls who played at cooking and made horseshoe shaped ovens from the red dirt mixed with water. The boys were mostly African as the white boys, like Hamish, went to school in Lusaka. Chrissie watched the boys swoop through the playground after a rag ball in a tangle of legs. She thought of Elijah. At the end of each day, while she waited for the school bus, Chrissie wandered off to the enclosure where the small animals were kept. She touched the rabbits' and guinea pigs' pink noses through the chicken wire and waited for the bush baby to peek out of its box. Sometimes she could see its eyes from inside the darkness, but it never came out, no matter how long she waited.

One afternoon, she got home to find Hamish in the swimming pool. Their mother had let him take a day off Lusaka Boys' School because he said he had a sore stomach. Normally Chrissie would be furious at the injustice, but she'd been so lonely without Elijah that she couldn't help grinning at the sight of her brother splashing through the green water, his blonde hair plastered darkly to his head.

'Come in, Chris, and I'll show you how to play Marco Polo,' he shouted. She peeled off her green school dress until she was in her pants and jumped into the water. When hunger drove them indoors, Samson was polishing the red tiles. He leaned on his broom and glared at their feet and the trail of muddy prints marring his shiny floor. They ran out again and stuck their toes under the outdoor tap while he watched them. Hamish was ready first and raced into the house to forage for food, but Chrissie lingered, turning her feet under the stream of water.

'Samson?' she said, after a while. 'Where's Elijah?'

'Elijah is sick.'

'Can I visit him?'

'No.'

Chrissie went anyway, once Samson was too busy in the house to notice her slip away. She went out through the veranda while he was in the kitchen, skirted the garden and doubled back to the servants' compound. The dirt yard was empty, the chickens huddled in their coop as if frightened of getting their feet wet in the puddles left by the latest downpour. Chrissie crept up to the door of the two-room shack and peered into the gloom. Elijah was lying in the corner on a camp bed her father had given Samson. Chrissie knew the camp bed was really uncomfortable and felt sorry for Elijah, but perhaps it was better than the mats his brothers and sisters slept on; at least he was up off the beaten earth floor and away from the snakes and *tsongololos*, fat black millipedes that curled into themselves like a liquorice wheel. Chrissie bent her face towards Elijah's. His eyes were closed and his skin looked like it had been dusted in ash from the wood fire. Chrissie sat on a low stool next to him and took his hand. After a while she noticed one of his little sisters watching her from the doorway. She waved at the little girl and the movement must have woken Elijah. He opened his eyes and smiled through cracked lips at Chrissie. She gave him some water from an enamel mug, tipping it carefully so the water wouldn't run out of his mouth.

'What's wrong with you?' she said.

He cleared his throat and when he spoke his voice sounded rusty. 'A witch has put a curse on me.' A tear slid down his cheek. 'We should not have gone to the graveyard.'

Chrissie felt as if a hand had reached into her stomach and twisted her insides. 'Don't be daft,' she said, using the same tone her mother used when Chrissie told her about a bad dream. But she remembered Nyirongo digging at the grave, emptying bones into the dirt, chanting under the moonlight, and what the villagers said about his powers. Maybe he had done this – not a witch. She patted Elijah's shoulder to comfort him and noticed his neck was bare. 'Where's your charm?' She touched her own neck.

'I dropped it in the graveyard when we ran away,' he said, his fingers going to his neck. 'Or maybe the owl, the *nbobo*, took it so the *nfiti* could come in the night to cast a spell to make me sick. The next day I was hot and cold and could not move from my bed. My sister Precious says I was bewitched so she took me to see Nyirongo.'

Elijah told Chrissie how he had been carried down to the village to the witchdoctor's hut. He had lain there in the darkness, shivering with fever and terror, while the witchdoctor took out a gourd and put some kind of greasy medicine into it. He had rubbed the outside of it with the fat and sung to it, shaken it, passed it around his head and told Precious to clap her hands together to show respect to the ancestor spirit.

'Chrissie, I wish you had been there with me, like at the graveyard. I would not have been so frightened.' Elijah tightened his grip on her hand and his eyes widened. 'Guess what? The gourd talked to me!' Chrissie frowned. 'Are you sure?'

'Yes, I'm telling you, I heard it myself. It had a scary voice, like an old woman, and Nyirongo called it *a Mai*, like we call our mother or our mother's sister.' Chrissie edged closer to her friend, transfixed by his words. The last vestiges of European scepticism she had been clinging to fell away as she saw the evidence of witchcraft in front of her: Elijah's ashy skin and staring eyes.

'What did it say, the scary voice?'

'It said a witch had come to the village who has used *nfumba*, bad magic, on me to make me sick.' Precious had started to cry and told Nyirongo that the witch must have put a curse on her too, and that is why she couldn't have babies and her husband had left her. The witchdoctor had agreed and told her no man would fall in love with her until the witch was killed. Precious had cried because not only did no man want her, but now her little brother was sick and maybe going to die. Precious had said she knew who the witch must be – the Barotse.

Chrissie shook her head. 'Do you mean Joseph? Don't be daft, he's not a witch!' She laughed, relieved. It was like Dad said: a lot of mumbo jumbo. Elijah tried to sit up and grimaced. Panting, he lay back down again and sweat ran from his hair. Chrissie dipped her fingers into the mug and sprinkled some water on his face. She put her hand on his forehead, like her mother did when one of them was sick. Elijah's skin was burning hot.

He pushed her hand away. 'You must listen to me! When the spirit in the gourd spoke again it said Precious was right, that Joseph is the *nfiti*. Then Nyirongo gave me magic to protect me.' Elijah held out the underside of his arm so Chrissie could see the cuts where the witchdoctor had rubbed in magic ointment. They looked sore; she would bring the little tin of pink Germolene from Mum's first aid box next time she came to see him. She curled her fingers around Elijah's again and wished she could do more. He pulled her towards him. 'Chrissie, I'm frightened.'

She edged closer. 'It'll be okay, don't worry.'

'The witchdoctor said if the *nfiti* is not caught and killed I will die, and a *nkhuli* will come.'

'What's that?' He looked as if he was about to fall asleep. She shook his fingers. 'What's the English word for it, Elijah?'

'I don't know it… when a big sickness comes… many people die… all my family will die and the rest of the village. Some are already getting sick.'

'An epidemic, you mean an epidemic?' They had been shown a film at school, lurid pictures of people with terrible sores and swollen body parts.

Elijah nodded and closed his eyes.

Chrissie ran all the way to the church on top of the hill. Father O'Brian was outside, playing football with some boys. When he came over, she buried her face in his shirt. The cloth was thick and coarse and smelled of the store: soap powder and dried fish. The priest put his hand on her head like a blessing.

'What is it my child?'

Chrissie stopped crying long enough to tell him that Elijah was sick. She knew the priest had access to proper medicine and that he was the nearest thing they had to a doctor.

She tugged at his shirt. 'Elijah said there's going to be an epidemic. Other families are sick too; he said that everyone is going to die!' Chrissie watched the priest run into the church and come out with his medicine bag. She looked up at the cross on top of the little white chapel and said a prayer.

'Please, Jesus, look after Elijah.'

COLD WAR

After their last fight, Robert and Evelyn stalked around each other like two cats forced to share the same territory, the silence between them heavy as a stone. They ate quickly so they could retire to their different corners of the bungalow. Evelyn felt betrayed and resentful that the intimacy they had shared in Pembroke had been a sham. She realised that Robert would never let go of his jealousy and suspected he was using it as a weapon, to control her and rob her of her youth and freedom. Evelyn tended her anger like a campfire, making sure the glowing embers never went out. She began to fantasise about what her life would be like if she were free of Robert's baleful stares. Even though they hardly exchanged a word for days, she was always aware of his brooding presence.

Robert had left early one morning and Evelyn was having breakfast on the veranda, relieved to be alone, when a battered pick-up truck came up the drive, its wheels sending up a spray of muddy rainwater. Father O'Brian climbed out and waved at Evelyn. Her mood lightened and she waved back. Since her night out in Lusaka, she hadn't dared to see Gerry at the school or have Joseph over for art classes; she had felt cut off from the world and was glad to see the priest's friendly face. She watched him skip around the puddles until he'd reached the safety of the stone steps. It had rained overnight and the orange marigolds planted along the path had been swept away. A deep rumble and boom in the iron sky made him look up and make a dash for the shelter of the veranda. Evelyn poured him a cup of tea. He sat down with her and didn't speak until he'd drained the cup.

'God, I needed that!' he said and held out his cup for a refill. 'I was up all night in the village drinking from the calabash and my head's thumping.'

Evelyn laughed. 'Did you find out any of their secrets this time?'

'As a matter of fact, I did. Which is why I'm here, visiting one of my lost sheep.'

Evelyn raised her eyebrows. 'Is that what I am? I didn't realise I was one of your flock.'

'Ah, we are all God's children, whether we like it or not.' He leaned towards her. 'We've missed you up at the mission. Sister Bernadette was getting quite used to you, you know.'

Evelyn shifted in her seat. She had wanted to send a note to Father O'Brian, or go and see him, but she'd been sidetracked by the plan to help Joseph get back into university to study art. Evelyn smiled at the memory of dancing in Joseph's arms, and how they had stolen looks at each other while his brothers joked and teased.

'Evelyn?' Father O'Brian was looking at her over his teacup.

'Sorry, Tom, I was a million miles away.'

'So I see. You were about to tell me why you've abandoned our wee clinic.'

'Oh Tom, I'm just no good at that sort of thing.'

Father O'Brian snorted. 'Nonsense! If an uneducated ninny from Ballymena like Sister Bernadette can bandage a few cuts and splash the iodine about, I'm sure a woman of your ability can too. Whether you want to or not is another matter. Perhaps you have other fish to fry.' He looked at her closely. 'Is there anything you'd like to tell me, my child?' He waited, but Evelyn refused to be drawn.

She set her cup down. 'Tom, I'm not a Roman Catholic, so I have no need to unburden myself to you. You won't get a confession out of me.'

'Ah, but they say confession is good for the soul, even a Protestant one.' He laughed and then winced. 'Oh, this head! Have you any whisky? There's a malaria epidemic going around and they say whisky cleans the blood.' Evelyn poured a tot into his cup and Father O'Brian sighed as the whisky took hold. He sat back in his chair and crossed his legs. After a while, he said, 'Why are you smiling at me in that knowing way, Evelyn Fielding?'

'When are you going to tell me what you're really here about? What are you up to?' she said.

'Well, as a matter of fact, there is something.'

She leaned forward. 'I knew it! Robert always said you should never trust a priest!'

'That's only the Jesuits.'

'Come on, then, out with it. You look exactly like my headmistress when she was about to read me the riot act.'

Father O'Brian held out his cup for another shot. 'Better looking, of course.'

'Fewer whiskers, anyway!'

They laughed. Evelyn kicked off her shoes and tucked her feet under her bottom. She'd missed Tom O'Brian; with his keen intelligence and warmth, he was good company, and Evelyn enjoyed their easy chats about nothing and everything. The colour had come back into his face and it glowed with ruddy health – or alcohol. His eyes were bright again and Evelyn could tell he was admiring her. She knew she was pretty and a priest was a man after all. She lifted the corners of her mouth and was glad she'd remembered to put on fresh lipstick this morning.

But instead of returning her smile, he became serious. 'You're right, there is something I need to talk to you about.' He rubbed his chin and she could hear the scrape of his stubble. 'There's trouble brewing in the village.'

Evelyn waited for him to go on.

'Joseph Makelele is in trouble, big trouble.'

The priest's head was framed by the hills, which were now darker blue from the rains and draped in thick cloud. Evelyn thought of the Yellow Shirts at the bottle shop in Lusaka and the mirrored sunglasses that hid their eyes as they watched and listened. Joseph had told her that Gerry had taken him along to various political rallies. Robert had warned Evelyn about Gerry's political activities being under suspicion. Were they coming for Joseph?

'You mean with the authorities?' Evelyn said.

Tom put his cup down on the table between them and studied

the Tree of India pattern. 'Nothing quite so straightforward, I'm afraid. You see, Joseph has been accused of being a witch.'

Evelyn laughed, relieved. 'A witch? But that's ridiculous!'

'Ridiculous to us, maybe, but the Africans believe in magic; they accept it unquestioningly, the way we do the telephone. I've spent my life trying to spread the word of God, but belief in witchcraft is as strong today as when I came out here as a young man in the Fifties.' Evelyn listened while the priest told her everything he'd gleaned from his nights around the calabash. Witchcraft – bad magic – was called *nfumba* and was always behind common misfortunes such as death, miscarriage, infertility, or an illness. 'Where we talk of bad luck, they believe a witch has been doing *matsenga* or bad magic tricks on them. Even a headache can be blamed on a witch who has come in the night while you are sleeping, cut off your head and used it as a football before putting it back at dawn.' Father O'Brian rubbed his forehead. 'I think they had a good game of footie with my old head last night.' He laughed and grew serious again. 'The thing that gets me is not the superstition and godlessness of it, but the way it's used for settling scores in a small community. The witchdoctor is nothing but a conman, happy to help someone pay out a grudge by pretending to sniff out a witch in return for a few pennies. Anyone can be a witch; the cousin who inherits the land you feel entitled to, or the stranger who doesn't fit in.'

'Like Joseph?'

'He's Barotse, not Chewa. Normally, that wouldn't matter – they're used to the student teachers coming from all over Zambia. But Joseph has obviously put someone's back up and that has prompted an accusation of witchcraft. It's malaria season and the village needs a scapegoat to blame it on. The children are getting sick and if one of them dies, Joseph will be forced to undergo a poison ordeal to prove he's not a witch.' Evelyn listened in growing horror as he described the practice – illegal but still carried out in secret at night – where the suspected witch must drink a potion made from the poisonous bark of the mwabvi tree. 'If Joseph vomits but survives he's in the clear, but if he dies, which is highly likely, everyone will know he's the witch. His throat will be cut to make sure he's dead, his body mutilated and left in the bush for the hyenas.'

Evelyn's throat felt as if it was clogged with dirt. She put her hand to her neck. 'Can't he just refuse to drink the poison?'

The priest shook his head. 'That's as good as admitting he's guilty and they'd cut his throat anyway.' The sky rumbled and rain fell in front of the veranda as suddenly as a curtain drop. It drummed against the corrugated iron roof and Evelyn had to raise her voice above the noise.

'You have to stop this. Tell them Joseph isn't a witch! You're the priest; they'll listen to you.'

He took her hand in both of his. His touch was gentle, like a blessing. 'I cannot stop it,' he said. 'Over the years, I've learned it the hard way. They'll listen to me about God and nod their heads and come to Mass and enjoy the singing, but they won't give up the traditional beliefs their ancestors have held for thousands of years. Rome was not built in a day, my child, and certainly not in twenty years by Tom O'Brian from Waterford.'

Evelyn wrenched her hand away. 'This is barbaric! There must be something I can do.'

He looked at her thoughtfully. 'As it happens, there is. You've taken an interest in the boy and that's why I came to you. They won't listen to me, but they respect Robert, in their eyes he's still the *Boma*. Robert must go to the headman and settle this. I would ask him myself, but we missionaries and the former colonial officers, well, we haven't always seen eye to eye. It would be better coming from you.'

Evelyn thought hard. She couldn't go to Robert and ask him to help. They had had too many fights about her friendship with Joseph. She would have to fix this on her own. She stood up and smoothed down the skirt of her dress. 'Thank you for telling me, Tom.'

The priest stood up to and took her hand. 'You'll help Joseph?'

'Yes, I'll make sure he's safe.'

FLIES

'Ready, kids?'

Chrissie looked up at her dad from the bottom of the empty swimming pool. He was standing at the edge with a giant box of Surf. This was the best bit, when he poured in the soap powder. Leaning on her broom to stop from slipping, she shuffled the green slime over towards Hamish. He was crouched over the drain, his hair slick and his brown back streaked with algae. Chrissie nudged him with her knee and giggled as he nearly fell over onto his bottom.

'Watch it, Chris! Can't you see I'm busy?'

'Come on, Dad's going to pour in the soap.' Hamish grunted but didn't stand up. She hunkered down next to him. 'What you got?' He moved aside to show her a dead rat, its coat still wet from the soupy water that had been let out of the pool so they could clean it. Chrissie leaned in for a closer look but she didn't touch it. 'What are you going to do with it?'

Hamish grinned at her. 'I was going to put it in your bed, but you've seen it now.' He stood up and wiped his hands on his shorts. 'Race you to the end of the pool!' They skated over the slime, pushing their brooms ahead of them, and shoving each other off course while their father poured in a stream of soap powder, turning magically to pale green foam as they churned through it.

'You look like a couple of mad curlers,' he shouted over their laughter.

'What are curlers?' Chrissie asked Hamish when they reached

the shallow end, knee-high in bubbles. He shrugged and began scrubbing the pool walls with the broom. She was scooping handfuls of frogspawn off the metal ladder and throwing them onto the pool's concrete surround to make a satisfying splat when a pair of small feet appeared at her eye level. Chrissie squinted up at Elijah's youngest brother. She felt a sense of foreboding like a heavy hand on her shoulder.

'*Bwanji!*' She said to the little boy but he only stared at her and scratched his stomach, which stuck out from under his shirt, swollen from a diet of maize and not enough meat. 'What's up, Jerusalem?' Chrissie said.

He pointed in the direction of the servants' quarters. ''Lijah says come quick.'

Chrissie scrambled out of the pool and nearly knocked her dad over in her hurry to get to Elijah. 'Sorry!' she said and nipped around him, pulling on the dress she'd left at the side of the pool. She heard him call out a question but ignored it, running as fast as she could towards the servants' compound.

When she got there, out of breath and unable to speak at first, Samson was sitting on a stool outside his house with a lot of other men. His face was wet and he didn't look up when Chrissie ducked past him into the room. It was full of women and there was a low steady keening coming from them. Elijah lay on his camp bed. Chrissie pushed through the crowd and stood between his mum and his big sister. Precious held out her hand and Chrissie took it.

'He is going to die,' she wailed. 'I could not protect my brother from the *nfiti* and now he is going to die.'

Elijah's eyes were closed. He tossed his head from side to side and mumbled. Chrissie knelt down next to him. A fly was drinking the salty sweat from the corner of his eye and she waved it away.

'Elijah, it's me.'

His eyelids flew open. 'Chrissie, you must get my *cibalili* back. I dropped it that night in Jeremiah village. You must get it back for me or I will die.'

She swallowed hard. 'Okay, I'll do it,' she whispered. Elijah closed his eyes and seemed to fall asleep in an instant.

Chrissie thought back to that night at the graveyard and

remembered that when she had looked back, Nyirongo had stooped to pick something up from the ground. He had the caul and would have kept it for its powerful magic. Chrissie knew what she had to do now: steal back the caul from Nyirongo. She pushed her way out of the room and began to run, her arms and legs still streaked with green slime.

It was cool and dark in the college under the newly thatched roof. Chrissie heard her flip-flops slapping against the concrete floors and took them off. She crept past a classroom where the students were singing in harmony *the man was crossing the road*. Their teacher clapped his hands and the rising swell of *red lorry yellow lorry* followed Chrissie down the corridor. When she reached the mailroom, she slipped inside without turning on the light. She could make out the dark outlines of a desk and a chair: Nyirongo's throne, where he sorted the mail. As her eyes grew accustomed to the gloom, she spied rolled up magazines and newspapers from Britain still in pale-blue airmail wrappers poking out of Nyirongo's bag under the table. She was in luck: he usually didn't let his bag out of his sight, but that also meant he wasn't far away and she'd have to be quick. Chrissie dropped to her knees and started scrabbling through the copies of *The Times Educational Supplement*, *Country Life* and *Punch* her dad always ordered from home. At the bottom of the bag she found what she was looking for: a leather pouch on a string. Chrissie tied Elijah's charm around her neck and tucked it out of sight. She was backing out on all fours when a hand gripped her ankle and yanked her out from under the table. When she spun onto her bottom Nyirongo's face was staring down at her. His eyes were bloodshot and the sharp smell of him was in her nose: a queasy mixture of coconut hair oil, sweat and sour beer.

He pulled her closer. 'Look what I've caught – a white rat trying to steal from me. Are you looking for sweets and comics?' He narrowed his eyes. 'What is that?' He was reaching for the charm around her neck when Chrissie kicked him hard. He gasped in pain and cupped his hands between his legs as she rolled sideways and away from him. She skittered like a crab out of the room while the witchdoctor lay curled up on the floor. At the door, she paused and wondered whether she should call for help; she'd been warned before that you weren't supposed to kick boys there but she also knew it was the most effective way to end a fight with one of them. Nyirongo was whimpering and she wondered again if she should call for help. Then he opened his eyes and what she saw in them made her run for her life.

Nyirongo staggered to his feet and roared after her: 'I will get you. You will be next!'

Chrissie ran all the way back to the compound, too terrified to look back. Any minute she expected to feel a hand clamp onto her shoulder, hot breath in her ear and strong arms lifting her off her feet. But she was alone in the red road with the empty blue sky; the only sound her own ragged breath as a stitch grew in her side. When she reached the shade of Elijah's house she bent over and put her hands on her knees to try and ease the twinge. When she straightened up she thought she could hear Father O'Brian using his church voice. There was a crowd of village men at the door looking in and she pushed past them to see the priest kneeling next to Elijah's bed. On the floor was a steel, kidney-shaped dish with a syringe and some little glass vials. Next to them, a wooden box with some Eucharist wafers, little bottles filled with what looked like oil, and balls of cotton wool. She crept closer. Father O'Brian shook something from one of the bottles and used his thumb to smear an oily cross on Elijah's forehead. The boy stared back at him without blinking. Chrissie took the charm from around her neck and got ready to give it to him. If only Father O'Brian would move out of the way, but he was chanting again.

'In nomine Patris et Filii et Spiritus Sancti. Amen.' The priest stroked his hand over Elijah's face, sighed and took off the silk scarf he wore for Mass. He leaned back on his heels and pinched the skin between his eyebrows. The priest looked old and tired.

Chrissie didn't have time to worry about Father O'Brian. She squeezed past him and whispered in Elijah's ear: 'I got it! Elijah, I got your *cibalili*. You should have seen stinky old Nyirongo's face! He nearly caught me, but I got away. I kicked him in the you-know-whats and you should have heard him scream.' She put the charm on Elijah's chest but he didn't wake up. There were flies around his eyes again so Chrissie brushed them away and shook him by the shoulder, but still he didn't open his eyes. 'Elijah! Wake up! You can get better now. I got your charm, see?'

Father O'Brian gently pulled her away from Elijah and held her. 'Elijah is in the arms of Jesus now, my child.'

Chrissie turned around to ask what he meant and saw that the tears were running down the priest's cheeks. Fear stabbed her in the stomach and she struggled to get away. A ball of fury expanded in her chest and she shouted: 'No!' Chrissie wrenched herself out of his arms and pushed past the wailing women until she was out in the bright blue day and began to run and run and run.

Later, when she opened her eyes there was a buzzing in her ears. Her head hurt and she wondered why she was lying under the mango tree instead of cleaning the pool with Hamish. She couldn't remember how she had got there. When she tried to get up her arms had no strength so she lay on her back again and waited for the ground to stop moving. Chrissie looked up into the tree and saw Elijah sitting on one of the branches fixing his chicken wire car. Next to him, a man with long hair and a beard in a white robe was eating a green mango. He swung his feet in their sandals and winked at her. Chrissie's eyes were heavy and she closed them. When she opened them Hamish was bending over her.

'What's up, Chris? Mum and Dad have been looking for you for ages. Are you sick?'

'Tell Jesus not to eat the green mangoes. They'll give him a sore tummy.'

'What are you talking about?' He put his hand on her forehead and a memory stirred before she closed her eyes again.

'Elijah,' she whispered.

'You're burning up. Wait here, I'm going to get the parents.'

Chrissie heard his footsteps running away and looked up. Jesus and Elijah waved at her. She smiled and closed her eyes again.

WITCH HUNT

The following evening, Evelyn was getting ready to go to bed when she heard tyres crunch outside in the drive. It couldn't be Robert: he had left that afternoon for up country and wouldn't be back for a week. Before leaving, he'd tried to breach the chasm that had opened up in their marriage.

Smiling at her for the first time in days, he'd said, 'Darling, let's call a truce, shall we? You're so much younger than me, and from a different world. I should have made allowances for you; you're new to Africa and can't be expected to know how things work or how people talk.' He put his arms around her and Evelyn felt her spine relaxing. She leaned her head into his chest and wished he had spoken earlier, before her anger had turned into a stone at the pit of her stomach. She had mustered a smile, wanting the coldness between them to be over but unable to summon up any real feelings of warmth for her husband. He didn't seem to notice and kissed her on the forehead before getting into the Land Rover. 'Are you feeling all right?' he said. 'Only, you look pale. Perhaps you should have a lie down.'

Evelyn bit her lip to stop the tears spilling and shook her head.

Robert smiled at her. 'I'm sorry I have to be away again so soon, and for so long. Another damned useless meeting first thing in Lusaka and then a tour of the district to see if there's been any progress on the court system. I've asked Sixpence to keep an eye on things while I'm away, check the perimeter fence at night. Things might get a bit lively in the village with the epidemic – there's bound to be a lot of drinking and nonsense. Any trouble, go next door to the Dochertys.' He stroked her face through the open window. 'I love you, Evelyn, more than my life.'

She couldn't meet his eyes. 'I love you too, darling.'

After Robert had left for Lusaka, Sixpence had brought Evelyn her meal in the dining room, but she had no appetite. The servant had shaken his head at her barely touched plate, but she didn't care. She went to her room and sat on the edge of her bed with the door closed, listening to him pad about the bungalow for what seemed like ages. Finally, the kitchen door had banged shut and she was alone. Through the window, she had watched the beam from Sixpence's torch move along the ground towards the servant's compound behind the house.

Now it was dark. She threw on her dressing gown and went outside to investigate the noise and saw Gerry standing in front of his car, the engine still running. His face was drawn and he kept glancing over his shoulder.

'It's Joseph,' he said. 'They're after him, a crowd of them. O'Brian was right. We've got to move now and get him out of here.'

Evelyn went cold despite the humid night air. She had gone to Gerry, not Robert, after Father O'Brian's visit, and they'd made a plan to get Joseph out of Chalimbana and into a safe place. But they hadn't moved quickly enough.

'I won't be a moment,' she said. In her room, she dressed quickly in practical khaki trousers and tennis shoes. She found a kit bag of Robert's and put in all the art materials she could find and some money. When she went to look for her keys, she left the bag on the floor of the bedroom in her haste. Outside, a soft wind with the memory of rain in it blew in from the hills and she shivered and pressed herself into the passenger seat of Gerry's car. An owl hooted and she heard drumming and a strange, high-pitched singing from the village. The hills were black and solid against a scattering of stars. She still wasn't used to the darkness at night. There were no street-lights, no traffic, and the only light came from her own veranda, where huge moths bashed their wings against the single bulb. Gerry fiddled with the ignition key, pumping the gas as the engine spluttered. Evelyn peered through the darkness towards Sixpence's quarters and saw with a jolt of fear that a yellow light shone from his window.

'Hurry up, Gerry.'

The engine sprang into life when she remembered the bag on her bedroom floor. 'Damn! I forgot the bag I packed for Joseph.'

'I'll get it, where is it?'

'My bedroom, just to the left of the sitting room.' He moved and she grabbed his arm. 'Wait, I'll come with you, it'll be quicker if I show you.'

When they came out of the bedroom together a few minutes later, Evelyn cried out. A lamp had been turned on in the sitting room. Sixpence stood in the middle of the room, holding a *panga*. When he saw her with Gerry, he lowered his arm.

'Madam?'

Evelyn tried to laugh but it sounded too loud, a false note in the room. 'Oh, Sixpence, you scared me! Mr Mann was just leaving. He left something here on his last visit. I'll just see him out. No need for you to stay up, you go on back to bed now.' Sixpence stared after her as she walked past him. In the car she said, 'Do you think he'll say anything to Robert? He's probably got the wrong idea, about you and me, I mean.'

Gerry swung the car out of the drive. 'I wouldn't worry about Sixpence – he's one of the old generation of Africans, still in thrall to his colonial master. He wouldn't dream of talking to the *bwana* about what he thinks he saw – it would be too awkward for him. Forget about it. Let's go, we're already late. Joseph is waiting for us. He'll think we've abandoned him.'

Gerry parked the car some distance away from the building where the trainee teachers slept. There was no answer when they knocked at Joseph's door.

'It's no use,' Gerry said. 'Maybe it's a false alarm and he's in the village getting pie-eyed with the rest of them on *shake-shake*. This whole thing is turning out to be a bit of a fiasco. Maybe we should go.'

Evelyn fought back her irritation with Gerry. 'Joseph doesn't drink. Try again,' Evelyn said. 'You're sure he was in danger?'

Gerry nodded. 'One of my students came and told me they were getting ready to grab him.'

Evelyn called softly through the door: 'Joseph, wake up! It's me, Evelyn.' She heard a spring creak and a moment later the door opened a crack. Joseph was wearing jeans but no shirt and his feet were bare. Without his long leather coat he looked younger, more vulnerable. Evelyn wanted to place her hand flat against his smooth chest, and feel the reassuring beat of his heart. Instead she clasped her hands. 'Joseph, you have to come with us.'

'You shouldn't be here,' he said. 'It isn't safe. They will be coming soon.'

'It's all right, Father O'Brian sent us to help you. He said you were in trouble. We've come to take you somewhere where no-one can hurt you.'

Joseph opened the door wider and they stepped inside. The room was bare, lit by a paraffin lamp on an upturned crate. A small window was covered with flour sacks and a truckle bed was tucked into the corner with an enamel basin and plastic jug underneath it. A pile of well-thumbed books sat on a desk made from a packing crate. Evelyn realised for the first time the gulf that lay between her life and Joseph's. The tiny room had none of the comforts she took for granted. But she could also see that every inch of the concrete breezeblock walls was covered in drawings. There was a series of pictures of children, both white and black. In one a white girl and a black boy were huddled round a fire, roasting lemons. She remembered her first day in Chalimbana when she had met the neighbours' children. In another, two children were peeking out of a bush, the leaves framing their watchful faces.

'It's Chrissie Docherty and her little friend, what's he called again?'

Joseph laughed his soft laugh. 'Elijah. They were playing spies.'

Gerry Mann put his hand on Evelyn's arm. 'Look, we don't have time for this. We've got to get him out of here.' He dropped the kit bag on the floor in front of Joseph's feet. 'Put your things in here and we'll get going.' Joseph packed away his few possessions and Evelyn took down the drawings while Gerry Mann stood guard at the window. He put his finger to his lips and turned down the kerosene lamp to an amber flicker. 'Quiet,' he whispered. 'I hear something!'

The three of them crouched by the window and peered through a gap in the sacking. They could hear shouts and drunken laughter and see lit branches blazing in the darkness. Evelyn saw the glint of metal and realised they were carrying the flat blades that were used to hack sugar cane. Chrissie remembered Piet Jacob saying, "There's been another panga murder," and she shivered. A man stepped out of the crowd and she thought she recognised him as the person who delivered the mail from England and Robert's newspaper.

'Isn't that the college messenger?' she asked Gerry.

'You're right, it's Nyirongo,' he said.

Joseph moaned and touched a silver disc strung around his neck. 'He is the witchdoctor. I found a pile of animal bones this morning when I opened my door. Now they have come for me and they will kill me.'

Evelyn put her arm around him and could feel him trembling. 'We'll get you away, you'll see.'

Gerry turned from the window. 'I don't think they know which room he's in. They've gone around the corner to try the doors at that side. This is our chance, come on.'

They made a dash for the door, leaving it open in their haste, but they heard voices. There was no time to reach the car so they dived behind some bushes. Evelyn crouched between Gerry and Joseph, her heart was hammering so loudly she thought someone would surely hear it and discover them. Her knee pressed against a sharp stone but she didn't dare move. She heard feet shuffling past and looked through the leaves. Nyirongo was on all fours and seemed to be sniffing the ground outside Joseph's room, while the others watched in a circle. He leapt to his feet and held up something in his hand.

'Look, the head of a rooster! My brothers and sisters,' he said. 'This is the house of the witch. Who lives here?' A young man stepped forward and Evelyn recognised one of the student teachers she'd seen with Joseph at the college.

'It is the home of Joseph Makelele.'

Nyirongo lifted up his torch and shadows distorted his features.

'This man is a Barotse. He has eaten all the dead people in his own land. Now he comes to put a fever curse on our children.' He threw back the door and roared: 'Be gone, witch!' He stalked into the room and came out with a piece of paper, which he waved in front of him. Evelyn couldn't see what he was holding, but it must be one of Joseph's drawings; she hadn't had time to take down them all down. Nyirongo handed the paper to a young woman who looked at it and shrieked. Evelyn shifted to get a better view. It was Precious. Evelyn remembered how the maid had found her dancing with Joseph, and how sullen it had made her.

'It is a picture of my brother Elijah,' Precious said. 'This is proof! This Barotse witch put a spell on him.' Nyirongo threw down his torch. He seemed to be listening to an invisible person and nodded his head and muttered in response. Evelyn knew it was all play-acting, but in the pool of darkness outside the flickering circle of torchlight she couldn't shake the terror that gripped her.

Nyirongo stretched out his arms like a preacher. 'The witch is not here. He has flown away to feast on the corpses in the burial ground. Right now, this hungry witch is eating the flesh and drinking the blood of our brothers and sisters, of our fathers and mothers, of our children.' An angry murmur rose from the crowd. Nyirongo waved the lit branch he was carrying. 'Come! Let us go to the graveyard and catch him. We will chop up this witch, and throw away the pieces for the hyenas to eat.'

The women began to ululate – the strange singing that Evelyn had heard earlier – and Nyirongo led them away. When the last flicker of torchlight had disappeared, Evelyn stood up on shaky legs. She realised she was clutching Joseph's hand. They ran to the car and wrenched open the doors. A warm yellow light spilled out around them and they climbed inside and sat in silence for a while.

'Where are you taking me?' Joseph said from the back seat.

Evelyn turned round and put her hand on his knee. 'Somewhere safe and far away from here. We've arranged it all with Father O'Brian.'

Joseph leaned his head back on the seat and closed his eyes, exhausted by the ordeal.

A Leopard in the Night

Evelyn opened her eyes to the sound of church bells. She stretched out in her narrow bed and in the confusion of half-sleep thought she was back in her old room in Farnham. Then a hoopoe started calling from the tree outside and she remembered where she was: the White Fathers' mission all the way down in Livingstone. She and Gerry had driven through the night to bring Joseph here, taking turns at the wheel. That journey though the African night! The darkness was so heavy, pressing in and around and on top of them like a blanket, the only light in the vastness of the bush coming from the car's headlights. Once, a leopard had leapt out in front of them, its round eyes glowing green before it melted into the dark. Hours passed with the wind roaring in at the windows; at last they'd seen the flicker of a torch in the road ahead, a figure waving them in off the road.

'Thank goodness you're here,' the priest had said when they jumped out of the car on stiff legs. Father John was a wiry Scot from the windswept and hard-drinking Outer Hebrides. 'I've been dying for a dram,' he had said, and explained that the priests in this mission house were only allowed to drink alcohol if they had visitors. 'There's been no-one near us for days; it's been Hell,' he said, as they followed him inside. Joseph had been shown to the guesthouse after they had eaten. Exhausted by the drive, Evelyn had left Gerry and the priest to empty a bottle of whisky and followed a nun to the women's quarters.

Evelyn had slept fitfully, and now the day had come to chase away the shadows. She left her room, slipped into the bathroom across from her room and ran water into an enormous cast-iron bath on claw legs. Evelyn smiled at the soap in the shape of a teddy bear and lay back in the hot water. It was so quiet. She must have slept late. Judging by the heat and the silence, it was after eight – mid-morning in Africa where the working day started at six.

Evelyn dressed in khaki slacks and a white linen shirt and wandered through the mission house. She called a tentative 'hello?' but the dining and sitting rooms were empty. Her stomach growled and she remembered she hadn't eaten anything since lunchtime the day before. There was a sudden clatter from the kitchen, as if a saucepan lid had been dropped, and she went to investigate. When she pushed open the kitchen door, the cook and a maid broke off their conversation and turned to look at her.

'Oh, I'm terribly sorry. I was wondering if I might have a sandwich or something?' The cook went to the fridge and brought out some ham, cut two doorsteps from a loaf, piled the whole lot together and handed it to her on a plate, all without a word. Evelyn stammered her thanks and fled out of the cool shadows into the brightness of the garden. She crossed the lawn to find the shade of a tree where she could eat in peace and noticed someone, perhaps a homesick priest, had planted English flowers: lupins and dahlias. Their pale petals looked colourless and out of place in the merciless sunshine. Evelyn closed her eyes and tried to think of the cool blue-greys and soft greens of England but the heat on her face made it impossible. She opened her eyes and was at once assaulted by the children's paintbox colours of Africa. If she ever took up her brushes here, she'd never need to uncap her tube of black to dampen down the vivid reds, yellows, greens and blues. Even African skin was not black but hues of ochre, sienna and purple, just as hers was not white but a kaleidoscope of pink, green and violet.

At the bottom of the garden, the delicate English flowers gave way to a border of brash orange marigolds, and a little further on a jacaranda tree scattered its blue flowers on the ground like spilt India ink. Evelyn sat down underneath it and kicked off her tennis shoes. Her toes dug into the dust and she admired how brown her feet had become. She picked up her sandwich and took a bite, leaning her head against the trunk of the tree and feeling her muscles soften. For the first time in months she was truly on her own. The latest silent war with Robert had exhausted her and, even when he was away on business, Sixpence was always around, watching her in the stifling bungalow. Evelyn stretched her arms above her head and listened to the leaves shushing in the breeze. A shadow fell over her and she looked up.

'Hello Evelyn, am I disturbing you?'

'Joseph! Not in the slightest.' Evelyn smiled up at him but could not see his face against the sky's blue glare. She patted the ground next to her and he sat down and drew up his knees. They listened to the grasshoppers scratching in the grass. A jacaranda blossom fell into Evelyn's lap and she brushed it away.

'How are you after last night?' she said.

Joseph picked up the blossom and twirled it between his fingers. 'I was not scared for myself but for you. I couldn't stand the thought of anyone hurting you.'

Evelyn turned her head to hide the smile that tugged at her mouth. When she looked back at Joseph she found his dark eyes studying her. She plucked the jacaranda flower from his hands and buried her nose in it. It had an unbearably pungent smell and the trumpet-shaped blossom felt sticky. She dropped it in the dust.

'You're very quiet,' she said.

Joseph looked towards the west, where the hills disappeared into the clouds. 'I was thinking about my village. At this time of the morning, the women light the fires for the porridge, and the boys and men bring home the cattle, pushing them with long sticks.' Joseph's simple picture and the longing in his voice made her eyes prick and her throat swell. In England, her mother would be sitting down to coffee; the apple tree in the garden would be in blossom and the clean smell of cut grass in the air.

'I miss my home too, sometimes,' Evelyn said. She got to her feet and pulled Joseph to his. 'We're both being far too gloomy for such a beautiful morning. Gerry said he'd take me to Victoria Falls today but I imagine he's sleeping off a hangover. Will you come with me instead?' She let her hands rest in his as they stood facing each other. In the morning light, his skin had a sheen like a blackbird's wing. She remembered his arms around her while they danced and how he'd shielded her with his body in the bottle shop.

Joseph grinned. 'I have never seen the falls. They were always too far away from my village, but everyone knows about them. In our language, we call them *Mosi-o-Tunya*, The Smoke that Thunders.'

She laughed. 'That's far more romantic than stuffy old Victoria Falls. David Livingstone had a lot to answer for.' They stopped at the kitchen back door and, bolder now she was with Joseph, Evelyn asked the servants to tell Mr Mann and Father John she was going to Victoria Falls for the day. The cook's eyes swivelled to Joseph before he nodded and carried on chopping up vegetables. Evelyn didn't care.

Gerry's keys were still in the ignition. Evelyn took the wheel and Joseph climbed in next to her. She put her foot down and sped down the empty road, the engine roaring and the hot air thrumming through the open windows. Evelyn had never felt freer: this was how she'd imagined her life in Africa. They stopped at a roadside stall and bought roasted corn on the cob and ate it hot while she drove with one hand on the wheel, swerving round potholes. When they came to villages, children ran alongside the car, laughing and calling out to them until they could no longer keep up.

They heard the roar of the falls miles before they got there. Spray hung like mist over the tropical jungle that grew at the side of the falls, nurtured by the steaming heat. Orchids pouted their fleshy lips at them as they made their way through the lush undergrowth, and Joseph held back creepers as they walked right up to the edge of the Zambezi River where a footbridge bridge spanned the abyss. Walls of water thundered down sheer drops; it was impossible to see where the falls met the pools. Within seconds Evelyn's clothes were plastered to her skin. She turned to Joseph and he raised his arms to show he was wet through too. They grinned at each other, the rushing din so loud it was pointless trying to shout, let alone talk. All around them the Zambezi emptied itself into a gaping chasm, as if the earth had cracked open in the river's path. Over it all, a rainbow arched, its end fading into the white madness below.

Evelyn closed her eyes and listened to the water throwing itself against the rocks. The noise was like a giant beating its fists against the inside of a cauldron. With her eyes still shut, she took a step forward and then another onto the bridge, as if pulled by the force of the falls. Her foot hit a stone and she stumbled and lost her balance, lurching forward against the safety rail. Her eyes flew open and she stared into the void, the wet breath of the falls all around her. The iron rail dug into her stomach and her feet left the ground as she pitched forward over the barrier. Hands grabbed her shoulders and yanked her backwards and she fell in a heap against Joseph.

He shouted above the din. 'I've got you. Are you all right?'

Evelyn was shaking too much to answer. Joseph put his arm around her and helped her sit on the ground with her back to the falls. She was aware that they were on a bridge suspended in the air, while death thundered below. When she looked up, an older white couple had stopped in front of them to stare, the woman's leathery face a scowl of distaste. Joseph started to move his arm but Evelyn grabbed his hand and made him stay, giving into a childish urge to stick her tongue out at the old bitch. Outraged, the woman marched off, her husband trailing in her wake.

On the way back, they stopped at another roadside stall and bought sugar cane juice, drinking it out of glass jars. A little girl came out of one of the huts with field mice roasted on sticks. Joseph bought two and ate one, his eyebrows raised at Evelyn. She shrugged and he handed her the other field mouse. She nibbled at the charred flesh and licked the grease from her fingers. They leaned against the car while they ate and Joseph asked her about London. Evelyn told him about the art galleries, the museums, Trafalgar Square and Buckingham Palace, but it wasn't until she mentioned the London Underground that his eyes widened and he asked for more details.

'A train that goes under the ground? How far under? Is it dark? Does it make the ground shake? Where does it go?' She took out her pocket diary with its map of the London Underground and showed it to him. He traced his fingers along the red of the Metropolitan line, the blue of Piccadilly. 'These colours all show the line of rail?'

'Yes, all the different routes, look here's the Piccadilly Line in dark blue and the Northern Line in black. Do you like it?'

He nodded. 'It's interesting, graphically.'

'Then keep it.'

'Are you sure?' But before she could answer he'd put the diary in his shirt pocket, where he kept his pencils and the little sketchpad he carried everywhere.

Back in the car she paused before starting the engine. 'Perhaps you'd like to go to London sometime, and see it for yourself? There are some wonderful art colleges there.'

'I would like that very much. But England is very far away, and expensive to get to. I'm afraid it's impossible.'

'Nothing is impossible, Joseph.' She smiled at him and shifted into second gear.

The sun was high in the sky and the horizon shimmered with heat when they passed a strange tree, its branches twisted grotesquely into the air like gnarled fingers grabbing for the clouds.

'It's a baobab tree, the upside down tree,' Joseph said when she pointed it out to him. 'My grandmother told us many stories about this tree. When the world was being made, it was the proudest tree and boasted it was better than the other trees.' He told her God wanted to teach the proud baobab a lesson so tore it out by the roots and tossed it into the sky. It landed upside down with its roots in the air and branches stuck into the earth. Joseph grinned at her. 'In Zambia, we aren't too keen on people who think they are a cut above the rest,' he said. 'They always get into hot water in my grandmother's stories.'

'The poor baobab, stuck forever like that,' Evelyn said.

'Oh, you mustn't feel sorry for it. You see, the baobab, even though it landed upside down, was so strong it survived and became the strongest tree in the whole of Africa.' Evelyn cut the engine and studied the tree in the sudden quiet. Its bare branches did look like roots, as if it were reaching up to claw at the sky.

'The upside down tree,' she said quietly.

Joseph laughed. 'That's a good name for it. I think this one is dead, but it won't fall down like other trees – the baobab rots from the inside out, so when it comes to the end of its life, it's hollow. The larger ones are used for shelter. I saw one once being used as a shop. But everything comes to an end: one day this tree will crumble to dust and disappear suddenly, as if it had never existed.'

Evelyn wanted to explore this odd tree. She drove the car off road and parked it under the tree and they got out. There was a door-sized hole in its trunk. She put out her hand – the bark was smooth to the touch, and warm, like a living creature.

Joseph laid his hand flat on the tree, next to hers. 'When I was a child, growing up in our village, my father used to make fishing nets from the bark.' He stripped off some of the tree's skin; it came away easily. 'You pound it with a stone and then you can make a rope with it. I used to help him.'

Evelyn waited for Joseph to go on. She had met his brothers of course, but he had never talked about his parents before today and she wanted more pictures to go with the one of his mother: waving the smoke out of her eyes as she blew on the embers, a cooking pot by her side, waiting for Joseph to come home.

She touched him lightly on the back. 'Tell me about your father.' Joseph turned to face her and they both leaned a shoulder against the tree. He told her he used to go fishing with his father on the lake near his village. They would cast the nets wide to catch fish, drying and selling them. Fishing paid for food and school fees for him and his brothers. Joseph was good at fishing and should have been on the lake more, but he was encouraged by the Presbyterian minister to stay on at the missionary school.

'My mother had ambitions for me: she didn't want me to be a fisherman like my father. Reverend Milne realised early on that I could draw and said it was a gift from God. It was him who persuaded my parents I should go to art college in Uganda.' Joseph traced a circle with his toes in the dust. 'Mr Milne is a good man. He's one of the reasons I want to train as a teacher. It's thanks to him that my brothers and I had an education and training, and that my two sisters stayed on at school and learned to read and write.'

He looked out to the west. 'Mr Milne is tall and thin – the school children call him Crane. He liked to walk with me and our long shadows would stretch out on the ground like Giacometti figures. I always remember the day he pointed to our shadows and said: *Do you see, Joseph, how we are all equal under the sun? In God's eyes there is no black and white.*'

Evelyn looked down at their hands so close they brushed

195

against each other. He is right: there is no difference, she thought.

'A good teacher can change lives,' Joseph said. 'But Mr Milne is getting old and when he leaves, there will be nobody to teach the children; nobody to show them there's more to life than herding cattle and scraping an existence from fishing.' Joseph opened his hands to show his palms. 'So, you see now why I must become a teacher. 'I know you and Gerry would like me to become an artist. But we are a young country, newly hatched, and we need teachers and engineers, doctors and nurses. Otherwise the children will have no future.'

Evelyn wanted to argue with him and tell him not to waste his talent; to leave teaching to others, but instead she said, 'Tell me why you left the village.'

Joseph dropped his hands. 'My father became ill and couldn't fish anymore, so there was no money and we moved to Lusaka, where my father got a job as a *Boma* clerk, and my mother cleaned houses for white families.' Joseph stopped talking. He looked up into the tree and Evelyn tilted back her head too. In the root-branches above, a hornbill peered down at them and gave its rasping bark before flying off. 'This is a bird that brings back luck,' he said.

Evelyn studied the side of his face, the curve of his brow bone and the thick fringe of eyelashes. 'Nothing bad could happen to us, not out here.' She touched him on the arm. 'Tell me what happened next.'

He rubbed his hand over his head and went on. 'I got a bursary and went to Uganda to study, but when I came back, my parents were struggling. My father had lost his job and my mother was working seven days a week, from dawn until midnight, for a pittance. I couldn't bear to see my mother turning into a ghost of herself. I told her I was going to the mines. She begged me not to go to Ndola; she said God didn't live there.' He grimaced. 'She was right.'

Joseph felt around his neck and untied the string with the coin on it and held it out to Evelyn so it swung from his fingers. 'Before I left my village, Mr Milne gave me this St Christopher medal.'

Evelyn caught the little tin disc in her palm and rubbed her finger over the figure of a man carrying the Christ child on his back. It was a strange thing for a Presbyterian minister to give.

Didn't they rather disapprove of the saints? But perhaps in Africa everyone needed a charm. She put the medal back in Joseph's cupped hand.

He stared at it for a few moments. 'I never forgot what Mr Milne told me about being equal: it stayed with me and helped me when I was working in the mines and being treated like a dog. I wore my medal when I was underground and the tunnel walls were pressing down on me, when the boss called me Boy, and when I was paid less than the white miners from South Africa.' A line of sweat had broken out on Joseph's forehead and he wiped it away with the back of his hand. Evelyn wanted to tell him to stop, that it was all right, she had heard enough, but she could tell he was back in the mines. 'I hated Ndola. My mother was right – God did not live there. Every morning I got up and looked out of the window of my shack at the rows of other shacks stretching as far as you can see. There was no lake and no trees, no grass or animals. Only dust. The other miners went to the company beer hall and spent their wages there, but I didn't. I worked until there was enough money to feed my mother and my brothers and sisters for a long time and then, one morning I couldn't go on. I knew I would rather die than go back under the ground, and I left. I wrote to Mr Milneto tell him I couldn't go on, and he wrote back and gave me Father O'Brian's and Mr Docherty's names. He told me I should go to see them in Chalimbana, where I could train to be a teacher.' He closed his fist over the medal. 'Now I will never become a teacher. If I go back to Chalimbana, Nyirongo and his cronies will make me drink poison to see if I am a witch. I don't know why they want to hurt me. I just want to live my life, draw, and look after my family.'

Evelyn put her hand over his clenched fist. 'I don't know either, but I do know you're a very special person – a gifted artist. That's why we all want to help you: me and Gerry, Father O'Brian, Jim Docherty and Mr Milne.'

Joseph moved closer. 'And what about you, Evelyn,' he said softly. 'Who will help you?'

Startled, she looked up at him. His eyes were so dark she could not see the pupils. Evelyn knew she shouldn't, but she took a step towards him. 'What do you mean?' she said.

'I see that you are sad and lonely. Even when you're with people you are alone. I see that you are lost.'

Her eyes smarted and her mouth worked to stop herself from crying.

'You are lost,' he said, 'But you will find your way, if you are brave and remember who you are.' He held out the medal to her and she traced the little figure of the man carrying the Holy Child. 'I want to give you this. It helped me remember who I was when I was lost. It will help you find your way too.'

Joseph lifted the St Christopher medal over Evelyn's head and moved her hair out of the way to tie the string. As the cool metal touched her skin, her head felt lighter, as if a heavy hand that had been pressing down on her skull had lifted. The song of the grass-hoppers grew louder and she heard the lonely call of a bird crying out to its mate. Joseph's fingers were gentle on the nape of her neck and she shivered as they trailed around her throat, coming to rest on her collarbones. Evelyn put both hands on Joseph's head, his beautifully shaped head, and studied the curl of his full lips and skin that was like dark honey. She pulled him towards her as the cicadas beat out their love tattoo and the sun climbed through the branches of the upside down tree.

They stumbled in the shade of the tree and tore at each other's clothes until they were standing naked together, an Adam and Eve who had found their way back to Eden. Joseph's fingers were long and cool as he ran them over her body and cupped her breasts. She laid her hands on his chest and pressed her mouth to the hollow of his throat. She tasted salt. He put his hands around the curve of her buttocks and lifted her up. Evelyn wrapped her legs around his waist and cried out. She moved her hips to urge him on. She bit at his neck, found his tongue: a current bolted through her as her eyes stared sightlessly into the green darkness of the tree. It was just the two of them as the world spun on its axis.

BABES IN THE WOOD

Gerry had to go back to work the following day and Evelyn seized her chance to be alone with Joseph.

'You go – I'll stay and make sure Joseph is safe,' she said. 'And Robert's away for a week so I won't be missed.'

'All right, I'll come back then to pick you up.'

'No need – Father John says Tom O'Brian is coming at the end of the week, so he can give me a lift back.' As Evelyn watched his car dwindle to a speck her heart felt as if it would burst out of her chest as she thought of a whole week with Joseph.

Every night that week, she left her bed and drifted through the garden past the jacaranda tree and into the guesthouse. He was always waiting for her, the lights doused, his dark eyes liquid in the shadows. Under the mosquito net, their lovemaking was made more intense by the knowledge that they would soon be apart. Afterwards they lay entwined and fantasised about a future together, a sweet, imaginary place where Evelyn was not married and they could live together happily, alone. Robert was never mentioned in these dream talks, nor Joseph's family in Lusaka. Joseph would fall asleep and Evelyn would slip back to the main house. They spent their days exploring. She borrowed the mission jeep and together they drove all over the veldt: the whole of Africa lay before them in the vivid, rainy-season hues of red and green. At the falls, in the dense rainforest that lined the Zambezi, they stole fevered embraces, hidden by the mist and the creepers that hung from trees like curtains. They ventured further into the jungle and discovered a deep pool they could dive into safely, leaving their clothes in a pile on a rock. The water was cool on their slippery limbs. Joseph teased her and they played like children, splashing and chasing each other in the dark green water. Evelyn had never felt so free or alive, and as she fell in love with Joseph, so she fell in love with Africa. After they had been swimming one day, their idyll came to an abrupt end. Evelyn's hair was still damp when they arrived back at the mission. The shadows were long on the grass and the sky was streaked with red as she walked over the lawn in her bare feet towards the main house. Joseph was under the jacaranda tree and she sensed him watching her. She turned and smiled at him, touching the front of her shirt, in front of her heart. When she turned back towards the house at first she didn't see Gerry waiting for her on the veranda. He was standing in the shadows and as she walked past him he caught her by the wrist. She dropped her shoes.

'Oh my God! You gave me a fright,' Evelyn said and twisted her arm away, rubbing the mark he had left. She glanced back towards the jacaranda tree but the setting sun was in her eyes and she couldn't tell if Joseph was still there.

'I'm sorry, I didn't mean to startle you. I've been waiting for you for hours. I need to talk to you.' She glanced at the house, looking for an escape. Gerry frowned. He took her by the shoulders and she could smell the whisky on his breath and tried to pull back, but his fingers dug deeper. 'Where have you been?' he said. 'I've been looking for you everywhere.'

'I was at Victoria Falls.'

Gerry released her and wiped the sweat out of his eyes. They were unfocused, as if he'd lost his train of thought. 'Never mind. There's something I need to tell you.' He took another step towards her and pulled her towards him clumsily, so her raised arms were crushed against his chest. His speech was blurred with whisky. 'Evelyn, I love you.'

She struggled but her arms were pinned. 'What?'

'I said I love you. I've fallen in love with you. I've been thinking about you all week, and I've made a decision: you have to leave that bastard of a husband and come away with me. I know you're not happy. I can make you happy. I've been offered a job in Lusaka, at the university. We could start a new life together, you and me.'

Evelyn's body still tingled from Joseph's touch. The thought of running away with Gerry was absurd; he was absurd. She laughed. His jaw dropped and she nearly laughed again. For a moment he looked bemused, and then his eyes switched focus to a point above her shoulder and his expression hardened. She turned and saw Joseph standing in the middle of the lawn, his shirt still unbuttoned all the way down to show his smooth chest, fists clenched and head down ready for a fight. Gerry touched her tousled, wet hair, taking in her untucked shirt. He picked up the St Christopher medal she wore around her neck and she saw understanding creep into his eyes. 'This is Joseph's medal – he told me once he never took it off. You were with him?'

She turned her head away and nodded.

With an odd little grunt, he pushed her away hard, and the sky tilted as she tripped off the edge of the veranda steps and fell backwards. He came down the steps and stood over her as she lay sprawled on the ground and turned and spat as if to get rid of a bad taste.

'You whore! Was he a good fuck? Did his big cock satisfy you?' He took a step towards her and raised his fist. Terrified, she scrambled backwards, her heels slipping in the dirt. Evelyn raised her arm in defence, cowered and closed her eyes, waiting for the blow. She heard footsteps running towards them, a shout and a smack. When she opened her eyes, Joseph was standing over Gerry, panting. Unable to trust her legs, she crawled towards Gerry where he lay on the ground, his face streaked with blood and mucus. He opened his eyes and groaned. Evelyn had been so frightened of him, but now she felt only pity. It must have shown in her face because he turned his head, as if she'd struck him. Gerry pushed her aside and pulled himself to his feet. Staggering to his car, he wrenched open the door and drove off, wheels spinning.

Evelyn sank back onto her heels and looked up at the purpling sky; it will be pitch black soon, she thought, and then this day will be over.

Joseph knelt beside her. 'Are you all right? Did he hurt you?'

Evelyn began to cry and he held her, and she didn't care that they would be seen together. When she was calmer, he helped her to her feet. She watched Gerry's car disappear in a cloud of dust as her body shook with rage and her tongue lay like a stone in her mouth. *Bastard!* No one had ever spoken to her like that before. She pulled back her hair into a ponytail and winced at the pain. Bruises in the shape of fingerprints were already blooming on her arms. Gerry was angry, perhaps angry enough to tell Robert. She moistened her lips, still tender and swollen from Joseph's lovemaking.

'I have to get home,' she said 'Before it's too late.'

POOR HELEN

Evelyn and Tom O'Brian left the Livingstone mission in the blue cool of dawn and drove in silence for a while. The priest had been morose since his arrival at the mission and had spent a lot of time alone, praying in the chapel or walking with his head bent as if studying the dusty track of his shoes. In the days after the fight on the lawn, Evelyn had been careful to avoid being seen alone with Joseph but she knew how servants talked and wondered if Tom had heard something. She hadn't offered an explanation about Gerry's sudden departure and he hadn't asked for one, and now the question hung over them as the ancient car ate up the miles to Lusaka.

His sigh broke the silence. 'Sometimes I wonder what good I'm doing out here, what good any of us are doing. That poor little mite.'

'What poor little mite?'

'A child I couldn't save from superstition and ignorance. His family used the witchdoctor's potions on him when he was sick, until it was too late, and that's when they sent for me.'

They returned to their silence. Evelyn glanced at his profile and longed to confide in him. Perhaps she could trust him – he was a priest after all and was used to confessions. She noticed how his biceps flexed under his short sleeves when he shifted gear. He was a man as well as a priest, with the same impulses and desires as everyone else; he would understand about love, how it could tilt the world on its axis and smash all the rules. Evelyn made up her mind to tell him about Joseph, but her throat closed over the words when she thought of the name Gerry had called her. She didn't know why she burned with shame when she remembered that word but not when she thought about Joseph.

Evelyn knew that in the eyes of Father O'Brian's church she had committed a terrible sin, but she couldn't imagine he would condemn her for falling in love. He would have to forgive her, wouldn't he? That was the wonderful thing about Catholicism: as long as you were sorry, your sins were forgiven. The thing is, she wasn't sorry, not in the slightest. For a split second she thought about Robert and felt a pang of regret, but she shook her head to get rid of the guilt. After all, it wasn't her fault: everyone knew you couldn't tell the heart not to feel, didn't they? She couldn't stop loving Joseph any more than she could stop breathing. Besides, she'd been so lonely, and whose fault was that if not Robert's? He'd brought her out here for a new life and had abandoned her: he only had himself to blame if she looked for comfort elsewhere. She should never have married him; she realised that now.

The door of her mind closed on her husband and she allowed herself to daydream about Joseph. She traced his name on the window of the car and rubbed it out with the heel of her hand. What she had done with him couldn't be a sin. Joseph had a pure soul: it was why everyone loved him. She closed her eyes and smiled at the memory of him, the salty taste of his skin on the tip of her tongue, the silken smoothness of his chest as he held her. He was young, like her. She deserved him. Something so beautiful couldn't be wrong, could it? God, if He did exist, wouldn't be so narrow-minded.

'Evelyn?' Tom said.

She kept her eyes closed and pretended to be asleep. She couldn't tell him, not yet; she wanted to keep what they had as a delicious secret. Her mind began to race as she remembered what she'd told Joseph when they'd said goodbye on their last night together: he would stay at the mission, to be safe, and when she got to Chalimbana, she would work out a way they could be together. Somehow or other, they would build a future together. He would become a famous artist and she would encourage him. She'd be his muse, his teacher, and his lover. She had whispered into his shoulder that they would live in a house surrounded by jacaranda trees and their a carpet of blue flowers. Evelyn thought about Joseph's honey-dark skin, so smooth her teeth had left little indents. The balloon inside her chest filled with air. *She didn't care. She didn't care. She didn't care.* Evelyn leant her head against the window and let the motion of the car send her to sleep.

When she woke up her neck was stiff. Tom O'Brian had pulled over to the side of the road and was watching her.

'Are you going to tell me what happened and why Gerry left in such a tearing hurry?' he said.

Evelyn straightened her back and stared out at the crouching trees. 'Why don't you tell me, Tom, since you're so up with kitchen gossip?'

He cut the engine. 'I'm worried about you, Evelyn. You're a bright young woman with not enough to do. If only you'd stayed on at the clinic you wouldn't have time for all these ... complications.' He waited for her to speak but she only stared out at the endless, empty terrain. Tom sighed. 'All right, I heard that Gerry took off with his tail between his legs and a bloody nose and that a certain handsome young man we both know was responsible.' He shifted in his seat. 'Will you turn round at least?' She did, knowing her eyes were red and her nose pink. His expression softened and he took her hand between his dry palms. 'If you're not going to tell me what happened to set those two cockerels fighting, that's up to you. Although I assume it's over a pretty little hen sitting not too far away from me, am I right?' She tried to pull her hand away but he held onto it. 'Evelyn, I'm not here to judge you, only to help. I've lived in Africa for more than twenty years and in that time I've seen pretty much everything. I'm not easily shocked.' After a while he let go her hand and reached for the ignition. 'Well if you're not going to talk to me, will you at least stop glaring out of the window and give me some of your chat before I die of boredom?'

Evelyn's shoulders dropped and she laughed. 'Only if you stop prying and promise not to lecture me anymore.' He grinned and she began to tell him about her trips to the Falls and the villages she'd seen, but the priest only nodded his head, and seemed to be half-listening. After a while, he turned off the main road onto a rutted track and they came to a scrappy collection of shacks in a litter-strewn yard.

'Wait here, I'll only be a few minutes,' he said. He took a sack from the boot and walked over to the nearest shack. A woman with a baby strapped to her back was pounding meal whilst a toddler played at her feet and an older child pushed a tyre round the dirt yard. The priest called out and when the woman turned round, Evelyn saw she was white. She gripped the dashboard and leaned forward to peer through the half-moons the windscreen wipers had cut through the dust and squashed insects. The woman's hair was a greasy straggle and a torn and faded dress hung off her thin frame. The toddler clung to her and she patted his hair, which was kinky but tipped with blonde. An elderly black woman came out of the shack and stood with her arms folded, watching while Tom opened the gate and placed a hand on the child's head. He put down his sack and the two children opened it up, pulling out clothes and toys. The priest put his arm around the white woman and she covered her eyes. Her shoulders were shaking. Evelyn could see he was talking to her and after a while the woman nodded and dried her eyes. When Tom got back into the car, he started the engine without a word.

'Who was that?' Evelyn said.

'Helen Armstrong, a poor soul who lost her way.' He passed her the map. 'Now, can you make sure we're on the right road to Lusaka? My sense of direction is hopeless.' Evelyn knew he wouldn't tell her any more.

When they reached the city, he dropped her at the Lusaka Club and leaned out of the window. 'Say hello to Jeanie for me, she runs the club. She'll look after you while I'm saying Mass. I'll pick you up in an hour or so.'

Jean Malcolm was behind the bar serving two black men in tennis whites. Evelyn caught her eye and she came over with a friendly look. She had a round, open face, freckles and sandy hair and smiled when she introduced herself.

'I haven't seen you in here before,' she said.

'No,' Evelyn said. 'I usually go to the Ridgeway.'

'Och, this is much nicer, more relaxed.' Evelyn smiled at her Scottish burr. It seemed you couldn't go anywhere in Zambia without bumping into one of Jim Docherty's countrymen. Jean tilted her head at the men. 'There's no colour bar like down in Rhodesia.' She tapped the newspaper on the counter and nodded at the two men. 'They're journalists, lovely lads.' Jean's finger landed on a grainy picture of a dark shape in the sky with the headline: *Witch Spotted Flying over Zambia-Rhodesia Border*. Only a few weeks ago Evelyn would have been shocked, now she pushed the paper away.

'Journalists?'

'Oh yes, they all come here, love the tennis.' She put a tumbler in front of her. 'G&T?' Evelyn nodded and Jean pouring a generous measure of gin and a splash of tonic. 'This used to be an all-whites club before independence, but everyone's welcome now, and that's the way it should be. Some people don't like the change since '64, but I think it's better.' Jean leaned on the counter. 'I remember when the blacks weren't allowed in a shop. They had to go to the hatch around the side. Terrible, when you think of it.'

Evelyn shook her head. 'That's awful. I don't understand why some people can behave like that. I can't get used to it.'

Jean smiled grimly. 'You will, once you've been here as long as me.'

'Have you been in Zambia long?'

Jean made a face. 'Years, don't like to think how many. Hugh came out to work in the tobacco but having to answer to a boss didn't suit him, so we took over this place. It's not so bad: I've got used to it. You do, don't you, if you're a woman? Just get on with things.' She took up a cloth and began to wipe down the counter. 'I like a blether with the customers, and my girls love the freedom. But I miss home, the shops and my own folk. Not to mention rain that doesn't skelp the hide off you.'

A little girl in a swimsuit and white blonde hair came running into the bar, her feet leaving wet prints on the floor. Evelyn smiled and thought of Chrissie Docherty.

'Susie Malcolm! Will you look at the state of my nice clean floor!' Jean said. But she came round from behind the counter and put her arms around the girl and kissed her until she squirmed free.

'Mum, can I please have a Fanta? The others want some too.'

Evelyn watched Jean's daughter walk carefully over to the

swimming pool, clutching an arm full of bottles. Some other children, tanned gold with the same white hair, broke off their games and ran towards her. She wondered what it would be like, to be a mother, to towel dry her own children wet from the swimming pool and kiss them until they ducked out of her arms.

She turned back to Jean. 'Tell me, are there any mixed race people around here?'

'The coloureds? Yes, of course, they live near the Indians, the other side of the city.'

'So that's tolerated, then, mixed race marriages between whites and blacks?'

Jean frowned. 'I don't know if you'd say that. Coloureds only marry other coloureds, and they don't really mix with the blacks or the whites. They look out for their own, keep themselves to themselves. Sad look about them as if they don't belong anywhere.' She topped up Evelyn's tumbler with gin. 'Most of them, they'll have a white great granddaddy, from when the men first came out here without the wives. Or some of the black girls will have babies that are light-skinned. Men come up to Zambia from SA to sleep with the local girls.'

Evelyn remembered the waitress at the bottle shop, how Gerry had put his arm round her and the blank look in her eyes. She stirred her drink without looking at Jean. 'What about a white woman and a black man, does that ever happen?'

Jean lowered her voice. 'Funny you should say that. A few years ago there was a big scandal in the club.' She glanced at the two journalists. 'It involved one of their workmates, a journalist at the *Times of Zambia*. He had an affair with one of the wives. She was young, no kids, bored out of her head of course, like so many of them here with all the servants and what not.'

She waved the gin bottle at Evelyn and she let her pour another jigger. 'Anyway, she ups and leaves her husband, a good-looking fellow, quite high up in Cable & Wireless, and runs off with this journalist. Went to live in his family compound, can you imagine that?'

Evelyn thought of the woman in the faded-print frock pounding mielie-meal with a baby tied around her back, and felt her stomach begin to roil.

Jean shook her head. 'Poor Helen. She can never come back now, of course. It's all right the other way round – but a white woman with a black man? No, that's too hard for both sides to accept.' She picked up the cloth again and sighed. 'Poor Helen,' she said again. 'She used to be so pretty and full of fun. I hear she has a hard life. I'll bet she regrets it now.'

Evelyn tried to imagine herself building a wooden fire to cook maize porridge in a blackened pot, hoeing in the field, or looking after children she'd given birth to in a shack, while all around her women watched her, their dark eyes darting and stabbing. Her forehead grew clammy and she put down her drink. She couldn't do this. Sweat prickled her neck. What if it had already started and there was a tiny bud growing inside her?

Jean frowned at her. 'Are you all right, dear? You've gone awfully pale. Have you eaten today? You shouldn't be drinking on an empty stomach in this heat, that's asking for trouble.'

Evelyn ran to the loo and vomited into the pan.

A Face at the Window

Chrissie vomited into the basin she was holding in her lap. Her mother rubbed her back and called her *chick* and *my wee hen*. She heaved again and sobbed when nothing came out. *It's sore!* Her mum put the basin on the floor and pulled the sheet up to her chin but Chrissie threw it off. *Hot, so hot.* A cold cloth was pressed to her forehead. Her mother switched off the bedside light and left the room, leaving her in darkness. Chrissie's breathing grew even and she closed her eyes. A murmur of voices and the door clicked shut. It was so quiet; she might fall asleep. The room began to go slowly round in circles but she didn't feel sick, only hot then cold then hot and cold. *Scritch, scritch, scritch.* There was something at the metal mosquito netting in the window. Chrissie thought of the bedtime story she and her sister begged their mother to read to them every night about the Hobyahs and Little Dog Toby. The Hobyahs were little goblins that stole into a little old man and little old woman's house every night. The little old man cut off their dog Toby's legs and head when he tried to warn them. Inside, the little dog was all yellow, like a sweet potato. Chrissie turned her head to find a cool bit of pillow. There weren't really any Hobyahs. Only Cat still thought that because she was the littlest. *Scritch, scritch, scritch.* If she kept her eyes shut it would go away. *Scritch, scritch, scritch.* Then a small creak as the window opened. Hamish! He was playing one of his tricks on her. Relieved, she let her eyes fly open and turned her head to shout at him.

Nyirongo stared at her from the window.

'*Eh-eh*. You still alive, little white rat? I'll get you some day. I have powerful medicine. I get everyone in the end. Your friend the Barotse thinks he has escaped from me, but I will get him too.' He jabbed his finger at her. 'And I will get you too, you will see, just like I got your little boyfriend Elijah.'

He bared his teeth at her and Chrissie whimpered and ducked under the bedcovers. When she poked her head out, he'd disappeared. The outside light shone on the window and she could see a corner had been cut away so that the metal screen curled up. There was a rustle, like dry paper scales moving across the tiles. She tore her eyes away from the window and sat up in bed to see what was in the corner, but it was too dark. There was a hiss and Chrissie screamed. Footsteps came running and the light popped on. She saw a black mamba slithering across the floor towards her bed. Something jumped on the floor. She screamed again and a frog hopped towards her. The snake opened its mouth wide enough to show the black skin inside, seized the frog in its jaws and began to gulp it down, its eyes bulging. Samson ran past in a blur of khaki, raised his machete and brought it down on the snake. Chrissie scrambled up to the headboard, as far away from the snake as possible, buried her face in her knees and began to cry. Samson pulled her onto to his lap, hushing and rocking her until her sobs quieted and she fell into a dark well of sleep.

Later, Chrissie woke to voices in the corridor. There were low ones, quiet and steady– her father and Samson – and a sharp frightened high one – her mother.

'How could this have happened, Jim? I thought you said they never came into the house, not the big ones.'

'Don't take on so, dear. There's no harm done and Chrissie is fine, thanks to Samson.'

There was a singsong murmur she couldn't make out – Samson. He had saved her. He had saved her when he could not save his Elijah. Chrissie began to cry again.

Her mother again: 'What a country! Chrissie ill with God knows what. I can't tell if it's malaria or hepatitis and no doctor will come out this far and they're no bloody good even if they did. And now

211

this. Why did you ever bring us to this Godforsaken place, Jim Docherty?' Chrissie heard the tap-tap of heels down the corridor. They must have been out, that's the only time her mother wore high heels. That was why Samson had come in when she screamed and not her mum or dad. Chrissie closed her eyes. Her head hurt and she wanted a drink of water. Samson was talking again and she tried to listen.

'Mr Docherty, this is bad magic.'

'Samson, not you too! I thought you were Jehovah's Witness? As if it wasn't bad enough having to deal with this mumbo-jumbo at work all day, now I have to deal with it at home too.'

'Mr Docherty, please listen to me. This must be a powerful witch to send a black mamba. These spells do not usually work on white people. You are all in terrible danger. You need protection.'

Chrissie knew Samson was right and tried to get out of bed to tell her father that he must believe him, but her legs were heavy, as if they were filled with sand. If only she had her Irish granny's caul. Something shifted on her neck and she put her hand up to find Elijah's *cibalili*. Samson must have put it on her. She stopped shivering and sank into the cool sheets, closing her eyes.

'Look, how many times do I have to tell you people...?' her father said. Chrissie heard him move away down the corridor with Samson. She began to dream of a bearded collie barking and a swarm of bees answering in singsong murmurs.

THE LAST TIME

Evelyn waited on the veranda for her husband to come home. Her hair was still damp and she had on a black dress Robert particularly liked. She nursed a tumbler of whisky and soda and watched as headlights moved up the road. Robert. She sipped her drink as the Land Rover drew closer. In the bath, lying in the tepid water, she had made up her mind to leave him. When she met Robert she'd been convinced that love – the love in story books full of moons and swoons and trembling desire – did not exist, or that if it did, it no longer mattered to her and she would never again need it or seek it out. She had decided, in that seedy London studio looking down on Patrick and Miranda on the mattress on the floor and watching their mouths shape those ugly words, that she was finished with love. She had tried it once and it had nearly broken her in two and she had vowed she would never again throw herself back into that vortex of pain. Robert, with his careful manners and kindness, had made her feel safe, as if she had sailed into a sheltered harbour from stormy seas. At first, Evelyn liked the way he looked at her, as if he were slightly distracted. He seemed to have no interest in what went on in her mind. It was such a relief after the ravenous way Patrick had torn into her thoughts, gnawing at the bones of them long after she'd given him up. Now she realised that far from being a pillar of strength, Robert had built a wall around the traumatised boy who had never got over the twin pains of his mother's infidelity and her death. Evelyn had to face up to it: despite the heady romance of their early days together, the flowers and elegant restaurants, they had been drawn to each other because they were both terrified of real intimacy and of the possibility of being hurt. They were like two rooks in a chess game that could only move in straight lines. It had only taken a nudge from Joseph to tip the delicate balance of their relationship and send the pieces crashing off the board.

But Joseph had saved her. This was love: so hot and radiant and maddening it was not to be denied. The force of it had pulled her over the edge and into the whirlpool and instead of smashing against the rocks or drowning, she had glided through its waters and found what she didn't know she had lost: her true self.

Evelyn shifted slightly in her seat, and stared unblinkingly at the headlights as they grew larger and brighter. Her fingers had turned white around the tumbler and she took another fiery sip of whisky. She was going to tell Robert it was over. It was the decent thing to do: she wouldn't funk it and slip off, leaving a note. No, she would say goodbye the best way she could, by giving him a last gift of tenderness. Evelyn watched her husband walk heavily up the steps; he looked tired. She reached up to him, opened her mouth to his kiss and pulled him down to the sofa, unbuckling his belt. His hands slid up her legs and he gasped as he found her naked under her dress. The chorus of insects from the darkness beyond the trees seemed to grow louder. *The last time, this is the last time*, Evelyn thought as he pulled back her hair and she arched her back, biting his shoulder to stifle a cry that matched his.

Afterwards, they watched the spider lilies open with a silent pop: their milk-white petals reaching for the moonlight. Robert took a sip from Evelyn's tumbler. He made a face and she took it from him.

'The ice has melted, I'll get you another. Then I want to talk to you about something,' Evelyn said. She stood up and straightened her dress, but he caught her hand and pulled her back down. Robert took her face in his hands and kissed her brow, her cheeks, nose, mouth, and the line of her jaw.

'I know I've been away a lot, and that I've been distant. You see, I still couldn't get it out of my head you might be seeing Gerry Mann.' She opened her mouth but Robert caught her hand and carried on. 'I know, I know, all utter nonsense. But, I've had time to think on this last trip, and I want us to start again.' He lifted her hand to his mouth. 'Things are going to be different now, I promise.'

Evelyn heard the rawness in his voice and knew he meant what he said, but it was too late for them now. If he'd spoken like this before, they might have had a chance, but now there was Joseph. She heard a rushing like water in her ears: it was the wind shushing through the eucalyptus trees, making the leaves rattle. She swung her feet to the ground. 'I'll go and get that drink for you.' Then she would tell him.

He held onto her arm. 'Don't move, Sixpence can get my drink. Christ! Sixpence! Do you think he saw us?'

Evelyn couldn't help laughing. 'It's a bit late now. Don't worry, he asked for the night off. He's gone to the village – a funeral I think he said.'

Robert rubbed his hand through his hair. 'This bloody epidemic. A child died last week – Elijah, the son of the Dochertys' houseboy.' Evelyn sat down again. She hadn't realised when she'd been looking at Joseph's drawings that the little boy in them was dead. Robert was still talking. 'He was only about eight or nine. It's what I've been dealing with all this time. The villagers want someone to blame and are sure there's a witch on the prowl, someone who cast a spell and caused the child's death – the usual bloody nonsense. Some things never change in Africa, no matter how much people like me have tried to bring about change. In my darker moments, I wonder if my life's work here has made any difference. When the last of us has gone, the bush will take back the roads and farms and the people will carry on as if we'd never been here.' He drained the last of her whisky. 'And to make matters worse, now little Chrissie Docherty has caught whatever's going round.'

Evelyn remembered Joseph's drawing: two faces peeking out of a bush, one white, and one black. She splashed more whisky into the glass and handed it to Robert. 'They were friends, Chrissie and Elijah. Poor little thing, she must be heartbroken.'

Robert turned the tumbler in hand. 'I doubt she'll be aware of much. She's in a bad way – she might not make it. Jim and Grace are out of their minds with worry.'

In the clinic up in the hills, when Tom O'Brian had talked about child mortality rates in Zambia, Evelyn had only half-listened. The diseases had such exotic names, they didn't seem quite real – bilharzia, sleeping sickness, hepatitis, cholera, malaria, elephantiasis – but oddly enough it had never occurred to her that anyone she knew would catch them, let alone a funny little scrap like Chrissie Docherty. Evelyn tried to picture Chrissie running around the compound in only her pants and flip-flops, but all she could see was the black outline of the Chalimbana hills.

The night air brought a distant drumming and she sat up and turned her head. 'What's that?'

Robert walked to the edge of the veranda and looked out over the dark valley, dotted with lights from their neighbours' houses. 'There's going to be trouble. There always is after a child dies.' He turned to face her. 'What did you want to talk about?'

A breeze came down off the hills and Evelyn shivered despite the sweat on her forehead. The news of Elijah's death and Chrissie's illness had unsettled her. Robert had had enough to deal with over the last few days. She would tell him tomorrow when he was rested. 'Never mind. Let's go inside.'

MR HEATH'S HELICOPTERS

Robert was right: trouble did come, right to their door. They were woken in the middle of the night by hammering. Groggy with sleep, Evelyn pulled on her dressing gown and followed Robert into the sitting room. She saw him go to the drawer where he kept his gun and hold it down by his side while he opened the door. Hamish Docherty stood on the doorstep in pyjamas and bare feet.

'Dad says I'm to warn you, Mr Fielding. There are people in our garden. Dad says they're dangerous. They don't like the helicopters.'

Evelyn came to stand next to her husband. 'What do you mean, Hamish? What does he mean, Robert?'

'Damn, I was afraid of this. Heath sold helicopters to the Southern Rhodesian Government just as Ian Smith has been putting down the rebels, the Patriotic Front. Some of the PF men have been spotted around here recently. And, to cap it all, the village elders hinted someone had been stirring things up, holding secret anti-government rallies – that bloody Gerry Mann, I shouldn't wonder. I'd turned a blind eye to his rabble rousing, but he's gone too far this time. The place is already a tinderbox with this business of the dead child.' He turned back to the boy, who was waiting on the doorstep. 'All right, Hamish, tell your father I'm coming.'

'Thanks, Mr Fielding.' Hamish ran back towards his house.

Evelyn poked her head out of the door and could see lights flickering through the Dochertys' fence and hear shouting. It reminded her of the night they saved Joseph, but this seemed less of an adventure and more frightening. She thought of the *panga* murders, of the man chopped into little pieces by the villagers. Evelyn retreated behind the screen door and went to find Robert. He had dressed quickly in khaki shorts and shirt and was lacing his boots over knee-length white socks.

'You look like something out of Rider Haggard,' she said.

'This uniform still means authority and the rule of law out here.' Robert went to the door. 'I want you to lock up and keep the lights off. Stay indoors, do you hear?'

She clung to his arm, afraid for him. 'Don't go, Robert,' she said. 'Let the police deal with this.'

'Evelyn, this is the bush – there's one policeman and he's probably drunk. Don't worry, I know these people. Stay here where you're safe.'

He had gone before she could stop him. Alone, Evelyn began pacing the floor. What if Robert didn't come back? What if the Dochertys were murdered, their throats cut? She'd heard the stories; everyone had heard the stories. Hadn't there had been a white woman pulled from her car and set on fire by a gang of men? She remembered what Gerry had told her: there were only 70,000 whites out of nearly five million people, in a country half the size of Europe. What were they doing here, any of them, in the middle of bloody nowhere? They'd all be murdered. Panic climbed out of the pit of her stomach clawed its way up her throat. The Dochertys' youngest was only four. And then there was Chrissie. Evelyn imagined her huddled under the bedcovers sick and terrified. She stopped pacing and tried to calm down. She couldn't stay here wringing her hands: she had to do something.

Evelyn let herself out of the house and crept up to the fence. There was a large crowd of more than a hundred as far as she could tell, shouting and waving *pangas* and hoes. They held burning torches and what looked like Guys, as if it were a sinister bonfire night. One of the figures was on fire, a placard around its neck: *Ted Heath Murderer*. Parts of the fence had been trampled flat and the lawn was filled with people. Her husband stood on the Dochertys' veranda steps next to Jim and was addressing the crowd but she couldn't hear what he was saying. One of the men stepped forward and began to shout and wave his arms about. It was that horrible man again, the so-called witchdoctor. Evelyn had already seen what he could do with a crowd. The Dochertys didn't stand a chance. She turned and ran toward the Land Rover. Gerry Mann had started this; he could damn well stop it.

Gerry opened the door to his bungalow, barefoot and bare-chested. Evelyn tried not to flinch at the smell of alcohol. She remembered the White Fathers' mission and how he had towered over her, his face twisted with disgust, and how terrified she had been. Now he just looked tired and drunk. He turned and lurched inside and she followed him.

Gerry picked up a nearly-empty bottle of Gordon's with its pretty yellow label patterned with juniper leaves and berries and waved it at her. 'Drink?' She shook her head. He shrugged and tipped the last of the gin into his glass and downed it neat.

'Gerry,' she said. 'You've got to help me.'

He swung round and stared at her. 'I've got to help you? That's a laugh. Why should I do anything for you?' He pointed his finger in her face. When she didn't back away, he dropped his hand and sat down heavily. 'What are you doing here, Evelyn?'

She sat down opposite him. 'There's trouble over at the Dochertys, some sort of political demonstration.'

He raised his glass and smiled blearily. 'I heard they were going to protest. About time they took some action. Good for them!'

'But, Gerry, the Dochertys are in danger.'

He shrugged. 'So what? The people have a right to protest. This is a democracy after all. I say, let them burn down Docherty's house. He's in the pay of the British Government; it's up to him to take the rap for their policies in Africa.' He glared at her, his eyes tiny and red. 'And now you're here to try and save your own skin. You're frightened they'll come after you and your *Boma* husband next.'

Evelyn tried to keep her voice steady. 'Gerry, listen to me. Whatever you think of me, you've got to do something to stop this before someone is hurt. It's turned ugly. That mob, they're drunk and armed. I saw some of your secondary school students, and those men we met at the bottle shop,' she tried to remember what he'd called them. 'Activists. You've got to come and talk to them, they'll listen to you.'

'Why should I? That smug bastard Jim Docherty's only got what was coming to him. He's just as bad as all those Old Etonians in Whitehall who still think the sun will never set over the British bloody Empire.'

Evelyn couldn't believe she'd once admired his rhetoric; it was all hot air, his personal grievances dressed up as a manifesto. But surely he wouldn't stand by and let his neighbours come to harm? She tried one last time.

'Gerry, for pity's sake, there are children in that house, one of them a little girl who is too sick to move.'

'So what? African children die every day and nobody cares. Anyway, the means justify the end.' He waved his drink and it slopped over the rim. 'Now, run along to your colonial husband, like a good little wife. I overestimated you, Evelyn. I should have known you'd never have the guts to leave him.' He was slurring his words now. 'In the end your sort always sticks together, looking after number one.'

Evelyn gave up and walked towards the door. She had been naive to think Gerry would help. Robert had been right about him all along and Gerry, for all his talk of a fairer world, was only concerned about himself. Robert was ten times the man he was. She turned to tell him that but he got in first.

'Here's a thought – why don't you get your precious Joseph to help you? He's your champion now. I have to hand it to you, Evelyn. You really have gone native.' She ran down the steps but his ugly laughter followed her into the night.

Evelyn revved the Land Rover and raced up the road, imagining the Dochertys slaughtered, their blood spattered over the walls of their bungalow. But when she pulled up at their house she saw Robert on the veranda, speaking to the crowd who seemed oddly quiet. She laid her forehead on the steering wheel and concentrated on breathing until she was steady enough to get out of the car. She could hear Robert's clear English voice resonating over the heads of the people standing silently on the lawn. Every now and then a murmur went up, like the sighing of the wind.

'Queen Elizabeth is a friend of Zambia. Didn't she give back to Zambians what was rightfully theirs? This country is already yours. You do not need to be rebels here.'

An older man stepped out of the crowd. 'If the British are our friends, then why did they give the helicopters to the Rhodesian *Boma*? The whites only look after each other.' *Mmmmhmmm* came from behind him.

Robert walked down the steps until he stood face-to-face with the older man, and put his hand on his shoulder. 'This was a mistake by Ted Heath. Queen Elizabeth will punish him for it. Daniel, as village elder, you know only too well what it is like when an impulsive, younger man acts on his own and upsets people with his foolishness.'

'This is true, *Maganga*.' Daniel turned and glared at some of the young men and they lowered their heads.

Robert opened his hands to show his palms. 'We have always lived in peace now and before independence. You ran your own affairs and only came to me if a dispute could not be settled.' *Mmmmhmmm*. The dense knot of people seemed to loosen as people turned to nod and speak to each other. 'Let's forget all about this unfortunate misunderstanding.'

Daniel nodded and shook hands with Robert. He turned to the people behind him and opened his arms like a priest giving a blessing and they began to leave. Soon, the only sign of the scene was the trampled fence.

As Robert stood there watching them leave, Evelyn saw that he was in command, and that this was natural to him. He seemed like a different man from the diffident stranger she'd met at the Soho gallery, somehow taller and broader. This was the role he was born and bred for, a role that he'd taken back for one night. She saw now that Africa was his home, but there was no longer a place in it for him, and she was desperately sad for him. Robert turned and said something inaudible to Jim; they were still laughing when he spotted Evelyn. She ran up the steps and he held open his arms.

'Darling, didn't I tell you to stay inside?' he said.

Robert sat down with a sigh and she perched on the arm of his chair.

Jim poured out three tumblers of whisky. 'Your husband is a

221

remarkable chap.' He handed Robert a drink. 'Masterful is the only word to describe him, bloody masterful.' Jim went round with the whisky bottle again. 'Are you still going hunting tomorrow?'

Robert yawned and indicated the hills where the sky was turning pale green. 'I was going to leave at dawn but it'll have to be after breakfast, unless I'm to fall asleep on the way.' He put his hand on Evelyn's back. 'Damn, I forgot to tell you about the hunting trip. It's been set up for weeks and I kept meaning to tell you but I've been so busy with this bloody epidemic. You don't mind do you, darling?'

Evelyn shook her head. She would tell him she was leaving when he came back. He was a good man, a brave man, but she didn't love him; she loved Joseph. She had to leave him, to save herself, and to take the gift she had been given.

'You're a brick,' he said and squeezed her hand. He turned to Jim. 'Tom O'Brian's coming on the hunt. Can I persuade you to join us as well? It'll be a chance for you get out into the wild and bag a nice fat impala for the pot.'

'I might be tempted.'

The men were discussing arrangements when the priest's car drew up.

Jim stood up. 'Speak of the devil. You're a bit early for the hunt.'

Tom O'Brian leapt up the steps, two at a time. 'Jim, you have to come quick. It's the college – it's on fire.'

It was like Bonfire Night. Every time one of the crates with audio equipment caught fire, the explosion sent sparks whooshing into the lightening sky and the crowd gasped and clapped their hands. There was a carnival atmosphere: the village women had come to watch the sky burst into stars and the children were running in and out of the adults' legs. Evelyn stood with Robert and Jim Docherty.

'Shouldn't we be passing buckets of water along to put the fire out?' she said.

Another crate went up. Jim didn't take his eyes off the fountain of sparks. 'No point, it's too far gone. By the time the fire brigade gets here from Lusaka there'll be nothing left but smoke and ash. Might as well enjoy the show.'

'But all that expensive equipment, the waste!' she said.

'The World Bank has it all insured,' Jim said. 'I'll just put in another order.'

Robert grinned. 'That's the spirit, Jim – more money for British suppliers.'

Evelyn couldn't understand why they were so relaxed. She would have been in despair if everything she'd worked for had gone up in smoke in one night.

'But it will take so long to rebuild everything,' she said to Jim. 'Your new language lab, it must have taken you years to set it up.'

His laughter was sour. 'What can you do? It's Africa. You either accept it or go mad.'

Later, back at her bungalow, Evelyn offered Father O'Brian tea. He'd come in while Robert was checking the grounds with Jim.

'I'd rather have a drop of whisky,' he said. They sipped their drinks and watched the jade sky turn red. Tom sighed and shifted in his seat. 'I never get tired of the sunrises here. I don't know how I'll cope when I'm back in Ireland and the rain is pelting down day after day. No wonder it's so bloody green.'

Evelyn frowned. 'There's no chance of that, is there?'

'What?'

'You going back to Ireland?'

He looked mournfully into his empty glass. 'The Church wants me to go home and recharge my batteries, whatever that's supposed to mean.' Evelyn poured him another measure and he grinned at her. 'This is all the recharging I need. They'll have to drag me out of Africa by my heels if they want me to leave. I've been here since I was just out of the seminary. What would I do back in Ireland? Count sheep and say the rosary?' Evelyn laughed and he put his hand on hers. He leaned towards her and spoke quietly. 'Joseph Makelele came to see me last night.'

A worm of excitement went through Evelyn. 'But it's not safe for him here.'

'That's what I told him. Nyirongo won't miss him twice. But he wouldn't listen, told me he couldn't stay away, that he's come back for the woman he loves. You wouldn't know anything about that would you?'

Evelyn stared at the hills, lavender in the morning light. Joseph had come back, for her. Her fingernails dug crescent moons into her palm. He'd risked everything to come and get her. As the sun rose, the hills were bathed in gold. Tom sighed and she turned to let him see her happiness. I am not afraid, she thought.

'Evelyn, listen to me,' he said. 'I'm not judging you, but you must be careful. I've sinned as much as the next person and I know what can happen when people fall in love.' She raised her eyebrows and he laughed. 'Don't look so surprised,' he said. 'I'm an ordinary man, not a celestial being sent down from heaven.'

Evelyn stood up. 'Tom, you're one of the most extraordinary people I've ever met. But you should mind your own business.'

He settled back in the armchair. 'Well, I'm afraid I can't do that. It's my job to be a nosy beggar.' She started to walk away but he caught at her hand again. 'I don't know what you think you're doing, but no good will come of it. For everyone's sake, you must send Joseph away. His family will turn their backs on him, and he'll never get a job or a place at university once the word is out that he's with a white woman. You could ruin his future. If you won't do it for me, do it for him.'

Evelyn's hand shook. She hadn't thought about what being together would mean for Joseph. 'What makes you think he'll come here?'

Tom gave her a long look. 'How could he stay away?'

SALT

Evelyn watched Robert over her coffee cup. She would tell him this morning that she was leaving. He looked up from his paper and smiled at her. This would be the last time they would sit together in peace. The sky was full of black clouds and the air was dense. Lighting crackled and a breath later, thunder rolled down from the hills.

'Do you have to go?' she said.

'I'm afraid so, the hunting party is ready. Listen.' He put down the paper and looked towards the hills. She heard a swelling wave of harmony from somewhere beyond the fence.

'What are they singing? I've never heard anything like it.'

'A hunting song.' He cocked his head and listened for a moment. 'They're asking their ancestors to guide their spears.'

Evelyn listened to the deep voices; the skin along her spine prickled. A sudden wind brought wood smoke with it: the early morning smell of Africa.

She tried to picture Joseph in London, wrapped up in a scarf to keep the cold away, standing in front of an easel in a life drawing class. But what if she couldn't persuade Joseph to leave Africa? How would they live if he couldn't study or get a job? Evelyn saw the white woman from the compound, the desperate way she had clung to Tom O'Brian, her sagging dress and shoes made from old tyres and children clinging to her legs.

Damn that interfering priest. If only Tom hadn't come round and put doubts in her mind. If only Robert hadn't been so vulnerable and tender and trusting last night, and then so noble and good and strong, it would be so much easier to tell him she was leaving. She took a gulp of coffee and scalded her tongue. She would tell him. She would. And then what? She squeezed her eyes shut as if to push the image of the woman in the compound out of her mind.

Robert didn't seem to notice. He picked up the *Times of Zambia* again and shook it out. She saw the headline: *Ndola Woman Gives Birth to Bird.*

'See there's been another murder, in Livingstone this time,' he said. 'Christ, this country's going hell in a handbasket. That's why it isn't safe for you to go off on your own like you did last night.' He frowned. 'Livingstone. Isn't that where you went while I was away? Some sort of retreat at Tom's holy HQ?' He raised his eyebrows at her over the newspaper. 'I'll have to watch out. You'll be turning Roman on me if we're not careful. Can't have you genuflecting in front of Reverend Waters at the Christmas service. He'd have a fit, the poor old dear.'

Evelyn put down her cup. 'How did it happen? The murder, I mean.'

Robert folded the paper and threw it on the table. 'Never mind that, I'd rather look at you. Come here.'

One last embrace before the pain. Evelyn went over and sat on his lap. She bent her head to kiss him and Joseph's medal came loose, hanging between them.

Robert took it between his fingers. 'Where did you get this horrible thing from?'

She thought quickly. 'Oh, Tom gave it to me.'

'More papist nonsense! It looks dreadful, a fairground trinket. Why don't you wear your pearls?'

Evelyn tucked the medal away. 'They're too good for every day. I don't want to lose them.' She kissed him to distract him and after a while he held her more tightly.

Sixpence chose that moment to appear on the veranda, his expression as stiff as an ebony mask. Evelyn scrambled off Robert's lap and went back to her chair. Sixpence padded silently around the table in his bare feet and put plates of scrambled egg and slices of pawpaw in front of them. Robert took a forkful of the eggs and made a face.

'Sixpence, how long have we been together?'

'Twenty years, boss.'

'Twenty years and you still haven't learned to season my eggs properly. I'll have to trade you in for a new model.' He winked at Evelyn. 'Pass me the salt darling,'

Evelyn was about to hand him the saltshaker when Sixpence shouted: 'No, boss!' and knocked it out of Robert's hand. It shattered on the floor. They all stared at the broken glass and salt scattered over the red tiles.

'What on earth do you think you're doing?' Evelyn said at last. She looked at Robert waiting for him to lay into Sixpence, but he just stared at her. His hands slowly clenched into fists and he narrowed his eyes at her. Evelyn laughed nervously. What was the matter with him? Why was he looking at her like that? She glanced at Sixpence but he stood with his head bent, like a messenger who has delivered bad news. In the distance, thunder rumbled and a gust of wind whipped rain into the veranda.

Evelyn touched one of Robert's hands. His knuckles were white. 'What is it?' she said. 'What's going on?' Sixpence went back inside the bungalow. When Robert spoke it was in the dry, matter-of-fact voice he used on official business.

'Where did you go last night'?

She went still. 'What do you mean?' He banged his fists on the table and she started.

'It's a simple question. Where did you go when I was with Jim Docherty? You needn't deny it, I saw you drive off in the car. Whom did you go to meet?'

Evelyn stared at him and said nothing.

He came to stand above her, his fists by his side. She shrank away from him instinctively, remembering the men in the sugar can field, Gerry in the same stance. She knew Robert would never hurt her, but she couldn't help herself. He put out his hand to her and she pushed back her chair to get away from him.

He stared at her, aghast. 'Do you really think I'd lay a finger on you? Is that the kind of man you think I am?' He wrenched open the screen door and went into the house. When he came back out, he was carrying his hunting rifle. Evelyn, desperate to find out what had upset him, tried to block his path, but he brushed her off and strode down the steps and over to the Land Rover. He threw the rifle into the jeep and got in after it, slamming the door.

She ran down the steps and stood at the window. 'What's happened? What are you doing? Where are you going?'

He put the engine into gear. 'Get out of the way.'

Evelyn stepped back and watched him drive off in a cloud of dust and exhaust fumes. She heard a movement behind her and turned round. It was Sixpence. For the first time he looked directly at her. She saw his mouth twist in contempt and something in the way he looked at her that she hadn't recognised until now: desire. Evelyn was suddenly aware of how alone and vulnerable she was. Sixpence moved closer. She stepped back and felt her ankle turn in a pothole left by the rain. Sixpence reached around her and caught her round the waist. Evelyn closed her eyes and turned her head. She could smell the cloves on his breath. He let her go and she stumbled again. When she opened her eyes, Sixpence had gone.

MULBERRIES

Evelyn was too frightened to go back into the house. Sixpence was behind the screen door, watching her. She took several deep breaths and looked at the hills; they had always calmed her before but they were threatening this morning, shrouded in sheets of rain. Robert might be back soon from wherever he'd gone. Evelyn didn't know what had got into him. One minute they'd been having breakfast and the next he'd stormed off. This wasn't what she'd planned for this morning. It was going to be brutally simple: she'd leave Robert and be with Joseph, and they'd work something out, somehow. Now she felt her resolve weakening. What if she wasn't strong enough for the storm that would break over them once the news was out?

Evelyn heard a sound from next door and saw Grace Docherty coming out with a bowl. She headed towards the mulberry bush between their houses and began picking the fruit.

Grateful for the distraction, Evelyn went to help her. 'How's Chrissie?'

Grace looked haggard. 'She hasn't eaten for days, just turns her head away when I bring her anything. But this morning she said she was hungry and asked for mulberries, so here I am.' Her hands trembled and when she reached to pick a berry off the top of the bush, the bowl went tumbling to the ground. Grace's shoulders slumped and she began to weep. 'I'm sorry. I thought I was going to lose her.'

Evelyn put her arms around her and led her to the Dochertys' veranda. 'Here, you sit down and have a rest, you're exhausted. I'll pick the berries and take them into Chrissie, sit with her for a while. How would that be?'

Grace nodded and laid her head back on the sofa and closed her eyes. 'Thank you.'

Chrissie was sleeping when Evelyn went in to her bedroom. Her little face was gaunt and pale, but her forehead was cool and her breathing even. Evelyn put the bowl of mulberries next to her bed and sat in the chair Grace had placed next to the bed. A sense of peace stole over her in the child's bedroom. A photograph was lying on the bedside table. Evelyn picked it up. It was of Chrissie and her friend Elijah. They were sitting in the flame tree. At the foot of the tree, the little one, Cat, sat in a doll's pram, grinning as she was pushed by an African toddler. Behind the pram, Hamish and Angus stood with their arms around a taller African boy. Evelyn propped the photograph against a water jug. Her mind had been troubled with doubts but now it cleared. Children were colour blind, and that was how it should be. She pictured Joseph standing next to the jacaranda tree, his hands loosely at his side. She was certain that they would be together again. Her eyes itched and she realised how tired she was after the broken night. Evelyn laid her head on the little girl's counterpane and fell asleep.

She woke around noon to find Chrissie staring at her from the bed, her pupils huge in her dark eyes.

Evelyn put her hand on Chrissie's forehead. 'How are you feeling?' The girl stared at her as if she hadn't heard her. When she spoke she sounded as if she were at the bottom of a well.

'You have to warn Joseph.'

'Ssshh, now, Joseph is safe. Father O'Brian is looking after him.'

Chrissie focused on Evelyn. She sat up and grabbed Evelyn's hand and wouldn't let it go. 'You must tell Joseph that Nyirongo is coming after him. He'll kill him just like he killed Elijah.' She pointed at the window. 'Nyirongo came to see me and said he's going to get Joseph. Tell Joseph to wear his charm. I didn't bring Elijah's back in time.'

Chrissie sank back onto the pillows, closed her eyes, and was asleep in an instant. Evelyn pulled the sheet up to her chin. The poor girl was delirious. All the same, she touched the St Christopher medal around her neck and wished Joseph were still wearing it.

Grace bustled in. 'Thanks for sitting with Chrissie. I'll take it from here. Oh, and Tom's next door to see you.'

The priest was waiting for Evelyn on her veranda. He watched her come up the steps. She realised her feet were bare and dirty, her hair a mess.

'Well, aren't you a sight for sore eyes?' he said.

Evelyn studied his long face, his thick head of white hair, and the kindness of his blue eyes. She would ask him if she could teach in the mission school. After sitting in the girl's bedroom, she knew more than ever that she had to leave Robert. She could teach while Joseph went to university in Lusaka. Evelyn pictured the children all gathered around under the shade of the big mango tree, reciting the alphabet. She would nurture their creativity; the bush with its colours and the vastness of its plains and skies was the perfect place to teach art. She didn't have to live a half-life any more: she could be happy. Here in Africa, with Joseph, she could be happy.

She put her arms around Tom and leaned her head on his shoulder.

He patted her on the back. 'If I'd known I would get such a warm welcome I'd have come earlier.' She wiped her eyes and smiled. 'You look worn out,' he said and led her to the sofa where they sat down. 'I'm tired myself. I've been putting out a fire at the clinic all morning. They tried to burn that down too. Well, they'll just have to rebuild it, brick by bloody brick. First the Dochertys, then the college, and now this – I don't know what's got into them.'

'I've been thinking,' Evelyn said. 'Maybe I could do some teaching, if you'll have me back.'

He raised his eyebrows. 'I thought you'd finished with my wee mission? But I'd be glad to have you back. The salary's not what you'd get back home but the children are a joy – they have a real thirst for learning. Bless you, you'll make a good teacher, although Sister Bernadette will miss you in the clinic.'

She put her arm through his. 'Thank you, Tom. You don't know how much this means to me.'

He nodded at the empty driveway. 'Now, where's that husband of yours? We're supposed to go hunting. Don't tell me he's gone off without me? I've been looking forward to this for weeks.'

Evelyn crossed the veranda and shaded her eyes as she looked out towards the road. 'I don't know where he's gone. I'm afraid we had a bit of a fight this morning, over nothing. He tore off just after breakfast in the strangest mood. I can't think what the matter is with him.' She glanced at the screen door to make sure Sixpence wasn't listening and lowered her voice. 'Something rather odd happened and I don't quite know what to make of it.' She told him about Sixpence knocking the salt out of Robert's hand, and his expression turned grim. 'What is it?' she said.

He shook his head. 'This is bad, this is very bad.'

'What do you mean? I wish you'd tell me. I feel as if everyone else knows something and I'm the only one in the dark.'

The priest wrinkled his forehead. 'Sixpence is Bemba, isn't he?'

'I have absolutely no idea.'

'I think he is. Robert brought him over after his stint in Malawi. But the Bemba, and the Chewa and a lot of the other tribes share a lot of the same superstitions.' He rubbed his chin and she could hear the bristles scraping against his hand. 'Let me remember how it goes, so. If a man comes back after a trip and his wife has been unfaithful to him, and she passes him salt and he eats it, he'll die as sure as if he's been fed poison. That's what they believe. Sixpence must think you... well he was trying to protect his master.'

Evelyn went cold. She remembered Sixpence staring after her and Gerry as they left her bedroom in the middle of the night.

'Tom, I'm afraid Sixpence may have got the wrong idea about Gerry and me. He saw us come out of my bedroom together when we were going to rescue Joseph, but we'd only gone in there to fetch a bag of supplies.'

The priest put his head in his hands. 'This is bad. Robert grew up here and he knows the African superstitions. And, I'm sure you know there's been talk about you and Gerry, so he'll have put it all together and gone to look for Mann.' He looked up at her. 'But hang on a minute, that can't be right. Robert was there the night you rescued Joseph – he was helping you, wasn't he?' Evelyn couldn't meet his eyes and the priest sighed wearily. 'You didn't ask him for his help, did you? You went to Gerry instead of your own husband.'

A breeze lifted the swing door from its hinges and it yawned open. Evelyn saw the empty rifle cupboard and she had a terrible thought. She clutched the priest's hand. 'The rifle – Robert took it when he left.'

'Well, he's going hunting.'

'Yes, but not then, he wasn't going hunting first thing. He said last night that he'd set out later.'

'So, where did he go?'

'He wouldn't say, but if you're right then he suspects Gerry.'

'Dear God!'

Tom ran down the steps towards his car and she shouted after him: 'Where are you going?'

'To find your husband and stop him doing something stupid.'

Evelyn hugged herself and looked out over the darkening hills. This wasn't what she'd planned. This shouldn't be happening. None of this should be happening.

She waited for what seemed like hours but when Tom came back she looked at her watch and saw he'd only been away for half an hour. Evelyn ran to meet him but he stayed in his car.

'Did you find Robert?'

He shook his head and stared through the windscreen, refusing to look at Evelyn. 'No, I didn't find him, but I saw Gerry Mann. He was fine – drunk as a lord and snoring fit to shake down the house, but alive and well. I went into the village and they said the *Boma* had collected the hunting party and left for the bush early. He must have calmed down.'

The priest looked at her and his expression softened and he muttered under his breath: 'God forgive me for a foolish old man.' He pinched the space between his eyes and sighed.

'Tom, I'm…'

He put up a hand. 'No, don't say anything. What I'm going to do now is catch up with the hunting party and bag myself a great big eland.' He put his hands on the wheel and met her eyes. 'And when I come back, we'll have a proper talk and you're going to behave like the good person I know you are.' Evelyn twisted her mouth to keep from crying. He placed his hand on her cheek and she looked at him through wet lashes.

His voice was gentle again. 'What you are not going to do is break Robert Fielding's heart. He already had it shattered as a child and it won't survive another blow. And when Joseph turns up on your doorstep, you're to send him away, for everyone's sake.'

WHERE THE ELANDS GRAZE

When Tom O'Brian came back later that day, Evelyn was having a nap. The sound of raised voices woke her up and she stumbled out onto the veranda, blinking in the harsh noon light, to find Sixpence on the lawn with the priest. Sixpence was on his knees, his head in his hands and wailing.

Evelyn ran down the steps. 'Whatever is the matter? Tom, what's going on?' She watched his long face crease with sorrow and his mouth open and shut without really taking in the words.

'It's Robert. The men took us to the *dambo* where the elands were grazing. I'm sorry, Evelyn, but before anyone could stop him, he stepped in front of the guns. I tried to stop the bleeding but I'm afraid there's nothing else I can do. He's still alive but he hasn't got long. He's been asking for you.' Evelyn turned away from him and looked at the hills and felt the world slow down. The blue glare from the afternoon sky sliced into her eyes and she flinched when the priest put his hand on her shoulder. 'You mustn't blame yourself.'

His words roused her. 'What did you say? I don't understand – why should I blame myself? It was an accident, a hunting accident. Robert would never...' Evelyn stopped and her scalp prickled with cold sweat. A terrible howling began. It was coming from her and she couldn't stop even though she covered her mouth with both hands. Tom put his arms around her and murmured *my child, my child*.

Evelyn could never remember the drive out to the dambo. Her eyes were fixed unseeing on the horizon and along to the thrum of the engine she told herself: *my fault, it's my fault – all my fault*. Robert was a good shot, a careful man who knew the bush and had been hunting since he was a child. When they reached camp, she saw he had been laid out in the shade, under a tree. She pulled open the car door and jumped out while the engine was still running. Evelyn stumbled and regained her footing, her breath ragged, her heart hammering as she ran towards her husband. The front of his bush shirt was stained and wet with blood. He must have heard her because he turned his head and opened his eyes, sunk in the hollows and shadows of his gaunt face. It was as if his life were draining out of him.

She knelt beside him. 'Robert, Robert...' But she couldn't find the words and took his hand and squeezed. He moistened his dry lips and tried to speak. 'What is it, my darling?' Evelyn said. He tried to speak but his voice was a dry whisper and she gave him a little water to drink. He closed his eyes to gather his strength and tried again.

'I'm sorry,' he said. 'It's the coward's way out, but I couldn't bear it, don't you see?' He licked his lips again. 'I knew you had to love him, to do what you did.' A spasm of pain sent his back into an arc and he gripped her hand. When it passed his face was beaded with sweat and he was panting. Evelyn sat quietly by his side and waited. Robert's voice, always firm and strong, was a dry whisper. 'What hurt most was that I realised you'd never loved me – not like that, and that you never would. There was nothing left but this.' He closed his eyes again and Evelyn bent to catch his last words. 'I'm sorry.' He gasped for breath and his brow furrowed in pain; then his face cleared and he was still.

Evelyn took him by the shoulders and shook him. 'Stop it, Robert! Stop it! It's me who is sorry. Robert!' She felt hands lifting her up and she turned and buried herself in Tom O'Brian's arms. He rocked her as she moaned, dry-eyed and afraid under the blackening clouds. The sky roared and the rains broke, soaking them both as they stood in front of Robert's body. Evelyn shielded her eyes from the sight and clung to the priest. 'What have I done?' she cried. 'What have I done?'

In the days following Robert's death, Evelyn only came out at night, to watch the spider lilies open. She sat wrapped in the darkness and waited for their delicate pop. Sometimes she touched their petals to see them close and open again. During the day she sat in her bedroom and watched a pair of weaverbirds flitting back and forwards with caterpillars in their beaks to the nest they had built just outside the window. She could hear the chicks peeping in the depth of the nest. One morning the nest was silent and the parents didn't come all day. She put her hand down into the sock-shaped nest and felt a cold little body. Something tickled her fingers and when she brought out her hand it was swarming with tiny ants. She started to weep. It was the first time she had been able to cry since Robert had died.

Evelyn hadn't cried when Gerry had come to the door and begged to speak to her. She'd let him in and sat in silence while he told her what had happened before the hunt.

'Fielding came round to my place ready to horsewhip me,' he said in a flat, metallic voice. 'He'd got it into his head that you and I, well that we'd been having an affair.' He twisted his hands together and laughed uncertainly but she didn't meet his eyes. 'I suppose he was half right – I wanted you so much, Evelyn, I still do.' But she only turned her head away. 'I'm sorry, now is not the time,' he said, his voice shaking. He stood up and helped himself to the whisky bottle from the sideboard. It seemed to give him a reckless courage. 'Ha! Can you believe the irony? That he would think that, after you made it clear you were too good for me.' He winced and reached for the bottle again. A little colour came back into his cheeks.

He was silent so long that Evelyn finally looked up. 'Go on. I want to hear you say it.'

His head snapped up and he blinked. 'It wasn't my fault – I was provoked. The arrogant bastard barged into my house like the colonial officer he's always been, spoke to me like I was a piece of shit on his shoes.' He glared at her as if daring her to agree. Evelyn stared back at him until he dropped his eyes. Gerry filled his glass again and took a deep swallow. 'Fielding was furious, wanted to fight me, fair and square, *outside now, Mann,* all that public school crap. I was drunk and angry, so I hit him where I knew it would hurt most.' Another slug of whisky and a desperate look as if he couldn't understand why the alcohol wasn't doing its job. 'I asked him if he knew his wife had gone native.' Evelyn drew in a breath but Gerry crashed on, too drunk and caught up in his confession to notice. He stood up and waved his arms as if talking to an imaginary Robert. 'I said to the old bastard: *Do you know a Joseph Makelele?*' Mann wiped his mouth and laughed. 'He didn't know what I meant at first but I could see it in his eyes – the understanding.' He passed his hands over his face and sat down heavily. 'It was like watching someone die in front of me.' He shook his head. 'I should have left it there but I wanted Fielding to hurt as much as I did. I said…' His voice faltered. 'I told him I'd seen you together and that he should check your neck, if he didn't believe me, because you wear Joseph's charm, a St Christopher medal, as a love token.' Evelyn's hand went to her throat and fingered the medal. Gerry was crying now, the tears running freely down his cheeks. 'I'll never forget the look in Robert's eyes. It was as if I'd stabbed him in the guts. It seemed to finish him off. He went barging out of my house and I followed, shouting I don't know what after him.' He wiped the sweat and tears off his face. 'I know, I know: I shouldn't have told him, but I didn't think the stupid bugger would go out and get himself shot.' His shoulders heaved. 'I'm sorry.'

She let him cry for a while then she stood up and opened the door. 'It's not your fault Robert's dead, it's mine. But you knew what you were doing,' she said coldly. 'What else could he do, a man like Robert, who had spent all his life in the old Africa, other than kill himself? You knew exactly what it would do to him.'

Gerry stumbled towards her, his arms outstretched. 'Evelyn, love, don't be like that! We can be friends again, put the past behind us. Don't worry, I'll never tell anyone what you did with Joseph. I'm sure it was only a moment of madness. I've succumbed to temptation myself, you know, with African girls. I understand the attraction. But that's all in the past and now you need a friend. I hate to think of you all alone out here. Come with me to Lusaka and we can start again together. I'm still in love with you.' He took her hand. His palm was moist. 'Let me look after you.'

Evelyn shook him off. 'Robert was right: you are a piece of shit.'

Over the next few days, Evelyn didn't answer the door to Gerry when he returned, or to Grace Docherty when she'd come round with a dish covered in a cloth. And when the college messenger pushed a letter through her door, it lay unopened on the floor for days. She lay on her bed, an arm shielding her eyes from the merciless sun, mind blank. Evelyn thought she'd never want to speak to anyone again, but when Tom O'Brian called her name through the screen door she let him in.

He picked up the letter and handed it to her. The franked stamp showed it was from London. She folded it in two and put it in her pocket without opening it. Tom led her carefully into the sitting room and Evelyn stared at her lap while he murmured words of comfort. She looked up when he spoke about God's forgiveness.

'In your eyes, I'm already damned, so I don't know why you're wasting your time on me,' she said and plucked at the material of her stained housecoat. 'I've caused the death of a good man I didn't deserve.'

The priest laid his hand on hers until her fingers stilled. 'God has a big heart, an endless love for his children. There is no sin that cannot be redeemed. Evelyn, you must not despair – that is the worst sin of all. Joseph and Robert had a part to play in this tragedy and they must take their share of responsibility. You've made mistakes but you can redeem yourself. To find forgiveness, to forgive yourself, you must make the rest of your life count.' His voice was gentle. 'I think you know what you have to do.'

Evelyn went to the bathroom and washed her hands and her face, watching the water swirl down the basin. Her eyes were red in the mirror, her face a white mask.

'I can't give him up,' she said to her reflection. 'He's all I have left.'

A BAD BUSINESS

Still fighting the last shreds of fever, Chrissie became dimly aware that something terrible had happened. *A bad business*. That's what everyone called it, and stopped talking as soon as she appeared. One night she was strong enough to get out of bed and went in search of a glass of water. She heard voices on the veranda and stood behind the screen door, listening, her thirst forgotten. Mr Jacobs was telling Dad to get some guard dogs.

'I've a couple of beauties on the farm, Danger and Domingo, two bloody big Ridgebacks. You might as well have them, I can't take them with me to Rhodesia. It's not safe around here, man, and with Fielding dead it'll only get worse. He was the only one who could keep order.'

Chrissie grabbed a handful of her nightie at her stomach. She'd never known anyone who had died before. A fly buzzed in her ear and she shook her head until it flew away. She heard her dad sigh.

'It's too bad about the Makelele boy being chased away. He'd have made an excellent teacher.'

'He must have been carrying on with one of the village girls,' Mr Jacobs's laughter was like the distant rumble of thunder. 'Young men, eh? *Ach*, I was one myself.'

Chrissie could hear the frown in her dad's voice. 'I heard rumours he was mixed up in politics. That bloody Gerry Mann, he will insist on stirring up the young men. One of my students said there were a couple of Yellow Shirts wandering about the village, drunk and asking questions about Joseph. Someone must have informed on him, and my money's on that snake Nyirongo.'

'Sounds like more trouble brewing.' Chrissie heard the sound of a beer bottle being slammed onto the glass tabletop. 'That settles it: I'll bring the dogs around tomorrow.'

'That's kind of you Piet, but we'd only have to find a new home for them. We'll be leaving here soon. I'm being posted to Madrid.'

'Grace will like that. Shops and restaurants and whatever and what have you.'

Chrissie heard her mother's voice. 'And good schools for the children, and doctors and dentists and parks where they can play safely that aren't full of snakes and disease. I can't wait.' Chrissie pushed open the door and went over to sit next to her. 'What are you doing out of bed?' Grace said, but she put arm around Chrissie and pulled her close.

'What are you all talking about, Mum?'

'It's nothing for you to worry about, chick. You should be in bed, – you're still not well. Off you go now.'

A few days later, Chrissie was finally allowed out of bed. The fever had lifted but had left her weak and she was lying on the veranda sofa trying to drink the disgusting glucose powder her mother had mixed with water. She was reading with Chomsky rumbling on her lap when Mr Jacobs came round again. Chrissie looked hopefully for the two dogs but the pick-up was empty. But he had brought her a bag of lychees and she nibbled at the sweet white flesh as she followed the farmer and her father down to the garage.

Mr Jacobs ran his hand along one of the Bentley's silver wings. 'She's a beauty, Jim.'

'1954 R Type. I've kept her in top condition. I'll give her to you for the price I paid.' Mr Jacobs got into the car and curled his big bare feet around the pedals and revved the engine.

Chrissie looked up at her dad, her eyes wide. 'Are you really going to sell the Bentley?' It was his most prized possession and the family photograph album was full of pictures of the children carefully posed in front of the vintage car, which was always fully in shot.

'Yes, I am,' her father said. 'Mr Jacobs is leaving Zambia and he needs a fine car like this to take him and Mrs Jacobs down to Rhodesia.' He put his arm around her shoulder and whispered: 'Don't worry, Chris. I've my eye on a Rolls Royce Silver Ghost, a real stunner. Just don't tell your mum.'

Chrissie giggled and leaned into his side. But when they started talking about cylinders and suspension and taking moveable assets across the border, she wandered off, bored. She'd been in bed for what seemed like ages and it was good to be outside, even if her legs were so weak it felt as if she'd forgotten how to walk. Chrissie crawled through the hole in the fence and came out at Mrs Fielding's bedroom window. There were funny sounds coming from inside. Her mother had warned her not to look through their neighbours' windows after she had caught her and Hamish playing spies with Elijah, but Mum was indoors and Dad was still busy with Mr Jacobs. Chrissie slowly peeked over the windowsill. What she saw made her turn and run.

*

Earlier that day, Evelyn had seen the Jacobs's pick-up drive up to the Docherty's house. She wasn't in the mood for company and if Lotte were there she'd come over and start asking questions. Evelyn still wasn't ready for the sympathy of other women, and she knew the Chalimbana gossip machine would be in full swing. She put down her book and went inside the bungalow.

She wandered through the empty house. Sixpence and Precious had disappeared since Robert's death and she was glad. She wanted to be alone and didn't miss them whispering about her in the shadows. Perhaps if she lost herself in drawing she'd be able to forget about Robert for a while at least. She had her head in a cupboard looking for her drawing materials when there was a knock at the front door and she sat back on her heels. Damn that Lotte Jacobs. Evelyn opened the door and her hand flew to her neck.

'Joseph.' They stared at each other, a breath apart. Evelyn heard a burst of male laughter and an engine rev next door. She took a quick look around and pulled Joseph inside the house. 'You shouldn't be here.'

'I could not stay away, when I heard what happened to Mr

Fielding. You should not be alone,' he said and bent his head to hers as if to kiss her.

Evelyn pulled back. 'You shouldn't be here. It's not safe. They're still looking for you, even more so now. A child died in the epidemic and they blame you.'

'I don't care,' he said. 'I don't want to hide anymore. I want to be with you. I have made up my mind. I've thought it all through. My family will come round in the end – you've met my brothers. And this is a new time, a new Zambia. There's no law that says we can't be married. I'll get a night job in the city and keep us both and go to art college during the day. Or we could move to England and start a new life there. Nothing else matters as long as we are together.'

But Evelyn knew that Tom had been right: if they stayed together and went public, Joseph would be shunned and his future as an artist would be ripped away. His marriage to a white woman would be seen as a betrayal of his own people. He must know this too, but here he was anyway: he didn't care about any of that. Her heart opened for the first time in days. Joseph loved her.

'Yes,' she said. 'Yes.'

Joseph put his hand at the base of her neck where the St Christopher medal sat under the yoke of her dress. 'You're still wearing it.' Evelyn put her hand over his; his skin was warm, his touch light. She remembered what Chrissie had told her, that Joseph needed his medal back for protection. It seemed silly, a child's superstition, but she untied the string.

'I want you to have this back. I'm not lost any more and I don't need it.' She took off the medal and he bent his head so she could put it on. Evelyn led Joseph into her bedroom and closed the door. He put his arms around her and unzipped her dress. It fell with a rustle to her feet and she stepped out of it. She reached behind her back and unsnapped her bra, wriggling out of her pants.

He touched her face. 'When I paint you, I will use colours and tones I have never needed before – violet for the shadows in your skin and pale green for the veins that show through here, where the blood runs cool,' he touched the inside of her elbow. He ran his hands down her back, over her waist, across her stomach. 'Your skin is like snow. It should be cold, but you're warm and soft.'

She lay down on the bed with her arms behind her head, watching him pull off his clothes and come towards her. He lay on top of her. As his hips began to move, she glanced over his shoulder at the window and saw Chrissie's face, her mouth open and her eyes wide.

*

Chrissie ran down the drive but by the time she got to the dirt road she was winded and slowed to a walk. She wanted to get as far away from what she'd seen as possible. Near the village, she saw mica glinting from the deep storm ditch on the side of the road and she climbed down to chip some off. It crumbled in her hands, leaving silver and gold flecks all over her fingers. She was so tired; maybe she'd have a sleep here. But when she lay back against the sloping ditch and closed her eyes, she saw Joseph naked on top of Mrs Fielding, and felt sick. Rage filled Chrissie and made her shake. How dare he do that *thing* to her? It was disgusting, dirty, what the wicked boys at school sniggered about; they were always trying to tell her stuff like that and she had tried not to listen. She hadn't really believed them. Not until now.

Chrissie heard voices and sat up to see two men up ahead in the road. She crouched back down in the ditch as they walked towards her. Her heart began to pound when she recognised Nyirongo and she ducked back down again. Their dusty feet stopped just above her and she tried to hold her breath so they wouldn't hear her. The two men were speaking in English but they were talking quietly and she couldn't make out what they were saying. She crept closer up the ditch and craned her head and saw Sixpence. His hands were working and he sounded angry.

'The Barotse witch has put a spell on my madam,' he said. 'He must be punished.'

'This witch has flown away,' Nyirongo said.

'No, no, he has come back. He came in a lorry last night. He is hiding at the lake. My brother saw him.'

'He escaped before with the help of the White Father and the Communist headmaster. But this time, I know how to catch him so he can't get away. I know some people who will be very interested when I tell them what you told me – that he has been at illegal meetings with this headmaster.'

244

Chrissie's leg cramped and she shifted, sending a tiny landslide scattering down the side of the ditch. Nyirongo stopped talking and she froze, not daring to breathe or look any higher. After a while she saw the two pairs of feet turn in different directions and walk away. She looked down at the pee that was trickling from under her dress. Once, what seemed a long time ago, she had been brave. Now she was terrified of Nyirongo, just like Elijah had been.

Chrissie waited for a long time to make sure they had gone. She should warn Joseph they were looking for him, but she was too scared to move. And, why should she? Joseph was supposed to be her friend but all the time he'd been coming to her garden he'd been trying to get close to Mrs Fielding. She dashed away a hot tear. Joseph didn't care about her at all; he'd tricked her. Chrissie remembered what they had looked like on the bed: his dark skin beaded with sweat, and how slowly he'd moved over Mrs Fielding's pale body, his back arched and his open mouth red and wet like a wound.

Chrissie's eyes grew heavy. She was so tired. Her mother would be cross when she got home and send her back to bed. She decided to rest in the ditch until she was sure Nyirongo had gone, and drifted off to sleep. When she woke later, the sun was high in the sky. Dazed with sleep, Chrissie scrambled out of the ditch and started walking home. Two men appeared in the shimmering heat haze ahead, like stick figures, and she stopped and shaded her eyes. Her chest fell and rose quickly but she stilled her breathing. It couldn't be them again: Nyirongo and Sixpence had split up and these men were both coming from the same direction, from the secondary school. As they drew closer she saw they were young men, loping along like hunting dogs, *pangas* swinging from their hands. They stopped in front of her, blocking her path.

'*Eh-eh*, white girl, where are you going in such a hurry?' One of them said. He wore a clean white shirt and black trousers and shiny black shoes, but when he smiled it was like seeing a Ridgeback bare its teeth. The other man squatted down to speak to her and took off mirrored sunglasses to reveal bloodshot eyes. Chrissie shrank back at the smell of sour maize beer on his breath.

His voice was a purr, thick with menace. 'Hey little sister, do you live here?' Chrissie couldn't help glancing towards her bungalow. When he looked over his shoulder in the same in the same direction, Chrissie took to her heels. She couldn't run very fast because she was still weak but didn't dare look back to see if they were coming after her. *I wish Elijah were here*, she thought as her breath started to catch in her throat. Together they would have turned this into an adventure. She'd been brave when she was with him but now she was on her own and being ill had made her weak. She heard the men calling after her and began to sob, her feet hardly lifting off the ground. It was like the dream she had sometimes where she was being chased but her legs wouldn't work properly. What would she do if Elijah were here? His charm on its string rubbed at her neck and it reminded her of the rough feel of dried mango stones. Their mango tree! Chrissie veered off the road and climbed up high into its cool dark branches. She sat with her knees up by her ears and tried to slow her breathing. The men walked underneath the tree, looking into the ditches either side of the road. She waited until she couldn't see them and then a while longer still to make sure they weren't coming back. Chrissie climbed down slowly. She jumped down the last bit and crunched onto the mango stones she and Elijah had thrown down. She began to cry as she trudged home.

Chrissie was nearly at her bungalow when she spotted some little blue cups that were used to wash out eyes and some tiny medicine bottles at the side of the road. They'd make perfect tea cups for her dolls. She was picking them out of a pile of yellow-stained cotton wool when someone grabbed her arm and hauled her to her feet.

'Look what we got here.'

It was the two men she'd run away from. They were standing over her, too close for her to duck round their legs. Chrissie pulled away but the one with the sunglasses wouldn't let her go.

'Don't be frightened, little sister. We will not hurt you. It is not you we want. We are looking for the Barotse, for Joseph Makelele. He's a bad person.' Her face closed like a fist and he laughed softly. 'I see you know this man, hmm? I know you do, you've been seen together.' His smile was wide and cold. 'Won't you help your big brother?' When she didn't answer, he tightened his grip. 'Tell me where he is.'

Chrissie knew she shouldn't tell, that it was important to stick up for your friends. That's what Hamish always said: it was wrong to tell tales. But Joseph wasn't her friend anymore and he never had been. He'd only pretended so he could do that dirty thing with Mrs Fielding. And if she told these men, they would let her go and not hurt her.

She pointed at the Fieldings' bungalow and said: 'He's in there.'

The man released her and tousled her hair. 'Thank you, little sister.'

Chrissie watched them walk over to the bungalow, their *pangas* held behind their backs. Joseph must have seen them coming because the door opened and he began to run. He took the veranda steps in one leap and tore across the lawn and down the road but they were too quick for him. The men raised their weapons and too late, Chrissie understood what she'd done.

She shouted: 'No, leave him alone!'

The men whipped their heads round but didn't break their stride until they were on Joseph. Chrissie stumbled towards them. Her legs folded just as the three men came together in a knot of tangled arms and kicking legs. She saw Joseph trying to get up and the flash of metal in the sun. The men struck and struck again. The swing door pushed open again and she saw Mrs Fielding run down the road screaming. Joseph's attackers jumped away from him and fled. Chrissie watched Mrs Fielding kneel down next to Joseph, who lay curled on his side. She was sobbing and crying out for help as a crimson stain spread over her yellow dress. Chrissie buried her head in her knees and put her hands around her ears. Keeping her eyes screwed shut she started to pray. *Our Father who art in Heaven, Hallowed be thy name...* What seemed a long time later, she opened her eyes. The road was empty except for a big dark red puddle in the dust. She walked towards it and saw a glint of silver at the edge: a medal on a string. Chrissie put it in her pocket. Flies hovered over the puddle. There was a whine behind her and one of the village dogs brushed past her. It crouched down and began to lap at the puddle. The flies were buzzing in her ears now and right inside her head, swarming over her eyes until the world turned black.

Chrissie stood in front of her bungalow and wondered how she had got there. The sun was beating down and there was a sharp pain like glass behind her eyes. There was something she had to tell her dad. What was it? Her stomach shifted and she swallowed a couple of times, trying not to be sick. Chomsky jumped down the steps and wound his furry body around her legs. Chrissie picked up the cat and pressed her face into its neck. She went into the cool of the house.

THE PROMISE

Pembroke Safari Lodge, May 1993

Chrissie stared at Evelyn, her hand over her mouth and her eyes filling. They were sitting in the shade of the jacaranda tree at the hottest time of the day. The lake shimmered like mica below them, too bright to look at for long. Chrissie rubbed her forehead as if waking from a dream of the past. Her memory was no longer a thousand shards from a broken mirror. She knew now what it was she had to tell her father: Joseph had been murdered. And it was all her fault. She'd betrayed him.

Her voice broke. 'I'm so sorry. I led those men to him.'

Evelyn frowned. 'You were only a child; you mustn't blame yourself. Joseph had seen them grab you through the window and was going to help you. When he saw they'd let you go, he made a run for it, but he didn't stand a chance.'

But Chrissie would not be comforted; it was all her fault. She had wanted those men to catch him, out of childish spite and white-hot jealousy. And cowardice. No wonder she had made herself forget: she'd been responsible for an innocent man's death, and had taken away Evelyn's chance of happiness. Shame crept through her and she squeezed her eyes tight shut, but that only brought back the images that were now so clear in her head. Nausea roiled in her stomach as she saw the pool of sticky blood, the crimson flower blooming on Evelyn's dress as she cradled her lover and called his name over and over again.

'If I had kept my mouth shut,' she said, 'they wouldn't have found him and beaten him to death. Joseph would be alive.'

Evelyn looked startled. 'But he is alive. He didn't die.'

Chrissie rubbed her eyes and tried to sort through the white noise in her head. 'But I saw him, I saw everything – the way they hacked at him with their *pangas*, and there was so much blood.' Chrissie swallowed as the scene came back to her: the rich iron smell, the flies greedily circling the red puddle, the village dog lapping at the pool as it coagulated in the sun. She groaned. 'I saw them kill him. I should have warned him they were armed, but I was too frightened.'

Evelyn took her hands in hers and made Chrissie look at her. 'Joseph is alive.' If it were true, then Chrissie had been saved.

'He didn't die?' Her voice was hoarse.

'No. Joseph did not die,' Evelyn said firmly.

Chrissie closed her eyes. 'Thank God.'

Evelyn squeezed her hands. 'I managed to drag Joseph to the Land Rover and took him to the mission clinic where they patched him up. He had a head wound, which is why there was so much blood, but he was lucky; when I came out, his attackers ran away before they could finish the job. They didn't want a witness. But it was horrible to see him like that – and later, at the clinic, I did think he was going to die. I'll tell you what happened.'

*

Evelyn cradled Joseph on her lap, unaware of the blood seeping through the thin cotton of her dress. His skin was ashy and he was so still, as if the life were draining out of him. *Not again, please God, not again.* Had she been so wicked that she was to be punished twice? But He was merciful, just as Tom had told her: a forgiving father. Only, for her prayer to work she must repent and truly mean it: she would have to make a real and lasting sacrifice to atone for her sins. Evelyn closed her eyes and put all her will and strength and love for Joseph into the desperate prayer. When she opened her eyes she searched his face for a sign of life. He was so still she had to bend her face to his to feel the lightest of breaths. His eyelids fluttered and flew open.

'My love,' was all he could manage before he fell unconscious.

At the clinic, Evelyn tended Joseph for days, bathing his forehead with cold cloths and helping Sister Bernadette to change his dressings and inject him with penicillin. She was terrified that his wounds would become infected and longed for a sterile hospital. Joseph shivered with fever, like a horse twitching away flies in the summer heat. Evelyn murmured comforting words to him but her mind was a burning dust bowl filled with a desolate, howling wind. *I am being punished for Robert. Joseph will die and I will die with him.*

On the third day, when the fever was at its peak and Joseph thrashed from side to side, Tom O'Brian arrived. He took one look at Joseph and sent for his wooden box with the little bottles of oil. The priest said the last rites while Evelyn paced the room and wept. When he had finished, he beckoned her to kneel with him beside Joseph's side.

'We can do no more for him. You must pray, my child. Put yourself into God's hands.'

Evelyn, drowning in grief, reached out for the priest's words as if they could rescue her. She bent her head and prayed all through the night. Towards dawn, Tom pulled himself to his feet with a sigh and stole out of the room. In the grey morning light, Evelyn stared at a picture of Jesus on the wall. His fingers were gently touching his exposed heart and his liquid eyes gazed down at her.

'If he lives, I will give Joseph up. I promise you,' she whispered to the sorrowing Christ. 'I will find a way to atone for Robert's death and I'll give up the only love I've ever known, if only you let him live, God damn you and your blasted eyes.' She heard a noise from the bed. She looked down and met Joseph's eyes. The fever had passed and his skin had taken on a golden glow from the sunlight that streamed through the window.

'Were you talking to me?' he said. 'I thought I heard your voice.' He closed his eyes again and Evelyn wept, already mourning her loss.

Evelyn waited until he was stronger and ready to leave the clinic before she told him it was over. The wound at his temple was beginning to heal but he would always have a scar. Already his body, young and strong, had recovered from the infection that had raged through him only days earlier. When she entered the room with his breakfast on that last day, Joseph was dressed and standing at the window.

'I will miss these hills when we go to England,' he said. She crossed the room and wrapped her arms around him, pressing her cheek against his back. His skin was warm through his shirt and she could feel the beat of his heart. He turned and took her face in his hands, like a priest offering the chalice up to God. 'My love,' he murmured, and kissed her. Evelyn closed her eyes and drank greedily, knowing this was the last time she would feel this tenderness from him. He pulled her close and she let herself sink into his arms and lean her head against his chest. After a while she broke away from him and led him to sit on the bed. She couldn't look at him and fixed her eyes on the hills, a blue pastel smudge on the horizon.

'We can't go to England,' she said.

He shrugged. 'I know, it would be too difficult now. You must stay in Africa and marry me, and I will work. I will look after you; I want to look after you.' Joseph took her hand and smiled at her and Evelyn thought her heart was going to break.

'No, that's not it, that's not it at all.' Her voice broke but she cleared her throat and went on. 'We can't be together any more. I'm sorry, we just can't. This is the end.' Evelyn wrenched her fingers from his and fled from the room before she changed her mind. Behind her, she heard a cry of visceral pain that made her think of the rasping cry of the hornbill when they had first kissed under the baobab tree. She stopped, her hand on the door. If she turned around now she would run to him and kiss away the agony, tell him of course they would be together forever, that she loved him, loved him more than her own life and happiness. That last thought gave her the strength to open the door and walk away from the only man she had ever loved.

*

Evelyn covered her eyes.

Chrissie gently reached for her other hand and held it in hers. 'I'm so sorry.'

They sat for a while in silence. Chrissie listened to the hum of the grasshoppers and farther away, the shuddering cries of flamingos at the lake. Chrissie let Evelyn's pain wash through her and felt her heart swell. What must it be like to give up so much? She didn't know if she would have the strength to make that kind of sacrifice.

'I came here to find answers, and you've given them to me,' Chrissie said. 'Thank you. And now I have something for you, something that belonged to Joseph.' She felt around her neck for the St Christopher medal she always wore, pulled it over her head and held it out to Evelyn. 'I couldn't remember where this came from, until now. It's yours really.'

Evelyn took it with trembling fingers. 'Where did you get this?'

'It was torn from Joseph's neck when he was attacked and I found it. I thought it was from my grandmother – she was always giving us little holy medals and I wore it to ward off the bad dreams, and the fear. But now I remember I picked it up from the ground, where Joseph had been attacked.' Chrissie rubbed her forehead as if to wipe away the newly awakened memory and the guilt that had come with it. 'I betrayed him. I'm so ashamed.'

Evelyn closed her hand over the medal. 'Listen to me, Chrissie. You were a child. Joseph didn't blame you. The first thing he asked when he was well enough to talk was if you were all right. He knew the danger he'd put himself in by coming to see me. Those men would have tracked him down sooner or later.'

Chrissie took a ragged breath. A weight that she'd been carrying around for years rolled off her chest.

Evelyn pressed the medal with the Christ Child and St Christopher against her lips. She tied it around her neck and touched the thin metal disc at her throat. She smiled at Chrissie. 'It was very brave of you to come all this way and face your past. I always knew you'd grow up into an interesting person and live your own life. It took me years to figure out how to do that, and by that time I'd made so many mistakes and hurt the people closest to me.' Evelyn's expression clouded with pain again.

'Joseph didn't give up so easily, of course, not after everything we'd been through together. After I left the clinic, he came to see me. I wouldn't let him in. I wouldn't look at him. I couldn't. I made him stand at the door, like a stranger, and told him we couldn't be together. He wouldn't accept it at first but I kept saying the same few words over and over: *I'm sorry, it's over*. I didn't explain why because I wanted him to be angry with me so he wouldn't come back, I wanted him to hate me.' She pushed back a strand of hair that had come loose. 'In the end, he went away and I didn't see him again for years.'

'That's heartbreaking,' Chrissie said.

'Yes, my heart was broken.' Evelyn's shoulders bowed for a moment and then she straightened again. 'But I had made a promise in exchange for Joseph's life. I had to face up to what I had done to Robert, and suffer the consequences. It's why I came here, to Pembroke. I wanted to do something good that Robert would have wanted. I inherited this place after he died, and quite a lot of money with it. There was a letter from Robert's sister, Pamela, telling me their father had died. She and his stepmother were bequeathed the house in England but there were instructions in the will for the lodge and the money from a trust to be released to Robert. Good old Pamela, and surprisingly, Clarissa. They could have fought it, kept the Fielding wealth in their family, but she and Clarissa thought it was only right that it went to me as his widow. I thought about refusing, of course, but Robert had always dreamed of restoring Pembroke, so I used it for that.

'Tom O'Brian pitched in when I told him what I wanted to do, put me in touch with builders and sent some White Fathers and lay workers to help me. We were an odd crew for the first few years.' Evelyn laughed softly. 'I took Robert's plans and built a clinic and a school, a farm, a village with sturdy houses and its own well and sanitation, and a safari business to give people jobs.' She sighed and shaded her eyes and looked over the valley. 'And here it is: my Eden, my Paradise Regained.'

Chrissie shaded her eyes and looked too. The flock of flamingos lifted as one and flew in a circle over the lake, in a honking, joyful cloud of pink and white. The hot, cloudless sky stretched above the valley, still green from the rains, and the ghostly, blue hills seemed to lean over the lake and the birds and the valley as if in a blessing.

'I understand,' Chrissie said. 'You came here to seek redemption.'

Evelyn folded her hands in her lap. 'That's what Tom O'Brian called it when I told him what I wanted to do. But I don't share his belief in a benign, forgiving God. I've never looked for forgiveness and I don't deserve it.'

'Reparation, then.'

'Yes, I like that, reparation. But there was another reason I came out here.'

There were footsteps from the path behind them and Chrissie turned round, expecting to see Tommo. Instead, she saw a tall young man. As he drew near she started and clutched the table. It was Joseph. She remembered the first day she'd met him outside the Chalimbana store, how he'd asked *where is the lake?* But that was twenty years ago, and this was a young man. Chrissie watched Evelyn take his hand and the tenderness that lit up her face, and she understood.

'He's your son.'

Evelyn smiled. 'Yes, this is my son, James.' She looked up at him. 'How was the safari, darling?'

'Oh you know,' he said, 'full of Americans taking photos of each other and complaining about the flies. But we saw a leopard, who sensibly stayed up in his tree, so that kept them happy.' James smiled with Joseph's wide, joyful smile and put his arm around his mother's shoulders. He pointed up into the branches of the jacaranda tree that spread its arms above them. 'Look, they're back.' Chrissie saw two yellow and black weaverbirds flitting back and forwards to their sock-shaped nest. She watched the little birds dipping in and out of their nest to feed their young and felt a stab of happiness.

When James went back into the house, Evelyn took up the threads of her story.

'When Robert died, my first instinct was to run home to England. But then the letter came, and I found out I was pregnant. I knew I couldn't leave Africa. I wanted James to grow up here, but in a safe place, where he would be accepted. I built this place as a sanctuary for my son, and now it is our home.'

'What about Joseph? Did you ever see him again?'

'Yes, I did. I heard he had been given a scholarship to finish his art degree – your father helped him before you left. Jim's a good man. After that, Joseph took up a place teaching fine art at the University of Zambia. I watched his career with such pride: he went abroad for post-graduate studies in France and Germany, and his fame grew with each state commission, and now he's one of the most respected artists in Africa.

'When James was about five and started asking about his father, I wrote to Joseph and sent him a photograph. He came straight away. By then he had married and had other children.' She touched the medal again. 'It was hard, seeing each other again, but I had James and that gave me strength. I never knew I had such strength until I became a mother. And I was grateful for my time with Joseph, no matter how brief. I have loved and been loved; I have built something worthwhile. I'm blessed.' Evelyn smiled and stood up. 'We still see Joseph from time to time, and he sends James drawings. There's quite a collection in our little art gallery. Come, I'll show you'

In the gallery, Chrissie looked at the framed pictures on the walls. They were line drawings in charcoal, powerful and alive: market sellers, miners, and women pounding maize. She stopped at one and touched the glass. Two children peeked out from a mulberry bush, their eyes bright with play. They looked happy. Tears pricked her eyes and she smiled as she thought of Joseph's voice, like water running over stones. *Hey, James Bond.*

STAY

Chrissie was on her balcony towelling her hair after a shower, an idea taking shape about a story about an undiscovered African artist that would be perfect for one of the Sunday colour supplements, when she spotted Johann striding across lawn. He looked up and saw her and stopped and shaded his eyes.

'Hey,' he called to her.

'Hey yourself.'

'One of the lionesses has had cubs. Do you want to come and see them?'

Chrissie tried not to show her excitement and leaned her arms on the railing. 'All right.'

The cub was soft in her arms; its eyes squeezed shut as it nuzzled and sucked at her fingers with little grunts and squeaks. Johann sat close to her to help her hold the wriggling cub and she could feel the heat from his body on her back. Chrissie kissed the cub's head and put it back with its mother. She turned to Johann to say something but he put a hand behind her head and pulled her into a kiss as soft and dark as the African night. She moved even closer to him. He released her only enough so that they were looking into each other's eyes.

'Don't go,' he said. 'Stay.'

Chrissie leaned her forehead on his shoulder and closed her eyes.

'I want to, but my life is in Scotland – my home, my family, my friends, my job.'

But even as she was listing the reasons she couldn't stay, she knew that Africa ran through her like an underground river. But she had to go home – didn't she? That was where she had worked so hard to put down roots after her restless, roaming childhood. Chrissie thought of the baobab tree, its roots reaching blindly for the sky, how it had been torn out of the ground and thrown back down. Instead of being weakened by its rootlessness, it had survived and grown into the strongest tree.

'How can you leave this place again?' Johann said, and tightened his arm around her.

She didn't want to give him an answer yet. They listened to a cicada chirrup to its mate and Chrissie thought again of all the reasons she shouldn't stay: Zambia was a mess. Lusaka had horrified her with its rich huddled behind security fences, the squalor of poverty in the rubbish piled up in the streets. And there were the villages, emptied by Aids of everyone but the very old and the very young. She remembered the last time she'd seen the Jacobs when they had fled Zambia.

*

It was the year after the Dochertys had left. Piet and Lotte had stopped off to visit them in Madrid on the way to Holland, the country of their ancestors, where they would be foreigners. It was 1975. Franco was in power and Chrissie was at a school full of rich Spanish children with double-barrelled Austrian names. Spain overwhelmed and enchanted her: the grand buildings like wedding cakes; the park with its lake and boats; the softness of spring and the sweetness of the first peaches, and the sharp cold of winter with the smell of chestnuts roasting in the streets. But she found the Spaniards harsh and imperious and missed Africa. In the incense-filled church every Sunday, old women in fur coats, their hair streaked blonde, looked her up and down disdainfully, their fans clacking against their chests, and in the crowded, cold streets, old men with hawk-like faces whispered obscenities in her ear as she hurried past them.

But here were old friends, friendly African faces. The Jacobs looked tanned and out of place in the Dochertys' nineteenth-century Madrid apartment with its high ceilings and windows looking out on to wrought iron balconies. Mr Jacobs, in a black suit, white shirt and tie, accepted a drink from her father.

'You got out just in time, *my bru.*' He shifted in his seat and pulled off his tie. '*Ach,* that's better. It's like wearing a noose.' He winked at Chrissie and took four of the oily chunks of the almond paste, *turrón,* off the plate she was offering him. 'These are *lekker.* Look at the size of you, *bokkie.* Hey, Lotte, did you see how big Chrissie got?'

Mrs Jacobs didn't turn around; she was too busy talking to Chrissie's mother. Chrissie could only make out bits and pieces of what they were saying. *A kaffir, can you imagine? I hear they used to... of course the servants all knew... she let us all down... that poor man... I hear she's...*

'*Ach,* the hens are too busy gabbing,' Mr Jacobs said to Chrissie. 'Come on, *popje,* let's see your muscles.' She flexed her biceps and Mr Jacobs whistled. 'I could have done with you on the farm instead of some of those lazy buggers.'

'What happened to the farm, Piet?' Chrissie's dad poured him some more brandy. The adults were going to watch flamenco and have dinner but that would be much later, when the night got under way and the *madrileños* came out to play. Mr Jacobs pulled Chrissie onto his knee and told her father how they had put off leaving again and again until his brother and his wife had been bound and tortured with smouldering branches.

'We don't know who they were – probably more of Mugabe's thugs from over the border, hiding out in the bush. Whoever they were, they burned off Jon's beard and drove a sharpened stick through his liver. They tied Maritje up and made her watch.'

Piet and Lotte Jacobs had left their own farm, driving south through the night to Rhodesia and down to Cape Town.

'We kept putting off leaving until one day a *wabenzie* came out to see us with a briefcase full of papers. The land was to be given back to the Zambians, he told us. Given back? That's a joke. My father and my grandfather dug that farm out of the scrubland. Now it'll turn back into bush. Those boys don't have a clue how to run a farm.' He shrugged and absentmindedly stroked Chrissie's hair. '*Ach,* there's no use crying over it. Zambia is finished for us. At least we're all right, unlike poor Jon and Maritje.'

'What did you do with the Bentley?' her father said.

'We drove it over the border into Rhodesia when we left. We had to sell it once we got to Cape Town. Pity, it was a beautiful car, man.'

'Good suspension, better than a Land Rover on those dirt roads,' her father said, and poured him another drink.

That night Chrissie had dreamt about Africa, her old dream about a black mamba. Once again, it reared up and swayed in front of her, its jaws open to show the blackness inside. She had woken and listened to rain pattering on the balcony and thought about Zambia. It would be the rainy season, the rains hammering on the corrugated iron roofs, churning the roads into a red river.

*

Now Chrissie stood up and walked away from Johann. With her back to him, she said, 'Zambia has changed. It's not the same as when I was a child here.'

'You could stay and help it change for the better.'

Chrissie shook her head. 'I'm not an aid worker or a missionary, I don't believe in meddling.' She thought of the last time she'd seen Father O'Brian. It was at Hamish's wedding and they'd all been tipsy. The priest had come over from Ireland, where he was reluctantly living out his retirement. His long face had creased with pleasure when he'd seen Chrissie. He'd stayed up half the night before the wedding with the Dochertys, talking and drinking and dancing. They were all like half-shut knives the next day but it had been worth it: she hadn't seen her mother so happy for years. In a quiet moment, Chrissie had asked the priest if he missed Africa and he'd looked sad.

Ah, Chrissie, looking back, I think we White Fathers did more harm than good. We're a practical lot and gave the fishermen new nets and boats, helped them plant small farms – after all, you can't preach to a starving man. We brought in teachers too, but the teachers and the fishermen had money, and with that they bought raw alcohol that made them go mad and half-kill each other. And with their new money they corrupted the village girls, turned them into prostitutes. I used to comfort myself with Christ's words: The poor are always with us. But sometimes I think we should never have been there. Still, I miss Africa. Every day.

And Chrissie knew now that she too had missed Africa, and all the time she had been growing up she had lived with the desolation of her loss without even being aware of it.

'I have to make a call,' she told Johann and went into the house. When she looked back, he stood with his arms crossed, waiting for her.

In her room, she picked up the phone and dialled.

'Duncan Cairns, BBC,' a tinny voice came down the line from Nairobi.

'Hello Duncan, it's Chrissie Docherty.'

'Chrissie! Good to hear from you. I hope you're calling to say you're staying in Africa.'

'Yes, I am, if you'll still help me.'

'Of course, I will. It'll be my pleasure. I could do with the company – and some help. I'm run off my feet here.' There was a pause and Chrissie listened to the crackling line. 'Tell, me,' Cairns said, 'what changed your mind?'

She looked out of the open window at Africa, its grasslands and hills and valleys and lakes and waterfalls and deserts and forests stretching all the way up to the tip of Spain. In the morning there would be the smell of wood smoke and the sound of singing as women pounded the maize, their babies snug on their backs.

'Just a feeling,' she said.

THE END

Acknowledgements

I'd like to thank a number of people who have helped me write this book: my parents and siblings; Ruby and Katrina Tweedie, Father Pat Harrity of the White Fathers, and former BBC East Africa correspondent Colin Blane for sharing their memories of Zambia; Philip Murnin, Carmen Reid and Debbie Hunter for reading the novel and for their insightful comments; my tireless and wonderful agent Jenny Brown; publisher Sara Hunt for her continuing support; Laura Waddell for her sensitive editing; Zoe Strachan and Dr Elizabeth Reeder of the University of Glasgow Creative Writing Department for their early encouragement; G2 Writers for their enthusiasm and feedback. And a special thanks to my loving husband Michael and son Adam.

THE AUTHOR

Maggie Ritchie's debut novel, *Paris Kiss* (2015), won the Curtis Brown Prize, was runner up for the Sceptre Prize and was longlisted in the Mslexia First Novel Competition. The German edition has appeared on bestseller charts, and the novel has also been translated into Czech.

Maggie graduated with Distinction from the University of Glasgow's MLitt in Creative Writing. A journalist, she grew up in Zambia, Spain and Venezuela before settling in Glasgow, where she lives with her husband and son.

@MallonRitchie
maggieritchie.com